Praise for *The Mountains Sing*

"[An] absorbing, stirring novel . . . Quế Mai contains her saga with a poet's discipline, crafting spare and unsparing sentences, and uplifts it with a poet's antenna for beauty in the most desolate circumstances . . . *The Mountains Sing* [is] a novel that, in more than one sense, remedies history."
—*The New York Times Book Review*

"A luminous, complex family narrative that spans nearly a century of Vietnamese history, from the French colonial period through the communist Viet Minh's rise to power, the separation between North and South Vietnam, the Vietnam War, all the way to the present day. Told alternately by Diệu Lan, born in 1920, and her granddaughter Hương, born in 1960, the novel resembles a choral performance with multiple voices."
—NPR

"A sweeping story that positions Vietnamese life within the rich and luminous history of national epics like *The Tale of Kiều* and the *Iliad*. Expansive in scope and feeling, *The Mountains Sing* is a feat of hope, an unflinchingly felt inquiry into the past, with the courageous storytelling of the present."
—Ocean Vuong, MacArthur Fellow and author of *On Earth We're Briefly Gorgeous*

"Good literature frees us from being trapped in our own skins by allowing us to identify with characters and see the world through their eyes. Reading this novel, I was moved by Nguyễn Phan Quế Mai's beautiful, even poetic, depictions of enduring courage. I came away with a deeper understanding of the war in which I fought."
—Karl Marlantes, bestselling author of *Matterhorn*, *What It Is Like to Go to War*, and *Deep River*

"A Vietnamese poet conjures history and fate in a luminous tale that resonates across generations as one family grapples with the psychic residue of war."
—*O, The Oprah Magazine*

"*The Mountains Sing* is an epic account of Việt Nam's painful 20th century history, both vast in scope and intimate in its telling. Through the travails of one family, Nguyễn Phan Quế Mai brings us close to the horrors of famine, war, and class struggle. But in this moving and riveting novel, she also shows us a postwar Việt Nam, a country of hope and renewal, home to a people who have never given up."
—Viet Thanh Nguyen, Pulitzer Prize–winning author of *The Sympathizer*

"A sweeping saga . . . Alternating between lyricism and blunt reality, Nguyễn Phan Quế Mai gives us a vivid look at Vietnam from within."
—*People*

"Nguyễn Phan Quế Mai's sweeping tale proves on every page that despite wartime tragedies and numbing ugliness, the human desire to forgive and thrive soars as high as the mountains. An essential read for Vietnamese and Vietnamese Americans searching to understand their grandparents and parents who lived through the war in Việt Nam."

—Thanhhà Lại, National Book Award–winning author of
Inside Out & Back Again and *Butterfly Yellow*

"Ultimately glorious in affirming the resilience of the human spirit."
—Julia Alvarez, bestselling author of *In the Time of the Butterflies* and *Afterlife*

"A mesmerizing, devastating, searing and utterly authentic and deeply human novel. Cannot recommend highly enough!"
—Lynn Novick, co-producer of *The Vietnam War* documentary

"I learned so much that I needed to know about Vietnam . . . This book, first and foremost, is one of the most significant contributions to literature."
—Natalie Jenner, author of the international bestseller *The Jane Austen Society*

"Such a good book . . . I was so impressed with it that I sent my mom a copy, and my mom is eighty-five!" —Andrea Nguyen, bestselling author of *The Pho Cookbook*

"A vast, epic historical novel set against the backdrop of the Việt Nam conflict through the eyes of the people themselves." —*Ms.* magazine

"The missing narrative of the American War in Vietnam."
—*Minneapolis Star Tribune*

"A poignant and vivid portrayal of a brutal slice of Vietnamese history from a perspective that is so rarely heard abroad: that of the Vietnamese themselves. We are starkly reminded of how those wars—and wars everywhere—wash over and drown both the guilty and innocent alike."
—Doreen Baingana, author of *Tropical Fish: Stories out of Entebbe*

"[A] panoramic epic . . . Like the work of Duong Thu Huong, who deserves the Nobel one day, this book brings to life a crucial part of Vietnamese history from within. Your heart will not leave this book untouched." —*Literary Hub*

"Epic in scope, and a celebration of the human spirit, *The Mountains Sing* is a story you won't soon forget." —*PopSugar*

"The structure is clever, the writing often evocative, the characters convincing and very touching and the whole narrative deeply engaging. And this is a first novel! Impressive."
—Sara Maitland, author of *Daughter of Jerusalem*, winner of the Somerset Maugham Award

"This poetic novel illustrates how their sacrifices ripple through [a] family."
—*Real Simple*

"Inspired by real-life events, Nguyễn Phan Quế Mai's story will thrill, shock and terrify the reader in equal measure. It will also inspire them with its life-affirming qualities of everyday heroism and survival against all the odds."
—Philip Caveney, author of the Sebastian Darke, Alec Devlin, and Movie Maniacs novels

"[Ms. Nguyen's] writing is gorgeous and vivid. As you read, you smell the cooking pots and incense around the characters, you run with them, hide with them, feel the searing pain in their bare feet, mourn with them, feel their fury at being attacked and witness the trauma that is etched into their civilian lives as one lash follows another . . . This book is so devastating in places as to be unbearable, but then the flow of the writing and the story brings you onto a wave of hope. Then you ride the resilience to the next trough, and so on, until you are nearing the end, wistfully, wishing to stick around longer to witness a good life for the adult Huong." —*Pittsburgh Post-Gazette*

"[Quế Mai's] vivid images, along with the simplicity of her prose, make the novel propulsive and haunting in its depiction of a deep, nuanced landscape." —*BookPage*

"A historical novel that portrays Vietnamese strength in the face of adversity . . . I came away at the end of the book with a new appreciation for the courage and resourcefulness of the Vietnamese." —*Washington Independent Review of Books*

"A gripping portrait of Việt Nam folded between a generational tale of love, loss, and above all else, the will to survive. Honest, alluring and hopeful, *The Mountains Sing* is a stunning work of historical fiction that lays bare history long forgotten."
—*Paperback Paris*

"In *The Mountains Sing*, Nguyễn Phan Quế Mai has found a true and clear voice in English that is rich and compelling the way only those who come to English as a second language can sometimes manage."
—Bruce Weigl, Pulitzer Prize finalist and author of the bestselling memoir *The Circle of Hanh*

"[A] masterful debut . . . Nguyễn writes vividly with profound psychological insight . . . [and] depicts emotional wounds and the resulting shifting familial dynamics with heartbreaking clarity . . . Nguyễn writes of Vietnamese history with such understanding and humanity that one can easily argue for *The Mountains Sing*'s status as the great Vietnamese novel of our time." —*DiaCRITICS*

"Animated by Mai's straightforward, sincere prose, Grandmother Dieu Lan and Granddaughter Huong take turns narrating their family's harrowing story, which at its essence is a search for harmony out of discord . . . The novel's overtures of betrayals, and subtonics of despair, give way time and again to a triumphant, beautiful song . . . Despite the famines, the bombings, and executions, *The Mountains Sing* maintains a sense of the sublime on every page. Mai's gentle prose always comes back to Grandma Dieu Lan's enduring harmony with the land, her history, and all of humankind." —*PopMatters*

"*The Mountains Sing* brings Vietnamese culture to life, steeped in beautiful language and tradition." —*The Campus*

"[A] harrowing and unflinching tale . . . A love letter, told honestly and poignantly, to the Vietnamese people, an homage to their dedication to remembrance, during and after a painful time." —*The Arts Fuse*

"A breathtaking multigenerational saga following the Trần family through Vietnam's turbulent twentieth century. Quế Mai's poetic eye illuminates the complex realities of living with devastating conflict and loss. *The Mountains Sing* is a vivid, mesmerizing, and essential feat of storytelling." —*The Magic Word* blog

"Quế Mai has written a timeless book of sadness and loss, and of gain and victory. Whether conscious[ly] or not, Quế Mai has spoken for generations outside of Vietnam, millions upon millions of people bombed out, put underground, forced to flee and desperate to live; people who are crazy yet lucid in their desire to not just escape and survive but to ultimately outlast and supersede the American war machine. It's a book for Americans too. Not a mirror for us by any manner, but a window, a view into what we have done and continue to do to so many." —*CounterPunch*

"An epic tale of family and Vietnamese history." —*Orange County* (CA) *Register*

"There is good reason that *The Mountains Sing*, the first novel in English by award-winning poet Nguyễn Phan Quế Mai, has been ranked among 'the most exciting writers to emerge in post-war Vietnam'—it is, in a word, breathtaking . . . decadent and heart wrenching, equal parts lush and vibrant in its unfamiliar setting . . . One of the most moving, and fundamentally eye-opening, novels I feel I will read in my lifetime."
—*The Nerd Daily*

"An engrossing story of family, adversity, war, loss, and triumph . . . Recalling Min Jin Lee and Lisa See, Nguyen displays a lush and captivating storyteller's gift as she effortlessly transports readers to another world, leaving them wishing for more. This may be Nguyen's first novel published here, but one can only hope it will not be the last."
—*Library Journal*, starred review

"Quế Mai tells the story of the war that tore apart Việt Nam, and of the generation lost to the war, by braiding around it two beautiful strands told by the older and younger generations of a family. This book is an act of love, compassion, and ultimately healing, and very much needed by all who survived the war."
—Thi Bui, author of *The Best We Could Do*

"A sweeping tale of one family's shifting fortunes in Vietnam across half a century . . . invitingly and gracefully told. [Nguyen] is particularly adept at weaving in folktales and aphorisms to create a vivid sense of place. A richly imagined story of severed bonds amid conflict."
—*Kirkus Reviews*, starred review

"Nguyễn Phan Quế Mai has written a wonderful, intricate story of the lives of a Vietnamese family trying to make it through generations of war. *The Mountains Sing* is a beautiful story of the simple challenge of keeping a family together and the courage of perseverance. It is told with the sureness of a master storyteller with a poet's spirit. A large and complicated story, marvelous to read."
—Larry Heinemann, author of *Paco's Story*,
winner of the National Book Award

"[L]yrical, sweeping . . . In a subtle coda, Nguyễn brilliantly explores the boundary between what a writer shares with the world and what remains between family. This brilliant, unsparing love letter to Vietnam will move readers."
—*Publishers Weekly*, starred review

"A story of loss and sorrow, of longing for peace and normalcy, and—above all—of the triumph of hope over despair, told in the authentic voices of a resilient and resourceful grandmother and her granddaughter."
—Mai Elliott, Pulitzer Prize finalist and author of
The Sacred Willow: Four Generations in the Life of a Vietnamese Family

"Over the last two decades we have been gifted with works by Vietnamese writers who have brought us into the consciousness of those that Americans saw only as backdrops for their own stories. Nguyễn Phan Quế Mai not only adds to that rich body of work, she daringly transcends it."

—Wayne Karlin, author of *Wandering Souls*,
winner of the Vietnam Veterans of America Excellence in the Arts Award

"[T]he ominous history of twentieth-century Vietnam told through four generations of a single family . . . Widely published in Vietnamese, poet, nonfiction writer, and translator Quế Mai's first novel in English balances the unrelenting devastation of war with redemptive moments of surprising humanity." —*Booklist*

"Deep human bonds of family, place, and memory are written of in ways that are often heartbreaking, but show the strength and persistence of those ties. This is a book that glows with spirit and those larger life forces that include love. I look forward to the day I can put this book in readers' hands."

—Rick Simonson, Elliott Bay Book Company, Seattle

"The author and poet . . . tells a comprehensive multigenerational tale, beginning in 1920s Vietnam and continuing through modern wartime. However, the larger history takes a back seat to family dynamics, demonstrating how different generations weather the burdens of conflict." —*The Washington Post*

"This moving saga has captivated readers with its authenticity and lyrical storytelling."

—Boston Public Radio

"Stunning . . . Filled with vivid characters and evocative depictions of the Vietnamese landscapes, both urban and rural . . . There's an important Vietnam War history lesson embedded here, as well, one that is not often available to American readers."

—*The Vietnam Veterans of America Book Review*

"Quế Mai opens a window into the other side of a controversial war, and we would do well to consider the lessons her characters teach." —*The Seattle Book Review*

"*The Mountains Sing* took my breath away. It moved me to my core. I was shaken, I was touched and, in spite of the tragedies in the book, I was inspired."

—WPSU Penn State Radio

International Praise

"*The Mountains Sing* not only portrays clearly the griefs of loss and separation brought about by war, it also praises family love, the value of hope and altruism."
—*Tuổi Trẻ News* (translated from Vietnamese)

"A Vietnamese novel that has moved Western readers."
—BBC News (translated from Vietnamese)

"Beautiful, heartbreaking and utterly essential." —*Saigoneer Bookshelf*

"This complex saga has a grand momentum . . . There is a compelling quality to the heightened emotions, the loss of life and culture, the strength and fortitude of the survivors, punctuated by the proverbs and aphorisms of old Vietnam. Our experience is enhanced by learning a nation's history from different points of view through the words of a skilled and impassioned writer." —*Otago Daily Times* (New Zealand)

"Quế Mai brings a poetic lyrical quality to her story . . . The story slowly and tantalisingly incorporates Vietnamese customs and language . . . As Vietnam becomes more important to Australia's strategic and economic future in Asia, it is hard to think of a gentler, more engaging way to understand its 20th century evolution."
—The Asia Society of Australia

"Authentic . . . The book has a very ingenious structure."
—ABC (Australia national radio)

"Told with poetic economy and intensity, *The Mountains Sing* is dominated by the formidable Diệu Lan and her granddaughter Hương, who find ways to pass on stories from the past—tales of survival in the face of invasion, atrocity and unimaginable loss— and remain determined to endure, as Vietnam changes radically around them, on the land of their ancestors." —*The Sydney Morning Herald*

"Good fiction can teach us about the truth of the world, and *The Mountains Sing* is a timely and moving novel that bears witness to the atrocities of the past, which remain as echoes in the present." —*The Saturday Paper* (Australia)

"From famine to war, Nguyễn Phan Quế Mai weaves into her epic novel *The Mountains Sing* stories of what her family and friends went through."
—*The Straits Times* (Singapore)

THE MOUNTAINS SING

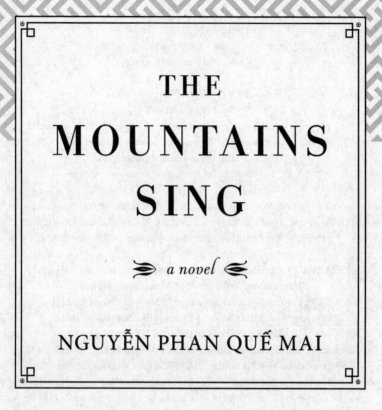

THE
MOUNTAINS
SING

a novel

NGUYỄN PHAN QUẾ MAI

ALGONQUIN BOOKS OF CHAPEL HILL   2021

Published by

ALGONQUIN BOOKS OF CHAPEL HILL
Post Office Box 2225
Chapel Hill, North Carolina 27515-2225

a division of
WORKMAN PUBLISHING
225 Varick Street
New York, New York 10014

First paperback edition, Algonquin Books of Chapel Hill, March 2021.
Originally published in hardcover by Algonquin Books of Chapel Hill in March 2020.
Printed in the United States of America.
Design by Anne Winslow.

This is a work of fiction. While, as in all fiction, the literary perceptions and insights
are based on experience, all names, characters, places, and incidents either are
products of the author's imagination or are used fictitiously.

LIBRARY OF CONGRESS CATALOGING-IN-PUBLICATION DATA
Names: Nguyễn, Phan Quế Mai, [date]– author.
Title: The mountains sing : a novel / Nguyễn Phan Quế Mai.
Description: First edition. | Chapel Hill, North Carolina :
Algonquin Books of Chapel Hill, 2020. |
Summary: "The multigenerational tale of the Trần family, set against the
backdrop of the Việt Nam War. Trần Diệu Lan, who was born in 1920,
was forced to flee her family farm with her six children during the Land Reform
as the Communist government rose in the North. Years later in Hà Nội,
her young granddaughter, Hương, comes of age as her parents and uncles
head off down the Hồ Chí Minh Trail to fight in a conflict that will tear
not just her beloved country but her family apart"—Provided by publisher.
Identifiers: LCCN 2019030591 | ISBN 9781616208189 (hardcover) |
ISBN 9781643750491 (ebook)
Subjects: LCSH: Vietnam War, 1961–1975—Fiction.
Classification: LCC PR9560.9.N45 M68 2020 | DDC 823/.92—dc23
LC record available at https://lccn.loc.gov/2019030591

ISBN 978-1-64375-135-1 (PB)

10 9 8 7 6 5 4 3

For my grandmother, who perished in the Great Hunger;
for my grandfather, who died because of the Land Reform;
and for my uncle, whose youth the Việt Nam War consumed.
For the millions of people, Vietnamese and non-Vietnamese,
who lost their lives in the war. May our planet never see
another armed conflict.

CONTENTS

The Tallest Mountains   *1*

Red on the White Grains   *3*

The Fortune Teller   *18*

Getting Up and Falling Down Again   *41*

The Great Hunger   *77*

My Father's Gift   *97*

The Land Reform   *131*

The Journey South   *149*

The Walk   *166*

My Mother's Secret   *199*

Destination   *231*

The Country Bumpkin Boy   *254*

The Way to Happiness   *281*

My Uncle Minh   *294*

Facing the Enemy   *325*

My Grandmother's Songs   *338*

THE TRẦN FAMILY TREE

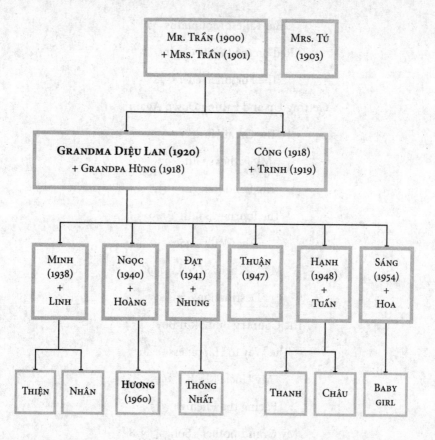

MR. TRẦN (1900)
+ MRS. TRẦN (1901)

MRS. TÚ (1903)

GRANDMA DIỆU LAN (1920)
+ GRANDPA HÙNG (1918)

CÔNG (1918)
+ TRINH (1919)

MINH (1938)
+
LINH

NGỌC (1940)
+
HOÀNG

ĐẠT (1941)
+
NHUNG

THUẬN (1947)

HẠNH (1948)
+
TUẤN

SÁNG (1954)
+
HOA

THIỆN

NHÂN

HƯƠNG (1960)

THỐNG NHẤT

THANH

CHÂU

BABY GIRL

The Tallest Mountains

Hà Nội, 2012

My grandmother used to tell me that when our ancestors die, they don't just disappear, they continue to watch over us. And now, I feel her watching me as I light a match, setting fire to three sticks of incense. On the ancestral altar, behind the wooden bell and plates of steaming food, my grandma's eyes glow as an orange-blue flame springs up, consuming the incense. I shake the incense to put out the fire. As it smolders, curtains of smoke and fragrance spiral toward Heaven, calling spirits of the dead to return.

"*Bà ơi*," I whisper, raising the incense above my head. Through the mist veiling the border between our two worlds, she smiles at me.

"I miss you, Grandma."

A breeze gusts through the open window, holding my face like Grandma's hands once did.

"Hương, my beloved granddaughter." The trees outside my window rustle her words. "I'm here with you, always."

I set the incense into the bowl in front of Grandma's portrait. Her gentle features radiate in the incense's perfume. I stare at the scars on her neck.

"Remember what I said, Darling?" Her voice murmurs on the restless branches. "The challenges faced by Vietnamese people throughout history are as tall as the tallest mountains. If you stand too close, you won't be able to see their peaks. Once you step away from the currents of life, you will have the full view. . . ."

Red on the White Grains

Hà Nội, 1972–1973

Grandma is holding my hand as we walk to school. The sun is a large egg yolk peeking through a row of tin-roofed houses. The sky is as blue as my mother's favorite shirt. I wonder where my mother is. Has she found my father?

I clutch my jacket's collar as the wind rips through the air, swirling up a dust cloud. Grandma bends, putting her handkerchief against my nose. My school bag dangles on her arm as she cups her palm against her face.

We resume walking as soon as the dust settles. I strain my ears but hear no bird. I search, but there isn't a single flower along our path. No grass around us, just piles of broken bricks and twisted metal.

"Guava, be careful." Grandma pulls me away from a bomb crater. She calls me by my nickname to guard me from evil spirits she

believes hover above the earth, looking for beautiful children to kidnap. She said that my real name, Hương, which means "fragrance,"
would attract them.

"When you come home today, you'll get our favorite food, Guava,"
Grandma tells me.

"Phở noodle soup?" Happiness makes me skip a step.

"Yes. . . . The bomb raids have stopped me from cooking. But it's
been quiet, so let's celebrate."

Before I can answer, a siren shatters our moments of peace. A
female voice blares from a loudspeaker tethered to a tree: "Attention
citizens! Attention citizens! American bombers are approaching Hà
Nội. One hundred kilometers away."

"Ôi trời đất ơi!" Grandma cries for Heaven and Earth. She runs,
pulling me along. Streams of people pour out of their homes, like ants
from broken nests. Far away, from the top of the Hà Nội Opera House,
sirens wail.

"Over there." Grandma rushes toward a bomb shelter dug into the
roadside. She pulls up the heavy concrete lid.

"No room," a voice shouts out from down below. Inside the round
pit just big enough for one person, a man half kneels, half stands.
Muddy water rises to his chest.

Grandma hurries to close the lid. She pulls me toward another
shelter.

"Attention citizens! Attention citizens! American bombers are
approaching Hà Nội. Sixty kilometers away. Armed forces get ready
to fight back." The female voice becomes more urgent. The sirens are
deafening.

Shelter after shelter is full. People dart in front of us like birds with
broken wings, abandoning bicycles, carts, shoulder bags. A small girl
stands alone, screaming for her parents.

"Attention citizens! Attention citizens! American bombers are approaching Hà Nội. Thirty kilometers away."

Clumsy with fear, I trip and fall.

Grandma pulls me up. She throws my school bag to the roadside, bending down for me to jump onto her back. She runs, her hands wrapping around my legs.

Thundering noise approaches. Explosions ring from afar. I hold on to Grandma's shoulders with sweaty hands, burying my face in her body.

"Attention citizens! Attention citizens! More American bombers are approaching Hà Nội. One hundred kilometers away."

"Run to the school. They won't bomb the school," Grandma shouts to a group of women lugging young children in their arms and on their backs. At fifty-two years of age, Grandma is strong. She dashes past the women, catching up with those ahead of us. Bounced up and down, I press my face against her long, black hair that smells like my mother's. As long as I can inhale her scent, I will be safe.

"Hương, run with me." Grandma has squatted down in front of my school, panting. She pulls me into the schoolyard. Next to a classroom, she flings herself down a vacant shelter. As I slide down next to her, water rises to my waist, gripping me with icy hands. It's so cold. The beginning of winter.

Grandma reaches up, closing the lid. She hugs me, the drum of her heart throbbing through my blood. I thank Buddha for the gift of this shelter, large enough to fit us both. I fear for my parents on the battle-fields. When will they come back? Have they seen Uncle Đạt, Uncle Thuận, and Uncle Sáng?

Explosions draw closer. The ground swings, as if it were a hammock. I press my palms against my ears. Water shoots up, drenching my face and hair, blurring my eyesight. Dust and stones rain through a small crack onto my head. Sounds of antiaircraft fire. Hà Nội is fighting back. More explosions. Sirens. Cries. An intense burning stench.

Grandma brings her hands together in front of her chest. *"Nam Mô A Di Đà Phật, Nam Mô Quan Thế Âm Bồ Tát."* Torrents of prayers to Buddha pour from her lips. I close my eyes, imitating her.

The bombs continue to roar. A minute of silence follows. A sharp screeching noise. I cringe. A powerful explosion hurls Grandma and me against the shelter's lid. Pain darkens my eyes.

I land feet-first on Grandma's stomach. Her eyes are closed, her hands a budding lotus flower in front of her chest. She prays as the thundering noise disappears and people's cries rise into the air.

"Grandma, I'm scared."

Her lips are blue, trembling from the cold. "I know, Guava. . . . I'm scared, too."

"Grandma, if they bomb the school, will . . . will this shelter collapse?"

She struggles against the confined space, pulling me into her arms. "I don't know, Darling."

"If it does, will we die, Grandma?"

She hugs me tight. "Guava, if they bomb this school, our shelter might collapse on us, but we'll only die if Buddha lets us die."

WE DIDN'T PERISH that day, in November 1972. After the sirens had signaled that it was safe, Grandma and I emerged, shivering thin leaves. We staggered out to the street. Several buildings had collapsed, their rubble spilling onto our path. We crawled over piles of debris, coughing. Billowing smoke and twirling dust burned my eyes.

I clutched Grandma's hand, watching women kneeling and howling next to dead bodies, whose faces had been concealed by tattered straw mats. The legs of those bodies were jutting toward us. Legs that were mangled, covered with blood. One small leg had a pink shoe dangling. The dead girl could have been my age.

Drenched, muddy, Grandma pulled me along, walking faster and faster, passing scattered body parts, passing houses that had crumbled.

Under the *bàng* tree, though, our house stood in glorious, incongruous sunlight. It had miraculously escaped damage. I broke away from Grandma, rushing ahead to hug the front door.

Grandma hurried to help me change and tucked me into bed. "Stay home, Guava. Jump down if the planes come." She pointed toward our bomb shelter, which my father had dug into the earthen floor next to the bedroom entrance. The shelter was large enough to hold us both, and it was dry. I felt better hiding here, under the watchful eyes of my ancestors, whose presence radiated from the family altar, perched on top of our bookshelf.

"But . . . where're you going, Grandma?" I asked.

"To my school, to see if my students need help." She pulled our thick blanket to my chin.

"Grandma, but it's not safe. . . ."

"It's just two blocks away, Guava. I'll run home as soon as I hear the siren. Promise to stay here?"

I nodded.

Grandma had headed for the door, but she returned to my bed, her hand warming my face. "Promise you won't wander outside?"

"*Cháu hứa.*" I smiled to assure her. She'd never allowed me to go anywhere alone, even during the months absent of bombs. She'd always been afraid that I'd get lost somehow. Was it true, I wondered, what my aunt and uncles had said, about Grandma being overprotective of me because terrible things had happened to her children?

As the door closed behind her, I got up, fetching my notebook. I dipped the tip of my pen into the ink bottle. "Beloved Mother and

Father," I wrote, in a new letter to my parents, wondering whether my words would ever reach them. They were moving with their troops and had no fixed addresses.

I WAS REREADING *Bạch Tuyết và bảy chú lùn*, immersed in the magical world of Snow White and her friends, the Seven Dwarfs, when Grandma came home, my school bag hanging off her arm. Her hands were bleeding, injured from trying to rescue people trapped under rubble. She pulled me into her bosom and held me tight.

That night, I crawled under our blanket, listening to Grandma's prayers and her wooden bell's rhythmic chime. She prayed for Buddha and Heaven to help end the war. She prayed for the safe return of my parents and uncles. I closed my eyes, joining Grandma in her prayer. Were my parents alive? Did they miss me as much as I missed them?

We wanted to stay home, but urgent announcements from public broadcasts ordered all citizens to evacuate Hà Nội. Grandma was to lead her students and their families to a remote place in the mountains where she'd continue her classes.

"Grandma, where're we going?" I asked.

"To Hòa Bình Village. The bombs won't be able to find us there, Guava."

I wondered who'd chosen such a lovely name for a village. *Hòa Bình* were the words carried on the wings of doves painted on the classroom walls at my school. *Hòa Bình* bore the blue color in my dream—the color of my parents returning home. *Hòa Bình* meant something simple, intangible, yet most valuable to us: *Peace*.

"Is the village far, Grandma? How will we get there?"

"On foot. It's only forty-one kilometers. Together we can manage, don't you think?"

"How about food? What will we eat?"

"Oh don't you worry. Farmers there will feed us what they have. In times of crisis, people are kind." Grandma smiled. "How about helping me pack?"

As we prepared for our trip, Grandma's voice rose up beside me in song. She had a splendid voice, as did my mother. They used to make up silly songs, singing and laughing. Oh how I missed those happy moments. Now, as Grandma sang, vast rice fields opened their green arms to receive me, storks lifted me up on their wings, rivers rolled me away on their currents.

Grandma spread out her traveling cloth. She piled our clothes in the middle, adding my notebook, pen, ink bottle, and her teaching materials. She placed her prayer bell on top, then tied the opposite corners of the cloth together, turning it into a carrying bag to be wrapped around her shoulder. On her other shoulder hung a long bamboo pipe filled with uncooked rice. She had already packed up my school bag with water and food for the road.

"How long will we be away, Grandma?"

"I'm not sure. Perhaps a couple of weeks?"

I stood next to the bookshelf, my hands running over the books' spines. Vietnamese fairytales, Russian fairytales, Nguyễn Kiên's *Daughter of the Bird Seller*, *Treasure Island* from a foreign author whose name I can't pronounce.

Grandma laughed, looking at the pile of books in my hands. "We can't bring so many, Guava. Pick one. We'll borrow some more when we get there."

"But do farmers read books, Grandma?"

"My parents were farmers, remember? They had all the books you could imagine."

I went through the bookshelf again and decided on Đoàn Giỏi's novel, *The Southern Land and Forests*. Perhaps my mother had arrived in *miền Nam*, that southern land, where she met my father. I had to know more about their destination—cut away from us by the French and now occupied by the Americans.

Grandma glued a note onto the front door, which told my parents and uncles that in case they returned, they could find us in Hòa Bình. I touched the front door before our departure. Through my fingertips, I felt my parents' and uncles' laughter. Now, looking back over the years, I still wonder what I would have brought along if I had known what would happen to us. Perhaps the black-and-white picture of my parents on their wedding day. But I also know that on the verge of death, there is no time for nostalgia.

At Grandma's school, we joined the throng of teachers, students, and their families, several with bicycles piled high with luggage, and walked, merging into the mass of people moving away from Hà Nội. Everyone wore dark clothes, and metal parts of vehicles were covered up to avoid reflection from the sun, for fear of attracting bombers. Nobody talked. I could only hear footsteps and the occasional cries of babies. Terror and worry carved lines into people's faces.

I was twelve years old when we started that forty-one-kilometer walk. The journey was difficult, but Grandma's hand warmed mine when the wind whipped its bitter cold against us. So that I wouldn't be hungry, Grandma handed me her food, pretending she was already full. She sang countless songs to calm my fears. When I was tired, Grandma carried me on her back, her long hair cupping my face. She bundled me into her jacket when it drizzled. Blood and blisters covered her feet as we finally got to Hòa Bình Village, nestled in a valley and surrounded by mountains.

We stayed with two elderly farmers—Mr. and Mrs. Tùng—who let Grandma and me sleep on the floor of their living room; there was no other space in their small home. On our first day at Hòa Bình,

Grandma found a worn path that zigzagged up the closest mountain and into a cave. Some villagers had chosen the cave as their bomb shelter; Grandma decided we must join them. Even though Mr. Tùng said the Americans would never bomb the village, Grandma and I spent the next day practicing climbing up and down the path, so many times that my legs felt like they had been hammered.

"Guava, we must be able to get up here, even during the night and without any light," Grandma said, standing inside the cave, puffing and panting. "And promise to never leave my side, promise?"

I watched butterflies fluttering around the entrance. I longed to explore. I'd seen the village's kids bathe naked in a pond, ride water buffaloes through muddy fields, and climb trees to reach for bird nests. I wanted to ask Grandma to let me join them, but she was looking at me with such worried eyes that I nodded.

As we settled into our temporary home, Grandma gave Mrs. Tùng our rice and some money, and we helped prepare the meals, picking vegetables from the garden, cleaning the dishes. "Ah, you're such a help," Mrs. Tùng told me, and I felt myself growing a little taller. Her home was different, but in a way, it was so much like mine in Hà Nội, with its windows sealed with black paper, to prevent American bombers from seeing any sign of our life at night.

Grandma looked graceful as she taught in the village temple's yard, her students squatting on the dirt floor, their faces bright. Her lesson wouldn't end until she'd finished teaching them one of her songs.

"The war might destroy our houses, but it can't extinguish our spirit," Grandma said. Her students and I burst into singing, so loud that our voices broke, and we sounded just like those frogs who joined us from nearby rice fields.

The Southern Land and Forests, set in 1945, had a fascinating beginning. Before my eyes, the South appeared so lush, the people happy and generous. They ate snakes and deer, hunted crocodiles, and gathered honey in dense mangrove forests. I underlined complicated words and exotic Southern terms, and Grandma explained them whenever she had time. I cried with An, who lost his parents as they ran away from the cruel French soldiers. I wondered why foreign armies kept invading our country. First it was the Chinese, the Mongolians, the French, the Japanese, and now the American imperialists.

As I escaped on an imaginary journey into the South, the bombs fell onto Hà Nội—the heart of our North. Whether it was day or night, at the clanging of a gong, Grandma would clutch my hand, pulling me toward the mountain. It took thirty minutes to climb, and I was never allowed to rest. By the time we reached the cave, gigantic metal birds would be thundering past us. I held on to Grandma, feeling thankful for the cave, yet hating it at the same time: from here I would watch my city being engulfed in flames.

A week after our arrival, an American airplane was shot and its pilot managed to fly his burning plane toward Hòa Bình. He ejected with a parachute. Other planes strafed and rocketed the area as they attempted to rescue him. Much later, we emerged from the mountain cave to see torn body parts strewn along winding village roads. Grandma covered my eyes as we arrived under a row of trees where human guts hung from the branches.

We passed the collapsed village temple. Sounds of a commotion rushed toward us, followed by a group of people who ushered a white man forward. Dressed in a dirty, green overall, the man had his hands tied behind his back. His head was bent low, but he was still taller than everyone around him. Blood ran down his face, and his blond hair was splattered with mud. Three Vietnamese soldiers walked behind him, their long guns pointed at the white man's back. On the right arm of the man's uniform the red, white, and blue of a small American flag burned my eyes.

"*Giết thằng phi công Mỹ. Giết nó đi, giết nó!*" someone suddenly shouted.

"Kill him! Kill that bastard American pilot," the crowd roared in agreement.

I clenched my fists. This man had bombed my city. The aggression of his country had torn my parents away from me.

"My whole family is dead because of you. Die!" a woman screamed, launching a rock at the American. I blinked as the rock thumped him in the chest.

"Order!" one of the soldiers shouted. Grandma and several others rushed to the sobbing woman, took her into their arms, and led her away.

"Justice will be served, Brothers and Sisters," the soldier told the crowd. "Please, we have to bring him to Hà Nội."

I watched the pilot as he walked past me. He didn't make a sound when the rock hit him; he just bent his head lower. I wasn't sure, but I thought I saw some tears trickling down his face, mixing with his blood. As the crowd followed him, shouting and screaming, I shuddered, wondering what would happen to my parents if they faced their enemy.

To CHASE AWAY fear, I buried myself in my book, which took me closer to my parents. I inhaled the scent of mangrove forests, sniffing the breeze from rivers crowded with fish and turtles. Food seemed to be abundant in the South. Such food would help my parents survive if they made it to their destination. But would the South still be this lush even with the American Army there? It seemed to destroy everything in its path.

Approaching the last pages, I held my breath. I wanted An to find his parents, but instead he joined the Việt Minh guerrillas to fight against the French. I told him not to, but he had already jumped into a sampan, rowing away, disappearing into the white space that expanded after the novel's last word.

"An should have tried harder to search for his parents," I told Grandma, pushing the book away.

"Well, in times of war, people are patriotic, ready to sacrifice their lives and their families for the common cause." She looked up from my torn shirt, which she was mending.

"You sound just like my teachers." I recalled the many lessons I'd learned about children considered heroes for blowing themselves up with bombs to kill French or American soldiers.

"Want to know what I really think?" Grandma leaned toward me. "I don't believe in violence. None of us has the right to take away the life of another human being."

TOWARD THE MIDDLE of December, whispers circulated that it was now safe to return home, that the American President Nixon would take a rest from the war to enjoy his Christmas holiday of peace and goodwill. People left their hiding places, flocking down to the roads that led them back to our capital city. Those who could afford it hired buffalo or cow carts or shared a truck. Those without money would walk the entire way.

We didn't join them. Grandma asked her students and their families to stay put. Buddha must have told her so. On December 18, 1972, we watched from inside the mountain cave as our city turned into a fireball.

Unlike the previous attacks, the bombings didn't cease. They continued throughout the next day and night. On the third day, Grandma and several adults ventured out to get food and water. It took Grandma so long to come back, and she brought Mr. and Mrs. Tùng with her. As Mrs. Tùng moaned about her knees, Mr. Tùng told us that the Americans were using their most powerful weapon on Hà Nội: B-52 bombers.

"They said they want to bomb us back to the Stone Age," he told us, gritting his teeth. "We won't let them."

Hà Nội burned and bombs fell for twelve days and nights. When the bombings finally stopped, it was so silent, I could hear bees buzzing on tree branches. And like those hard-working bees, Grandma returned to her class and the villagers to their fields.

A week later, a group of soldiers arrived. Standing on the temple's remaining steps, a soldier had a smile stretching wide across his gaunt face. "We've defeated those evil bombers!" He pumped his fist. "Our defense troops shot down eighty-one enemy airplanes, thirty-four of them B-52 bombers."

Cheers erupted around me. It was now safe for us to go home. People hugged each other, crying and laughing.

"I'll never forget your kindness," Grandma told our hosts. *"Một miếng khi đói bằng một gói khi no."* One bite when starving equals one bundle when full.

"Lá lành đùm lá rách," Mrs. Tùng replied. Intact leaves safeguard ripped leaves. "You're welcome to stay with us at any time." She clutched Grandma's hand.

I smiled, enchanted whenever proverbs were embedded in conversations. Grandma had told me proverbs were the essence of our ancestors' wisdom, passed orally from one generation to the next, even before our written language existed.

Our hearts bursting with hope, we walked many hours to return to Hà Nội.

I had expected victory but destruction hit my eyes everywhere I looked. A large part of my beautiful city had been reduced to rubble. Bombs had been dropped onto Khâm Thiên—my street—and on the nearby Bạch Mai Hospital where my mother had worked, killing many people. Later, I would go back to class, empty of my fifteen friends.

And our house! It was gone. Our *bàng* tree lay sprawled across the rubble. Grandma sank to her knees. Howls escaped from deep inside her, piercing through the stench of rotting bodies, merging into a wailing sea of sorrow.

I cried with Grandma as we pushed away broken bricks and slabs of concrete. Our fingers bled as we searched for anything salvageable. We found several of my books, two of Grandma's textbooks, and some scattered rice. Grandma picked up each grain as if it were a jewel. That night in my schoolyard, we huddled against the wind with people who had also lost their homes to cook our shared meal of rice mixed with dirt and stained with blood.

WATCHING GRANDMA THEN, nobody could imagine that she was once considered *cành vàng lá ngọc*—a jade leaf on a branch of gold.

Three months earlier, as my mother got ready to go to the battlefield, she told me Grandma had been born into one of the richest families in Nghệ An Province.

"She's been through great hardships and is the toughest woman I know. Stay close to her and you'll be all right," my mother said, packing her clothes into a green knapsack. Trained as a doctor, she had volunteered to go south, to look for my father, who'd traveled deep into the jungles with his troops and hadn't sent back any news for the past four years. "I'll find him and bring him back to you," she told me, and I believed her, for she'd always achieved whatever she set out to do. Yet

Grandma said it was an impossible task. She tried to stop my mother from going, to no avail.

As my mother left, Heaven cried his farewell in big drops of rain. My mother poked her face out of a departing truck, shouting, *"Hương ơi, mẹ yêu con!"* It was the first time she said she loved me, and I feared it'd be the last. The rain swept across us and swallowed her up into its swirling mouth.

That night and for the next many nights, to dry my tears, Grandma opened the door of her childhood to me. Her stories scooped me up and delivered me to the hilltop of Nghệ An where I could fill my lungs with the fragrance of rice fields, sink my eyes into the Lam River, and become a green dot on the Trường Sơn mountain range. In her stories, I tasted the sweetness of *sim* berries on my tongue, felt grasshoppers kicking in my hands, and slept in a hammock under a sky woven by shimmering stars.

I was astonished when Grandma told me how her life had been cursed by a fortune-teller's prediction, and how she had survived the French occupation, the Japanese invasion, the Great Hunger, and the Land Reform.

As the war continued, it was Grandma's stories that kept me and my hopes alive. I realized that the world was indeed unfair, and that I had to bring Grandma back to her village to seek justice, perhaps even to take revenge.

The Fortune Teller

Nghệ An Province, 1930–1942

Guava, remember how we used to wander around the Old Quarter of Hà Nội? We often stopped in front of a house on Hàng Gai. I didn't know anyone who lived there on Silk Street, but we stood in front of the house, peering through its gate. Remember how beautiful everything was? Wooden doors featured exquisite carvings of flowers and birds, lacquered shutters gleamed under the sun, and ceramic dragons soared atop the roof's curving edges. The house was a traditional *năm gian*, with five wooden sections, remember? And there was a front yard paved with red bricks.

Now I can tell you the reason I lingered in front of that house: it looks just like my childhood home in Nghệ An. As I stood there with you, I could almost hear the happy chatter of my parents, my brother Công, and Auntie Tú.

Ah, you ask me why I never mentioned to you about having a brother and an aunt. I'll tell you about them soon, but don't you want to visit my childhood home first?

To go there, you and I will need to travel three hundred kilometers from Hà Nội. We'll follow the national highway, passing Nam Định, Ninh Bình, and Thanh Hóa provinces. Then we'll turn left at a pagoda called Phú Định, crossing several communes before arriving at Vĩnh Phúc, a village in the North of Việt Nam. The name of this village is special, Guava, as it means "Forever Blessed."

At Vĩnh Phúc, anyone will gladly show you to the gate of our ancestral home—the Trần family's house. They'll walk with you along the village road, passing a pagoda with the ends of its roof curving like the fingers of a splendid dancer, passing ponds where children and buffaloes splash around. During summer, you'll gasp at clouds of purple flowers blooming on *xoan* trees and at red *gạo* flowers sailing through the air like burning boats. During the rice harvest season, the village road will spread out its golden carpet of straws to welcome you.

In the middle of the village, you'll arrive in front of a large estate surrounded by a garden filled with fruit trees. Peeking through the gate, you'll see a house similar to the one we saw on Silk Street, only more charming and much larger. The people who take you there will ask whether you're related to the Trần family. If you tell them the truth, Guava, they'll be astonished. The Trần family members have either died, been killed, or disappeared. You'll learn that seven families have occupied this building since 1955, none of them our relatives.

My beloved granddaughter, don't look so shocked. Do you understand why I've decided to tell you about our family? If our stories survive, we will not die, even when our bodies are no longer here on this earth.

The Trần family's house is where I was born, got married, and gave birth to your mother Ngọc, your uncles Đạt, Thuận, Sáng, and your aunt Hạnh. You didn't know this, but I have another son, Minh. He's my first-born, and I love him very, very much. But I don't know whether he's dead or alive. He was taken away from me seventeen years ago, and I haven't seen him since.

I'll explain what happened to him later, but first, let me take you back to one particular summer day in May 1930, when I was ten years old.

I WAS STARTLED awake by the sound of thudding, deep in the heart of the night, a rhythmic, hollow clunking. "Who's making so much noise at this hour?" I complained, turning sideways, to find Mrs. Tú, the housekeeper, snoring next to me. Her name, Tú, means "refined beauty," but if you met her, you might be frightened at first. A deep scar zigzagged from her mouth to her left eye. On her right cheek, flesh had melted into a mass of wrinkles. Mrs. Tú wasn't born that way, though. Years ago, before I popped out from my mother's stomach, a fire had gobbled up most of Vĩnh Phúc Village, reducing Mrs. Tú's house to ashes, killing her husband and her two sons, burning her almost to death. My mother brought Mrs. Tú to our home and nursed her back to health. When Mrs. Tú recovered, she decided to stay and work for us. Over the years, she became part of our family.

Years later, Guava, it was Mrs. Tú who risked her life to save mine and your mother's.

That early morning, though, the sight of our housekeeper calmed the frantic wings inside my stomach. I was thankful she'd agreed to leave her room to keep me company for the last few nights.

"Wake up, Auntie Tú. What's that noise?" I whispered, but she continued to snore.

The thuds got more urgent. I yawned, hoisting myself up. Fumbling in the dark, I found my wooden clogs. Leaving my bedroom, I clip-clopped into a long corridor that ran past a large room, which stored our fields' harvests. With my hands, I felt my way forward. Careful as I was, I still bumped my head on the *đàn nhị* and was startled at the low hum its two strings made. I cursed my brother for hanging the musical instrument so low, as if the awful wailing sounds he made with those strings weren't enough. I passed the living room, where a kerosene lamp glowed on a table, spreading light onto a lacquered sofa inlaid with mother-of-pearl. A wooden platform rose up on its four strong legs—the *phản* divan, where my father often sat and entertained his guests. Massive pillars made of precious *lim* wood ran all the way from the brick floor to the ceiling. High up, another kerosene lamp eyed me from the family altar. Two lacquered panels on the wall bore poetry written exquisitely in *Nôm*—the ancient Vietnamese script.

Following the noise, I emerged into the front yard. There, bathed in moonlight, my father was raising a large wooden pestle, hammering it on a stone mortar. His square face and muscled arms shone with sweat. He was pounding rice, but why hadn't he asked his workers to help?

Not far from him, my mother squatted on a stool, holding a bamboo tray, tossing pounded rice. Her hands jerked back and forth, forcing the husks to fly out. She looked so graceful in her movements that if it wasn't for the sheet of rice fluttering in front of her, you would think she was dancing.

Then, I remembered our family tradition: my parents always prepared the first batch of rice from a new harvest by themselves and offered it to our ancestors. They had begun harvesting our fields the day before, piling the fruit of their work under the longan tree.

"Mama. Papa." I skipped down the five steps that flowed from the front veranda to the brick yard.

"Did we wake you up, Diệu Lan?" My father reached for a towel and swept it across his face. A chorus of insect songs rose from the garden behind his back. Muffled sounds of cows and water buffaloes echoed from stalls that ran deep into the side garden, but the chickens remained quiet inside their bamboo cages.

"Kitten, go back to bed." Unlike my father, my mother was superstitious and called me by my nickname, to guard me from evil spirits.

"Ah. My lot is ready." My father scooped his mortar's contents into a bamboo basket. An aroma of rice perfume blossomed into my lungs as I helped him.

I carried the basket to my mother, who was inspecting the white seeds on her bamboo tray, before pouring them into a ceramic urn.

"How's Master Thịnh, Diệu Lan?" My father's voice rose above the pounding rhythms. He'd been so busy, we hadn't had much time to talk.

"He's wonderful, Papa." Master Thịnh was a scholar my parents had just hired to teach my brother Công and me. The only school in my entire district was too far away and reserved for boys. Công and I had always studied at home with our tutor. My father had recently gone all the way to Hà Nội and brought back Master Thịnh, who appeared at our gate with a buffalo cart full of books. While most girls in my village were taught only how to cook, clean, obey, and work in the fields, here I was, learning how to read and write with a scholar who had traveled far, even to France. I was beginning to enjoy the adventures his books gave me. Master Thịnh lived with us, in the western wing of the house.

"I'm glad he's teaching you and Công French," said my father.

"But I don't see why they should learn it," my mother said, and I couldn't agree more. The French were occupying our country. I'd seen French soldiers beating farmers on our village road. Sometimes they'd come into our home, searching for weapons. In our province, farmers and workers had been demonstrating against them. My parents didn't get involved. They feared violence and believed the French would eventually return our country to us, without bloodshed.

My father stopped pounding and lowered his voice. "You know that I hate those foreigners. They've been here more than sixty damn years too long, robbing us blind with their duties and taxes, killing innocent people. But we can only kick them out if we understand them."

"Is Emperor Bảo Đại doing just that? Studying in France to liberate us from them?" my mother asked, holding out her tray as I poured pounded rice onto it.

"People say the French are turning him into their puppet, though. Wouldn't it be ideal for them, ruling us via our own emperor?" my father answered, and resumed pounding.

We finished our work. A rooster flapped his wings from our side garden, tossing a buoyant song high up. Other roosters followed, chorusing to call the sun to wake.

Drum sounds echoed from the village pagoda, signaling that the fifth time interval had finished, that it was five o'clock in the morning.

Mrs. Tú hurried down the yard. She pulled me into her arms. "Why aren't you in bed, Kitten?"

"I'm a little farmer today, Auntie." I sniffed the sweet smell of areca nuts and betel leaves emanating from her clothes.

She smiled and turned to my mother. "Sorry, Sister, I overslept."

"Not at all, Sister. You worked so late last night."

Receiving the urn, which brimmed with white rice from my mother, Mrs. Tú hurried across the yard, toward the kitchen.

A pink glow pushed through the eastern horizon. Birds sang on tree branches. The first sunrays glimmered on the husks under my feet. I held the broom, sweeping sunlight into a pile.

My mother carried a tray to my father, who sat on the veranda steps. She poured steaming green tea into jade cups.

"Good morning."

I looked up to see Master Thịnh stepping out, his eyes smiling under bushy eyebrows. "Oh how I love to wake up early here, to this fresh air," he said, taking a deep breath. Class wasn't starting soon, yet he'd already donned his turban, black tunic, and white pants.

My father laughed. "Please, join us for some tea."

Squatting down between my parents, I had a sip of my father's tea. A bitter taste bit into my tongue, yet a fragrant sweetness lingered in my throat.

"Master Thịnh, I was just wondering about Hà Nội. . . . It must be a fascinating place," my mother said as she handed my teacher a cup. Like most people in our village, she hadn't been to the capital city.

"Hà Nội? Oh, yes, it's special. And very ancient, too. Nearly one thousand years old." Master Thịnh's eyes became dreamy. "My family lives in the Old Quarter. There, small lanes weave through a maze of old, slanting houses. But you only know the Old Quarter if you remember its thirty-six main streets. Each has a life of its own—Silk Street, Silver Street, Tin Street, Shoe Street, Bamboo Street, Coal Street, Copper Street, Salt Street, Coffin Street, Cotton Street, Traditional Medicine Street . . ."

My eyes widened as my teacher recounted all the names from memory.

Master Thịnh went on to say that his family had a house on Silver Street. His father was a silversmith who wanted him to continue the family tradition. "But the busy city life isn't for me. I'm lucky my younger brother Vượng is there to shoulder that task, so I can enjoy this wonderful country life while teaching delightful children." He smiled at me.

I thought it was clever of Master Thịnh's parents to name his sons Thịnh and Vượng, which, together, mean prosperity. As Master Thịnh talked about Hà Nội and his family, I tried to remember his every word. I had no idea what I did then would help save my life twenty-five years later.

"G'morning."

I turned. My brother was standing in the doorway, yawning and stretching like a cat. Two years older than me, Công was tall and well built. His skin was a golden brown from his days playing outside, riding buffaloes and catching crickets.

"Up so early?" Master Thịnh asked, sipping his tea.

"Yes, Master. Got to study while the brain is fresh."

"*Có công mài sắt có ngày nên kim,*" my teacher said, beaming. Ah, the proverb that I'd heard countless times: Perseverance grinds iron into needles. Upon hearing it again, the happy feeling inside me dropped like a stone. When it came to studying, Công worked much harder than me and I believed he was much better. He could remember all those confusing ancient Vietnamese, Chinese, and French characters. On top of that, he didn't need an abacus to do his arithmetic.

As if to rescue me, a group of nine men appeared at our gate. Clad in brown shirts and black pants, they were holding sickles in their hands. On their heads sat *nón lá*—conical hats woven with bamboo and palm leaves. These men had worked for my parents for many years.

"Please, join us for some tea," my father said.

Công and I raced inside the house to fetch new cups.

Then my brother and I rolled up our pants and got down to our chores. On the farm, which my father had taken over from his parents, Công fed the pigs and I the chickens. My parents had shown us that the greatest joy of being a farmer was to get our hands dirty in the company of plants and animals.

I played with the chicks until my mother's call rolled toward me. She was carrying a tray heaped with food from our family altar out to the veranda, followed by Mrs. Tú, who lifted another tray.

Surrounded by my family, I held the sweetness of the new rice harvest in my mouth. My teacher and the nine men kept nodding their heads, complimenting Mrs. Tú's and my mother's cooking.

After breakfast, my father went with some workers to the fields while my mother worked with the rest in the yard. She'd asked me to go back to bed, but I sat at my desk, opening my books. In the study, Master Thịnh was teaching Công. It'd be my turn to learn in the afternoon, and I wanted my teacher to say I was more intelligent than my brother.

A cooling wind gushed through the open window. Outside, sunlight poured gold and silver onto swaying leaves. Through the fence of flowering hibiscus that bordered my house and the village lane, I saw an old man stooping.

He was dragging his feet, guided by a walking cane. The flaps of his white tunic fluttered like butterfly wings. A black headband crowned his silvery hair. I recognized him to be Mr. Túc, the famous fortune-teller of my village.

Like all my friends, I both feared and admired the old man. I often lurked in front of his home, watching crowds of people who'd traveled from faraway places to receive his predictions. Some emerged from his house delirious with happiness, others brimming with tears. Although many people worshiped Mr. Túc, nobody knew exactly where he got his fortune-telling magic. Some whispered that when he was seven years old, Mr. Túc went swimming in the village pond. The greenish *Thủy Quái*—the Water Devil—caught his legs, pulled him into the mud, and tried to drown him. None of his friends had noticed he'd gone missing until a column of water arose, shooting up a boy who was punching his fists and kicking his legs. They watched in astonishment as Túc plopped back down into the water and swam calmly to shore. When the boy came home, many people rushed to him to ask about his fight with the Water Devil. Later, they would come back again and again for his fortune-telling magic.

What was he doing here, at this time of the day, leaving his customers behind?

I hoisted myself up to the window frame, jumping softly down to the garden beneath. A few grasshoppers sprang up, their rough skin brushing against my calves. Crouching low, I watched as Mr. Túc stopped in front of our gate.

"*Chào ông Túc*." Delight jumped out of my mother's mouth as she rushed over to meet him.

"*Chào bà*. How busy you are! Is the harvest good?"

"It's not bad, Mr. Túc. At least our rice wasn't destroyed by storms like last year." My mother put down her basket, helping the fortune-teller across the bustling yard.

Determined to know the reason for the fortune-teller's visit, I sneaked into the living room and sat on the wooden *phản*, behind the old man's back. My mother was pouring tea, offering him a steaming cup.

"Mr. Túc, thanks for coming. With our business growing, we need to build a large storeroom. Perhaps on the front garden." My mother poured herself a cup. "Do you think the location is auspicious?"

Just then, something scurried in front of me.

"*Ahhh!*" I leaped away from the *phản*.

"What's that?" The old man flinched.

"A huge rat." The animal had vanished, but I still rushed to my mother.

She laughed. "Our harvest is disturbing them, Kitten. They'll soon go back to their burrows."

The fortune-teller suddenly straightened his back. "Tell me who this girl is, Madam Trần." He looked me up and down.

"This is Diệu Lan, my daughter."

I folded my arms in front of my chest, bowing my respect to the old man.

"Come here, little girl." The fortune-teller knitted his brows. "Something about you is making me very . . . very curious. Sit here, that's right. Show me your palms. Spread them wide and hold them still."

I did what I was told. Waves of excitement rolled through me. Surely my friends would be very jealous that Mr. Túc offered to read my future.

The old man leaned back in the wooden armchair with dragon heads carved into the armrests. He squinted, scrutinizing the lines and marks on my palms. All of a sudden, his eyes popped open, as if registering a shock.

"So, Mr. Túc, what do her palms say?" My mother grabbed a paper fan, sending a breeze toward the fortune-teller and me.

"Give me another minute." Mr. Túc lifted my hands even closer to his eyes. He peered at the lines, touching them with his index finger. It tickled. I would have laughed if he hadn't looked so serious.

My mother poured more tea.

"So?" she asked when he looked up.

"Madam Trần, I don't think you'd want to know."

"Why not, Sir?" My mother's hand and the teapot stopped midair.

"Perhaps it's better for you not to."

"In that case, I'm very curious." My mother leaned over the table, her forehead wrinkled with concern.

The old man studied my face, his stare sending chills down my spine. "Madam Trần, if you must know . . . your daughter will have a very hard life. She'll remain rich for a while, but will lose everything and become a wandering beggar in a faraway city."

The teapot slipped from my mother's hands, shattering steaming tea onto the floor.

"*Mẹ!*" I rushed to her.

She stepped away from the broken mess, pulling me into her arms. "Mr. Túc, are you sure?"

"The palms say so, Madam Trần. I'm sorry."

My mother gripped my shoulders.

MY MOTHER NEVER saw Mr. Túc again and forbade me to set foot near his house. His prediction so terrified her that she secretly took me to countless temples and pagodas to pray for blessings. As I watched her burn stacks of hell money for unseen ghosts and offer roast piglets to invisible devils, I resented the old man.

Two years later, when I turned twelve, Mr. Túc died of old age. His funeral was one of the largest our village had ever witnessed. People from countless regions came to pay their respects. They talked and talked about how true his predictions had turned out to be.

Still, I didn't see how he could be right about my future. How could I possibly become a beggar? My family was by far the richest in our village. Our stalls were filled with animals, our fields with rice and vegetables. With our buffalo cart, my father had started transporting our produce to Hà Nội, where he sold it for high profits to select restaurants. At night, when I listened to the *click-clack* sounds of my mother's abacus, I knew we had plenty of money. Although we had to pay all types of taxes to the French and to the Emperor, my parents worked hard.

Mr. Túc's prediction eventually faded like a drop of black ink diluted in a pond, leaving me a carefree girl. With my friends, I ran across fields, chasing grasshoppers and locusts, exploring streams, paddies, and gardens, climbing trees, and peeking into bird nests to spy on the hatching of eggs. With my family, I piled into my father's buffalo cart, heading toward colorful weekend markets or to Nam Đàn Forest, where Công and I galloped in the green space. Oh Guava, if I close my eyes and take a deep breath now, I can still taste the sweetness of purple *sim* berries, the richness of yellow mountain guavas, the sour bite of wild bamboo fruit.

Sometimes my father drove us even further, so that we could see the rice fields rolling out their silky carpets, dotted by fluttering wings of storks, the Lam River glimmering in the sun, and the Trường Sơn Mountains soaring like dragons ready to take flight. My childhood, let me tell you, was both like, and unlike, any other.

I studied hard under the guidance of Master Thịnh, who spent five years with us, and who was my father's best friend. Night after night, the two men sat on the veranda, sipping tea, composing poems. *Ca dao*—our folk poetry—had taken root in my father's life via his mother's lullabies. As with many farmers, for my father the act of composing poems was as natural as plowing a patch of field.

Meanwhile, all my girlfriends were getting married to men chosen by their parents. When she was thirteen, my best friend Hồng had to marry a man twice her age. His wife had died, and he needed someone to work in his field. That was how most women were regarded in those days, Guava.

My mother made sure things were different for me. She and my father encouraged me to be independent and speak my own mind. They even agreed when I refused to discolor my teeth. Do you know that in those days black teeth were considered essential for women? Those with white teeth were regarded as improper. But I was horrified at the pain my friends had to endure while their teeth were being softened by lime juice and lacquered with black dye. Master Thịnh's books had given me other ideas of beauty.

It was customary for the eldest son to inherit the family business, but my brother Công wanted me to be involved. The elders in my village often said if the French hadn't abolished the royal exams, Công would have passed them, become a mandarin of the imperial court, and brought honor to our village. But Công always shook his head at such ideas. He loved our fields, and he was falling in love with Trinh, daughter of the village chief. They got married when I turned sixteen, and Trinh became the big sister I always wished to have.

In my village, there was someone in charge of collecting taxes for the French. Nicknamed Wicked Ghost, he had a meaty face, narrow eyes, and a bald, shiny head. We all dreaded the sight of him and his whip, made out of the strongest jungle vines. Wicked Ghost whipped those who couldn't pay in time, taking their belongings in place of the money they owed, and he lashed his wife. I avoided him and never dared to look directly at him. Little did I know that I would have to face him one day.

When I was seventeen, I met a young man. Hùng. My parents had known his family for years. After finishing his studies in Hà Nội, Hùng came back to our village and taught at a new school in our district.

Until the day I met Hùng, I didn't like boys. Well, I liked picking on them, just as I enjoyed picking on my brother. So, you could well imagine how Hùng reacted when he first visited my home. We argued.

Yes, we did. We argued.

"Don't you think we should kick the French out right away?" Hùng fumed at me. "The atrocities they're committing against our people must be stopped!"

"Haven't you heard?" I threw my words back at him. "They've promised to return our country to us. If we wait a few more years, we'll have our homeland back without bloodshed."

"Ah, you trust those foreigners too much. They're pacifying us with their words, words that they'll soon swallow." Hùng went on to tell me how the French wanted to keep Việt Nam backward, uncivilized, and impoverished. How they extracted our natural resources, transporting them home. How they fed Vietnamese opium to blunt our sharp minds. They were never going to let us be free.

As we talked, I was amazed. Men I knew outside my home didn't bother with women's opinions, considering us unworthy of conversation, saying that *"Đàn bà đái không qua ngọn cỏ"*—Women can't pee higher than the tips of grass blades. So when Hùng looked into my eyes and said he didn't agree with me, I liked it. I realized how genuine and handsome he was. His eyes radiated excitement, his lips curled up like a half-smiling moon.

I fell in love with your grandpa then. I still see his love every day, looking at you, Guava. You have his eyes, his nose, his smile. Sometimes when I'm talking to you, I feel I'm talking to him, too.

We married that year, the Year of the Buffalo, 1937. At my parents' request, Hùng went against tradition and moved into our house. Our eldest son, your Uncle Minh, was born in 1938, followed by your mother, Ngọc, two years later, then your Uncle Đạt in 1941.

Now, looking back, these were the happiest years of my life. I thought happiness had burrowed deep under my skin and no one could take it away from me.

Then, one day during the winter of 1942, my life changed.

I REMEMBER THAT day, so vividly, from the moment I bent down to my children, the lamp in my hand illuminating their faces. Minh, four years old then, had his arm slung over Đạt, who'd just turned one. Both had kicked away their thick blanket.

In a far corner of my large childhood bed, Ngọc was muttering in her sleep. Guava, you know how beautiful your mother is now, but you don't know how pretty she was as a little girl—milky skin, long eyelashes, rosy lips. Wrapped in a silk quilt, she was a fairy coming out of her cocoon.

"I'll miss you, babies," I whispered. In a few hours, I'd be leaving them for the first time, to go to Hà Nội for twelve long days. I wanted to scoop them up, holding them close. Instead I pulled the blanket over the chests of my sons, then slipped away as winter rain sluiced down our roof.

The lamp's flickering guided me back to my room, which used to be the old storeroom.

"Diệu Lan, are you up?" A soft voice. Oh, no, I'd woken my husband. I blew out the lamp, gliding into bed.

"What time are you leaving, em?" Hùng's chin was on my face. He covered me with the warmth of our quilt.

"At the start of the fifth time interval." Around three in the morning.

"I wish you'a let me go instead. Women shouldn't be on the road."

"Oh, don't be silly, anh Hùng." I brushed away his idea with a quiet laugh. "Papa and Brother Công will take care of me. Besides, I need to pay respect to Master Thịnh."

With this trip to Hà Nội, I'd get to visit my childhood teacher, who had been ill, and see his house on Silver Street. This would also be my chance to help my father. Business hadn't been easy. With the spread of World War II, the Japanese had arrived. They'd been ruling us through the French, burdening us with yet another layer of taxes and duties.

"But Hà Nội is a long way, em," Hùng insisted. "As I said, a teacher at my school has heard stories about Japanese soldiers robbing villages up North, attacking civilians."

"Ah, these are just rumors, don't you think, *anh*?"

"It might be true. This crazy war is giving the Japs too much power."

"You worry too much." I pulled the blanket to cover Hùng's arm. "As I've told you many times, Papa knows the roads." I reminded him that the Northern region rumored to have troubles was near the Chinese border, far from where we'd be traveling.

"But promise you'll be careful?" Hùng begged.

I thought it was unnecessary for him to worry about the trip. The Japanese had said on the radio that Asians ought to love Asians, and they were not here to fight. They said they'd help Việt Nam establish its independence. I'd seen with my own eyes how polite Japanese soldiers were. A group of them had passed by our village. The sight of their brown uniforms, shiny boots, and dangling swords scared me at first. But timidly, they knocked on our house gate, asking my mother if they could use our yard to eat their lunch. They were so young, these soldiers, and friendly, too. They played with my children, kicking featherballs high into the air, laughing just as Vietnamese boys laughed.

I let a current of sleep pull me away, waking a bit later to the sounds of faint murmurs, hurried footsteps, and the thumping of buffalo feet against the yard's surface. I fumbled in complete darkness for the bag of clothes I'd kept near the bedroom entrance and sneaked out.

On the veranda, under the glow of three large kerosene lamps, my parents, Công, his wife Trinh, and Mrs. Tú were piling sacks of potatoes onto a long cart. The cart sat on large wheels, its wooden frame crowned by sheets of woven palm leaves.

Out in the rain, a pair of water buffaloes were munching fresh grass, their horns' arcs towering above their heads.

Rushing toward my family members to lend them a hand, I knocked my knee against the cart's side and nearly tumbled down into the yard.

"Hey, watch out." Công snatched my arms, pulling me to safety.

"You okay?" Trinh looked up from the sack she was cradling.

"I'm drunk from sleeping too much," I said in embarrassment.

"Come on, Diệu Lan, you were up late last night breast-feeding Đạt." Mrs. Tú handed a sack to my father, who stood inside the cart.

"It's good you're weaning Đạt by going on this trip." My mother bent to pick up a sack. "He's already thirteen months."

The thought of feeding Đạt sent a painful sensation to my chest. My breasts started to well up with milk. "He doesn't want to wean," I blurted.

"I know where he got his genes from." My father chuckled. "I was still drinking from my mother at four years old. She tried different ways to wean me. Nothing worked. Until one day . . ."

"What happened?" Công asked.

"She ate a couple of bird's eye chilies. Picked from our garden, they were ripe red, hot as fire. Her milk was so spicy, I spit it out and never went near it again."

Our laughter filled the veranda, mingling with the fragrance of fresh earth stirred up by the rain.

"*Shhh*. The neighbors will think we're crazy, laughing at this hour of the morning." Mrs. Tú tried to suppress her giggles between her black teeth.

"I bet they wish they had some of our craziness." Trinh swept the floor with a large broom.

I couldn't agree more.

The rain had eased into a light drizzle. With all the sacks safely stored inside the cart, my father and Công secured additional palm-leaf sheets around the frame, turning it into a cozy carriage. The ride to Hà Nội would take five days and nights, and we had to be prepared for worse weather. If these potatoes were to sell to the best restaurants there, they had to be top quality. As clever as he was, when my father imported new seedlings from Europe many years earlier, he didn't know they'd help make our family fortune.

My father and Công placed a wooden board above the sacks. Trinh and I lowered a thick palm-leaf sheet, which became the cart's back door. We pushed the cart out to the yard, tethering it to the buffaloes with a yoke.

Mrs. Tú lugged large hampers of food and water into the cart. My mother pushed a fat envelope into my pocket. "For Master Thịnh's medicine."

Drumbeats from the village temple cut through darkness, their echoes rippling like waves. Time to depart.

Guava, when I turned to get my bag, someone was holding it. Guess who it was? Your Grandpa Hùng.

"Shouldn't you be in bed, *anh*?" I laughed.

"Have to see you off," he whispered into my ear.

My mother helped my father put on his raincoat, an imported product he'd purchased in Hà Nội. She secured a *nón lá* on his head.

"Let's go." My father hopped onto the cart's front.

My mother clutched my hands. "Take care on the road, won't you?"

"I'll cook Đạt many types of porridge. He'll eat plenty," Mrs. Tú said.

"I'll send the kids to sleep with fairy tales," Trinh added.

As the buffaloes heaved us away, I poked my head out, my words woven into the rain. "I'll bring home exciting stories about Hà Nội."

Soon, we were riding on the bumpy village road. The cart's wheels clicked noisily against thick mud.

"Try to get some sleep, children." My father's voice boomed through the palm-leaf sheets.

"Papa, call me when you want to swap places." Công's voice turned toward me, "Sleep, Sister."

I lay down. As the cart rocked and swayed, I found myself wide awake with thoughts about my father out there in the cold.

I fumbled for a raincoat. Lifting the layers of sheets, I faced the solid backs of the moving buffaloes. A glow of light in front of the animals' heads let me know the cart had turned onto a larger road.

I made out my father's hand holding two small ropes that ran parallel to the buffaloes' bodies and connected to their noses. His other hand was clutching a torch that he'd also gotten from Hà Nội. I admired its stable light as I settled down next to him.

"Can I hold that torch for you, Papa?" I asked as the drizzle slapped its chill onto my face.

"Want to hold these ropes instead?"

Surprise bloomed inside my chest. I'd never dared dreaming about driving our buffalo cart. Back then women were considered dirty because we menstruated. Once I saw a man beat his daughter because she'd crossed the driver's seat of his cart. He believed she'd bring bad luck and cause the cart to tumble.

"It's not difficult." My father thrust the ropes into my hands. "Pull them backward hard if you want the buffaloes to stop. Pull to the left to go left, and vice versa. Relax your hands otherwise."

I clutched the ropes tight and gave them a tug. My whole body tingled at the excitement of being in control.

"Doing great." My father cast a halo onto the road. "See the puddle there? Pull to one side. Here you go. Good, good."

Leaning over, he put his *nón lá* on my head.

"No, you wear it, Papa!"

"If you fall sick, who'll take care of us on this trip, huh?" He secured the hat's silk strap under my chin.

We turned onto a rutted road before merging onto the national highway. My father explained that the road used to be called Đường Cái Quan, built by our emperors and upgraded by the French to serve their colonial needs. At occasional checkpoints we had to stop to show our travel permit. Stationed by the French, the guards there scrutinized our papers, inspecting our cart, looking for weapons we could be transporting for the Việt Minh guerrillas who were rising up against them.

My father knew how to handle those guards, and soon I relaxed. The highway was almost empty at this hour. For the long while that we traveled, we only passed a cart pulled by a skinny cow and a group of farmers lugging baskets piled high with vegetables.

"Just straight ahead and we'll be in Hà Nội." My father leaned back beside me.

From afar, a rooster called out his morning greetings. Daybreak gleamed on the horizon. The rain ceased, leaving a thick mist in the air. Large bushes lined up along the roadside, their silhouettes looking like gigantic animals ready to pounce.

The cart climbed onto a hilly part of the highway, where I cast my eyes beyond the thick lines of trees, beyond emerald rice fields, toward clusters of houses with wisps of white smoke unfurling above their roofs. Down there, mothers and sisters were preparing breakfast for their families.

I realized no one was living next to the highway, and for us to buy food or water we'd have to turn into village roads that occasionally cut into our path.

The buffaloes whipped their tails, chasing away flies that hovered above their fat bottoms. I loosened the ropes, thinking that once I returned home, I needed to take my whole family across this vast countryside.

"Diệu Lan . . ." my father said just as my eyes widened at the sight of a commotion ahead. Where trees had thinned, I could see a group of houses burning like torches and columns of black smoke funneling into the cloudy sky. I heard the wails of women and children, the screams of men, and shouts in a strange language. I pulled the ropes hard. The buffaloes stopped, craning their necks, listening.

I turned to my father. Fear had frozen on his face.

"Japanese. Japanese soldiers," he mumbled with unblinking eyes. I glanced back at the burning village. Men were marching out of its glow, toward the highway, their bayonets held high.

"Go back! Go back!" My father snatched the ropes from my hands. The cart quickly turned.

"Look, Papa, look." I pointed ahead.

A large shadow was creeping along the road, bayonets gleaming like tigers' eyes. Sandwiched between two groups of Japanese soldiers, we had nowhere to run, no village road nearby to turn the cart into. I couldn't see the soldiers clearly yet but knew they were advancing quickly, their footsteps sending tremors onto the road.

"Công. Get up!" My father reached into the cart, shaking my brother.

"What's wrong?" Công sprang up.

"Hurry. Take your sister. Hide by the roadside. Choose the thickest bush. Whatever happens, don't come out until I say so." My father turned to me. "Go."

I jumped, fell, and rolled down onto the mud-spattered road, the *nón lá* crushed beneath me, crackling like hundreds of cockroaches being popped. Crouching down, Công dragged me toward a deep trench that ran along the roadside and pulled me into a bush. I lost my sandals in the trench. Thorns burrowed into my naked feet. Twigs dug into my scalp. I bit my lip, desperate to stay silent.

Holding our breaths, we watched our father from tiny gaps among the leaves. He'd spun the buffaloes around. At his order, the animals advanced toward Hà Nội. Following Công, I crept from one thick bush to another. We stayed low, letting the sounds of the buffalo footsteps guide us.

The thumping of the buffalo hooves softened. From our hiding place, I could see that the first group of Japanese soldiers had gathered on the highway, blocking my father's way, while the second group was coming up from behind.

My father approached the first group.

"Stop! What's in that cart?" a man roared in badly accented Vietnamese. He looked almost like a local except for the way he'd tucked his pants into his high boots. Somebody must have punched him in the eye, for it was swollen and black. He was carrying a rifle, as well as a sword.

"Potatoes, Sir. I'm taking potatoes to Hà Nội." My father's voice was calm and polite.

"Hasn't your mother taught you manners?" the black-eyed man shouted. "You Vietnamese must bow down to us. Bow, bow down low!"

Công held me tightly in his arms. "Don't make any sound. They'll kill us." He cupped his palm against my mouth.

My father got down from his cart, bent his body low, and bowed to the Japanese.

My eyes darted toward the second group of soldiers, who were reaching the cart. They were dragging several young women by their hair. The women's shirts and pants were ripped, exposing pale breasts and upper legs. Blood was running down their inner thighs.

"Show us what you have in that cart." Black Eye flicked his fingers.

My father lifted up the cart's back door, heaving away the wooden board. Black Eye and several of his comrades inspected the cart's contents.

"Sir, these potatoes are for my customers in Hà Nội."

"Damn your customers!" Black Eye lifted his rifle and aimed at the inside of the cart. Torrents of bullets deafened my ears. Potatoes jumped from the cart like injured fish. The remaining soldiers threw back their heads, laughing raucously. I tasted blood on my tongue; I'd bitten into my lip.

Getting Up and Falling Down Again

Hà Nội, 1973–1975

The bombings had stopped. I was surprised by how blue the sky was, even when it was raining.

Grandma and I knelt on the site of our collapsed house, piling broken bricks into a pair of bamboo baskets. Our hands became the color of brick; so did our clothes. Nearby, a bomb crater was half-filled with rainwater. It gazed at me with its single murky eye.

I thought about the American pilot. Did he drop this bomb? What had happened to him, and did he have a daughter like me?

The baskets were full. Grandma reached for a bamboo pole, balancing it on her shoulder. She bent, hooking the pole onto thick ropes that held the baskets. I winced as she stood up, hoisting the baskets onto her skinny frame, staggering toward the bomb crater, the toes of her bare feet splaying out. I caught up with her and helped her dump the baskets' contents into the murky eye. Water splashed up.

Around us, men, women, and children, with torn clothes and ghostly faces, were doing the same thing, filling the eye from hell with the remains of their homes.

"*Mẹ Diệu Lan ơi, Hương ơi!*" A voice called out to us.

The brick shards fell away from my hands. My mother. She was back.

I stood up, stumbled, and ran forward. In the afternoon's failing light, my mother was pushing a bicycle; something perched on its back saddle.

"*Mẹ!*" I cried out for her.

We got closer. My eyes found her face, and my feet stopped. It was my aunt Hạnh, not my mother.

Auntie Hạnh leaned her bike against a pile of rubble and rushed toward me. She knelt, taking me into her arms. Her tears trickled on my face. "Oh, Little Hương. Hasn't your Mama come back?"

I shook my head, burying my face into my aunt's chest, searching for my mother's warmth. Auntie Hạnh was Grandma's fifth child, eight years younger than my mother. She lived far away, in Thanh Hóa Province, in her husband's hometown.

"Hạnh." Grandma arrived, embracing us both.

"I was insane with worry." Auntie Hạnh touched Grandma's face, body, and arms as if to make sure nothing was missing.

"Ah, you silly girl. It's not easy to kill this old water buffalo." Grandma laughed. Her voice leaped upward, free. I felt myself smiling, too.

Helping Auntie Hạnh push the bike forward, I eyed the brown sack on the back saddle. Hunger gnawed my stomach, but I shouldn't expect my aunt to bring us food. Her husband, Uncle Tuấn, had gone to war. She taught at a primary school and worked alone in her paddy field; whatever she earned had to stretch thin since her children were young and her parents-in-law sick.

"How long did it take you to cycle all the way here, Hạnh?" asked Grandma.

"Just a little over a day and a night, Mama."

"Don't do it again, please. It's long and dangerous."

"You once walked more than three hundred kilometers, remember, Mama?"

As we approached the bomb crater, our neighbors stopped us, asking Auntie Hạnh many questions.

I didn't hear what they said because I lagged behind to study my aunt from the back. She looked just like my mother then, with velvety hair flowing down to her slender waist. Oh how I longed to run my fingers through my mother's hair again. We'd always washed our hair together, under the shade of our *bàng* tree. Those days seemed like a dream away; even our beloved tree was now just a memory.

"Who's taking care of your kids, Hạnh? How are little Thanh and Châu?" Grandma asked once we were by ourselves again.

"They can take care of themselves fine, Mama. You should see how tall they are now."

We reached the pile of rubble that had been our home. Auntie Hạnh rested her bike against the broken *bàng* trunk. Grandma had planted this tree when she built the house. The *bàng* had decorated our front door each spring with emerald buds, each summer with tangy fruit, each autumn with red leaves of fire, and each winter with a web of slender branches. Now its roots protruded into the air like raised, burned hands.

"Oh my tree. My home." Auntie Hạnh caressed the torn bark.

"*Trong cái rủi có cái may*," said Grandma. Good luck hides inside bad luck. "We'll plant another tree and build another house."

Aunt Hạnh dried her eyes with the sleeve of her shirt. "So, where have you been sleeping?"

I pointed toward the patch of dirt, our former backyard. Grandma's friends had cut away some *bàng* branches, hammering them down into the earth like tent poles. The branches now bore the corners of a plastic sheet, to make the roof of our shelter. A tattered straw mat made the floor, three unbroken bricks our cooking stove, a tin bucket our cooking pot. I'd been gathering dry twigs and leaves for fuel.

Auntie Hạnh shook her head. She unhooked the rubber cord that tethered the brown sack to her bike. "Just some rice and sweet potatoes."

I helped her free the bundle, my mouth watering at the thought of food.

"You have many mouths to feed, Hạnh," said Grandma. "Hương and I, we have our food stamps."

"But Mama, people say many government stores have been destroyed, that there isn't much food left to buy."

"Well, you have your children and parents-in-law to feed. Don't bring anything next time."

I stole a glance at Grandma. Every morning she woke up before the sun, standing in long lines in front of government stores. Mostly she returned home empty-handed. If we were lucky, she'd come back with a handful of manioc. Rarely could Grandma get us a cup of uncooked rice, and even then, it was often stale and infested with insects.

Grandma helped Auntie Hạnh carry the sack into our shelter. I ran ahead, straightening the straw mat. Putting the sack down, Grandma reached for a bottle of water, handing it to my aunt, who took a long drink.

Rummaging through the sack, Auntie Hạnh winked at me. "Look what I have for you."

A book! Tô Hoài's *Adventures of a Cricket*.

"One of my favorites." Auntie Hạnh smiled.

"It's wonderful, at least not a work of propaganda," said Grandma.

I was tempted to start reading straight away, but Auntie Hạnh pulled another package out of the sack, giving it to me.

"Cookies?" I gasped, wanting to rip it open but not daring. I told myself not to show my aunt I was hungry.

"Your uncle Tuấn brought these back for us." Auntie Hạnh stretched her legs. "Cookies from Russia, can you believe it?"

"Tuấn came home for a visit? How is he?" Grandma asked as hope swelled in my chest. Perhaps my parents and uncles would soon be back to see us, too.

"Skinny as a firewood stick, but he brought some good news. He said we're negotiating with the Americans, to restore peace to our land. Mama . . . on the way here, I heard about the Paris Peace Accords from the public radio's broadcast."

"Yes," said Grandma. "It's great, but . . ."

"But what?"

"The war will only end once all of our loved ones are home."

I looked away, the longing for my parents and uncles heavy in my chest. Something that felt like fear churned. Many of my friends had received bad news from the battlefields. Such news ignited more anger. Some boys at my school, those too young to enlist, had cut their hands, using their blood to write letters to the Army, volunteering to become soldiers. I hoped the war was really ending, bringing home my parents, uncles, and everyone I knew.

"Ah, Guava." Auntie Hạnh tickled me. "No sharing?" She eyed the package in my hands.

I tore off the wrapping. The cookies lay in neat rows, each engraved with delicate patterns.

I offered them first to my aunt and Grandma, then ate as slowly as I could, letting each bite dissolve on my tongue. Years later, when a friend asked what sweet food tasted like to me, I thought about those cookies and said: Happiness.

In our makeshift home, Grandma and my aunt seemed to forget about their worries. They chatted about old times, giggling together. Around us, wisps of smoke rose from our neighbors' shelters, entwining into the red glow of sunset. Out on the neighborhood lane, some of my friends were chasing each other, their laughter spiraling above the smoke. They called me to join them, but I didn't. With Auntie Hạnh by my side, it felt almost as if my mother were back.

That night, I slept between the two women, their soft voices drifting me into a dream. In it, my mother was running toward me, my father alongside her. As I called their names, my mother bent down, scooping me up. She smelled just like Auntie Hạnh. My father embraced us both, laughing, saying he'd never let us out of his sight again.

I woke up to find myself blanketed by Grandma's clothes. It was cold; the moon was out, trembling above the mist. Grandma and Auntie Hạnh were clearing away the rubble. They were humming a song. Their voices felt like summer on my face.

Every day, Grandma urged Auntie Hạnh to go home, but she stayed and worked. She worked as I went back to school and Grandma to her class. She worked until the debris had been cleared away and our shack built. Thanks to the kindness of those we knew and those we didn't, we now had a better shelter: rusty tin sheets over bamboo poles. We no longer had to sleep outside in the whipping rain of winter.

Once my aunt was sure Grandma and I would be all right, she wiped her tears, leading her bike out to the dirt path. To prepare for her journey, Grandma had stayed up the night before, cooking a small bucket of rice, pressing the rice into balls, sprinkling them with crushed peanuts and salt. I didn't know how Grandma managed to find those peanuts; they were as rare and valuable as gold.

We watched Auntie Hạnh cycle away.

"Be careful, Daughter," Grandma murmured, only for her and me to hear. She lifted her face up to the sky, as if fearing bombs would be dropped onto the roads where her daughter would be traveling.

I lost myself in *Adventures of a Cricket*. I wished I could be Mèn the cricket, leaving his nest to venture out into the world, to see the vastness of nature, meet all types of people, have a taste of independence, cause mischief, and make new friends. In the world of Mèn, there was no war. It seemed only humans waged wars on each other, making each other suffer.

More than a week after Auntie Hạnh's departure, I walked home from school with Grandma, gossiping about my friends along the way. She still didn't allow me to go anywhere without her; she'd picked me up after her class.

Our neighborhood lane stretched out in front of us, filled with soggy mud, dotted by pieces of broken brick. We advanced slowly, stepping onto whatever brick islands our feet could find. Grandma gripped my hand in case I slipped.

"*Bà Diệu Lan,*" someone called Grandma's name. I turned to see our neighbor Mr. Tập waving at us. "Two soldiers came looking for you," he said. "I sent them to your house. I thought you were home."

Grandma thanked the man, gripped my hand tighter, and hurried forward.

In front of us stood a yard—our communal washing area—the only place in our neighborhood where we could collect clean water that dripped from a slimy tap. Kids and their empty buckets made up a long line. As we approached, the children sprang up. Abandoning the buckets and jostling each other, they hurtled toward us.

Sơn, the boy who won most of our racing games, pulled at Grandma's shirt. "Grandma, the soldiers asked about you. They—"

"They said they wanted to wait for you," my friend Thủy interrupted. Several voices buzzed up around us like bees.

"Wait. One person at a time, please," said Grandma. "Now, where are the soldiers?"

"Over there. Over there!" Several hands pointed at Mrs. Như's shack, which sat across from ours.

I struggled with my plastic sandals. Thủy dragged me forward. Grandma was already rushing ahead. She slipped on the mud, tried to stand, and fell again. When I arrived at her side, two soldiers were already pulling her up. We helped Grandma wipe off the mud, but she brushed our hands away, telling us she was fine.

The soldiers stood tall and thin in their dark green uniforms. One was older, with deep wrinkles around his eyes. The other one was young, as young as the high school boys who'd just left my school for the battlefields.

"Dạ, xin chào," the older soldier offered Grandma his polite greeting. "We're looking for the family of Comrade Nguyễn Hoàng Thuận."

Nguyễn Hoàng Thuận was Grandma's fourth child. My Uncle Thuận.

Grandma clutched my hand, leading the soldiers toward our home. The neighborhood kids followed, their whispers mushrooming around us. The older soldier reminded them about their water-collecting duties. They understood his hint and scattered.

"Tell me later . . . about the news they bring." Thủy breathed her words into my ear before dashing away.

Inside our shack, I fetched a towel for Grandma and spread out the straw mat, wondering whether the soldiers knew my parents and other uncles.

Grandma invited the men to sit. They bowed their thanks, taking off their rubber sandals. I eyed the footwear, appreciating the secret of their sturdiness: my father had told me soldiers' sandals were made out of thrown-away tires.

Sitting cross-legged on the mat, the men undid their hats, placing them onto their laps. The hats were the color of their uniforms and each had a brilliant gold star on the front. My parents and uncles wore the same when they went south.

Grandma poured some water into the bucket, placing it on the three bricks. I kindled a fire.

She took a deep breath before turning back to the soldiers. "I hope you didn't have to wait long."

"It wasn't that long, Mother," one soldier said. He called Grandma "Mother," just like my uncles did.

The soldiers were now asking for my name and my grade.

"I'm Hương. I'm thirteen and in grade six, Uncles."

"Ah, you're tall for your age," exclaimed the older soldier.

The younger one laid down a dark green knapsack. It looked full, and I hoped it contained a letter from Uncle Thuận. Grandma had told me there was rarely any postal service from the battlefields, so our best chance of getting some news from my uncles and parents was when one of their comrades returned to the North, bringing us a letter or depositing it into a post box somewhere.

"I must be crazy!" Grandma gave out a sudden laugh. "I'm trying to make tea, yet we have no tea leaves. This has never happened . . ." Her voice quivered with nervousness, but I didn't know why.

"It's fine, Mother. We just had a drink at your neighbor's."

Grandma fumbled for the water bottle. "Sorry, we only have one cup."

I turned to the stove, feeding the fire a couple of twigs. It roared, sending tiny sparks into the air. We couldn't waste such a fire, I told myself, reaching into Auntie Hạnh's sack, groping around for the last handful of rice. This would be sufficient for two bowls of watery porridge. I released the rice into the bucket, watching it slide through a curtain of steam.

The older soldier cleared his throat. "Mother, we heard about the bombing but didn't think it was this bad."

Silence followed. I added water to the pot. The fire bathed me in its warmth.

"Mother, we're here with news about your son, Comrade Nguyễn Hoàng Thuận."

"How's Thuận? Is he well?" Grandma gripped the hem of her shirt, her fingers trembling.

Instead of answering, both men got up, kneeling. The younger soldier unlaced the knapsack. With both hands, he lifted a soldier's uniform while the older man held up several letters.

"Mother . . ." They offered the uniform and the letters to Grandma.

"No!"

"Comrade Nguyễn Hoàng Thuận was brave." I could only catch these few words. Everything around me spun into a blur. I crawled toward Grandma. She was crying, her shoulders heaving.

"We're sorry, Mother. Comrade Thuận was ambushed. He fought courageously."

Grandma reached for my uncle's uniform. She buried her face in his clothes. "*Thuận ơi, ơi con ơi. Con về với mẹ đi con ơi!*"—she wailed his name, asking him to come back to her.

I clung onto Grandma. My Uncle Thuận was dead. Uncle Thuận, who'd tossed me into the air and tickled me until I rolled around laughing. Uncle Thuận, who'd climbed countless *sấu* trees to pick the ripest fruit for me, who'd made the most beautiful paper kites for me to fly.

"Mother, we know how terrible you must feel. But we assure you your son didn't die in vain. We, as his comrades, will wipe out the enemy."

Grandma shook her head as if not wanting to hear more. "Did you . . . did you know Thuận well?"

"We belonged to the same unit, Mother. Comrade Thuận was a brother to us. He was kind to everyone."

Grandma ran her fingers over the letters, tracing the handwriting of her son.

"There's one more." The older soldier held out another letter. "For his girlfriend, Miss Thu."

Grandma cupped the letter in her palms. She swallowed hard. "Thuận wanted to marry her. I was already saving for their happy day. Our happy day."

"We know, Mother. Thuận told us he couldn't wait to hear you sing at his wedding."

"I'll go see Thu tomorrow," Grandma said. "Would you . . . would you like something to eat?"

"Thank you, but we need to go." The older man smiled weakly. "We're here on a training course, Mother. Our commander asked us to see you first."

Grandma nodded. "Stay safe . . . so you can see your families again."

The soldiers bent their heads. Outside, a strong gust of wind ripped through the air, clashing against our tin roof. On the neighborhood lane, a young boy called for his mother, his cries fading into the distance.

I turned back to the fire. It had dwindled, leaving behind half-burned, smoldering twigs. I could hear nothing now, and felt nothing except for the tightening grip of winter.

GRANDMA AND I set up an altar for Uncle Thuận. We no longer had a photo of him. His knapsack and clothes sat in front of his incense bowl. Grandma stayed up three nights to pray for my uncle's soul to reach Heaven. Her murmurs, the wooden bell's rhythmic chime, and incense smoke filled our hut.

I woke up after the third night to see Grandma in front of our home, gazing up at the sky, Uncle Thuận's letters in her hands—letters I'd learned by heart. I only needed to close my eyes for his words to appear before me, leading me into Trường Sơn jungles where he journeyed under tall trees, where butterflies flittered and monkeys jumped from one branch to the next, where his laughter rose as he caught fish from streams and picked *tàu bay* plants to eat. There was no fear, no fighting, no death in his letters. Only hope, love of life, and the longing for home. He was just a young man who believed his future was ahead of him.

I went to Grandma, embracing her. The sky was as clear as a mirror, and I sensed Uncle Thuận was up there with my ancestors, watching over us.

We'd hoped for the war to end, but it continued. If Grandma was sorrowful and fearful, she never let me see it again. One day, after looking long and hard at my thin body, our cold kitchen, and our ragged home, she told me she wanted to quit her teaching job, which paid next to nothing. At first I thought I'd heard it wrong, but then her students started appearing, pleading with Grandma to change her mind.

"Please, Grandma, don't quit!" I insisted the next day as she picked me up from school.

"Shh." She put a finger to her lip, eyeing the teachers who stood close by.

At home, she lowered herself onto the straw mat. "Now we can talk. But let's keep our voices low."

"You can't quit teaching, Grandma. Don't you see how much your students love you?"

She reached for our comb, running it through my hair. "Yes, I'll miss my students. But I can't stand brainwashing their innocent minds with propaganda. We aren't just teachers, we're servants of the Party."

"But where will you work, Grandma?"

"Can you keep a secret?" She brought her mouth to my ear. "I'm going to trade on the black market, to buy us food and rebuild our home. To save for the return of your parents and uncles. And I'll be free, no longer somebody's servant."

"You'll become a *con buôn*—a trader? But that's . . . that's bad. . . ." My eyes widened, the words of my ethics teacher ringing in my ears: "As a socialist country, we honor workers and farmers. We must sweep bourgeoisie and traders away from our society. They are leeches living on people's blood."

"Ha, it seems you've been brainwashed, too." Grandma snorted. "There's nothing wrong with being a trader, and you can bet I'm going to become one. In fact, I've already traded my gold earrings for some stuff to sell."

I reached for her ears and gasped. Her only valuable belonging, which she'd saved for Uncle Thuận's wedding, had disappeared.

"You traded the earrings for what, Grandma?"

"Let me see." She counted her fingers. "Sandals, towels, batteries, soap, bicycle tires. Best-selling items on the black market."

"But where are they?" I looked around our empty shack.

"At a friend's house. In the Old Quarter. They'd be confiscated if I carried them around."

"But isn't it illegal, Grandma? I heard only government stores are supposed to trade—"

"Guava." She interrupted me, taking my face into her hands. "I'm not going to do something bad, believe me."

I looked into Grandma's eyes and saw determination. But would her new job get us into trouble?

"We need food," Grandma told me. "People need these items. Besides, we have to prepare for the future, for the return of your parents and uncles. We can't live forever like this." She patted our bed, the straw mat. It looked miserable, glued to the earthen floor.

"Grandma, but if something happens to you—"

"Nothing will. I'll be very, very careful." She kissed my hair then pointed at a pot dangling from the roof of our cooking area. "Guess what I have for us?"

"Rice?" My stomach rumbled.

"Better. Wait and see." She winked at me. "I got you a gift, too, but can't remember where I put it."

I jumped up and peeled away the straw mat. Nothing. I looked under our pillows. There was nothing under our clothes and among our bowls and chopsticks, either.

"Look harder." Grandma giggled.

Finally, I found my gift, wrapped and hidden under the pile of dry branches for cooking fuel. A book. *Pinocchio, the Adventures of a Little Wooden Boy.* Squatting on the mat, I opened the pages, which transported me to Italy, where Geppetto the woodcarver discovered a piece of wood that could talk.

A delicious smell rose from the kitchen. I lifted my eyes. Grandma's thin body bent down to the fire. She'd always encouraged me to read far and wide, unlike my friends' parents who pushed their children to memorize textbooks. She'd always done the best for me. I was a bad granddaughter for doubting her.

I came to her, eyeing the pan. Beef. Paper-thin slices of it were sizzling.

"There's one thing I don't like about becoming a trader." Grandma squinted her eyes against the smoke. "I won't be home often to look after you."

"I can look after myself, Grandma. Remember how you panicked the other night? It wasn't necessary."

As Grandma turned around to chop more onions, my fingers became a pair of chopsticks, lifting several slices of beef, ferrying them into my mouth. My tongue burned, my eyes watered, but my stomach cheered.

I quickly wiped my mouth before Grandma could catch me. She tossed pieces of ginger and onions into the beef, her chopsticks danced, mixing them together.

"I'm sorry." She added a dash of fish sauce into the beef. "But I'd gone to Thủy's house and her mother said she hadn't seen you."

"I was playing in her backyard, Grandma. Please, stop worrying about me."

"Guava, I promised your mother to take care of you. I can't let anything happen—"

"Don't you see how big and strong I've become?" I pulled her up, showing her that the height of our shoulders matched. "And should somebody try to kidnap me, I'd kick their buttock." I poked my finger into Grandma's stomach. Quick as lightning, she jumped back, her hand blocking mine.

I kicked into her groin. She raised her leg, blocking my leg.

"All right, all right. I shouldn't have forgotten I've taught you the moves of Kick-Poke-Chop." Grandma laughed. "Let me finish cooking, or else everything will burn."

GRANDMA'S NEW JOB gave me freedom. She was gone most of the day, and I didn't need to be home. After school, I spent most of my time with Thủy, skipping ropes, lying in her hammock gossiping, venturing out to see different parts of Hà Nội. We even walked all the way to the Red River, dipping our feet into the water, the wind whistling in our hair.

As Grandma turned into a professional *con buôn*, the Old Quarter became the maze of her secret operations. She had no stall, nor did she carry any of the goods with her. With a *nón lá* resting on her head, shielding her from the sun, she hung around government stores, looking for customers. Negotiations were conducted in whispers. Once the price was agreed upon, Grandma took her customer somewhere else, where the item was handed over and money paid. All the while, everyone involved had to be watchful. They would scatter and abort the sale whenever a policeman or government guard appeared.

By now, American planes had vanished from Hà Nội's sky. Grandma made the most out of the opportunity by working day and night. Dark rings appeared around her eyes. Her skin was scorched by the sun, and she had blisters on her feet. In exchange for the danger she faced, she brought home food, clothes, and books for me. And whenever she was home, she sang.

"As long as I have my voice, I'm still alive," she had told me as she recounted how she'd carried Uncle Sáng three hundred kilometers to Hà Nội, on foot. My uncle was a baby then. He was a soldier now. Where was he fighting and was he surviving? Were my parents surviving?

"Grandma," I asked one night. "How come Auntie Hoa hasn't

visited us for a while?" Auntie Hoa was Uncle Sáng's wife and lived in an apartment near the Hà Nội Opera House. Her parents were high-ranking Communist officials.

"I think we won't see her for quite a while longer." Grandma was eating her dinner after a long day of work. It was nearly midnight. She picked up some water spinach with her chopsticks, dipped it into fish sauce, and popped it into her mouth.

"How come? Isn't she supposed to take care of you when Uncle Sáng is away, Grandma?"

"She belongs to a different class. A higher class. So I guess she isn't bound by any rule." Grandma shrugged as her chopsticks ferried a couple of tiny shrimps, which I'd cooked with juicy star fruit.

She smacked her lips after chewing. "Delicious, you're becoming a chef."

"Grandma," I insisted. "I know Auntie Hoa holds an important Party position, but we're still her family, right?"

"Right, but it doesn't mean she's allowed to show us compassion. Rumors travel far these days, and she knows I'm trading. I'm sure she won't visit us for a while. People could run into trouble if they're caught associating with me."

"That's why our neighbors don't visit us anymore, except for Mrs. Nhân. I don't mind but when it comes to Auntie . . ."

"It doesn't matter, Guava. Nothing matters when I have you."

A FEW DAYS later, I went to Thủy's shack, bringing her a small plate of *bánh cuốn* Grandma and I had cooked together. These crepes—thin layers of steamed rice flour wrapped around minced pork and finely chopped mushroom—were her favorite.

"She's not here," her mother said before I could step inside.

"I've got something for her, Auntie." I lifted the *bánh cuốn*.

"We already ate." She turned away, leaving me desolate in her yard. I tried to think of the reasons for her rudeness. Perhaps I'd forgotten to bow my greetings when I last saw her?

Next day at school, Thủy avoided me.

"What's going on?" I caught up with her on the way home.

She kept on walking.

I blocked her path. "Did I do something wrong?"

She tried to get around me but I reached for her arm. "I saved some *bánh cuốn* for you—"

"I don't want your food." She pulled herself away from me. "Please, you shouldn't visit me anymore."

"It's your parents, isn't it? They don't want us to be friends because of my Grandma's job. . . ."

She bent her head. When she looked up, a proverb spilled out of her mouth, *"Cá không ăn muối cá ươn, con cãi cha mẹ trăm đường con hư."* Fish failing to absorb salt spoils; children defying parents ruin themselves hundreds of ways.

As she left, I wondered whether she expected me to defy my grandmother to earn her friendship.

That night, I planned to try to convince Grandma to quit trading, only to see her come home with a smile as wide as a river. "A book from America," she told me, unwrapping a bundle, revealing more than a hundred pages of text, all hand-written. "It cost quite a fortune, but I thought you might like to read it. The novel is called *Little House in the Big Woods*, very famous in America."

"Why should I read something from the country that bombed us?" I looked toward Thủy's house, hoping she'd change her mind.

"You know . . . not all Americans are bad. Many have been demonstrating against the war." Grandma picked up the first page, reading it out loud. The book began with "Once upon a time," just like a fairy-tale, and brought me immediately into the mysterious world of an American girl called Laura and her house made of logs, surrounded by great, dark forests where wolves, bears, and deer lived.

"Who translated this book, Grandma?" I fingered the pages, touching the path that would lead me into the country I knew little about, although its actions were changing my whole life.

"A professor. He was sent to Russia to study American literature, to see into the minds of American people, to help us defeat their army. He practiced his English by translating this book."

"This is his handwriting?"

"His family hand-copied it, to sell. . . ."

LITTLE HOUSE IN the Big Woods helped me forget about Thủy and allowed me to become friends with Laura, with whom I sat listening to her father's music and stories. Just like my father, Pa was funny and enjoyed working with his hands. Just like my mother, Ma was attentive and loved to cook.

I adored Laura but also envied her. While my world was full of longing, hers was filled with the presence of her parents, her sisters Mary and Carrie, as well as her dog Jack. But just like me, Laura had her own angst. She feared for her father as he crossed the dark forest, went to town to sell furs and didn't come back for an entire night. She was terrified for her mother when they ran into a bear, which could have killed them both.

I had heard rumors that American people liked to rule other races, that they didn't have feelings like us, but now I knew they loved their families, and they also had to work hard to earn their food. They enjoyed dancing, music, and storytelling, just like us.

TOWARD THE END of March 1973, news of American troops withdrawing from Sài Gòn reached Hà Nội. During class time, my teachers showed pictures of tall foreign men boarding their planes. We clapped our hands, singing songs of victory. It seemed the war was definitely ending, now that we'd defeated the American invaders.

At home though, Grandma wasn't so excited. She knew from information circulating in the Old Quarter that fighting was still taking place. With the Americans gone, the war was now among Vietnamese ourselves, the North against the South.

Whenever I saw a soldier visiting our neighborhood, I was petrified. I tried to focus on my studies, read my books, and pray.

And I stayed close to Grandma. After dinner and homework, I'd take a little nap and wake up when she came home. While she washed up and ate, I was right by her side, telling her about school and hearing about her days. At government stores, she told me, there wasn't enough food. Arguments often exploded as people fought for a place in the long lines. More and more people were getting up in the middle of the night to queue, then sell their places to others. People had to offer bribes to get a better cut of meat or some rice without the generous addition of maggots. Everyone around us was doing whatever they could to survive, to live.

Grandma and I saved as much as we could. Each night, I helped her count the coins and wrinkled notes she'd brought home. Each was black with the sweat of her labor.

One early evening, Grandma came home with a bicycle. Running my hands over its rusty handlebars, I laughed. In my neighborhood, only Mr. Lượng owned a bicycle, and he was a Party official. I hoped Grandma would let me use her bike sometimes; Thủy would faint from being jealous. She still wouldn't talk to me, and I'd tried not to look her way. My friends were now Laura the American girl, Pinocchio the wooden boy, and Mèn the cricket.

Grandma showed me a certificate issued by the Hà Nội Department of Public Security that said she was the bike's rightful owner. On the bike frame dangled a number plate made of metal, which read 3R-3953. We hugged each other, jumping up and down. To celebrate, Grandma took the evening off and rode me to Silk Street. The moon, round and bright, followed us. We rejoiced at the sight of the five-section wooden house. Under moonlight, it stood ancient and dreamlike—the wooden doors that bore exquisite carvings of flowers and birds, the ceramic dragons and phoenixes that soared atop the roof's curving ends. Did the home of my ancestors survive the bombings, too? When would I be able to go there and touch the remnants of Grandma's childhood?

Now Grandma could get around faster and serve more customers. She expanded her business to sell winter jackets, raincoats, and radios. Some of those were even imported from China and Russia.

Her trading job helped Grandma learn news about the war. She told me the Northern Army was advancing further south and winning battles. Yet I feared my parents would never come home. We'd heard nothing from or about them. Out of my remaining uncles, only Uncle Đạt had managed to send back a letter, saying how much he missed us. He was okay and heading to Sài Gòn. I wondered how hard it was for Miss Nhung, his girlfriend. She'd been together with my uncle since high school and worked as an accountant. She was one of the few who didn't care about Grandma being a trader. Miss Nhung visited us often, and when Grandma wasn't home, she taught me to ride her bike. I hoped Uncle Đạt would soon come back and marry her.

Months passed. I turned fourteen. Grandma worked and worked.

One night, she pulled me close. "I think we have enough to build our-selves a very simple brick house."

My eyes grew large. By now, our shack could barely stand against a strong wind. The tin sheets became blazing heaters during hot days and leaked whenever it rained.

"I might need to borrow, but we'll be able to repay," said Grandma. "Let's plan for three bedrooms."

"On this?" I looked around our small shack.

"We'll build into the backyard. We need one room for your parents, one for Đạt and Nhung, and one for you and me, you see." She smiled at me. "Do you want to draw a plan for our house? Just a simple one. What do you think we need?"

"A bomb shelter!"

"Oh yes, it's most important. Shall we have it at the entrance of our bedroom?"

"But we need three, Grandma."

"Ah, for the three bedrooms. Such a thinker you are. How about a living and dining room where we can eat and talk?"

"And a kitchen and a washroom?"

"And the best corner, somewhere light and airy, for your study desk?"

"That could be next to our bedroom window."

Just like that, the two of us made the plan for our house. I sketched it and each night, Grandma and I refined it together. We made sure our windows were high up, to avoid spying eyes. Once our drawing was complete, Grandma brought it to the Old Quarter, where an archi-tect drew a more complex plan based on ours. He added details for electric wiring and plumbing, even though we rarely had electricity, and no water could reach our house.

I couldn't wait for it to be built. Thủy was still living in her shack, for sure she'd want to pay a visit.

A few weeks later, Grandma came back from work, grinning. "Found a team of construction workers. Got the permits to buy cement and bricks."

"We need permits, Grandma?"

"Without them, materials would be confiscated on their way here." She brought her mouth to my ear, her breath tickling me. "We need to build very quickly. The neighbors will be very curious. If anyone asks anything, tell them to come to me."

I nodded.

"I've been to the People's Committee Unit to get us the clearance to rebuild." Grandma showed me a document with a fiery red stamp. "Had to beg for it. They wanted to know where the money came from. As they were grilling me, Trương—Thuận's former classmate—walked in. Trương told his comrades to give me a break. He said I'd sent my four children to war to protect this country from the American invaders, and I should be allowed to rebuild my home."

I looked up at Uncle Thuận's altar. Perhaps his spirit had blessed us.

"Trương was helpful," sighed Grandma, "but I should've told him he was wrong."

"Wrong? What do you mean, Grandma?"

"I didn't send your uncles and mother to war, Guava. I nearly lost them when they were little. I didn't want them out of my sight. Ever!"

I squeezed Grandma's hands. We looked out to our neighborhood, where shanties sat silent in the dark.

"There's a hurdle we have to cross. Trương told me, in private, that to ease the jealousy of those around us, we should do something for the neighborhood."

"Should we offer them food?"

"Good thinking, Guava. But I'd like our help to last a bit longer. What do you think if we have a well dug and a pump installed where the water tap is?"

I jumped up, excited at the idea. "The line for water has been ridiculous. I bet our neighbors will be overjoyed."

"Don't bet on it yet. I'll need to convince them."

SEVERAL WEEKS LATER, Grandma came home early and hurried through dinner. I clapped my hands when she said I could come along to the weekly citizen meeting.

The People's Committee Office used to be housed in a charming French-style villa with spacious balconies and large wooden windows. Flattened by bombs, it was now a box of cement and bricks. "Rebuilt in the Soviet style," Grandma told me.

My neighbors poured into the stuffy meeting room and sat in rows of chairs. I looked over at Grandma, and her calmness quelled the butterflies in my stomach. She looked graceful despite her sun-roasted skin and bony frame. Her face glowed with confidence. Her long hair was rolled up and pinned behind the nape of her neck, revealing her scars.

"Thank you for coming." Mr. Phong, the head of the People's Committee Unit cleared his voice, and the crowd grew silent. "We have many items to discuss tonight, but first, one of our neighbors has a proposal."

Murmurs rose as Grandma stepped up to the front.

"I'd like to thank you all for your kindness during the past years." Grandma looked around the room. "When my children and I came here, we were country bumpkins, and you opened your arms to receive us. You helped make this neighborhood our home."

Our neighbors stopped talking. I could see that they were drawn by Grandma's sincere words.

"As you know," Grandma continued, "our communal water supply has been giving us problems. We spend hours each day waiting in line, and there hasn't been enough water to go around. I've been thinking about an alternative supply, so I asked a technician to visit our neighborhood. He gathered samples of our underground water, especially under the communal washing area." Grandma passed a stack of papers around. "In your hands are results of the water tests. If drawn from more than fifty meters below the ground level, the water is good, safe for us to use." She paused to give her listeners time to scan the papers. People started whispering again, but this time they were nodding their heads.

"With these results," said Grandma, "I'd like to make a proposal. Instead of relying on the public water supply, we should have a system to draw underground water out for us. A well and a manual pump would do the job."

"This sounds grand, but it costs a lot of money," a neighbor said aloud.

"We don't have enough to eat, how can we afford it?" another one asked.

Grandma raised her hand. "As a token of my gratefulness to this community, I'd like to pay for all the costs involved."

Voices mushroomed all around us. At first, people's eyes seemed to light up, but as they talked among themselves, their eyes dimmed. Heads began to shake.

"We can't accept money from a *con buôn!*" Mr. Tân, an elderly neighbor sprang to his feet. "Bourgeoisie and traders are leeches that suck the life out of our economy."

"Her money is dirty." Mrs. Quỳnh, a middle-aged woman pointed her finger toward Grandma's face.

"She can afford to throw her money away, money she earns without doing any real work," said someone else.

I saw myself in the angry sneers targeted at Grandma. I'd held strong feelings about her job, only to have my eyes opened by her entrepreneurship, hard work, and determination.

I had to be Mèn the cricket who was brave and stood up for his own beliefs. I found myself on my feet. "Please, may I speak? My name is Hương. I'm Grandma Diệu Lan's granddaughter. My parents have gone to the battlefields, and Grandma takes care of me. I live with her, and I'm aware of what she does." I looked at Grandma and smiled. "Grandma Diệu Lan works harder than anyone I know. She barely sleeps. Just look at the blisters on her feet and they'll tell you that she doesn't exploit anyone. Every cent she wants to donate to this neighborhood has been hard-earned money."

A tear rolled down Grandma's face. Silence enveloped the room.

"Children don't lie." Mrs. Nhân stood up. She was the only person here who'd remained friendly to us. "Don't think about propaganda, please. Think about the benefits this would give your own family. Your children will have more time to play. You will have more time to relax. The water will be much safer. No more lining up from four in the morning. No more fighting about who got a fuller bucket."

People started murmuring together again.

"All right, all right." Mr. Phong raised his hands to silence the crowd. "Let's have a secret ballot. There're paper, pens, and a box on the table over there. Write down your wish, yes or no to Mrs. Diệu Lan's offer, and put it into the box. The majority decision will be the final one."

As the neighbors made their way to the table, Grandma found me. "I guess from today I shouldn't call you Guava anymore. You're a young lady now, Hương."

I beamed. "I love my baby name, but yes, Hương would be nice."

I squeezed Grandma's shoulders as Mr. Phong read the result aloud. "Out of forty-one people present here tonight . . . thirty-six agreed to

Mrs. Diệu Lan's proposal." He turned to Grandma. "On behalf of our neighborhood, thank you."

A FEW DAYS later, a group of men built a well and installed a manual pump. Even little children could use it to fill their buckets. Instead of waiting for their turn to collect water from the slimy tap, kids now washed themselves in front of their homes, tossing rainbows of water over each other, laughing.

Construction materials started to fill our shack. Mrs. Nhân came by one late evening, bringing a book of astrology. She sat with Grandma by the oil lamp, scrutinizing complicated-looking charts, comparing them against our birthdays.

"The date of the Ox, the hour of Dragon is an auspicious start," Mrs. Nhân said, and Grandma nodded.

Grandma stayed home to supervise the construction. Every day, returning from school, I had to push through a crowd of curious onlookers to be able to get inside.

The workers and Grandma labored day and night. More than two months later, our new house stood, gleaming under the sun. Grandma could only afford to build one floor, but all the rooms we'd planned were there, the way we'd mapped them out.

Grandma smiled as I dashed from one room to the next. There was so much light. I loved my writing corner, the bedrooms, and the living-dining room that opened into the kitchen. I adored the entrance door with its solid wood panels and the windows that let me see a piece of the sky.

I continued to share a bed with Grandma, leaving the other rooms empty. They were there for my parents and uncles to come back to.

Grandma brought home a young *bàng* tree. We planted it in our tiny front yard, on the same spot where the old tree once stood. Every day, I watered it and watched it grow. I couldn't wait for my mother to return, for the tree to shade us as we washed our hair.

As we now had a secure roof over our heads, Grandma came home from the market just after sunset once a week. We spent the entire evening practicing meditation and the swift moves of Kick-Poke-Chop self-defense.

"Calm your mind and build your inner strength," she told me.

Grandma kept working extra hard. Gradually and secretly, she brought home pieces of furniture: my study desk and chair, a book-shelf, a wooden *phản* for the living area, three bamboo beds, and a dining set. They were old and rickety, but we treasured them. We kept the bookshelf next to my study corner and filled it with stories that would take me to faraway places.

"Do you want a job, Hương?" Grandma asked one night that summer as we unrolled our straw mat under the *bàng* tree. It was too hot to stay inside. The neighbors were also out on the lane, paper fans flapping in their hands.

I didn't answer, fearing she'd ask me to become a trader.

Grandma flicked her paper fan. "A friend of mine is making quite a bit of money raising chickens and pigs. All in her little apartment. We have more space than she does."

"Pigs and chickens? Here?"

"Why not? We can keep the chickens in the washroom and the pigs under the *phản*. It'll work, believe me. My farming experiences will come in handy."

To prepare for the animals' arrival, Grandma had another window cut high up into our washroom's wall, to give light and air. She had a multilayer bamboo shelf made. "For the chickens to sleep on and lay their eggs," she explained.

I went with Grandma to pick up ten newly hatched chicks, who stood in a bamboo cage, chirping all the way to our home. The piglets were delivered to us during the night. As soon as I saw them, their names came to my mind. The white piglet with scattered dark spots was Black Dots, and the black piglet with the cute face was Pink Nose. While the chicks were confined to the washroom, we let the pigs roam around our living-dining area.

Now I no longer minded that Thủy had stopped speaking to me. The animals became my most loyal friends. The chicks sang for me when I picked them up, fed them, and cleaned their stall. Black Dots and Pink Nose rubbed their wet mouths against my feet and fell asleep in my arms.

STILL, I MISSED my parents dearly. During the years that she was gone, I imagined seeing my mother again every day. I imagined disappearing into her embrace, into the river of her hair, into her soft breasts. I imagined our voices rising like kites from under the shade of our new *bàng* tree.

I missed how my mother had filled our home with her singing voice, how gracefully she'd danced, how she'd led me along by my fingers, twirling me around her so my shirt would flare. Whenever I was sad, I told myself to be strong, like my mother. She never cried or showed fear. Once we found a snake under our bed and, while I stood there shrieking, she bent and picked it up by the tip of its tail, flinging it out of the open window.

By the beginning of 1975, rumors spread that the war was really ending, and I imagined my mother flying me down the streets of Hà Nội on the back of Grandma's bicycle. We would scream at the top of our lungs as the bike rushed us into a brilliant summer, into red *phượng* flowers, into purple *bằng lăng* petals that blossomed above pavements punctured by bomb shelters. We would stop at the Lake of the Returned Sword, delighting in the delirious coldness of Tràng Tiền ice cream.

In my dreams, my mother always returned with my father. He was tall and handsome. Sometimes he would rush toward me on his two feet; sometimes he struggled on a single leg, leaning on a crutch. Sometimes he embraced me with his two strong arms, and at other times he had no arms at all, just two lumps of soft flesh protruding from his shoulders. But he always laughed as he called my name: "Here's Hương, my daughter."

At the end of March 1975, our city was hit by an unseasonal storm. Heaven dumped bucket after bucket of water over our heads, turning our neighborhood lane into a twisting, blackish river.

Grandma and I sat on our *phản*, counting the money she'd made that day. Strange noises made us turn toward the door, noises other than the rattling of the wind and rain.

"What's that, Grandma?" I asked.

The strange noises boomed again. Faintly, I heard a human voice. Grandma dropped the money, rushing forward.

I jumped down, too. My toes hit the snout of Black Dots, who squealed.

"I'm coming." Grandma pulled the door open. In the dim light of our oil lamp, a thin shadow stood, its hair a tangled mess, its clothes dangling shreds of rags.

The wind tore in, snatching away the light of our lamp.

"*Bà ơi.*" I called for Grandma. The shadow must be a ghost whose grave was unearthed by the storm. The ghosts in the stories I'd been reading were hungry; they sucked people's souls to fill their stomachs.

Grandma was saying something. The wind was howling louder, the ghosts cackling. I hung on to the *phản*, my body as stiff as a tree trunk.

I opened my mouth to call for Grandma to come back, but words were stuck to my throat.

I heard the door closing, moans, footsteps. "Hương," Grandma called. "Your mother is back. Give us some light."

My mother? Could this be true? I fumbled in darkness, searching for the box of matchsticks. I struck one and a fire sprang up, wobbled, and died. I tried another. It didn't ignite. For the third time, I struck three sticks against the side of the matchbox. Holding the fire, I turned.

A woman stood, her head on Grandma's shoulder. Her eyes were closed. Her face was red and swollen, her hair glued against her skull.

"Hương, your mother is home. She's home!" Grandma sobbed.

The fire ate into my fingers. I dropped the matchsticks onto the floor. I didn't feel any pain, for I'd seen the deep anguish on the woman's face. My mother's face.

"Mẹ." I struggled against darkness, rushing to her. My cheek was hot against her chest. My hands clung to her bony frame. "Mẹ, mẹ ơi."

My mother's fingers trembled over my nose, mouth, eyes. "Hương. Oh, my darling. Hương . . ."

The tears that I'd buried inside of me burst. I cried for the years we'd been apart, for Uncle Thuận's death, for the deaths of my classmates, for myself and the fact that I no longer had any real friends.

Grandma relit the lamp. She pushed the money on the phản aside. I helped my mother lie down, drying her with a towel. She shivered under my hands.

As Grandma went to get a change of clothes for my mother, I kissed her forehead. A fever seared through her skin. She moaned.

"You'll be better soon now that you're with us, Mama." I ran the towel along her legs, wiping away the mud, eyeing the large bruises imprinted on her skin. "How did you get home, Mama? Where've you been?" I wanted to ask about my father but feared the answer.

"Hương." My mother opened her eyes. "Your Papa . . . Did your Papa come back?"

My heart paused in its beat. The lamp stopped flickering. "Mama, you didn't find him? You didn't see him?"

A tear slid out of my mother's eye. As she shook her head, I stood up. I walked to the room Grandma had reserved for my parents, putting my face against its door. My mother had led me to believe that she could find my father and bring him back to me. I had believed she could do anything she wanted to.

"I'm sorry, Hương." Her voice was a bare whisper.

The door was hard and cold against my forehead. I wanted to break it open.

"Now the war is ending, Hoàng will be back any day. He'll be back," Grandma's voice said.

"Did you ever get a letter from him?" my mother asked.

"Not yet, Daughter. Perhaps he found no way to send it."

"How about my brothers, Mama?"

"I'm sure they're fine, and they'll be home soon." I turned to see Grandma sitting my mother up, giving her a glass of water. I looked up in the direction of Uncle Thuận's altar, feeling thankful for the darkness: it had concealed the truth from my mother, for now.

As I helped Grandma change my mother, I eyed her protruding ribs. The bruises were not just on her legs, they marked their presence on her back, chest, and thighs. What had happened to her?

Grandma brought a towel and a pail of warm water. As I cleaned my mother's face and hands, she lay there, her eyes tightly shut, her body shuddering. I turned away. I didn't want to look at her, nor pity her. Where had my strong and determined mother gone? She didn't ask about Grandma and me, how we were doing and how we'd survived the bombings.

"Let her rest," Grandma whispered, pulling a blanket to my mother's chest. As she started cooking, I went out to our young *bàng* tree. The rain had died into the earth. A half-moon dangled from the sky. I closed my eyes and saw myself as a child, my mother combing my hair, her singing voice the wind in my ears.

Grandma came out. She embraced me, her arms felt as solid as tree roots, holding me up. "I'm sorry your Mama isn't well, Hương. We must be the pillars for her to lean on."

"She used to be my pillar, Grandma."

"I know, but you're a strong woman now. . . . She needs you."

I looked up at the moon and tried to let its soft light calm me. Perhaps it was wrong of me to feel disappointed at my mother. At least she'd tried to find my father and bring him back. Grandma had said that it was an impossible task.

"Don't tell her about your Uncle Thuận yet," said Grandma. "When she sleeps tonight, I'll bring Thuận's belongings into our room."

I nodded and buried my face into Grandma's hair. Years later, looking back through the journeys of my life, I understood the fear Grandma must have carried, not knowing what would happen the next day to her children. Yet she had to appear strong, for only those who faced battles were entitled to trauma.

That night, after Grandma had fed her a bowl of phở, I sat guarding my mother. I thought that if I watched her closely enough, she wouldn't disappear again. I believed that if I told her how much I'd missed her, she'd once again be the mother I knew.

But as a fifteen-year-old girl, I couldn't imagine how the war had swallowed my mother into its stomach, churning her into someone different before spitting her out. I couldn't understand how she could scream so loud in her sleep, about bullets, shooting, running, and death. There were words I didn't understand. And I couldn't understand how my father's name could sound so sad on her lips.

In the days that followed, several neighbors came to visit my mother. To my surprise, she didn't get out of bed or sit up. She only nodded or shook her head at their questions, her face sad and empty. She did the same with her friends and colleagues from the Bạch Mai Hospital. After a while, they all left, whispering that she was exhausted and needed to rest.

But I knew it was more than that. Sometimes when I was alone with her, her shoulders trembled. She must have been crying, but still, no sounds emerged. They only came during the night, when she slept, her body shaking with nightmares.

Fearing my mother would hurt herself in her sleep, I moved into her room. She didn't want me to be on the same bed, so I unrolled a straw mat onto the floor. I'd been a good sleeper, but no longer.

Once, deep into the night, I heard her whispering in jumbled sentences about a baby. Hair stood up on the back of my neck as she said she'd killed it. I covered my ears. For sure my mother wasn't a murderer. For sure she'd helped deliver the baby, who didn't survive.

The next morning, I told Grandma what I'd heard. She pulled me close. "Your Mama is a doctor. Accidents happen. Don't think too much about it."

Grandma and I tried to nurse my mother back to her own self, by cooking the food she used to love. Yet she ate as if she were chewing sand. She said she was tired when we attempted conversations with her. She turned away whenever I came into her room. She was home, but not home, for she was so lost in the war, she forgot I was her own daughter.

I gave her the recent letters I'd written to her and my father, but she left them there, unopened, next to her pillow.

Grandma had to return to her job. I stopped going to school, to stay close to my mother. There was enough dry food for me to cook, and Grandma often brought us meat, fish, and vegetables early in the morning.

Our days passed quietly. There was no laughter, no talk as I'd hoped.

"Go with her for a walk, she'll feel better," Grandma told me.

But my mother shook her head whenever I suggested the idea. "Let me sleep." She turned away from me again.

One afternoon, as the sun pulled its light across the sky, I held a comb in my hand. Crawling over to my mother who lay on the *phản*, I wondered if she'd push me away.

Her shoulders quivered as I touched her. Untangling the stubborn knots in her hair, I talked. I told her about the books I'd read. I chatted about her friends, who still lived in temporary shacks across from us. Their children had such hungry eyes, sniffing the smell rising from our kitchen. They were the same children who refused food whenever I brought it to them, saying their parents didn't allow them to receive anything from us.

My mother stopped shaking when I finished combing, but her back was still turned toward me. I swallowed my disappointment, moved to the kitchen, and started a fire. Instead of cooking dinner, I found myself grilling a bunch of dried *bồ kết* fruit. Their perfume reminded me of our happy times when my mother and I washed our hair under the old *bàng* tree.

The *bồ kết* sizzled, flowering their fragrance into the air. From the corner of my eye, I saw my mother turn. Her gaze followed my hands as I filled a pot with water, crushed the roasted fruit, and dropped them into the pot. She watched as I broke dry branches, feeding them to the fire, keeping the stew from boiling over.

"Thank you, Daughter." Her whisper startled me. I turned to see her behind me, the stove's flame dancing in her eyes.

"For you to wash your hair, Mama."

She nodded. "I can take care of it now. Go outside and play."

I didn't want to go, but my mother's eyes told me to. Standing under the *bàng* tree, I felt abandoned. Tiptoeing to the entrance door, I peeked inside.

My mother was lugging a bucket into the kitchen. It looked heavy, and I knew it was half-filled with cold water. She lifted the pot of *bồ kết* from the stove, pouring the liquid stew into the bucket, sending steam swirling up around her. She mixed the hair wash, testing its warmth with her elbow.

My mother looked her old self when she sat in a stream of sunlight, tilting her head forward. She scooped up the mixed *bồ kết* stew, letting it run through her hair. A river of light wove its way down a river of black.

Enthralled by the scene, I was stunned when her sobs came, so suddenly and unexpectedly. Her hands clutched her shoulders. She rolled into a ball on the floor, her body shaking.

My fingernails dug into my palms. I didn't care what war meant. I just wanted it to return my mother to me, give me back my father and my uncles, and make our family whole again.

The Great Hunger

Nghệ An, 1942–1948

Guava, tell me how you like this short poem.

> Quiet pond
> a frog leaps into
> the sound of water

You think it's beautiful? I do, too. The poem is a haiku written by a famous Japanese poet named Matsuo Bashō, who lived in the sixteenth century. I found Mr. Bashō's poems a few years ago, when I'd become a teacher and decided to learn about the Japanese. I wanted to understand why Japanese soldiers had done what they did in our country. The books I read told me that many Japanese are Buddhists like us.

They worship their ancestors and love their families. Like us, they like to cook and eat, and dance, and sing.

Before I read those books, I'd watched the Japanese man—Black Eye—in the winter of 1942. I'd tried to believe that he had some goodness inside of him and that he would let my father go.

Do you really want to know what happened to your great-grandpa? All right. Hold my hand as I go on.

Black Eye advanced. He reached into the cart, and flung a sack of potatoes onto the road. The soldiers kicked open the sack, chopped the potatoes into pieces. I watched my father closely as he put the wooden board back onto the cart. Oh, I watched him—the tanned hands that had held me against his chin, the eyes that had lit up whenever they saw my smile, the lips that had told me countless legends and fairy tales of my village.

Several men from the two groups of soldiers were talking to each other in a language I couldn't understand. It sounded soft and lyrical. Surely, the people who held such a language on their tongues couldn't be brutal toward others.

The women were pushed forward. They scrambled frantically into the cart like mice being chased into a hole, hurried by the glinting bayonets. My father stood by, helping them up, sorrow heavy on his face.

"Tell me who the potatoes are really for?" Black Eye roared, shoving his hand against my father's chest, pushing him away from the cart. "For the Việt Minh guerrillas who just killed my comrades?"

"No, Sir. They're for my customers in Hà Nội."

"Ah, for the French, the invaders of your country?" Black Eye laughed. He turned as if about to walk away. But in a swift movement, he spun around, his sword cutting a deadly arc across the air. "Traitor!"

I stood frozen as fountains of blood spouted out of my father's neck. His head thumped down the road, rolling, his eyes wide with terror. As Công pressed his palm tight against my mouth, my father's arms writhed in the air. His body crumpled.

The world around me spun as I tried to run toward my father. Công held me back, whispering that the Japanese would kill us.

I looked on helplessly as a Japanese soldier jumped onto the front of the cart, turning it around. He lifted his feet, kicking the rumps of the buffaloes. The cart's wheels rolled over the headless body of my beloved father.

OH, GUAVA, I'M sorry for the tears you're shedding for your great-grandpa. I'm sorry. I'm so sorry. . . .

I didn't want to tell you about his death, but you and I have seen enough death and violence to know that there's only one way we can talk about wars: honestly. Only through honesty can we learn about the truth.

In seeking the truth about the Japanese, I read as much as I could about them. I found out that, during World War II, Japanese troops beat, hurt, and murdered thousands and thousands of people across Asia.

The more I read, the more I became afraid of wars. Wars have the power to turn graceful and cultured people into monsters.

My father was unlucky to meet one of those monsters. He died so that Công and I could live on. He died protecting us.

We brought my father home. My mother leaned against me as we knelt by his coffin, our heads white with funeral bands. The *đàn nhị* two-string instrument wailed in Công's hands. He played for the entire three days and nights of mourning, the days and nights that saw our home packed with people who came to pay respect to my father. Only then did I learn how many people he'd helped.

I didn't want to say good-bye but the time came. The *đàn nhị* music led the funeral procession to the rice fields where my father was laid to rest. Công played until a dune of soil covered the coffin, the last incense burned out, and the sun died on the horizon.

Công didn't utter a single word during the entire funeral, but when he returned home, he stood in the front yard, the *đàn nhị* raised high above his head. His scream tore into the night as he shattered the instrument onto the brick floor. His wife, Trinh, and Mrs. Tú gathered the broken pieces, trying to put them back together, but he would never play again.

I blamed myself for my father's death. If I hadn't been driving the cart, we would have gone faster, and my father wouldn't have met Black Eye. Your grandpa Hùng didn't let me succumb to my sorrow. "It was not your fault, you were just helping Papa," he said. "Besides, he wouldn't want you to be sad. He would want you to celebrate his life."

My mother was like a tree uprooted. She would just sit there on the *phản*, her gaze distant and empty. Minh, Ngọc, and Đạt didn't leave her alone, though. They surrounded her, becoming the soil of her life, demanding that she grow new roots. "Grandma, play with us," they said, pulling her arms, leading her out of the house and into their childhood games.

We told each other not to venture out of our village. We had to stay away from the fighting among the Việt Minh, the French, and the Japanese, which was growing more intense. We'd hoped for the war to end, but it was escalating. Three years after my father's death, the war found us at our home.

THIS TIME, THE war came in the form of *Nạn đói năm Ất Dậu*—the Great Famine of 1945—which killed two million of our countrymen. Rather than being a vicious tiger gobbling us down, the hunger was a python that squeezed out our energy, until there was nothing left of us except skin and bones.

By April 1945, I was so weak that I didn't care whether I lived or died.

"Diệu Lan, wake up, Diệu Lan!" One morning, I heard Mrs. Tú's call. I wished the housekeeper would leave me alone. But then, a sound made me open my eyes.

It was the faint cries of your mother. A five-year-old baby then, Ngọc was resting her head on my stomach. Next to her, your uncle Đạt, barely four, lay silent. Your uncle Minh called me. I slowly turned and gazed at him: a hollowed face, dark rings around sunken, yellow-ish eyes; he was a seven-year-old skeleton.

I sobbed, gathering the children into my arms.

"Mama, I'm so hungry," Minh whimpered.

Mrs. Tú held out a bowl. Steam rose from her hands but no smell of food.

"Banana roots, perhaps the last ones your mother and I could find," she said. Her skinny arms trembled and I knew she, too, was starving.

I scooped up the black stew, blowing it to cool, feeding the chil-dren, and when they'd had enough, I shared the rest with Mrs. Tú. The banana roots tasted bland in my mouth, but I was grateful for each bite.

As Mrs. Tú lay down, lulling the children to sleep, I looked at what remained of our house. In my brother's room, an old blanket had been folded neatly and piled on top of two worn pillows. Above a cracked cabinet, the *đàn nhị* poked out its broken pieces. I wondered whether our lives would stay like the instrument, shattered and unable to sing. The living room was barren, except for a makeshift bench. What had the Japanese done to our furniture? They'd invaded our village, calling us sympathizers of the Việt Minh. They beat up people for no reason, taking away everything of value: money, jewelry, furniture, pigs, cows, buffaloes, chickens. They robbed us of all our food. They made all villagers uproot our rice and crops, to grow jute and cotton for them. Our family could no longer pay our workers. All around my village, people had gone crazy with hunger. The last drops of water had been scooped out of ponds to catch any remaining fish and snails. No insect could escape human hands. Edible plants were dug up for their trunks, leaves, and roots. It didn't help that a terrible drought had ravaged our whole region, sucking our fields and creeks dry.

My dear husband wasn't home. His mother had died from starvation. His father was growing weak but refused to come and stay with us, believing that his wife's soul still lingered at home and needed company. Hùng had told me he hoped to find something to eat on the way to his father, but I didn't know what. There was no food for sale at the market. Nobody had anything left to sell.

We'd longed for food to reach us from the south, but nothing. Japan and America had been fighting in other parts of the world, and now American bombs had exploded onto our land, destroying shipping lines, ports, roads, and railways.

I had to do something to keep my babies alive.

In the garden, naked of greenery, my mother squatted on bleached soil, poking a stick into the earth. I staggered toward her. "Mama, where are Brother Công and Sister Trinh?"

She lifted her haggard face. Most of her hair had turned white, thinning on her skull. "They went to the fields."

I thought about the cracked fields and hundreds of hungry villagers out there, searching.

"Have you eaten yet, Mama?"

"Yes, banana roots."

Picking up a stick, I started digging with her. Dry soil pushed back against my hands. Surely a manioc or sweet potato was hiding somewhere. This part of the garden used to teem with those plump roots.

After a long while, my mother said, "We have to go look for food."

"But where, Mama?"

"The forest. There'll be wild fruits and insects."

"But that's too far away."

"Fifteen kilometers, maybe."

"It takes three hours at least. I'm not sure we can make it."

"Listen, Diệu Lan. Every patch of earth close by has been dug up. We must go further. *Còn nước còn tát.*" While there's still water, we will scoop. "The forest is our remaining hope."

"I'll go, Mama. You stay here—"

"No! We'll go together." My mother clutched my shoulder. "Without food, the children will die. They'll die, don't you understand?"

In the kitchen, I filled a bamboo pipe with water, looping its string around my shoulder, then picked up a chopping knife. Reaching for two *nón lá*, I put one on my head and gave the other to my mother.

We unlocked our gate, stepped out and secured it again. A horrific stench made me gag. Nearby, a rotting corpse lay face down on the dirt road, green flies buzzing around it. A bit further on, the body of a mother embraced her baby in their death. Several corpses were scattered in the basin of our dried-up village pond.

"Madam Trần. Help us!" A desperate call rang out from a pile of corpses. A woman with bleeding lips stretched out her palm. On her bare chest lay a boy—a skeleton of skin and bones.

"I have no food left." My mother bent down, tears trickling down her face.

"So hungry," the woman whimpered, pulling herself and her son closer to us.

"We only have water." I lifted the bamboo pipe. The woman swallowed in big gulps.

As I nursed water into the boy's mouth, my children's faces flickered in my mind. We needed to hurry and get back to them.

My mother had squatted down, howling. In front of her was the body of Mr. Tiến, who'd worked for us for many years. His wife and son were next to him, their heads on his chest. They died a horrific death, pain still spilling from their gaping mouths.

I pulled my mother up and away. There were people everywhere, lying by the roadside, dying, begging. A few tried to snatch our legs as we wobbled past them, but they were too weak to hold on.

Except for the feeble sounds of humans, the village was quiet. There were no animals left to make a noise. Everything was brown and bleached. Even the landscape was dying.

"Don't stop anymore, Mama." I pulled her away as a woman tried to hold on to her feet.

"Give her some water."

"We don't have much, Mama."

"Damn it. Give it to her!"

I eased the liquid into the woman's mouth. She nodded her thanks, closing her eyes, resting her face on the sun-scorched soil.

We tried to walk faster, passing huts filled with murmurs of children, passing piles of rotting bodies, passing hands that reached out to us, trembling in their calling. We swallowed our tears and walked as if we were blind, as if we had hearts of stone.

Holding on to each other, we wobbled together toward Nam Đàn forest. Thoughts about Minh, Đạt, and Ngọc gave me strength. But the farther we walked, the weaker I felt. My mother was slower and slower with each step. The sun beat down on us, blanching the surroundings into a blur.

Yet we walked. We walked, leaning on each other. We walked, muttering to each other that we had to make it, to bring food back for the children.

Exhausted, I led my mother over to a large tree, barren of leaves. We took off our hats, letting the brown trunk receive our tired backs.

Using the knife, I dug. The earth was as hard as rock. All I could find were some grass roots. I handed them to my mother, who wiped them clean. She ate a few and gave me the rest. With the bitterness of the roots between my jaws, I eyed the horizon, where trees layered into a velvet of green. Hidden inside that greenness could be our saviors: grasshoppers, crickets, sim berries, and mountain guavas.

"Mama, wait for me here. I'll come back with something to eat."

My mother shook her head. "Since your father's death, I can't be the one who stays behind. If death comes, it'll have to take me first."

"It was not your fault, Mama! It was mine. If it weren't for me, we wouldn't have encountered those murderers. I slowed us down by driving the cart."

"No, Diệu Lan. Your father wouldn't want you to think that way. He loved you more than his life."

"You're more than life to him, too, Mama. Stop blaming yourself, please."

My mother bent her head. "I have something to show you." Her hands trembled as she unhooked the safety pin that closed her pocket.

I blinked, thinking that hunger must be making me hallucinate. In my mother's palm was the Trần's family treasure—a large ruby framed by solid gold and fixed to a gold chain.

"I managed to hide it from the Japanese." My mother handed it to me.

I cupped the precious item of jewelry to my face, hearing my ancestors' lullabies echoing from it. My father had received the necklace from his parents. He'd proudly shown it to Công and me. Guava, the necklace had enchanted me so much that I had named your mother— my first daughter—Ngọc, which means ruby.

"Diệu Lan." My mother swallowed hard. "I'd promised your father I'd safeguard this, to be able to pass it on to you and your brother. But now . . . if somebody offers some food. . . ."

I nodded, returning the necklace to my mother, who carefully put it back into her pocket, securing it with the safety pin.

Holding on to each other, we dragged our aching bones toward the forest. It looked close but was an ocean away from us. We'd left our wooden clogs somewhere along the road, for they'd become too heavy, and now sharp stones dug into our naked feet.

Just when I thought I'd collapse and die, swaying trees welcomed me into their arms.

I broke away from my mother, rushing onto a worn path that zigzagged through the forest. But instead of finding joy, I found more corpses, of children, women, and men. All around them, fruit trees had been cut down or uprooted. No sight of birds, fruit, flowers, or butterflies. No sound except flies' buzzing.

My mother pulled my arm, leading me deeper into the forest. In front of a large, thorny bush, she bent down, pushing away low branches.

A narrow opening.

"A path, created by your father." My mother's lips curled into a rare smile. In his final years, my father used to take my mother here for a walk, just the two of them. They'd come home with nuts and mushrooms, wild hens, and once, a wild pig.

We put aside our *nón lá* hats, pressed our stomachs against the ground, and wriggled our way through. On the other side was a tiny path, almost hidden among the trees.

I opened my eyes wide, seeking food. Only tree roots and fallen branches met my gaze. Other people had been there, before us.

"Go deeper, go on." My mother led me through a maze of passages. Finding nothing to eat still, we walked further and further. My feet trembled under me, but my mother kept forcing the way forward, as if she had gained new strength. We journeyed so deep into the belly of the forest that I no longer knew where we were.

"Will you find the way back, Mama?" I panted, staring at a dense bush we'd just crawled through.

My mother didn't answer. She walked to a green wall in front of us. It looked thick, woven by intertwining jungle vines.

"There used to be a corn field . . . behind this." She coughed, pushing the vines away, trying to take a peek, but the wall was too thick.

"Why didn't you tell us earlier, Mama?"

"I was sure I wouldn't remember the way." She clutched her stomach, squatting down. "Perhaps nothing grows there anymore. Perhaps . . . perhaps other people have found it."

I listened to sounds from the other side. Was that a bird singing? If there were birds, there must be food.

I handed my mother the pipe, telling her to drink. There was only a mouthful of water left, and I wanted her to have it. Holding up the knife, I thrashed at the green wall. The knife sprang back at me, narrowly missing my face.

"Cut . . . one by . . . one." My mother lay down on the ground.

I nodded, wondering how long it'd take to make a hole. As I worked, blisters swelled up under my skin. It took many chops to defeat one single vine. My arms ached, my hands started to bleed. "Food for the children," I told myself, raising the knife, my body bent forward, sweat stinging my eyes.

I don't remember how long it took me to chop enough vines to create a small opening, but I do remember what I saw through it: a field of corn plants.

"Food, Mama! Food." Throwing the knife aside, I slipped through, pulling my mother behind me.

We faced the field together. On top of dry soil stood hundreds of plants, skinny and yellowish. My eyes searched among the leaves and my heartbeats quickened. Ears of corn. "Who owns this, Mama?" I looked around.

"No idea . . . Your father found this by chance."

We crawled toward the middle of the field. Hunger didn't let us travel far. My hands and legs were shaking. I held my breath, reached up, picking a corn ear. The size of my bony arm, it felt solid in my grip. I tore away the outer husks, my mouth drooling at the sight of corn seeds: milky, perfectly white, like rows of baby teeth.

I lifted the corn to my mother's mouth. We shared the delicious food. My stomach rumbled. The hair on my arms stood up at the pleasure of eating.

"Chew carefully," whispered my mother. "Our stomachs have been empty for too long. Eating too much and too fast can kill us."

I nodded, taking another bite, wondering how I could stop myself.

"Ahh. You thieves!" A voice thundered, sending a shudder from my head to my toes. The half-eaten corn rolled down to the soil.

Clutching my mother's shoulders, I looked up to see a towering man. A meaty face, narrow eyes. A bald, shiny head. Wicked Ghost!

Remember what I told you about this man, Guava?

"Please, Sir . . ." My mother trembled.

Wicked Ghost answered by raising his whip. Pain surged through my neck and back. I watched in terror as the whip landed on my mother's head with a swishing sound.

"No. Please." I shielded her with my arms. The whip slashed across my shoulders.

"Forgive us, Sir." My mother brought her head to the ground, kowtowing to Wicked Ghost.

He turned his whip on her, spattering blood into the air. "Forgive and let you steal all my corn? Forgive and see the mob come out here and make me hungry?"

His kick sent her sprawling.

"Mama!" I jumped toward her. Pieces of flesh had been ripped away from her skull and neck. Blood was streaming down her face. I reached for Wicked Ghost's feet with both of my hands. "Don't beat my Mama, I beg you. I'm the one that took her here. I'm the one who stole your corn."

The whip lashed down, knocking me to the ground.

WHEN I CAME to, the sun was setting, drenching me in its thick, red light. I wiggled, but my legs and wrists were bound. I'd been roped and tied to a large tree trunk.

"Mẹ ơi!" I called. My frantic eyes found my mother. She was several body lengths away, a heap on the dirt. Her long hair covered a part of her face. Blood had caked on her head and around her mouth.

"Mẹ ơi!"

She didn't move. No lifting of the head. No flinching of the skin. I launched myself toward her but the ropes held me back.

I drifted from a cold night into the heat of a blazing morning. I called but my mother didn't make a sound. I cried until the world faded into darkness as deep as a grave.

Intense pain shot through my body. Opening my eyes, I realized I was being dragged across the forest. A stick-thin man was clutching me by my ankles, pulling me forward. He was huffing and puffing, his stomach bulging out in a peculiar way.

"Somebody, please help!" I croaked.

The man dropped my legs. "Shush, be quiet if you want to live, Diệu Lan."

My heart was in my throat when I heard my name. Crouching down low, the man got closer to me. A dried bottle-gourd dangled on a string in front of his chest. I could see his face now: weather-beaten and haggard.

"Who are you?" I wriggled away from him.

"Run, Diệu Lan." He unlooped the string of his bottle-gourd, giving me his water. "Get out of here, before Wicked Ghost finds you."

"My mother . . ." I turned back to the road we'd just traveled. "Please help her."

"I'm sorry . . . Madam Trần . . . she's no more."

"No!"

"Shush. They'll hear you. Leave now or they'll catch you."

I tried to stand up. "Take me back to my mother. Take me back now! She can't be dead."

"Diệu Lan, listen to me." The man gripped my shoulder. "Please . . . believe me. I work for Wicked Ghost, but I am indebted to your parents. My wife nearly died in childbirth. Your parents found a doctor. They saved her, and they saved my son. If Madam Trần was alive, I wouldn't have left her there."

The man's words were sincere, and they cut into me deeper than any whip. Wicked Ghost had killed my mother. Blood had to be paid by blood.

"My name is Hải. Your brother Công knows me." The man nursed water into my mouth. "I'm sorry I came too late. I'll find your mother a good resting place, I swear." He pulled something out of his shirt.

Ears of corn. They were the reason for his bulging belly. As he put the corn into my pockets, I remembered something. Something that made me cry out in anguish.

"What is it, Diệu Lan?"

"Uncle . . . my mother had a gold and ruby necklace in her pocket. If I'd remembered to offer it to Wicked Ghost—"

"Then you could have saved her?" Mr. Hải shook his head. "If you assume so, you don't know him at all. That man is beyond evil. And did he give you the chance to think?" He pointed at the path to my right. "It'll lead you back home, hurry."

As I wobbled forward, Mr. Hải disappeared into the trees. I told myself not to forget his name. Hải means ocean, a deserving name for a man whose compassion ran deep.

I don't know how I found my way out of the forest and how long it took me to get home, but I know that Mr. Hải saved your mother and uncles, Guava. The ears of corn he gave me enabled them to survive two more weeks, until a kind Catholic priest came to our village, bringing some food. Later, the Việt Minh helped our villagers attack the Japanese and French rice supplies.

But help came too late for many. The Great Hunger claimed more than half of Vĩnh Phúc. Many families had no one left to carry their name forward.

The Great Hunger gobbled down such a big part of my life, taking away not just my mother but also my sister-in-law, Trinh.

Oh, Guava, I used to think that we were the ones in charge of our destinies, but I learned then that, in time of war, normal citizens were nothing but leaves that would fall in the thousands or millions in the surge of a single storm.

For months after my mother's death, whenever I slept, I saw her slumped against cracked soil. I'd wake up screaming, telling her that

I was sorry for not being able to save her. I was twenty-five years old, and had seen both my parents murdered.

Mr. Hải came to visit us after the Great Hunger. I knelt before him to thank him. He took Công, Hùng, Mrs. Tú, and me to my mother's grave. He'd laid her in a corner of Nam Đàn forest where wildflowers blossomed through all four seasons.

Mr. Hải told me he'd searched my mother's pockets as well as her surroundings but couldn't find the necklace. He helped us retrace the path my mother and I had taken before we reached the cornfield. We looked under the bushes and fallen leaves, hoping to find that remarkable piece of jewelry. But there was no hope. Many people were there, taking away and burying dead bodies. Any of them could have found our family treasure and kept it for themselves.

Oh, Guava, I wish I still had your great-grandma's necklace to give you. It was the Trần family's heritage.

We returned Mr. Hải's kindness by giving him a piece of our field. He tried to refuse it, but we didn't let him. If there was someone from our village whom we could trust, it was this man who had risked his life to save ours. Years later, when we rebuilt our family business, Mr. Hải became the supervisor of our workers.

I knew Mr. Hải was kind and brave, but I didn't know that one day he would once again be our savior.

So, you must be wondering what happened to Wicked Ghost. When I came home from the cornfield, Hùng and Công sharpened a chopping knife. They found Wicked Ghost drunk and alone in his house. Wicked Ghost was crazy; he dared Hùng and Công to kill him. He said that my mother had died of hunger. He said he knew nothing about the necklace. Hùng and Công could have hurt him easily, but they turned away. They weren't as evil as Wicked Ghost, you see. Anyway, after the Great Hunger, Wicked Ghost could no longer harm anyone else. He was always drunk, talking and crying to himself. Perhaps the spirits of those he killed had come back to haunt him. *Gieo gió gặt bão*—He who sows the wind will reap the storm.

In 1946, one year after my mother's death, Wicked Ghost disappeared. It was rumored that he, his wife, and their young daughter had moved to the wife's village, somewhere in the middle region. I didn't care where he'd gone, I was just glad that he left. Years later, when I became a Buddhist, I learned that I should forgive people for their wrongs, but when it comes to Wicked Ghost, I can't, Guava. I don't ever want to breathe the same air as such a terrible man.

During the following years, we worked hard. Công and I put into practice all the skills my parents had taught us. We grew crops that were in high demand. We saved and invested. We buried jars of dry food in the garden, so that we'd never go hungry again. Over time, our family business started to blossom. Our cattle stalls were once more alive with animals, our fields green with all types of rice and vegetables.

My love for your grandpa blossomed, too. In the Year of the Pig, 1947, I gave birth to your Uncle Thuận, followed by your Aunt Hạnh one year later—in the Year of the Mouse, 1948. I turned twenty-eight that year and was already blessed with five children, and I wanted to have many more.

I remember clearly the summer I gave birth to Hạnh. It was hot and humid. The air vibrated with cicadas' cries. Following the *nằm ổ* custom, I was confined to my bed for the whole month, a bucket of hot coals constantly smoldering under my bed. Hot coals were meant to ward off evil spirits, but the heat was almost unbearable. My whole body stank and itched; I was forbidden to take a bath or wash my hair.

Three weeks into *nằm ổ*, I was going mad. One morning, after breastfeeding Hạnh and putting her to sleep, I wrapped a scarf around my neck and snuck out of my room. Inhaling fresh air deep into my lungs, I walked along the corridor, passing my brother's bedroom. Arriving at the living room where new furniture was gleaming, I looked for my parents. There they were, high up on the altar, behind bowls of incense.

"So skillful!" A child's voice flowed toward me, together with the rhythmic tick-tick sound of a featherball being kicked. Ngọc, Minh, and Đạt were counting, together: "*Một trăm bảy mươi mốt.*" One-hundred and seventy-one times! Could someone kick the ball so many times without dropping it? I stood up, bowed to the altar, and went out to the front yard. Squinting, I saw the children standing in a circle.

Dressed in shorts, Minh was bare-chested, sweat glistening on his skin. He was balancing on one leg, his other leg kicking a featherball. My brother Công had found the best feathers and pinned them to a rubber base, to make the ball. My children had become his children.

As the featherball fell, Minh's foot raised to meet it with a happy click. The ball fluttered upward, once again.

"You're so good," I said. The children turned. Minh dropped the ball and in an instant, all of them darted over to me.

"Mama, Mama," they cheered, their embraces tightening around me.

I knelt down, wiping droplets of sweat from their faces. "Play in the shade." I led them into the shadow of the longan tree.

"Why are you out here, Mama?" Ngọc stared at me. "Grandma Tú said you have to stay in your room."

I had to laugh. Guava, at a young age, your mother was already *bé hạt tiêu*—a little hot pepper.

"I'll ask for her permission then." I hurried across the yard before emerging into the coolness of Mrs. Tú's room.

"*Dì Tú ơi*," I called. She was squatting on a straw mat, Thuận in her arms.

"What're you doing here?" She frowned.

"*Mẹ*." Thuận babbled, craning at me.

"Mama is here. Here's Mama." I cooed, reaching out for Thuận. Just over one year old, he looked adorable with a single tuft of black hair crowning his head. His father had cut his hair according to the traditional *trái đào* hairstyle.

"Why have you left your room? Bad winds will make you sick."

"It's been three weeks, Auntie." I tickled Thuận's neck with my nose. He giggled.

Mrs. Tú walked toward a large wooden trunk, where fruits picked from our garden were kept to ripen. There, you could easily find tiny yellow *thị* fruit radiating delicious fragrance, papayas reddening under layers of jute bags, and juicy *na* fruit opening like flowers.

Mrs. Tú fetched a golden banana and returned to the straw mat. Thuận crawled out of my arms and onto her lap. She laughed, peeling the fruit. Thuận clutched it with both hands, munching.

"Smells good." I gave Mrs. Tú a begging look.

"You know you can't eat raw fruit yet. Not yet. Go back to your room." She stood up again. "I'll bring you a bowl of black chicken and herb soup."

Black chicken and herb soup, again? It was supposed to help my body regain strength. It'd tasted delicious at first, but the herbs— stewed *ngải cứu* leaves—were overwhelming. I shuddered.

Instead of protesting, though, I watched Mrs. Tú walk across the room. Unlike the children, she'd never recovered from the Great Hunger. She'd lost most of her hair. If it weren't for her, things would have been worse for us.

Returning with a long-sleeved shirt, she made me put it on. She unrolled the sleeves until they covered my fingers. Wrapping a thick scarf around my neck, ears, and head, she spun me around. Once she was sure there was no more exposed skin where evil spirits could attack me, she pushed me lovingly out of her room.

Walking past the side garden, I caught sight of bent backs. My husband and brother were chatting away while working on a square patch of young rice plants. The planting season had come and they'd transformed a part of our garden into the hatching place for rice seedlings.

The children ran past me. "Mama, want some green guavas?" Minh asked.

"Oh, yes, please." Saliva gushed to my mouth, but I knew I'd have to hide those fruits from Mrs. Tú.

The children skirted around the kitchen, headed for the thick fence in the back. There, they would crawl through a secret hole to get to the plot of land my parents had given Mrs. Tú to build her own home, but on which she'd grown fruit trees instead.

I sank into the cradle of our front yard. It was mid-morning and the sun was drawing its ball of fire across the sky. An ox cart rolled past our gate. My village was alive around me. I inhaled its energy deep into my lungs.

My Father's Gift

Hà Nội, 1975

"Be patient. Be patient." I laughed. Pushing Black Dots and Pink Nose out of the way, I dumped bran mixed with chopped water spinach into their trough. The animals buried their mouths in the food, chomping, their tails wagging.

"Hương, are you home? Anybody home?" a voice called. Wiping my hands against my pants, I rushed to the door, pulling it open. Auntie Duyên. She stood slender in the morning light.

"I still can't believe how much you've grown." She beamed. "What a pretty young woman you've become, and you're getting fat."

"It's great to see you, Auntie." I grinned, happy that Auntie Duyên called me fat. Everyone I knew was trying to gain weight, but how could they, with so little food?

At the dining table, I pulled out a chair for Auntie Duyên and ran to the kitchen. With my aunt here, it was almost as if my father were home. Auntie Duyên was the only sibling my father had. Their parents had died young. They did odd jobs to support each other growing up.

Bringing back a pot of green tea, I found my aunt in front of Uncle Thuận's altar, incense sticks smoldering between her palms. She bowed her head in silence. Grandma had taken apart the altar only to have her secret revealed: a friend of my mother had passed by when Grandma wasn't home, telling my mother how sorry he was for her loss. I would never forget how long my mother had cried, clutching Uncle Thuận's clothes against her chest. I'm not proud of this now, but at that time I felt as if all the rivers of her tears had flown toward the spirit of my uncle, leaving her motherhood for me dry.

Auntie Duyên sat down at the table. "Is your mother feeling better? Is she home?"

I nodded, trying not to spill the tea as I poured it. "Mama . . . I think she's sleeping." I gestured toward my parents' bedroom.

Auntie Duyên looked up at the clock. "Let me try and talk to her again." She emptied her cup, then carried the teapot into the room.

I wondered how long it'd take for Aunt Duyên to come out, the corners of her mouth sagging with disappointment. My mother had managed to disappoint all of her visitors, including her younger sister. Poor Auntie Hạnh, who'd traveled all the way from Thanh Hóa Province, just to see her.

I tried to read my textbooks, but words were empty and colorless. I had to go back to school soon, otherwise I'd be kicked out. The door to my mother's room was still closed. Pretending to sweep the floor, I tiptoed across to it, putting my ear against the wood. Murmurs and occasional sobbing. My mother's voice. I closed my eyes, listening, but the murmurs melted into the air before their meaning could reach me.

The clock struck eleven. I lit the coal stove, boiling water for a spinach soup. In a clay pot, I stewed a couple of mullets with fish sauce, chili, and pepper. Pouring rice into another pot, I washed it carefully to get rid of any rice weevil. Normally I had to mix corn, manioc, or sweet potato with rice to fill our stomachs, but we were having a special guest today. So, rice for lunch. I hoped Auntie Duyên would appreciate the food. It had to be difficult for her. She worked in a garment factory and was being paid in food coupons. Like my father and uncles, her husband had gone to the battlefield. She lived by the Red River, and had to take care of two young children.

Noon approached. The fish simmered. The air smelled so delicious, I put out my tongue to lick it. I tasted the spinach soup. It was so yummy I had to have another spoonful. Glancing first at my mother's bedroom, I reached for the rice pot. Just one spoon, one only.

Putting the rice into my mouth, I was yet to chew when a sound clicked at the front door. "Hương, I'm home." Grandma's voice. I swallowed so fast, the rice glided like fire down my throat. I kicked the spoon into a kitchen corner, wiping my mouth against my shirtsleeve.

"Is the food ready? I'm starving." Grandma pushed her bike inside.

My smile must be crooked. I signaled toward the bedroom. "Auntie Duyên is here. She got Mama to talk."

Grandma brought a finger to her lips. "Let them."

I ferried bowls and chopsticks to the table. My mother was talking, she must be feeling better. I imagined our meal to be a happy reunion lunch, where I'd sit next to her, she'd praise my cooking, fill my bowl, and urge me to eat; her tender voice would tell me to stop worrying about her and go back to class.

But when Auntie Duyên and my mother came to the table, a heavy silence shrouded our meal. Grandma tried to keep the conversation flowing by asking Auntie Duyên about her job.

"We're producing by quota." My aunt sighed. "Our garments are piling up in the warehouse. We can't sell, but production has to go on."

"The government wants to control the economy, but how can they?" Grandma put some fish into Aunt Duyên's bowl. "Our medical system is suffering, too. I just visited a friend at the Bạch Mai Hospital; it's so crowded. They need more doctors there." She turned to my mother. "Ngọc, I ran into your colleagues who said they can't wait to have you back."

"They told you that because they love to lie." My mother's sharp words startled me.

A minute of silence followed.

"They care about you, Daughter. All of us do. We all want to help you get better."

"Get better?" Laughter spilled from my mother's mouth; her eyes were red. "If I were as strong as you, for sure I'd be better. You left us behind when running away from your goddamn village, remember?"

"Come on, Ngọc. That was a long time ago. I didn't have any choice." Grandma's lips quivered.

"You had a choice. Every mother has a choice!"

I had never seen my mother so angry.

"Sister Ngọc . . ." Auntie Duyên reached for my mother's hand.

"No, you don't get it. If my mother hadn't run away, perhaps all of my brothers would be alive now. Thuận is dead. Đạt and Sáng might not be coming back. Brother Thuận is dead. He is dead!" Tears trembled on my mother's cheeks.

"I'm sorry, Daughter," Grandma whispered. "Let me make it up to you. Tell me what I should do."

"You can do nothing for me now." My mother brought her hands to her face. "Nothing! I'm finished. Fouled and finished. Nobody could make me clean again."

I stared at my mother. Her words made no sense to me.

"Ngọc." Grandma put down her bowl and chopsticks. "You must have gone through terrible things. Let me help—"

"If you can help, tell me how you do this." Anger flashed in my mother's eyes. "Tell me how you can go on. Tell me how you can eat when Thuận's body is cold under the ground."

"Enough!" Grandma slammed the table so hard, it shook. "You can't even imagine how much it hurts to have a dead son."

"Oh, you bet I can. I know exactly how it feels and that's why I can't understand how you can sit here, eating like this."

"Stop fighting," I screamed. "Stop it!"

I WAS AT my desk, crying, when Auntie Duyên came to me. "I'm sorry I stirred up bad emotions. Your mother . . . she needs time."

"What happened to her, Auntie? What did she say to you?"

Auntie Duyên dried my tears with the back of her hand. "You'll understand one day, Darling. . . . What I can tell you is that as a doctor, your mother saved many lives. She worked at makeshift clinics along the Hồ Chí Minh Trail. She operated on soldiers, sometimes without the help of pain-relief medicine. Wherever she was, she tried to look for your father and uncles, but it was in vain."

"What else did she tell you? What turned her into such a horrible person?"

"Oh Hương, the war . . . it's worse than we could ever imagine."

"Did she kill anybody?"

"What? Why did you say that?"

"In her sleep, she cried about a baby. Once she said she'd killed him."

"No . . . that was just a nightmare." Auntie Duyên shook her head. "Believe me, your mother is a good person."

"You talked for hours with her. Please, what else did she say?"

"I'll leave it to your mother to tell her own story to you once you're old enough, Hương. Whatever happened, please know that she loves you very, very much. She cares about you more than you'll ever know. And she's very thankful that you've tried to take care of her."

"Did she even notice?"

"Of course she did." Auntie Duyên bit her lip. "There is . . . there's something she asked me to tell you."

"She can't talk to me herself?"

My aunt reached for my arm. "Hương, your mother wants to come to my place and stay for a short while. She needs time to—"

"She wants to abandon me again?" I stood up.

"Oh, Hương, don't think like that. Your mother needs help. I can be there for her. My home is not much, but I can take long walks with her by the river. Being close to nature would be good for her."

I turned away. My mother confided in Auntie Duyên, but not in me. She didn't trust me. She didn't think I was good enough as a daughter.

AFTER MY MOTHER had departed with Auntie Duyên, I went out to the backyard, *Little House in the Big Woods* in my hands. How lucky for this American girl to be anchored by her parents, while mine had drifted so far away. I turned to the final page, where Laura had been tucked snugly in her bed, with her mother in her rocking chair knitting and her father's music and singing voice filling their cozy home with happiness.

I ground my teeth, ripped the last page from the book, and tore it to pieces. I thought I'd feel satisfied by my revenge but as the scraps of paper flittered down to my feet like dead butterflies, my tears followed.

I went back to school, struggled, and did badly on my tests.

Grandma was shocked at the results, but I didn't care. She was the one who'd chased my mother away.

Grandma became quiet; my mother's words had hurt her deeply. She'd taken care of me, and now I should show my loyalty by comforting her, but I couldn't bring myself to do so, fearing I would betray my mother. My mother didn't care much about me, though. Whenever I brought her the food baskets Grandma had prepared, she looked at me with such vacant eyes that I wondered if it was truly my mother sitting there.

I tried talking to Auntie Duyên, but she didn't tell me anything new. She kept saying that my mother needed time, and that she'd get better soon.

On April 30, 1975, news of the Northern Army taking over Sài Gòn came, bringing torrents of people out of their homes. The Resistance War against America had truly ended. Việt Nam was now united. The North and the South had again become the body of one nation. People were singing, dancing, twirling our flag in their hands. The red flag, centered by a yellow star, soared like flames along each street, each road, each winding lane. Speeches and songs blared from public speakers, praising the heroism of the North Vietnamese Army, applauding our people for defeating the Americans and their Southern regime.

Looking back, I wish I had understood more fully the significance of this day. It marked the end of a bloodbath that flooded our country for nearly twenty years, drowning more than three million people, leaving millions of others injured, traumatized, and displaced. Once, I read an article about the bombs that had been dropped during our war and the number stunned me: seven million tons.

Yet on the day the war ended, Grandma and I didn't celebrate. For us, peace would only arrive when all our loved ones had returned home. Our house was the only one in the neighborhood without the red flag unfurling above its front door. Grandma knelt in front of our family altar, the wooden stick in her hand knocking rhythmically against her prayer bell. I was next to her, my eyes closed, my hands in front of my chest. I prayed for my father, Uncle Đạt, and Uncle Sáng to come home, and that they wouldn't bring any ghosts of war back with them.

WHILE GRANDMA URGED me to go to school, she stayed home during the next days. She spent money lavishly, preparing different types of food, ready for a big welcome home party.

Exactly one week after Unification Day, I got up early and prayed with Grandma. While she prepared breakfast—another sumptuous meal, just in case—I carried a pair of empty tin pails out of the door. I greeted Mrs. Nhân, who was out in her front yard doing her morning exercise.

Several women were squatting around the well, washing buckets of clothes, when I arrived. I passed them, heading for the water pump.

"A returning soldier," someone murmured behind my back.

I turned. A slim figure was moving down our neighborhood's lane. He had the same build, the same height as my father.

"He looks just like my brother," someone else said.

Crashing sounds rang up around me as the women knocked over their buckets, rushing toward the man. I pushed ahead but was too slow. A crowd had already surrounded the soldier when I approached.

"*Chú Sáng, chú Sáng về rồi!*" a kid's voice called out cheerfully. My Uncle Sáng. He was back.

"*Chào các bác, các cô, các cháu.*" He greeted the men, women, and children around him.

"Your mother is lucky, Sáng." Mr. Tùng patted my uncle's shoulder.

Mrs. Thương, an elderly lady, clutched his hand. "Have you seen my sons Thắng and Lợi?"

Uncle Sáng shook his head. "Now the war has ended, they'll be back soon."

"I hope so." The lady mumbled, turning away, wiping her tears.

"Here's Hương, your niece." Someone ushered me forward, and I sank into Uncle Sáng's embrace.

"Look at you, you're nearly as tall as me," my uncle said as I took a deep breath, telling myself not to cry. Uncle Sáng was back, really back. My father and Uncle Đạt would return soon and everything would be fine.

"WHAT A STUPID, stupid thing you did." I sat frozen next to Grandma as Uncle Sáng paced back and forth in our living room, berating her. His boots squeaked under his heavy footsteps. He raised his feet, sending the pigs scurrying away. "I can't believe you quit teaching to become a trader."

"Calm down, Son. I'm not doing anything bad." Grandma poured a cup of tea for my uncle.

"Nothing bad?" Uncle Sáng walked to Grandma. He put his mouth against her ear. "I've become a Party member. My mother can't be a con buôn."

"Oh, so you've joined the league, have you?" Grandma snorted. "I don't see how anyone should care. My business is my business. Yours is yours."

"It's not as simple as you think," hissed my uncle. "My comrades and I, we've risked our lives to bring justice to the people of this country. We've shed our blood so our people are free from foreign invasion. Free from exploiters and bourgeoisie."

As my uncle went on preaching, Grandma stood up, moving toward her stove. She carried plates and bowls of food to the table: steamed rice rolls, phở noodle soup, glutinous rice with coconut milk, and fish porridge. Seeing that she was determined to celebrate her son's return, I got up and helped her.

". . . you are ruining my chance for a leadership position, Mama. I'll become a laughing stock in front of my comrades. Now I can't discipline anyone anymore because—"

"Because you can't discipline your own mother?" Grandma looked up from the chopsticks she was distributing. "Come on, Sáng. You haven't seen me for years. Sit down and enjoy our first meal."

Only now did Uncle Sáng stop walking. He stared at the food, his nostrils flaring. He turned away, but not quickly enough. I saw him swallow.

"Uncle Sáng, please," I told him. "Grandma has been cooking your favorite dishes all week, just in case you came home."

My uncle walked back and forth a few more times. He checked to see if our door was closed and locked. He put his ear against it, then peered out from a crack as if to make sure no one was spying. He glanced up at our windows.

He walked to the table. "All right," he whispered, "only this time and only because I don't want little Hương to be sad." He dove into the food. He was silent throughout his meal, but when he finished, he let out a gigantic belch.

Grandma and I were still eating when he stood up, his boots knocking against the chairs' legs. When he opened his mouth, his words rolled out, as if from a stranger's tongue, "Mama, if you love me, quit your trading job and go back to teaching. Until you do, I can't visit you anymore."

• • •

GRANDMA LOOKED DEFEATED after Uncle Sáng left. She put away the food and quietly returned to the market.

What had happened that made Uncle Sáng change so much? He'd always been caring toward Grandma. He'd often folded colored papers into animals for me and my friends. During the Mid-Autumn Festival, he'd slivered bamboo and made different paper lanterns: a cat, a fish, a tiger, a star, a flower. The lanterns he made for me always won a prize at the Light Parade around the Lake of the Returned Sword. He'd learned the skills from the artisan who took care of him when he first got to Hà Nội with Grandma.

I gave Grandma a glass of water when she came home. "You okay? I couldn't believe how rude Uncle Sáng was."

"He's been brainwashed by propaganda." She sat down on the *phản*. "Given what happened to his father, I've warned him about the dangers of politics. Yet he doesn't want to listen." She sighed. "People say *mưa dầm thấm lâu*." Soft and persistent rain penetrates the earth better than a storm. I need to be patient with him."

She turned the glass in her hands. "As for your mother, Hương, I've been thinking . . . that we need to make more effort. Keep talking to her. Your voice will lead her back to us."

"She doesn't care, Grandma. I don't want to visit her anymore." I stood up, wanting to walk away from my mother's problems.

Grandma reached for my hand. "Hương, if we don't help her, nobody can. Promise you'll never give up on her?"

FROM THEN ON, whenever I visited Auntie Duyên's house, I brought books along to read and homework to do, so as to fill the silence between my mother and me.

A few weeks later, I got a letter. I was so surprised, I kept opening

the envelope, pulling out a note, reading it, smiling to myself, returning it to the envelope, only to open it again.

"Whose letter is that?" my mother suddenly asked, sitting a few
arm's lengths away from me as usual.

"I don't know, Mama."

She arched her eyebrows.

"Want to know what it says?" I asked, and without waiting for her
answer, I cleared my throat.

Dear Hương, have you noticed that summer has arrived?
Phượng flowers are lighting up their torches alongside the
streets. I dream about the day when I can walk with you under
the red sky.

I held up the note. "Found it inside my bag. I don't know who put
it there."

"You have a secret admirer then." My mother actually smiled as
she said these words.

"Perhaps someone is playing a trick on me?"

"I don't think so," she said. "I also received such letters when I was
your age."

"Really? How many? And who sent them to you?"

The smile on her face vanished. She turned, looking out of the
window.

"Don't you want to come home, Mama?"

Silence.

"Mama, please. Come home. I need you."

"I can't. . . . You shouldn't be around me now. I'm no good."

"Auntie Duyên said you're going back to work. But why at her factory? You're a doctor. You loved your job."

"I can't be a doctor anymore." She twisted her fingers. "It'd bring back too many painful memories."

"What memories, Mama?"

"Oh Hương, I can't tell you. Let's just say that I went through terrible, terrible things. Things that I don't wish to happen to anyone."

"Mama, if you can't tell me, talk to Grandma. She can help you."

"No," whispered my mother. She bent her head, her shoulders quivering. "I'm sorry I couldn't bring your Papa back to you, Hương. I made him join the damn Army. He wanted to chop his finger off so he wouldn't have to enlist. He talked about going into hiding to avoid fighting. But I told him he was a coward, that as a man he had to defend our country and get rid of foreign invaders."

I stared at my mother. Had she gone mad?

I shook my head. "Grandma told me everyone had to go. Papa didn't have a choice."

"Yes, he did have a choice. Damn it, he did!" She clenched her fists.

"Papa will come back. He will—"

"Will he? It's been three months since the war ended, Hương."

Three months. We would've heard from him by now if he were still alive; she wanted to tell me that but couldn't bring herself to say it.

As anger filled my chest, tears filled my eyes. I didn't know the woman in front of me anymore. Perhaps she did send my father to war. Perhaps she did kill babies in the battlefields.

I headed for the door, then whirled around. "I hope Papa comes back, because if he doesn't, I'm never going to forgive you. Never, ever!"

At home, I asked Grandma whether my mother had truly convinced my father to join the Army.

"No man could escape, Hương," she exclaimed. "I don't know why your mother is blaming herself. It's true some people cut off their fingers or went into hiding, but everyone I knew who did that suffered severe punishment. They all had to become soldiers in the end. Would I have let your uncles go if there had been a chance for them to escape?"

"But she must have told Papa to go, that's why she feels guilty."

"It was a very different time when your father left." Grandma sighed. "Innocent souls had died because of the bombings. Hà Nội was boiling with anger. There were waves of people volunteering to fight. Like many others, your mother was patriotic."

I thought about the young boys at my school who had lied about their age, to be able to enter the Army. Yet it wasn't easy to accept that my mother had helped push my father into the furnace of war.

I went outside, gazing up at the starless sky. "Come home, Papa. Come home and make things right between Mama and me."

I BURIED MYSELF in books, trying to forget my longings and anger. I had to focus on my studies. Grandma was doing everything she could to give me a chance for a good education, and I had to grab that chance. In three years, I would finish high school and face the university entrance exam.

In August, five months after my mother's return, I was selected to attend one of Hà Nội's top schools, Chu Văn An.

This school had luckily survived the bombings. Its ancient buildings proudly stood, looking out over West Lake. From my classroom, I could see fishermen rowing their bamboo boats with their feet, their hands gathering shimmering nets. I could watch women lowering themselves into the water, disappearing completely under rippling circles as they searched for snails.

My new school was much further away from home, so Grandma bought me a bike. Among fifty-four classmates, I was one of the only two who had bicycles. The rest had to walk, regardless of how far away they lived.

My classmates knew Grandma was a trader and didn't want to be seen with me outside class. No one would come to my house.

I didn't care. My heart wasn't at school. It was at home where I could read those so-called anticommunist books that had been banned, but that Grandma still purchased for me. Home was a place of calmness: practicing self-defense techniques with Grandma and playing with our animals. I'd begged Grandma not to sell Black Dots and Pink Nose and she'd found a way: they became mother pigs, giving birth to twenty-two piglets during their first season. We sold fifteen piglets, making a handsome profit. Grandma converted the third bedroom into a pigsty, after moving Uncle Đạt's bed to my parents' room. "We'll figure things out when your uncle returns," she said.

AUTUMN ARRIVED. I hoped that Grandma would help bring my mother home, but something else was on her mind. One day, she returned from work, excited.

"Hương, guess what? I'm getting another grandchild. Your Auntie Hoa is pregnant. Oh, I can't believe it."

"That's great news, Grandma, but how did you find out?" Neither Uncle Sáng nor Auntie Hoa had contacted us. They'd only seen my mother once.

Grandma winked. "A friend of mine has been visiting your uncle on my behalf."

She started cooking, happy songs returning to her lips.

I was doing my homework when her voice boomed through the door. "Hương, help me bring some food to your Auntie Hoa."

I went out to see her piling boxes of sticky rice, charcoal-grilled fish, and stir-fried vegetables into a bag. "These will give Hoa plenty of milk."

"I don't want to see her, Grandma. Besides, I have a test tomorrow." I headed back to my desk.

"It's a quick trip." Grandma's voice followed me. "Please . . . I'll bring you there with my bike."

I rolled my eyes. I didn't understand how Grandma could be so forgiving about Uncle Sáng. She should be helping my mother, instead of him.

I was in bed, reading Xuân Quỳnh's poetry, when Grandma came to me.

"It looks like someone is done with preparing for the test." She smiled.

I flipped another page, feeling bad that I'd lied about the test. But it was boiling hot outside and Uncle Sáng's preaching stank.

"Hương. The baby is your cousin . . ."

"If you want to give them food, do it yourself."

"I can't. That's why I need your help."

"Why can't you? Oh I remember." I cleared my throat, imitating Uncle's Sáng's voice. "I've become a Party member. My mother can't be a *con buôn*."

Grandma grimaced. "I don't ask a lot from you, but this is the one duty you're going to help me with."

"I'm no longer a baby buffalo for you to lead me by my nose." I returned to my book, wishing I could disappear into its pages.

"Hương! I didn't bring you up to talk like that. You need to be respectful."

"Respectful?" I sat up. "Perhaps respect no longer exists in this family." I thought about how Uncle Sáng, his wife, and my mother had behaved.

Grandma's face darkened. I was sure she'd slap me or shout at me, but she quietly retreated from my room.

I lay down, humming, thinking I'd won Grandma over for once, but she appeared, the *nón lá* on her head, the food bag in her arm.

"You'll understand why I do this once you become a mother." She pulled me up. I wanted to resist, but the look in her eyes silenced me.

When we arrived at the concrete building where my aunt and uncle lived, Grandma sent me upstairs alone, hiding her face under her *nón lá*. "Meet me on Tràng Tiền Street when you're done," she said.

I watched her pedal away, her shadow tiny against approaching darkness.

I bit my lip to stop myself from screaming as I entered the gloomy, filthy staircase. I wanted to rip the bag open, devouring the food myself. I was tired of my duty: to Grandma, to my mother, to my relatives.

I knocked on the apartment door. No answer. I waited. "Uncle Sáng," I called.

Silence.

"It's good you're not home," I said, turned, and was about to walk away when a whisper raced past my ears. "Hương, is that you?"

The door had creaked open. Auntie Hoa was poking out her face, scanning left and right. In a flash, she reached for my hand, pulling me inside. The door shut quietly behind us.

"Did anyone see you come up?" She frowned, her stomach bulging under her mismatched pajamas.

"Don't think so. Why?" I didn't address her with a respectful title, yet she didn't even notice; her eyes were on the food bag.

"Come. We're just having dinner." She pulled me further into her apartment. We passed a room where piles of books sat on the floor. *Theories of Marxism-Leninism*, the cover of one book said. *Capitalism*

Is Shuddering before Its Death was the title of another one. *The American Empire Is Only a Paper Tiger* was a book with the name of its publisher printed in a large font: the Truth Publishing House.

To my right was the empty kitchen. To my left were a bathroom and another room, barely furnished. Grandma had told me Uncle Sáng had given away his beautiful furniture, to show that he belonged to the working class. There was plenty of space to raise chickens and pigs, but there were no animal sounds.

We stepped into a big room.

My uncle was sitting on a reed mat. In his undershirt and shorts, he looked shockingly thin. In front of him were two plates of food: manioc and boiled water spinach. People who worked for the government were paid in food coupons, but the coupons weren't enough. Uncle Sáng should raise animals like us, instead of reading those propaganda books.

"*Chào chú.*" I greeted him.

"Hương. You here alone? Where's Grandma?"

"Down there on the street."

He breathed out a sigh of relief.

"She sent you some food." The bag felt much heavier now; it contained many hours of Grandma's labor and her love for her youngest son.

Uncle Sáng and Auntie Hoa exchanged glances. A moment passed. My uncle cleared his throat. "Just put it down. Lean it against the wall. Yes, yes. It's fine there."

I dropped the bag.

"Hương," my uncle said. "Tell Grandma it's good she's careful, that she sent you instead of coming herself."

I didn't answer. I just needed to get out of there.

• • •

A week later, I arrived home from school and was unlocking the front door when a bell clanged behind my back. I turned to see a man in a yellow hat who was perched on a bicycle, a bag slung over his shoulder, an envelope in his hand. A postman.

"Eh, is this the house of Mrs. . . . . Mrs. Trần Diệu Lan?"

"Yes, Uncle, she's my grandma," I said.

"A letter for her. From Sài Gòn."

I leaned my bike against the door. "Sài Gòn?"

The man nodded, handing me the envelope.

I glanced at the neat writing on its front. "From my Auntie Hạnh. Do you . . . do you have another letter for us?"

"Don't think so, but let me check." The postman pulled a stack of envelopes out from his bag, going through them. "Nothing else."

I watched until he and his bike disappeared from our lane, hoping he'd turn back to tell me that he was wrong, that there was another letter for Grandma and me.

The pigs, piglets, and chickens greeted me with hungry complaints as soon as I swung the door open. I peered at the letter. Perhaps Auntie Hạnh had gone to Sài Gòn to look for my father and Uncle Đạt. Perhaps she'd met them there.

I wanted to know what my aunt had written, but feared the news. I had to find Grandma.

I hurried to feed the animals, then raced toward the Old Quarter on my bike. Around me, autumn was ripening. Golden light poured from the deep, blue sky. Red and yellow leaves swayed, drifting down from tree branches, covering pavements, rustling under people's feet.

In the Old Quarter I rode from Silk Street to Silver Street, from Cotton Street to Onion Street. I returned to Traditional Medicine Street, biked along Coffin Street and ended up on Bamboo Street.

There were thirty-six streets here, and Grandma could be on any of them. She could be any of the people I saw, scurrying by, their faces hidden under their *nón lá*.

My heart jumped as I caught sight of two guards, their armbands bright red. I pressed the brake, gripping the handle, about to turn around when one of the guards pointed at me. "You! Come here."

I got down from my bike, leading it toward him. "Hello, Uncle." I held my breath, hoping my face wasn't red with fright.

"Papers," the guard shouted, towering above me.

I opened my bag, giving him the bike's ownership paper and my ID.

The other guard, short and chubby, edged closer and had a look. "So you're rich, eh, Younger Sister, having this bike in your name."

"Where did you get it?" demanded the tall guard, looking me up and down.

"My grandma brought it for me, Uncle."

The chubby guard winked at me. "Call us Brother." He eyed my chest.

The tall guard frowned. "Your grandma, huh? How the hell could she afford this?" He kicked the bike. It shook and rattled. I gripped the handle, hanging on, feeling like he'd kicked me in the stomach.

"She's a teacher, Uncle. She works hard." I was polite, yet the Kick-Poke-Chop moves flashed through my mind.

"Look." The chubby guard elbowed the tall guard, gesturing toward a middle-aged woman who was struggling on her bicycle. "Take that bike if it's not in her name. I'll handle this one."

As the tall guard jumped out on to the road, shouting at the woman, the chubby one studied my papers. He caressed my picture on the ID, his fingernails black with dirt. "Pretty, but prettier in real life."

"Uncle, can I please go now? I'm late for class."

"Ah, I see, 173 Khâm Thiên Street," he read my address aloud and looked me straight in the eyes. "Be home tonight. I'll come by for a visit."

"Visit? Why, Uncle?"

"I said call me Brother," he hissed, then lowered his voice. "Let's just say I'm doing you a favor. You'll be safe, going out with me."

I avoided his eyes while putting the papers back into my bag. *Calm your mind,* I told myself, repeating Grandma's words as I cycled away. *Build your inner strength.*

Finding a lane, I turned into it. My legs wobbled as if they were mud. I parked the bike near an older woman who was squatting on the pavement, a bamboo basket in front of her.

"Green tea, green tea. Would you like some green tea?" she called out to me.

"Yes, please, but not too strong, Grandma." I studied the bike. Luckily, the kick didn't do much damage. I unbent the chain's metal cover.

"Better lock it." The lady lifted the cloth that covered her basket, pouring steaming tea into a cup. "Thieves lurk around every corner these days."

She gave me a low stool, handing me the cup. The softness in her eyes told me that she was kind, and could be trusted. Leaning over to her, I whispered, "I'm Hương, I'm looking for my grandmother. She trades around here."

"What's her name?" the lady whispered back, then asked in a loud voice, "Should I add water to your tea? It's strong."

"Yes, please," I said aloud, then lowered my voice. "Her name is Diệu Lan."

She studied my face and looked away. "Green tea, green tea," she called out to a passer-by.

I took a sip. The tea scalded my mouth. "If you know where she is, please tell me. It's urgent," I begged.

"Green tea, green tea," she called louder, then lifted her *nón lá*, pretending to fan herself so she could hide her mouth. "How do I know you're her granddaughter?"

I reached into my school bag. "Here . . . a letter from my aunt."

She sneaked a look. "Wait here." Picking up her basket, she hoisted it against her waist, disappearing around the corner. After I'd finished my cup, she came back, gathering her stool. Without being told, I pushed my bike, following her. Salt Street was quiet when we got there. The tea seller chose a corner. I sat down opposite her.

"Guava, you all right?"

I turned to see Grandma's face and wrinkled forehead.

I stood up. "Auntie Hạnh sent you a letter."

Grandma sat down, tearing the envelope open. She scanned the pages, a sigh of relief escaping her.

"What does it say, Grandma?"

"Why don't you read it aloud? I'm sure Mrs. Uyên here wants to hear it."

"Read here?" I glanced around. A few people were walking nearby. A man sat a few houses away, smoking a bamboo pipe; streaks of whiteness untangling themselves above his head, before vanishing into the air.

"Why not? Go ahead." Grandma stretched her legs, sipping her tea. I cleared my voice.

Dear Mama, Sister Ngọc, and Hương,

Sorry I didn't have the chance to tell you about our moving to Sài Gòn. Tuấn returned from the war and was sent back to the South again, this time to manage a factory. He asked us to join him, and I had to quickly sell our land and house and pack as much as I could. With Thanh and Châu and my parents-in-law, I boarded the train, traveling for three days. I had to pinch myself when we arrived at the city once called Pearl of the Far East.

I had expected Sài Gòn to be rich, but oh my, it was beyond my imagination. Avenues as big as rice fields, buildings taller than the tallest trees I'd ever seen in my life. The people here, their fashionable clothes and southern accents make me feel such a country bumpkin.

Do you know that Sài Gòn's name has just been changed to Hồ Chí Minh City? We're told to use this new name. I'm putting down both Sài Gòn and HCM City as my address, though, just in case.

Anyhow, Tuấn said there's much to be done. People who worked for the Americans or for the Southern government are being sent to reeducation camps. When our army was about to take over the city in April 1975, a lot of them tried to escape overseas by planes and ships. Many abandoned their houses, just like that. As we're linked to the army, we got to stay in one of those houses. It's a two-story home, as big as a mansion.

I LOOKED UP at Grandma. The next two paragraphs were black. It seemed somebody had dipped a thick brush into an ink bottle and hurriedly painted over them.

"Go on, ignore the censored part," Grandma urged me.

"Censored?"

"You think Hạnh smeared ink on her letter in such a way? She's always taken great care of her handwriting." She brought her mouth to my ear. "The higher ones spy on our letters. The parts they don't like are blackened out."

"Oh." I studied the censored paragraphs, unable to make out a word.

I started my teaching job at a school close to our house, where Thanh and Châu are studying. Many teachers here have been sent from the North, and we're using textbooks published in Hà Nội. Our task is to erase remnants of the old regime.

Mama, I hope Brother Đạt and Brother Hoàng are back. Please let me know immediately if there's any news. And please, write me right away if you hear anything about Brother Minh. I pray for their safe returns. I'll try to look for them here.

I bit my lip. There was no good news.

Sister Ngọc, I hope you're feeling better. I'm sorry for not being able to stay longer when I visited last time. But I want to be back soon, to talk to you, like we used to. Please let me know if there is something I can do.

Mama, when you see Thanh and Châu again, you'll be surprised by how adept they are at Kick-Poke-Chop self-defense. I've been teaching them, and am reminded of those wonderful days we had with Master Văn. Mama, I hope you're taking good care, and that you aren't working too hard.

And Hương, thank you for being such a good girl, for looking after Grandma and your Mama. How are your studies? Are you still the only student who got the Excellence Award from your school? Write me soon, promise?

Mama, Sister Ngọc, Hương, I can't wait to have you visit me here. We could spend the entire day shopping at Bến Thành

Market and sample all types of Southern food. It's an amazing city, really.

With all my love,

Hạnh.

The tea seller praised Auntie Hạnh for doing so well in the South, but Grandma said she didn't like some of the changes mentioned in my aunt's letter, such as reeducation camps and the abolishment of the South's well-established education system.

Grandma decided to go home early with me. She led the way, weaving us into tiny lanes that cut across the Old Quarter. When we turned into a large road, I paused at the sight of several guards clutching the arms of a struggling man, dragging him along. Grandma told me to keep going.

When Grandma stopped, I realized we were in front of the legendary Tràng Tiền store. Here, the most delicious ice cream had been made for generations. I didn't dare think we'd buy something, but Grandma told me to choose as many sticks as I wanted. I went for three different types: chocolate, young sticky rice, and coconut. Grandma bought two for herself, both mung bean.

"Let's go somewhere nice," said Grandma.

"Hoàn Kiếm Lake?"

"You read my mind."

A short distance away, the Lake of the Returned Sword sparkled in front of us like a gigantic mirror. I pushed the bike along the dirt path that snaked around the shore, passing bomb shelters with lids overgrown by sprawling grass.

"Grandma, the man who was being pulled away by the guards, what do you think he did?" I asked.

"His pants . . . The cuffs were too wide. Too flared. He was being punished for trying to look like Western hippies."

I looked down at my pants. Thankfully, the cuffs were narrow.

"The government wants to control us, Hương. People have been arrested and put into prison. Promise you'll be careful? If they find reasons to take your bike away one day, let them. Don't fight them, promise?"

I nodded, wondering how I'd handle the guard if he came to our home, looking for me.

We sat on a stone bench, under an ancient tree with its many branches reaching down to the lake's surface, yellowing leaves flitting in the wind. A short distance away, in the midst of the water, the Turtle Tower glimmered in the afternoon light, moss greening its walls. Atop the tower, figures of dragons and phoenixes soared up to the sky. On a tiny island near the tower, the Ngọc Sơn Temple rose above a thick clump of trees.

It was a blessing that this ancient site had escaped the bombings.

I watched the water's surface, hoping for a glimpse of one of the gigantic turtles that lived in this lake. When I was little, Grandma had told me the legend of the Lake of the Returned Sword. Hundreds of years ago, when China's Ming Dynasty invaded Việt Nam, Heaven helped the Vietnamese by sending a magical sword. A poor fisherman found the sword many kilometers away from Hà Nội and brought it to Emperor Lê Lợi, who used the sword to defeat the powerful Ming Army. When peace came, the Emperor went boating on this lake. A huge turtle appeared before him, spoke in a human voice, asking the Emperor to return the sword. "The world will only be at peace if all people let go of their weapons," the turtle said. Astonished, the Emperor held out his beloved sword. The turtle took it with his mouth, disappearing under water. From then on, the lake was named Hoàn Kiếm—the Lake of the Returned Sword.

The ancient legend couldn't be truer. If both Americans and Vietnamese had laid down their weapons, no one would have had to die.

Grandma's eyes were dreamy. "Mrs. Uyên, the tea seller, once saw a Great-Grandparent Turtle emerging from this lake. When she got home, her daughter-in-law gave birth to a son."

Grandma and everyone I knew had such respect for the Hoàn Kiếm turtles that they called them *Cụ Rùa*—Great-Grandparent Turtle.

I took a bite of my ice cream. "It's true then, whoever sees a Great-Grandparent Turtle in this lake will be blessed. But how many Great-Grandparent Turtles still live here, Grandma?"

"Nobody knows. We only know they're rare."

I shifted my gaze to the Ngọc Sơn Temple. Grandma and I had been there many times, praying to Heaven and admiring the remains of a Great-Grandfather Turtle. He weighed 250 kilograms and was more than two meters long. According to experts, he was 900 years old.

Resting my head on Grandma's shoulder, I wished I could tell her how sorry I was for the fight we'd had. From now on, I had to be kinder to her.

Twilight sprinkled its golden rays onto us as I cycled home with Grandma. As we turned onto our lane, I saw that a crowd had gathered in front of our house.

Grandma jumped down before her bike stopped completely. She pushed herself into the crowd, disappearing from my view.

"Can't believe he made it back," a woman said.

"He's lucky to be alive," said a man.

My bike crashed to the ground.

"Please, let me through." I squeezed myself between bodies, my arms opening the way. Someone shoved me to the left, another to the right. I struggled to breathe, my head spinning. I inched forward and eventually found myself closer to a small clearing in the middle of the circle.

Squashed behind some people, I stood on my toes, looking over their shoulders. My eyes found Grandma. She was kneeling in front of a metal chair that sat on two large wheels, holding hands with someone whose body was obscured by the wheelchair's back.

"Grandma," I called. The people in front turned. They mumbled, giving way. Someone pulled me down, and I knelt next to Grandma. I blinked and saw a blurred but familiar face.

"Hương, Little Hương." A voice I knew called my name.

"Papa!" Flashes of light flared up around me. Light that faded into a dark tunnel, pulling me into its depth.

I FLOATED ON a bed of clouds. An immense blue sea surrounded me, waves bobbing under a layer of mist. A black dot appeared, grew larger, then turned into a Great-Grandfather Turtle. The turtle was swimming next to me now, his head held high, his mouth opening. I tried to speak, but only muffled sounds came. "Hương," the turtle said, his eyes glowing, water glistening on his head. Breathing noisily through his nose, he flicked his tongue; something cool lapped against my forehead.

"*Hương, Hương ơi!*" Someone called my name from a faraway distance. I tried to move and the mist started to evaporate. The turtle disappeared and I was inside our home. The clouds became our wooden *phản*, and the turtle's tongue, a wet cloth on my forehead.

"Guava, do you feel better?" my grandmother said.

"What happened, Grandma?"

"You fainted, my darling." She nursed sugary water into my mouth.

Memory rushed back. "Papa!"

I looked around. There he was. The hollowed eyes, the gaunt face, the beard and rough skin. Wearing an army shirt, he was sitting in the wheelchair. Two scar-ridden stumps—the remains of his legs—protruded out from a pair of army pants that had been cut short.

The man grinned, and I heard myself cry.

He was not my father, but Uncle Đạt.

"Hương," said my uncle. "I frightened you, didn't I? Sorry."

I shook my head, tears rolling down my cheeks.

Grandma caressed my face. "You scared me so, Guava."

"Uncle Đạt, I'm so glad you're back," I managed to say.

"Me, too. My Guava. My Little Hương. But you're not little anymore. You've grown so much."

"Sorry about your legs." I glanced toward the stumps. "Do they hurt?"

"Not anymore." My uncle pushed himself closer to the *phản*. He reached for my hand, held it up, whacking it against his stumps. "See? I don't feel any pain."

"What happened, Son?" asked Grandma.

"I stepped on a land mine, Mama. Not such a big deal." My uncle shrugged.

"We're lucky you made it home." Grandma squeezed his hand.

Uncle Đạt smiled at me. "I have something for you, young lady. I'm glad . . . so glad to finally deliver my promise." Unbuttoning his breast pocket, my uncle pulled out a tiny bundle, kissed it, brought it to his chest, and looked up to Heaven. He closed his eyes for a long while before turning to me, the bundle in the nest of his palms.

I picked it up, staring at the blackish outer layers of plastic and paper. "Who is it from, Uncle?"

"Your father." My uncle beamed.

"You saw him?" I sat right up.

"Oh, many years ago. Let me see . . . seven years and two months, to be exact. It was in August 1968, when we were both heading south."

"Have you seen him again? You know where he is?"

"Nope, but I bet he'll be back before you know it."

As I sat there, unable to move, Grandma nudged me. "Don't you want to open it?"

My hands trembled as I peeled away the layers of wrapping.

A bird. An exquisitely carved bird. Chiseled from wood, it stood on a square base, its wings open, its neck craning forward as if ready to burst into a song.

"Your father carved it himself." Uncle Đạt grinned. "This type of bird used to sing for us as we walked for months and months to get to the battlefields."

"Does it have a name, Uncle?" I brought the bird to my face. It smelled like my father, like his laughter.

"Sơn ca."

"A splendid name." Grandma smiled at me. "Sơn ca means 'The Mountain Sings.'"

"Believe me, this bird can sing," said Uncle Đạt. "Whenever it did, all the mountains around me seemed to be singing, too. My comrades used to tell tales about the Sơn ca. They said the Sơn ca's songs can reach Heaven, and souls of the dead can return in the Sơn ca's singing."

"What a special bird, Uncle."

Uncle Đạt nodded. "This wooden bird was my travel companion during the last seven years, Hương. It climbed countless mountains with me, swam through rivers, dived into underground tunnels, and survived the bombs."

"That's how it got these watermarks." Grandma admired the bird's wings. "I know your father has clever hands, Hương. I didn't know he was such an artist."

"Thank you, Uncle Đạt."

"Come on, Hương. I'm the thankful one. This Sơn ca saved me. I promised your father to bring it back to you in one piece. I had to stay alive, to be able to do this," he pointed at the bird. "See the words under the base?"

I turned the Sơn ca and tears ran down my cheeks. My fingers traced my father's message: CON GÁI, CON LÀ MÁU NÓNG TRONG TIM CHA.

"Treasure this bird, Hương," said Uncle Đạt. "There aren't many left. I saw plenty of them at first. But then the bombs and the chemical sprayed by the enemy silenced them."

"Chemical?" asked Grandma.

"Yes, they dumped plenty of it onto our forests and jungles. To make leaves fall off trees, so they could see us soldiers from the North. But whatever they sprayed also killed small living things. I didn't know what the chemical was called, until after the war. It has a beautiful name: Agent Orange."

WHEN DINNER WAS READY, I pushed Uncle Đạt's wheelchair to the table. Grandma and I glanced at each other. He sat too low.

"We can move you onto this." Grandma pulled a dining chair.

"If you two are strong enough." Uncle Đạt tried to laugh.

"You bet." I stepped to his right, Grandma to his left.

"Now, hold on to these useless pieces of meat." Uncle Đạt gestured toward the remaining parts of his thighs.

Grandma slid her hand under one stump, her other hand supporting Uncle Đạt's back. I followed, shivering when my fingers touched the soft flesh.

"One, two, three." We counted together, struggled, but managed to shift Uncle Đạt.

"Oho, you girls are good." Uncle Đạt clapped his hands.

"It's not difficult." I sat down, picking up his bowl.

He waved his hand. "Don't fill it with rice yet." He looked around. "You have some liquor, Mama?"

"Liquor? I don't remember that you drink, Đạt."

"Well . . . you know, sometimes the stuff helps ease things."

"Sorry, we don't have any."

"Hmm, perhaps up there?" My uncle looked up at our family altar. "I'm sure Papa, Uncle Công, and Thuận wouldn't mind sharing their drinks."

"They didn't drink, Đạt. I've never offered them liquor."

"Fine." Uncle Đạt's face drooped. "Go ahead and eat. I can't without a drink first."

"Wait." I stood up. "Perhaps Mrs. Nhân has some. Let me go across the road."

Thankfully, our neighbor was as helpful as usual. She gave me a bottle of rice liquor, whispering, "My husband brewed it himself, but don't tell anyone."

Back at our house, Grandma fetched a small cup. Uncle Đạt filled it, emptying it in one gulp. He smacked his lips. "This stuff is good, real good." He picked up the bottle, sniffed it and filled the cup again. "Can you ask where she bought it?"

"Her husband made it himself," I blurted out, and regretted it immediately. "Oops, Mrs. Nhân told me not to tell anyone."

"It's a secret then," Uncle Đạt chuckled, tossing another cupful down his throat. He leaned toward me. "But I can only keep it a secret if they teach me how to make this." The pungent smell from his mouth made me grimace.

"Have some food before it gets too cold." Grandma put a piece of grilled beef into Uncle Đạt's bowl.

He chewed and swallowed. "*Mmm*, this tastes divine. I haven't had meat for so long. . . ."

"There's plenty. Eat all you want." Grandma rearranged the plates so the beef was in front of Uncle Đạt. He picked up another piece, dipping it into salt mixed with lemon juice and ground pepper.

"You seem to be doing really well, Mama." He looked around. "This grand house, the bicycles, the pigs, piglets. . . ."

"Grandma works very hard," I said.

"Didn't imagine her teaching job would pay that much." He drained another cup.

"Of course it didn't. We would've been struggling now if I'd continued teaching." Grandma grabbed the bottle, filling the cup. "That's enough for today, Son." She stood up.

"You what?" Uncle Đạt was so shocked about Grandma quitting her job that he didn't seem to notice her walking away with the bottle.

"I've become a *con buôn*." Grandma reached up, depositing the bottle into the kitchen cabinet. She closed the door.

"Hey, I need that," my uncle protested, but Grandma was already returning to the table. She ladled vegetables into his bowl.

"Remember how you used to love this? Spinach cooked with dry shrimp." Her voice sounded choked.

"Yeah, I remember. It's delicious, thanks." He bent his head. "So, you became a trader, huh? It's brave of you."

"It's saving us." Grandma scooped rice into his bowl.

"Grandma's trading keeps me at school, Uncle. Many of my friends have had to drop out and work instead."

My uncle nodded. "So, where do you trade, Mama?"

"Around the Old Quarter. I've done it for a few years now."

"You're a pro then." He drained the cup. "Think you'll hire an invalid as your assistant?"

"Đạt!"

"I'm serious, Mama. I need a job. Me, minus my two legs." Uncle Đạt's voice quivered. But he cleared his throat and quickly gained his composure.

"I'm serious, too, Son." Grandma caressed his hand. "You're my life. I'll take care of you. You'll get a job, I promise."

"Thanks." My uncle picked up his chopsticks.

Grandma scooped more food into my bowl. "Now, tell me why it took you so long to get home. It's October now. You could've been home six months ago."

"It's a long story. I don't want to talk about it now. Please, can I have some more of that liquor?"

Grandma sighed. I thought she'd say no, but she stood up.

She put the bottle down. "Just finish your food and you can drink."

GRANDMA SLEPT SOUNDLY next to me. My mind was alive with images: of my father dashing through jungles under the bombs, of butterflies and birds falling in a rain of Agent Orange, of my father crouching and chiseling the wooden bird, of his hand carving his message to me onto the bird's base: "Daughter, you are the warm blood in my heart."

The Land Reform

Nghệ An, 1955

G uava, one afternoon in March 1955, your grandfather came home, looking drunk. He leaned onto the doorframe, trying to take off his shoes.

"How many cups of rice liquor did your friends force on you, *anh* Hùng?" I asked, untying his shoes. Some of Hùng's friends brewed their own liquor but he wasn't a drinker. Not at all.

"No friends . . . I was called to a meeting." Hùng struggled toward the bedroom. The way he talked, I knew the meeting wasn't related to the school where he worked. It was to do with his political activities. Ten years earlier, after the Việt Minh saved us from the Great Hunger, Hùng had become an underground Việt Minh member, writing

leaflets and documents, calling on our fellow citizens to unite in supporting the Việt Minh troops.

I followed Hùng into the bedroom and helped him settle into bed.
He shivered under the blanket; his forehead burnt with a fever. If he
hadn't drunk, perhaps he'd been caught by some bad wind.

"What was the meeting about, *anh*?" I slid a softer pillow under
his head.

"They challenged me about what I'd said. So I had to explain why
we need democracy. Why multiple political parties should be allowed
so that we could run real elections."

Hùng hadn't hidden his opinion from anyone. He was determined to
help resurrect our homeland from the remnants of war. The Việt Minh
had become popular by liberating the North and forcing Emperor Bảo
Đại to abdicate, and by then triumphing over the French in 1954, at
the battle of Điện Biên Phủ. But Hùng wasn't keen that the Việt Minh
had followed the path of the Chinese and Russian Communists by ruling our North with a single political party. By that time, the Russian
Communist leader, Stalin, had sent millions of Russians to labor camps.
He killed millions of others to consolidate his power.

"I bet they didn't like what you told them." I frowned.

"They called me a traitor." He clutched his stomach, curling up like
a shrimp.

"Who did?"

He closed his eyes. "Doesn't matter."

I reached for his stomach. "What did you drink or eat, *anh*?"

"They served us homemade juice." He winced. "I couldn't tell what
it was."

I wished my brother was home, but he'd taken the children to visit
our relatives. As I rushed to the kitchen to make ginger tea for Hùng,
my feet felt as if they were tethered to boulders. Just last night, Công

had reminded Hùng to be careful, but Hùng had knocked his fist against the table. "Brother," he said, "only through democracy can we ensure that there'll be no abuse of power."

When I returned to the bedroom with the tea and a cool towel for his head, Hùng's breathing was ragged and rapid. He drank the tea but asked for water. I brought him a large cup. He gulped it down.

"Would you like some more?" I asked, alarmed.

He shook his head, his fever warming the towel in my hand.

"Let me go get Mr. Nguyên." I stood up, ready to race out to find the healer.

"No need." Hùng looked up at me. His eyes were strange. The pupils were small, too small. "I'll . . . I'll be fine. Just need a good sleep." The muscles on his face started to twitch.

"We need Mr. Nguyên." I ran out of the room, shouting.

Mrs. Tú hobbled toward me. "What's wrong, Diệu Lan?"

"*Anh* Hùng is very ill. Please watch him, Auntie. I'll be back soon." I would've liked to stay with my husband, but Mrs. Tú had twisted her ankle the day before.

I dashed out to the village road, praying while running. When I reached the healer's house, he wasn't there.

"Are you all right?" his son, Việt, asked. "My father is out with his friends."

I told Việt about Hùng.

"Let's go find him." Việt grabbed the wooden box his father always carried while visiting patients. We raced out into the village, running from one house to the next.

It took us a long time to find Mr. Nguyên and rush him to my house.

Entering the front yard, I heard Mrs. Tú's voice. "*Hùng ơi, con ơi!*" she was wailing. My feet started to give way beneath me.

Việt snatched my arm, pulling me along. We burst into the bedroom. Hùng was convulsing violently under the grip of Mrs. Tú. His eyes rolled back in their sockets. Foam bubbled at his mouth.

"Stay calm, women! Stop screaming." Mr. Nguyên ordered Việt to loosen Hùng's clothing. We held him down so he wouldn't hurt himself or fall out of bed.

The healer checked Hùng's breathing, eyes, and chest. He clutched Hùng's hand, turning the palm up, listening to the pulse. Through my tears, I saw his eyes widen.

"Poison. Don't touch the foam," he shouted. "Make him vomit. Turn him!" He hurried to wrap his hands with a cloth. "Mrs. Tú, go wash your hands with soap. Get me some warm water."

Việt and I turned Hùng onto his stomach, tilting his head down to the floor. The healer forced open Hùng's mouth, trying to induce him to vomit. Not much came out.

Mrs. Tú rushed into the room with a jug of water. We returned Hùng to his back. I wiped his mouth and caressed him with my voice. By now his tremors were easing, but he felt limp in my hands. His eyes had stopped rolling, and I caught the flicker of desperation in his eyes.

"Hold on, *anh* Hùng. Look at me. Talk to me!" I commanded, yet he didn't reply. His eyes were closing.

"Mr. Nguyên, please . . . ," I begged. The healer had opened the wooden box, scooped powders into a bowl and mixed them with water.

We sat Hùng up. Mr. Nguyên fed him the concoction, but it flowed back out. Hùng could no longer swallow. He could no longer respond.

Wrapping our hands with cloths, we opened Hùng's mouth, trying to force the medicine down, but it didn't work. Mr. Nguyên shook his head. "Diệu Lan. I'm sorry. I'm afraid we are too late."

I got down on my knees. "Please save him, Mr. Nguyên. I beg you!"

The healer pulled me up, his eyes sorrowful. "It's too strong, the poison Hùng took."

"No! Please save him. Save him!"

I lay my face on Hùng's heart. But he was silent. Silent as a piece of paper that had been erased of all its words.

Công was miserable and furious when he got back. He beat his fists against his chest, talking about revenge. He tracked down those people who were with Hùng at their meeting. They denied any responsibility and threatened to put Công in prison if he didn't stop making accusations.

I should have pursued it further, Guava. I should've tried to find the one who killed your grandpa and bring him to justice, but I was a coward. I was fearful for Công's safety, as well as my children's.

But Công was stubborn. He went to the authorities. I had to come with him, to make sure he wouldn't be arrested.

"Nobody killed your brother-in-law," one official told Công, eyeing me. "Perhaps he took his own life."

"That healer Nguyên is crazy," snarled another official. "What proof do you have? Pursue it further and we'll put you and that insane healer of yours in prison. Defamation against the Party is a serious crime."

I begged Công to go home. I knew it wasn't true that Hùng had committed suicide. He loved us, Guava, and he loved his life.

Soon, we heard plenty of rumors that the Việt Minh was getting rid of its anticommunist members, as well as intellectuals and the rich. The Party had to belong to farmers and workers, not to a member of the bourgeoisie like Hùng.

I don't know whether these rumors were true, but I do know that politics is as dirty as sewage. I don't ever want to set my foot near it again.

I can't tell you how wrecked we were by your grandpa's death. Your Uncle Minh, seventeen by then, had been very close to him. So were your mother, your Uncle Đạt, Uncle Thuận, and Auntie Hạnh. Sáng was the only one who didn't know what was going on. He was just four months old.

I had to stay strong for my children, but for a long time afterward, I felt like a broken shell. I know now that true love is rare and once we find our true love, we must hold on to it. I just wish that when Hùng was alive, I'd told him more often that I loved him.

Công swore to stay out of politics and never to support the government again. He poured his energy into our family business, which had been prospering under his leadership. He passed his skills to Minh and the two of them spent a lot of time together. We all worked hard and managed to hire additional workers. Our fields continued to be lush and our cattle stalls full.

I thought we were getting back on our feet. I was sure we'd received enough bad luck and Heaven would spare us from further turbulence.

But I was wrong.

In October 1955, just seven months after your grandpa's funeral, something else crashed down onto our heads.

"DIỆU LAN, CAN you keep a secret?" asked Mrs. Tú in the kitchen as I poured shredded crabmeat into a clay pot filled with rice porridge. Food for Sáng. I'd just come back from the field, and wanted to feed him before going out to lunch. One of my mother's friends was turning seventy and had invited me to come over.

"What secret, Auntie?"

"Remember Thương?" Mrs. Tú whispered. "She worked as the cook for the Đinh family. I ran into her this morning at the market. She told me the Đinhs have left. They're trying to cross the border, to go to the South."

How strange, I thought. The South had been cut away from us over a year before, in June 1954, by something called the Geneva Agreements. The Communists ran the North, but in the South, Ngô Đình Diệm was in charge, supported by the French and the Americans. Most of those who worked for the French or were Catholics had moved south. As far as I knew, the Đinhs hated the French. They weren't Catholics. Since the Great Hunger, they'd prospered and become the richest clan in Vĩnh Phúc Village. Besides, the North-South border had already been closed. How could they even get to the South?

Mrs. Tú edged next to me. She lowered her voice further. "Diệu Lan, I think you should listen to this. Thương said Madam Đinh told her the Communists have started some crazy thing called the Land Reform. Landless farmers are encouraged to rise against rich land-owners. That's why the Đinhs left."

I squinted through a curtain of woodsmoke, ladling the porridge into a bowl. "I heard about the Land Reform, Auntie, but we have nothing to worry about. Remember how much rice, silver, and gold we donated to the Việt Minh?" I closed my eyes, trying to make myself believe what I was about to say. "The Party will protect us against any uprising. After all, together with other landowners, we financed their troops."

"I know, Diệu Lan. But I'm worried."

"We'll be fine, Auntie. We work as hard as everyone else. We give people jobs. We've done nothing wrong. Công and I already talked about this. . . . And Auntie, we can't just leave. The workers and their families depend on us. The graves of my parents are here to be looked after. Besides, how can we just abandon everything? My parents and grandparents built all this with their lives. We can't just run away because of some rumors."

Mrs. Tú nodded.

Holding the bowl, I walked out of the kitchen. In the yard, the longan tree was blooming, its blossoms spreading a dome of pearls atop its green canopy. Instead of bringing joy to my heart, the sight reminded me that life's peaceful moments could be as short-lived as flowers—gone with a strong gust of wind. The news of the Đinhs' departure could be a warning sign.

"Mama, look."

I turned to see Đạt, sunlight on his shoulder, rushing toward me. Fourteen years old then, he was taller than me, and well built. Thuận, eight, and Hạnh, seven, ran after him. Carrying bags in their hands, they were coming home from school.

Đạt opened his palm and showed me a shivering bird. It was feather-less, its wings drooping by its side. "A *sẻ* bird, Mama. I found it under a tree."

"I saw it first." Hạnh shook her head.

"No, I did first." Thuận's face reddened.

"How about all of you found it at the same time?" I couldn't help but laugh. "Bring the poor creature back to the tree. Its mother must be looking. If you can't find the mother, feed it water and insects."

"Let me see, let me see." A voice flew through the gate. Guava, your Mama Ngọc. She was a pretty girl of fifteen then. Glowing skin, deep dimples on her cheeks, her schoolbag in her hand.

The children squatted down, studying the bird and debating what to do next. I hurried inside, to my bedroom. Sáng was already standing up in his cot, crying.

"Mama's here," I cooed, placing the porridge down and picking him up. My baby, he was so cute, with those big eyes and chubby face.

Villagers who passed by for a visit often pinched his cheeks, saying how much he looked like his father.

"*Mẹ, mẹ,*" Sáng babbled, lifting my shirt. He was nearly one year, yet I hadn't weaned him. I knew he'd be my last baby.

As soon as he'd satisfied his thirst, he pointed at the porridge.

"You're really hungry, aren't you?" I chuckled.

Once Sáng finished eating, I changed into my favorite green silk blouse. Công had ordered it for me from the famous Vạn Phúc Silk Village, where people had been weaving silk for over a thousand years. The fabric was exquisite, made of several layers, with the ancient Vietnamese word *Phúc*—Blessings—woven into it many times over. The shirt was thick, perfect for the cool autumn weather.

While doing the last button, I cocked my head. I heard voices and the sound of running feet.

"*Đả đảo địa chủ cường hào!*" Screams flooded through my half-open window: Down with wicked landowners!

Rushing to the window, I pushed my hands against the wooden shutters, opening them wide.

A group of people armed with bricks, knives, large sticks, and angry faces were dragging Minh and Công across the yard. In their brown farmer clothes, my brother and son were shoeless, their feet spattered with mud and blood, their shirts and pants torn, their hands tied behind their backs. They were being pulled by the hair as well as their arms. Less than an hour ago, I'd been with them in the rice field.

"Minh, Brother Công!" I wailed.

The crowd turned their attention to me.

"Catch her. That's the rich bitch. The wicked landowner!" a woman shouted, pointing at my face. She had a large protruding forehead and teeth that looked like those of a rabbit. I recognized her as the butcher at our village market. She had a reputation for cheating her customers.

Later, much later, I found out that the Việt Minh deliberately chose *bần cố nông*—landless farmers who were fed up or angry with life—to lead the Land Reform movement.

"Kill them all, the wicked landowners!" the mob was chanting. Many of them were pointing their fingers at me.

I turned, picked Sáng up, frantically looking for somewhere to hide. I crawled into a corner, Sáng clutched tight against my chest. My baby. I needed to protect my baby.

The door crashed open. Two men and the butcher-woman charged in. Anger and excitement glinted in their eyes.

"There she is, the bitch!" shouted the woman, baring her teeth. "Get her. Bring her outside."

Someone grabbed my hair, pulling me up. As I screamed, the woman snatched Sáng away from me. The men twisted and roped my hands behind my back.

"Outside, bitch!" one man roared.

"Look how fat she is. Fat from farmers' blood," said the other man.

I was pulled and pushed along the corridor, across the living room. I howled for my children as someone flung me down the five steps. I struggled to open my eyes and saw Minh writhing on the floor.

"*Mẹ ơi*," he called for me. Behind him, Công's face was white with fear.

"Down with wicked landowners!" The mass of people surrounded us, chanting their vicious words, their faces contorted by anger.

My children's cries rose high above the noise. Through gaps among the moving legs, I saw Ngọc, Đạt, Thuận, and Hạnh huddled in Mrs. Tú's arms.

"Where's my baby Sáng, where is he?" I screamed.

"Kill them all, the wicked landowners." The crowd's rage swallowed my voice.

"I beg you, please let them go." Công bent forward, knocking his head onto the brickyard. "I'm in charge of this household. This woman and her son are innocent. Please . . . let them go."

I sobbed. It pained me to see my brother shaking. The torn patches of his shirt and pants revealed areas of bleeding flesh.

From the village road, drumbeats started to surge into the yard. The crowd shifted, giving way to children who marched toward us, their hands knocking on red drums clutched against their stomachs. Guava, some of those children had been students of your grandpa. Some had been friends of your uncles and your mother. For sure they would help our family. For sure some of the people around me would help us.

The crowd cheered, and the children got more excited. The thudding of their feet against the yard sent tremors through my bones. I saw the cruel glint in everyone's eyes. I saw their satisfied smiles. The drummers advanced and lined up in front of us. As the drumming stopped, a boy raised his foot and kicked Công straight in the face.

I screamed.

A woman lurched forward, a brick held high in her hand. "Shut up, wicked landlord, or else I'll crash this down on your stupid head!"

I bowed my head low. When I looked up, chairs were being carried out of our house and arranged into a row between the drummers and us. Some people were led to the chairs. They were Mrs. Tú, Mr. Hải, and the six farmers who worked for us. I begged Mr. Hải with my eyes. He'd rescued me from Wicked Ghost, could he save us today?

A man with a thin face emerged. Dressed like a farmer, but with skin as fair as of those who'd stayed most of their lives outside the sun. He introduced himself as the head of the People's Agricultural Reform Tribunal. He said he was a farmer, but the way he looked and acted told me otherwise.

The man cleared his throat. "Today is significant for all of us. The Land Reform has arrived at Vĩnh Phúc Village. For hundreds of years, rich landlords have exploited us poor farmers. Today, we stand up against their exploitation. Today, we're here to take back our rights!"

The drums rolled and the people shouted, "Down with wicked landowners."

"For generations, these rich bourgeoisie *ngồi mát ăn bát vàng*—sat in cool shadows and ate from their golden bowls—while we, the poor, have had to bend our backs under the sun to work for them and to serve them," the official shouted.

Drumrolls. Angry screams.

"Now it's your turn to seek justice." The man turned to face Mrs. Tú, Mr. Hải, and the workers. "Denounce them. Tell us how they've exploited you."

Drumrolls. Angry shouts.

"They never exploited me. They treated me as family," Mrs. Tú said, weeping.

"You fool! They've brainwashed you." The butcher-woman jumped forward. She was the one who snatched Sáng from my arms. Where was he? What did she do with him?

"It's true," said Mr. Thanh, one of our longest-serving employees. "They pay us well. They send our children to school."

"They never insulted us," said Mr. Hải.

"We're lucky to be working for them. Luckier than most people," Mr. Hà, another worker, said.

"Shut up! You're naïve and stupid," shouted a man, stepping up to the front. He raised a large stick in his hands and bared his yellow teeth. "Can't you see that they got rich on your sweat and blood? They exploited you and brainwashed you."

"They've poisoned your minds," yelled someone else.

"At other villages around us, terrible crimes by landowners have been revealed. Exploitation, beating, even rape," barked the yellow-toothed man. "Think hard. Did they rape you, beat you up, starve you?" He raised his stick higher and brought it down onto Minh's head, knocking him to the ground.

I wriggled toward my son, but somebody kicked me and pulled me back.

The official paced back and forth. "These landowners are born evil. At your neighboring Vĩnh Tiến village, a woman has denounced her own father. She said he'd raped her one hundred and fifty-nine times. One hundred and fifty-nine times! His own daughter."

The man paused, looking at us. "That evil landlord was executed, shot in the head. His daughter received a large share of his land to compensate for her suffering." He turned to Mrs. Tú and the workers, grinding each word between his teeth. "Now, don't be afraid. These Trần people, they can't get rich out of thin air. Look at their big house, big garden, fields, cattle. They must have been earning from someone's blood and sweat."

"I know how hard they work," Mrs. Tú wailed. Beside her, Mr. Lộc, the eldest worker, had wet his pants. "My husband and sons died in a fire," said Mrs. Tú. "The Trầns took care of me. They saved my life. They're my family now."

"Take her away. She's useless." The official shook his head. Mrs. Tú was pulled up and pushed away. She ran toward the children.

Next, the official turned to the seven men who sat on the chairs. "Make your choice now, Brothers. Keep sitting here like idiots or condemn them and get a share of their properties. We are here to help, don't you get it? We're here to undo the injustice they brought upon you."

One of our younger workers, Thông, lifted his head and scanned our faces. He grimaced. "They exploited us!" He shot to his feet. "We're poor and they're rich."

The crowd cheered and punched their fists.

"They made us work long hours. They didn't pay us enough. They made sure we remained poor so that we continued to serve them," Thông shouted.

The crowd roared.

"All of this wealth belongs to us, Brothers." Thông looked at the remaining men. "It's our right to take back the results of our labor."

"No, it's not true!" Mr. Thanh stood up. "The Trầns gave my family food during the Great Hunger. They helped so many when everyone was starving." He turned to the crowd. "You, and you, and you." He pointed at the faces in front of him. "I saw you here receiving their rice. I heard you tell Madam Trần you'd be grateful for the rest of your lives." His voice turned into a yell. "Anyone here, speak up if this family didn't try to save you during the Great Hunger."

The crowd grew silent. Even my children stopped crying.

Mr. Thanh turned to Thông. *"Đừng ăn cháo đái bát."* Don't eat porridge then piss into the bowl.

"Enough!" the official shouted into Mr. Thanh's face. "They've brainwashed you more than anyone."

"Down with wicked landowners." The shouts and the drumrolls were weaker this time.

"Rich landowners, how cunning they are." The official coughed and spat onto the yard. "Well, they can't get away with this. We're going to hold an open tribunal against them."

The drums rolled louder.

"We're going to divide their properties. Landless farmers will get a share!" the official roared and the crowd roared with him.

"Please, take everything you want," cried Công. "Denounce me if you must, but let my sister and her son go. Please let them go. I beg you. Let them go."

Another man, also fair-skinned, whispered to the official, who nodded.

"Take these two away." He pointed at Công and Minh. "Keep an eye on this evil woman." He gestured toward me. "We'll come back for her. Don't let her escape."

"No!" Công hollered. "Minh is just a kid. He knows nothing."

"Please, I beg you. Don't take my brother and my son away, please." I bowed to the crowd.

The official flicked his hand. Several men reached down, pulling Công and Minh up. My brother turned to look at me, tears and blood trickling down his face. "Don't worry, Sister, we'll come back soon. We did nothing wrong. Just take care of yourself and the kids . . ."

"Mama!" Minh struggled to free himself.

I tried to get up and run after them, but strong hands held me back. In the blink of an eye, my son and brother disappeared behind the yard's fence.

FIREFLIES HOVERED. THEY looked like burning eyes of devils who'd taken over our world. I blinked, but the darkness was too deep for me to see. I wriggled, but the ropes that tied my hands and legs were too strong. I sobbed but was dried of tears.

How many hours ago did the crowd come back, frightening me with their shouts? But they ignored me, the helpless woman who was roped against the thick trunk of the *na* tree. They charged into the cattle stalls, taking away our cows, buffaloes, pigs, and chickens. They mobbed the house, carrying away the sofa, chairs, beds, and cabinets. My brother and I had bought those with the sweat of our labor. I studied the mob's faces. I knew them all: the farmers of my village. Out of our seven workers, only Thông—the person who denounced us—came back. He avoided my eyes.

How many hours ago was a fire lit in our front yard? The mob had cheered, carrying our books outside, tearing them up, feeding them to the blazing flames. Remnants of the feudal system, they'd called my literary treasures. Our village pagoda was burned down, too, columns of smoke twisting up to the sky. Gone was our sacred place of worship.

How many hours ago did I last hear my children's cries? They were huddled inside the house like animals. Mrs. Tú was with them. Would she abandon us like everyone else?

All afternoon and evening, I remained bound to the tree trunk. To make sure that the children and I couldn't escape, an armed guard had been stationed at our gate and another at our front door. At first, I'd seen them smoking and heard their curses. But now things had gone quiet. Perhaps they'd fallen asleep.

"*Mẹ ơi, cha ơi, anh Hùng ơi, chị Trinh ơi.*" I silently prayed for the spirits of my mother, father, husband, and sister-in-law to come back and help rescue Công and Minh.

I was fearful but also very angry with myself. If I hadn't been so naïve, perhaps we would have had time to escape. If I hadn't been so involved with the new planting season, perhaps I would've learned a thing or two about the secretive plan to punish us.

A cracking sound. I strained my ears. The crunch of dry leaves being crushed underfoot. My heart thumped.

"Diệu Lan." The soft voice of Mrs. Tú.

"Auntie, I'm here."

I felt my savior creeping toward me in the dark, then her breath warm against my ear. "Take your children. Leave now." Tender hands reached for mine. Cold metal brushed against my skin. A pair of scissors released me from the grip of the ropes.

Mrs. Tú pulled me into her. We trembled in each other's arms.

"Auntie, I can't leave. Minh and Brother Công . . ."

"Diệu Lan . . ." Hot tears rolled from her eyes onto my face. "Mr. Hải sent us a message. They killed Công. You must leave now. They'll come for you."

"No!"

Mrs. Tú's hand cupped my mouth. I shook my head. My brother couldn't be dead. Just this morning, he was right next to me, talking and laughing. He'd never hurt anyone. No one should hurt him.

"Diệu Lan, run away before they find out about Minh. He escaped."

I gasped. Even in the midst of my grief, I felt a moment of elation.

Mrs. Tú pulled my arm. We crawled over fallen leaves, damp earth, and dew-soaked vegetables. I bumped against low tree branches but kept going.

"Mama's coming." "Mama, is that you?" I rejoiced at the sounds of these whispers. My hand felt a half-open door. I eased myself into the kitchen, and, fumbling in darkness, touched the teary faces of Ngọc, Đạt, Thuận, and Hạnh. I embraced them, willing them to melt into my body, so that we'd never be apart again.

"Baby Sáng, where's he?"

"Here. He's sleeping, Mama," Ngọc said, and I reached out for the warmth of my son.

"You have to go," said Mrs. Tú.

"Auntie, but Minh might come back to look for us," I said.

"He's run far away, Diệu Lan," Mrs. Tú whispered into my ear. "Stay here and you'll die. I beg you." She turned away from me. "Children, remember what we agreed? Crawl in single file. Hold the ankle of the person in front."

"Yes, Grandma."

"The guards are outside. Don't speak out there." Mrs. Tú's hands reached for me. She tied Sáng to my chest with her carrying cloth. "Diệu Lan, lead the children through the secret hole in the back fence to get to my plot of land. Run away from there."

"Won't you come with us, Auntie?" My throat tightened.

Her fingers were soft against my tears. "They'll burn this house without anyone here. They'll smash the family altar. I need to stay. To guard the graves of your parents."

"Grandma Tú, Grandma Tú." The children started to cry.

"*Shhh*, they'll hear us." Mrs. Tú sniffed. "Grandma will see you all again soon. Be strong and help your Mama. Come back to me when it's safe."

"But Auntie, how will I find Minh?" I asked.

My savior caressed my face. "Heaven will light the way for you to find each other, Diệu Lan. Try to bear your destiny, my child." Her hands left me. "Đạt, you're the eldest boy now. Take care of your siblings. Keep this food bag safe."

"Yes, Grandma." Đạt sobbed.

Darkness was our ally as we slithered across the back garden and through the fence. Darkness held us in its mouth as we ran through the rice fields, crossing several streams to get to the next hamlet.

Terrified, we ran.

The Journey South

Hà Nội, 1975

I t was pitch dark when I woke up. Grandma was snoring beside me. I fumbled around, found the Sơn ca, and clutched it tightly in my hand. I lay there for a long time, thinking about the ordeals each of my family members had had to go through. If I had a wish, I would want nothing fancy, just a normal day when all of us could be together as a family; a day where we could just cook, eat, talk, and laugh. I wondered how many people around the world were having such a normal day and didn't know how special and sacred it was.

Knowing I could no longer sleep, I lifted the mosquito net, tiptoed toward the bedroom door, and closed it behind me. In the kitchen, a shadow startled me.

"Uncle Đạt," I whispered, "couldn't you sleep?"

"No," a whisper came back.

I put the bird on the table, lit an oil lamp, and got us each a glass of water. In his wheelchair, my uncle looked like a shriveled old man. Yet he was only thirty-four.

"Want to go back to bed, Uncle? I can help you."

He shook his head. "Can't sleep much these days."

"How come?" I sat down next to him, pushing the glass into his hand.

"Nightmares and stuff, you know." He took a sip. "Don't worry about me, though. Go back to bed."

"I can't sleep either. . . . Uncle Đạt . . . thanks for saving me last night."

The chubby guard had come. So arrogant, he'd expected me to go out with him. He didn't have a chance since my uncle was there to face him for me.

"I guess I scared the hell out of him, huh?" Uncle Đạt chuckled. "Bet he won't return."

"I'm glad." I smiled. "But Uncle, please be careful. Grandma said those who dare to challenge the authorities are imprisoned—"

"That guy and the authorities? No way. He's just a prick trying to scare people. Excuse my foul language." My uncle shook his head. "They wouldn't dare touch me though. We veterans with our big mouths."

I drank my water slowly, trying to sort out the jumble in my mind. "Uncle, after my father gave you the bird, you didn't see him again? You didn't hear from him at all?"

"No. I'm sorry, Hương. The battlefields were vast, you know. I didn't run into Thuận, Sáng, or your mother either."

"I'm sure Mama and Uncle Sáng will come see you tomorrow. They'll be so happy you're finally home."

"Happy? You think they'll be happy seeing me like this?"

"Things will get better, Uncle."

He laughed, his laughter one of the saddest sounds I'd ever heard. "For months, I'd been thinking . . . that I shouldn't come home at all. That I couldn't face my friends and family like this, that I couldn't burden those I love." He looked up at the window, above which a wedge of the moon was suspended in the black sky.

"Please, Uncle." I fought back tears. "We'll take care of you."

He slumped down in his wheelchair.

"Uncle, I was just hoping . . . that you'd tell me about your trip south and how you met up with my father."

"Now?" He glanced up at the clock, which showed two a.m. "It's a long story. Don't you have school tomorrow?"

"Uncle, please. I've waited so long for news about my father. I need to imagine how it was for him."

"I need a real drink." Uncle Đạt eyed the cabinet. "Too bad I emptied the whole thing last night."

"Ha, wait a second." I jumped up. Rummaging the cabinet, I held up the bottle, now full. "Grandma bought it last night . . . after you'd gone to bed." I giggled. "She knew you might need it."

"My old Mama," chuckled my uncle. "She's someone special."

UNCLE ĐẠT IGNORED the cup I brought him and drank straight from the bottle. He bent his head for a long while. And then he began to talk. Now, thinking back, I realize how hard it must have been for him to dredge up these memories, trying to help the niece who searched for her father in her uncle's journey south.

"Yes, you were just a little girl when it all began," he said. "Back in 1968, an urgent order came for all men to enlist. Grandma tried all she could to stop us from going, but we had no choice. Sáng was just fourteen then so he didn't have to go yet, but your father, Thuận, and I were drafted.

"We were taken to a training camp at Ba Vì Mountain. Each of us had a knapsack to be filled with rocks. Each knapsack had to weigh at least twenty kilograms. We spent weeks climbing the mountain with the knapsack. Up and down, down and up, every single day. We practiced climbing during the night as well. Little did we know that we were preparing for the toughest walk of our lives."

Uncle Đạt shook his head. "We had to walk to the battlefields, more than a thousand kilometers away. Our mission was to wipe out the Americans and their ally, the South Vietnamese Army. I hadn't known this, but other countries such as Australia, South Korea, New Zealand, and Thailand also sent troops to fight with the Americans."

I shuddered. "You must have been afraid, Uncle?"

"Not really, our spirits were high. If we didn't fight back, we'd be bombed to dust and our North taken over. Before we started our journey, your father, Thuận, and I got separated into different companies. Thuận told me that as we'd survived the Land Reform, nothing could kill us—we were invincible. Your father joked that upon our return, he'd hold a joint wedding for Thuận and me. He'd seen how much our girlfriends—Thu and Nhung—wept as they saw us off.

"We hugged each other so tightly as we said good-bye. We weren't told exactly where we were heading."

Uncle Đạt stopped speaking. I was afraid it was too difficult for him to continue, but he cleared his throat.

"The North Vietnamese Army didn't have many cars, trucks, or trains, you know, and enemy bombs were targeting the roads. So it was better to walk through jungles and forests, climbing over the Trường Sơn mountain range. In fact, hundreds of thousands of Northern soldiers went south this way, forcing a network through jungles, now called the Hồ Chí Minh Trail.

"I was told it'd take six months to walk, and we each had to carry many things—clothes for all types of weather, medicine, bandages, a hammock, a fold-up spade, sandals, cooking and eating utensils. . . . On my left shoulder I carried five kilograms of rice in my *ruột tượng*, a long bag made out of cloth. On my right was an AK-47, an assault rifle supplied by the Russians. Around my waist, I had two hundred rounds of ammunition and a canteen of water."

Uncle Đạt closed his eyes. "Winter had set in when my comrades and I started our walk. It was wet and cold. The Army had a slogan for us: '*Đi không dấu, nấu không khói, nói không tiếng.*'" Advance without a trace, cook without smoke, talk without sound.

"Enemy planes were trying to find us, so we had to keep our movements secret. We walked at night and hid during the day. We camouflaged ourselves with green leaves and small branches so as to blend into the surroundings. Our stoves were deep holes that had to be covered and connected to long vents to dissipate the smoke."

"It sounds terribly dangerous, Uncle."

"Yes, it was. Walking in total darkness was a big challenge. It would be fatal to get lost. When a new day came, we set up camp and rested. Whenever I sat down, I found leeches clinging to my skin."

I shivered. I had read about those parasites, which sucked so much blood, they swelled up and became round balls.

"Bombing raids were frequent, so whenever we stopped, we had to find or dig shelters before we could string our hammocks between trees. Each hammock had a piece of canvas to shield us in case it rained, which was often. The canvas was important, let me tell you. It'd wrap a soldier's body after he died; it'd be our shroud.

"In the beginning, for every five walking days, we had one to rest. Rest days were something to look forward to. If I wasn't on duty, I could sleep, hunt, fish, or gather edible plants. On rest days, our captain would send a squad of twelve soldiers to an army camp nearby to bring back food supplies for the next five walking days. Together with the Russians, the Chinese Communists supported our fight against the Americans, so we also got food from the Chinese."

I closed my eyes and tried to picture my father fishing at a stream deep inside the jungle.

"But our bodies weren't made for the harsh jungle conditions, Hương," continued my uncle. "One month into the walk, many of my comrades were falling ill. I was exhausted. Luckily, spring arrived to save me. Flowers burst out their brilliant colors. Sunlight was as gold as honey. The air smelled of life, rather than death and explosives. Birds, the same type that your father carved as a gift for you, sang."

"You met my father then?"

"No, I first met sốt rét—malaria. Bouts of fever hit me, yet I felt so cold, I shivered uncontrollably. My bones seemed to crumble under me, I'd never experienced such pain. I couldn't walk and had to lie on my hammock by the roadside, waiting and waiting to get better.

"At first, when someone fell ill, the soldiers in his company would carry him forward. But my comrades were so weak, too—those that were left. There was a clinic where the men in my unit wanted to take me, but I refused because it was too far away. I told them I'd soon recover and catch up. So my comrades left me food, water, medicine, and said their good-byes."

"Uncle, if you'd let them bring you to the clinic, my mother could have been there."

"She hadn't joined the Army at that time yet, Hương. Do you know where she was stationed?"

I shook my head. "She hasn't told us much. She just said that she'd gone through terrible things. Things she doesn't wish to happen to anyone."

"Doctors had one of the most dangerous jobs on the battlefields,

Hương. They needed to find ways to conceal their clinics from enemy planes. Their job was not only to save lives but also to protect patients. Whenever the enemy attacked, they had to move patients down to shelters or over mountains to set up new clinics. Sometimes they even had to pick up their guns to fight."

That stopped me. I hadn't thought about this. I swallowed. "Uncle, do you think my mother could have delivered babies in the battlefields?"

"Why do you ask?"

"I'm just . . . just curious."

"For sure your mother could have delivered babies, Hương. Doctors from the North had to help civilians who'd fled their villages."

I nodded, a heavy burden lifted from my chest. "Now that you're here, Uncle, I hope she'll come home."

I went to the kitchen, bringing back a bowl of roasted peanuts. Uncle Đạt tossed a few into his mouth, chewing noisily. "Grandma told me your mother moved to Duyên's house because it's peaceful there. What's the real reason?"

"She had a big fight with Grandma." I turned the bowl in my hand.

"About what?"

"She said that if Grandma hadn't run away from her village, perhaps all of you wouldn't have had to go to the battlefields and Uncle Thuận wouldn't have died."

"What?" Uncle Đạt looked up to the altar, shaking his head. "Grandma saved us by running away. Besides, had we remained at the village, we would've been drafted as well."

"So you don't blame Grandma at all for what happened?"

"Blame? No way. On the contrary, I feel like I'm not good enough to deserve her. I don't know why your mother would say such hurtful things."

"Uncle, please . . . don't be upset when you see my mother. I want her to move back with us."

"I want her home, too, Hương. Don't you worry."

I picked up the Sơn ca, cupping it to my face. "Uncle, so what happened next?"

Uncle Đạt sighed and took a drink from his bottle. "Malaria is a terrible thing to have. It makes you so weak. I just lay there in my hammock, shivering and burning with fever as flocks of people passed silently by me. The days and nights dragged on, and still, I couldn't get up. Whenever a company set up camp where I was, they helped cook my rice and gave me some greens. They were tired, hungry, and sick, too, and I felt so useless.

"One morning, a man shook me from my blurriness. I thought it was only a dream, but Hoàng was standing in front of me."

"My father?"

"Yes, it was him. He was grinning from ear to ear. 'Ah, I can't believe this dead log turned into my brother-in-law,' he told me."

"How was he, Uncle? Very thin?"

"He was thinner but looked okay. He was growing a beard, too. He said that your mother used to shave him so he was keeping the beard for her, as a gift."

I couldn't help but smile. "He still managed to joke?"

"He's a rare spirit, I know."

"Tell me more about him, Uncle."

"He showed me the Sơn ca he'd carved for you. He went on and on about how much he missed you and your mother. He said he regretted he'd never told you how much he loved you, and that you meant the world to him."

"Why hasn't he come back, Uncle? Do you think something happened to him?"

"It took me a while, you see? He might be home any time now."

I nodded. Uncle Đạt's return gave me hope.

"That day, your father cooked and fed me breakfast, lunch, and dinner. For the first time in weeks, I got to eat fresh meat. He also managed to find medicine for me. He stayed by my side, whispering to me about you and your mother, and about our happy times in Hà Nội. As the sun began to set, he pulled the Sơn ca out of his breast pocket, asking me to give it to you if I made it home first."

I held the bird tightly, a tear sliding down my cheek.

"I didn't want to see darkness, but it came. Time to say good-bye. Your father poured all the rice from his cloth bag into mine. He went to a stream nearby and filled my canteen, disinfecting it with one of our medicine tablets. He gave me his big, brotherly hug. He joked that whoever got home first would have to buy the other a round of beer.

"Around half an hour . . ." My uncle quickly glanced at me. He cleared his voice. "Hmm . . . as I said, I wished your father could stay. I tried to get up from my hammock, thinking I was strong enough to join his troops, but my feet collapsed under me. I couldn't be his burden, so I lay there, watching him leave. Two weeks . . . two weeks after his departure, American planes arrived. Bombs darkened the sky. Explosions turned the world upside down. Jungles were uprooted and burned like wild grass."

I looked up to our family altar and prayed.

"Your father's medicine gave me strength to crawl into a cave and hide inside. His food helped me survive the bombing days.

"As soon as I got better, I staggered out of the cave. Enemy planes were gone, and I couldn't believe my eyes: hundreds of soldiers were silently moving past me, on the same trail the bombs had destroyed. Groups of Youth Brigade volunteers, most of them women, were repairing the trail; their first task was to find unexploded bombs and defuse them.

"I joined up with another unit, and now we were walking during the day as well as night. It was by pure chance that Thành, your Auntie Hạnh's classmate, was one of my new comrades.

"Along our way south, I saw bomb craters, so many that it seemed flocks of gigantic animals had rushed by, leaving their footsteps carved into the earth. Sometimes when we were trekking, I felt a light rain being sprayed from airplanes overhead. Plants around us shriveled instantly, large trees dropping their leaves. Everything around us just withered. To protect ourselves, our commander ordered us to take out our handkerchiefs, pee onto them, and put them against our noses. We walked on."

My uncle held the bottle with both hands, staring at it.

"It was depressing whenever we passed a destroyed area. No birds, butterflies, flowers, or green trees. The howling wind sounded like the cackling of angry ghosts.

"It was more dangerous, too, as the enemy could see us more easily from above. I'd never touched a dead person before the war, except my father, but now I was constantly digging graves, burying my comrades."

I reached for my uncle's arm.

"Thành and I became best friends. We told each other we had to survive, to get back to our families. Thành showed me his wristband made of tiny wooden beads. His mother had walked the Yên Tử Mountain's thousands of steps, to reach the sacred Yên Tử Pagoda where she received the wristband from the head monk whose blessing she believed would protect her son from harm. I showed Thành my lucky charm: the Sơn ca bird."

My uncle took another sip of the liquor.

"After many weeks, we arrived in Quảng Bình, a central province. As we stood on a riverbank, my jaw dropped. In front of me, hundreds of sampans glided on the emerald water. They'd come to pick us up, bringing us into the famous Phong Nha caves. We rowed under thousands of magical-looking rock formations that hung low, glimmering like domes of stars above the flickering light of torches."

"The caves sound stunning, Uncle."

He nodded. "Yes. . . . For a little while it felt as if we'd left the war to enter the world of peace. There were no more bombs and bullets, no more death. Just water lapping against our boats. I smelled the sweetness of peace in those caves, Hương. I inhaled it, and I longed for peace.

"When we arrived at the heart of Phong Nha, I found thousands of soldiers resting on sandy beaches along the riverbanks. I tried to find Thuận and your father, but they weren't there.

"Phong Nha isn't a cave—it's a gigantic system of caves. Where I rested, sunlight poured in through cracks between high mountains, twinkling on the rock formations. The mountains shielded us. At night, artists who'd traveled all the way from Hà Nội sang, danced, and read poetry to us. For the first time in months, we were able to talk and laugh freely. We no longer had to be afraid of our own voices.

"I had one of the best nights of my life in that cave. I could hold a girl performer's hands, inhaling her hair's perfume. When I fell asleep on the riverbank, amidst the water's gentle lapping sounds, I dreamed of Nhung." Uncle Đạt gulped down his liquor.

Miss Nhung? Last night, my uncle's girlfriend had arrived shortly after our dinner. She'd waited for him seven long years, and I'd thought he would be happy to see her. But he avoided her eyes and only answered what she asked. Grandma was still boiling water for her tea when my uncle said he was exhausted and needed to sleep. After he'd gone to bed, Grandma tried to console Miss Nhung, but she left, crying. Had the girl performer made Uncle Đạt change his mind about Miss Nhung?

"The cave was so peaceful, Hương, that I wanted to stay there, forever. I imagined getting married and raising my children there. But when morning came, we had to leave.

"To help us get to the South, the Hồ Chí Minh Trail cut through both Laos and Cambodia. But the American bombs found us there. We brought the war into our neighbors' homes."

I saw myself in the girls and boys in our neighboring countries who had to run for shelters during bombings. Years later, I was to learn that hundreds of thousands of Laotians and Cambodians perished in the war known internationally as "the Việt Nam War," but called by the current Vietnamese government "the Resistance War against America to Save the Nation." Regardless of its name, even today the war continues to kill children in Việt Nam, Laos, and Cambodia, with millions of tons of unexploded ordnance still buried in the belly of the earth.

My uncle swallowed. "Soon, we moved back onto Vietnamese soil, into southern areas controlled by the enemy. Thành and I stayed close. I hung on to my lucky charm, and I pulled the little bird out night after night, whispering to it. By this time, the war had cut down more than half of my company. There were just around fifty of us left.

"I had to be alert and careful all the time. In a war, the smallest mistake or negligence could cost a man his life, Hương.

"Once, we stopped at a stream to get drinking water. One of my comrades made a sign. He gestured toward the stream, then pointed at his nose. I cupped some water into my palms, sniffing it. It smelled of soap. Our captain sent a small group of us upstream. We sneaked through the jungle, keeping a safe distance from the stream's bank.

After a while, we heard muffled laughter. Creeping closer, I saw a group of soldiers through gaps in the foliage."

My uncle stopped speaking. The oil lamp flickered.

"There were around ten shirtless men washing themselves on the opposite shore. They were young, these foreigners, perhaps just eighteen or nineteen. Some were white and had blond hair, while the others were so black, their skin looked like it'd been smoothed with charcoal. Two boys were just standing in the middle of the stream, splashing water at each other, laughing. Dappled sunlight glimmered on their bodies, glittering on the stream's surface. The air smelled fresh and happy. It was such a peaceful sight that I just watched, entranced.

"Rounds of gunfire shook me. In the blink of an eye, the foreign boys had fallen backward into the stream. They howled, kicking up water. Their handsome faces twisted into pictures of horror. I stayed frozen as more bullets pierced through them, blowing their flesh into the air.

"Hương, watching the blood of those men seep down the stream, I suddenly thought about their mothers and sisters. I thought about tears and sorrow. I thought about you, Grandma, your mother, and Hạnh.

"I had hated the Americans and their allies so much before that day. I hated them for dropping bombs on our people, killing innocent civilians. But from that day, I hated the war."

What my uncle said made me think. I had resented America, too. But by reading their books, I saw the other side of them—their humanity. Somehow I was sure that if people were willing to read each other, and see the light of other cultures, there would be no war on earth.

"Perhaps it was my sympathy for the enemy that later saved me." Uncle Đạt shook his head. "Once, I was journeying alone through a forest to deliver an important message to a close-by camp. Then I heard the sounds of an approaching helicopter.

"I ran, trying to find a hiding place, but there was nowhere to hide, so I lay down and covered my body with rotten leaves.

"The helicopter floated into my view, and in its open door stood a white man, tall and broad-shouldered. He was studying the forest beneath, his hands clutching an M-60 machine gun."

I gasped.

"The foreigner pointed the gun at me. I was sure he saw me. The helicopter blades had blown the leaves covering me away. I held my breath, waiting for the sounds of gunfire, waiting for terrifying pain to sear through my flesh, waiting for death to take me away. But the man just stared at me—then he shook his head and flicked his hand. The helicopter slowly floated away, and above me was nothing but the brilliant sky.

"I still wonder who that man was and why he didn't shoot me. Perhaps he didn't see that I had a weapon, for I had hidden my AK-47 behind my back. Perhaps he was sick of killing or had turned against the war. Or perhaps he simply thought I was dead, but I know that isn't true. In that instant we looked into each other's eyes as if into mirrors.

"But war isn't kindness or sympathy, Hương. War is death, sorrow, and misery. I know, because I wound up at one of the worst battle-fields, near Núi Bà Đen—the Black Virgin Mountain, northwest of Sài Gòn. We thought we were safe in the shelters dug under large bamboo groves, near the mountain's foot, but the enemy quickly located us. They bombarded us with artillery before sending in their ground troops. The battle only ended when we shot down two of their helicopters. After the enemy had withdrawn, I thought our captain would order us to move away, to find another hiding spot, but for some reason he decided that we'd stay the night. He sent some soldiers out, to form a circle of protection around us, and a team up to the Cambodian border to buy a pig. We had to celebrate our victory, he decided. We'd been hungry for days, so he wanted us to gain strength for another difficult journey.

"When the meal was ready, we squatted on the ground, about to enjoy our feast. As soon as we picked up our chopsticks, noise rumbled from the sky. I thought it was thunder.

"'B-52 bombers!' someone shouted. We sprang up, running for our lives. I pulled Thành along, dashing for a nearby bomb shelter. It was a large one, dug for common use.

"I dived down, Thành followed, together with six other men. Explosions lifted us off the ground, flinging us about like pebbles. My ears went deaf, my vision black. Rocks and soil rained down on us. More explosions came. I thought the shelter would give way and collapse on us, but all of a sudden, the bombing stopped.

"Things became quiet. I could hear my frantic heartbeat and the crackle of a fire. I smelled dust and a burning stench."

My uncle gazed at the oil lamp. His face twitched.

"But I knew it wasn't over yet. The Americans liked to carpet bomb with their B-52s. The second attack would come soon. I longed for the security of my honeycombed-rock shelter, where I'd been earlier. 'I'm going back to my place,' I shouted. 'Comrade Thành, come with me!'

"'No, you go ahead.' Thành's voice trembled. He didn't want to risk being hit while running outside.

"Two of my comrades followed, but not Thành. The ground was strewn with rocks, bamboo branches, and pieces of the delicious pork we'd prepared but hadn't had time to eat. I could hardly see where I was going. Finally, I found my shelter and jumped down. The other two men ran toward their own. Soon, the second round of bombing hit.

"Later, when silence returned to the bamboo forest, my company gathered. The B-52 bombs had killed more than half of us. Thirty-six young men died that night, including four people with whom I'd shared the common shelter. Some were crushed beyond recognition. Some were blown into pieces. I could only recognize Thành by his beaded bracelet.

"I'd already buried many comrades along the way, but that night was the hardest. Disfigured bodies and unrecognizable body parts . . . Thirty-six men in an unmarked mass grave . . . I agonized for the family of my best friend, a man so shy he hadn't even held a girl's hand yet. There were no tears of good-bye. It was forbidden for us to show sadness. If we expressed emotion, it could only be hatred toward the enemy."

My uncle clenched his fists. I held onto the Sơn ca.

After a while Uncle Đạt spoke again. "As we moved away, thunder exploded above our heads. Lightning ripped open the black sky. The rain punished me with its cold lashes. For the first time in years, I allowed myself to cry, because the rain could hide my sorrow. With the exploding thunder, I was able to beat my fists against my chest and scream. I hated myself for not pulling Thành along as I escaped the common shelter. I could have saved him."

I wanted to tell my uncle not to blame himself but feared I'd interrupt his thoughts. Perhaps he had to untangle his feelings on his own, by talking out loud, so that he could understand how it was to be alive, and to be dead at the same time.

"I've been thinking about Thành's family now that I'm back here in Hà Nội, Hương. . . . I must visit them. I want to tell them what a unique person he was, but I fear they'll ask me where his body is buried.

"I can't fucking remember . . . The bamboo forest was enormous, and we'd made no headstone. There were no nametags on the Northern soldiers I'd seen rotting in forests, on roads, dirt paths, floating in creeks and rivers.

"I could've become one of those unknown bodies easily, I swear. Once, I wrote my name, date of birth, and our address onto a piece of paper, stuffing it into the tiny glass bottle of my penicillin antibiotics, and kept it in my pants' pocket. I was determined not to become another unknown body, you know, but when I crossed a river, the strong current took the bottle away.

"The Sơn ca bird stayed in my breast pocket, though. It brought me incredible luck. Until, on one of the last days of the war, I stepped on a land mine. The whole world became blank.

"I woke up in a medical clinic. When I looked down and saw the stumps of my legs, I wished I'd died. What use is a man without his legs? What use is a man who has to rely on others to feed him?"

Uncle Đạt picked up the liquor and finished it. He wiped his mouth with the back of his hand, banging the empty bottle onto the table.

"I'm sorry, Uncle. I'm so sorry."

Uncle Đạt turned to me, his face wet with tears.

"I'm sorry, too, Hương. I don't know what happened to your father, but I do know that wherever he is, he loves you, very, very much."

The Walk

Nghệ An-Thanh Hóa, 1955

Guava, I need you to understand why I didn't tell you about your grandpa, your great uncle Công, and your uncle Minh until now. In your schoolbooks, you won't find anything about the Land Reform nor about the internal fighting of the Việt Minh. A part of our country's history has been erased, together with the lives of countless people. We're forbidden to talk about events that relate to past mistakes or the wrongdoing of those in power, for they give themselves the right to rewrite history. But you're old enough to know that history will write itself in people's memories, and as long as those memories live on, we can have faith that we can do better.

So, what happened that day, after we ran away from the village of our ancestors? . . .

A COLD DROPLET splattered onto my forehead. I opened my eyes to find myself slumped on dew-soaked grass. My five children lay around me, snuggled against each other. Watching their innocent faces, my stomach clenched. My brother was dead. Those who killed him wanted to uproot and erase our family. I couldn't let that happen. I had to continue carrying the torch of my brother's life forward, and seek justice for his death one day.

I studied our surroundings, yearning for a glimpse of Minh, but nothing. Young rice plants rolled out their green carpets. Clumps of trees and faraway villages dotted the horizon. Nearby, a stream gushed.

It didn't look right. Farmers of my region were known to be industrious, always arriving at their fields before sunrise. That morning, though the sun was up, the fields were empty. It must have been the Land Reform that had forced people to abandon their work.

The previous night, we'd run for our lives. We'd heard shouts and cries bursting out of the villages we passed. Torches and flames that lit up the skyline looked like tongues of demons. We ran, stumbled, got up and kept going, until our legs gave way and we collapsed on this patch of grass.

Now hunger pulled me toward the sound of water. I knelt, put my face into the stream, and drank. The pain from my feet throbbed. I'd been pulled away so suddenly and had no shoes on. Thorns had burrowed deep into my soles. Thankfully, all the children, except for Sáng, had sandals.

A wild banana plant stood on the stream's bank, but it bore no fruit. I searched, but there was no sweet potato, cassava, or other vegetable nearby. I remembered from the Great Famine that the banana plant could keep us alive, though: Peeling away outer layers, I found its white core. Food for my children.

Something moved. A mud crab half the size of my palm. It climbed onto a rock, sunbathing. Quiet as a cat, I inched forward, caught it, and broke it into parts.

As Sáng nursed hungrily, I opened the cloth bag Mrs. Tú had given us. A bunch of bananas, three ripe *na* fruit, and a handful of sesame seed candies. Their perfume flowered, like her love for us. We had to survive to come back to her.

I nudged the children. Thuận and Hạnh turned away. Ngọc and Đạt sat up, rubbing sleep from their eyes. I led them to the stream. "Wash and have a drink first."

Back on the patch of grass, I offered them the banana stalk.

"But that's pig's food," said Đạt.

"If pigs can eat it, so can we." I smiled and bit into the stalk. Juicy and crunchy, it relieved me of thirst.

Ngọc took a bite and nodded. "Delicious."

Đạt shook his head but gave in, biting down. His face softened as he ate.

I picked up a crab leg, popping it into my mouth. "Try," I told the children, who shuddered. "It's going to be a long walk."

"Where're we going, Mama?" Đạt asked.

"To Hà Nội." I'd thought hard and long about this. In the capital city, I'd look for my childhood teacher. Master Thịnh and his family would surely help us. Maybe I could find a job.

"But that's far away," said Ngọc.

"Yes, three hundred kilometers." I crunched the crab between my teeth, grinding it hard, forgetting to swallow.

"How are we going to get there?" Đạt stopped chewing.

"We'll follow the national highway."

"But how exactly?" Đạt's eyebrows had become two question marks.

"We'll walk." It'd be too risky to hitchhike, and I had no money with me. All of it was gone, stolen by the mob. I'd watched them desperately as they carried my money trunk away. They were like wolves, fighting for it.

"Walk? Three hundred kilometers?" both children cried out in unison.

"*Shhh*. Let's get further away, and we'll see."

"Will we find Brother Minh soon, Mama? What will happen if those evil people catch him?" Đạt looked at me with tears in his eyes. He was so close to Minh. They'd shared the same bed, climbed the same trees, chased the same soccer ball.

"We'll see him again, Son. He's fast. Nobody can catch him."

Ngọc gave me a wrinkled piece of paper. "Mr. Hải's note. We found it next to our open window, wrapped around a small rock. I read it for Mrs. Tú."

My fingers trembled.

Urgent! Diệu Lan, take the children, run away. Công was killed before my eyes. Minh escaped. You must go fast, don't wait for him. They have a quota of how many people to execute. Please go. Hurry!

My tears fell onto the hurried words, smudging them. What had we ever done wrong? Why was I under a death sentence?

The sounds of distant drums and shouts startled us. The Land Reform was waking up from its night's sleep.

Thuận and Hạnh sat right up when another round of drumbeats boomed. Holding on to each other, we scurried away.

At midday, we stopped under a tree, collapsing under its shade. It looked safe to take a break here. Behind us was a row of thick bushes that lined the bank of another stream.

Sáng lifted my blouse, looking for milk. Ngọc shared the rest of the banana stalk with Đạt. Thuận and Hạnh fought for a bigger *na* fruit. We were hungry, yet more than half of the food was gone.

I explained to the children that we needed to flee far away, that we couldn't go to our relatives because our villagers knew all of them well. Ngọc nodded, studying the black spots in my soles. Using a long thorn, she managed to take out the smaller thorns that had burrowed into my feet.

"Sister Ngọc will make a good doctor," Hạnh and Thuận cheered.

"Wait, Mama." Đạt took the remaining food out of the cloth bag, then tore the bag into long pieces and wrapped them around my feet. Now I had shoes, made out of love.

Looking at the children, the desire not just to live, but to *thrive,* surged into my heart. If those evil people wanted me to surrender, they couldn't be more wrong. As long as I was a mother, I would never, ever give up.

For hours we walked, soaked by the rain of a sudden storm, roasted by a blazing sun, hungry, tired, the children whimpering, until Đạt said, "Look, Mama."

A man. Standing in the paddy next to our path, he was bending, his face hidden under a *nón lá*, his body shielded by an *áo tơi*—a coat woven from dry *tơi* leaves and bamboo strings.

I stopped walking, as did the children.

"Should we hide?" whispered Ngọc.

The farmer straightened his back, tossing a chunk of weeds into the stream. As he swung his arm, I realized "he" was a woman.

Her eyes met mine.

"Stay quiet, children. Let Mama do the talking." I struggled forward. "Hello, Sister."

The woman nodded, tipping her hat backward. "Where did you come from?" She studied our clothes.

"We . . . we just paid a visit to our relatives over there." I pointed in the direction of a village to our far right.

"Thiên Sơn Village? I live there. Who did you visit?"

"Who? Oh . . . my uncle. He's getting old and weak."

"Is your uncle Mr. Trương or Mr. Thảo?"

How stupid of me to pick the closest village. Now the woman would find out that we were running away.

I stayed rooted as she climbed onto our path, advancing toward us.

"It's not a good time to be wandering around." She took off her stiff coat, laying it down onto the grass. She proceeded to peel off her brown, long-sleeved outer shirt. I had always worn the same type of shirt in the fields, to protect myself from the sun.

"Your clothes and your children's clothes . . ." The woman shook her head. "They look too expensive for you to be safe." She glanced around us.

I dropped my gaze to my green blouse. Despite some small tears and splatters of mud, the silk sparkled. The woman was right, I didn't look like a poor farmer.

"Wear this. It's a crazy time." The woman gave me her outer shirt and helped me put it on. "Make your kids look poor, too." She sank her hands into a mud pocket and wiped them onto the children.

Thuận and Hạnh jerked back, but Đạt and Ngọc calmed them.

"Go to a big city. Find somewhere to hide," the woman whispered. "I wish you luck."

"Sister . . . how do we get to the national highway?"

She pointed ahead. "But don't go near the village over there. There're lots of vicious dogs."

Ngọc and Đạt bowed their thanks to the woman, who cupped their faces with her palms. "Take care of yourselves." She pushed them away and stood there, watching us. When we had gone a short distance,

I looked back and saw her standing in the same spot, her *nón lá* a gleaming white flower in a vast green.

"MAMA, I'M SCARED." Hạnh clutched my hand as we curled up onto a patch of grass. Above our heads, clusters of stars and an orange wedge of a moon lit up the sky. But Heaven's light was too far away to reach us. Where we lay, darkness trapped us in its cocoon.

"Don't be, my love. I'm here." I kissed Hạnh's wet cheeks.

"I'm hungry, Mama," Thuận said.

"We'll find something to eat tomorrow. Try to get some sleep." We'd been running for three days. There was no more food. I'd found some mud crabs and snails but couldn't give them raw to the children anymore. Đạt and Hạnh had been hit by bouts of diarrhea. Ngọc had some kind of fever.

"Your tummy hurts?" I reached for Đạt.

"It's better now, Mama." His voice was as tired as an old man's. He curled like a shrimp, Sáng between us. My baby had cried for a long time before falling asleep. I could no longer produce enough milk for him.

It pained me to think about the long way ahead. We'd found the national highway and been walking on a path parallel to it, but hunger and exhaustion were slowing us down.

"Mama, I'm hungry." Again Thuận's voice rose into the dark.

"Shut up, I'm trying to sleep," Hạnh scolded him.

"*Shhh*. Let me sing. Let me sing you a lullaby. . . ."

"The one about the crane, Mama."

"*À à ơi . . . con cò mà đi ăn đêm, đậu phải cành mềm lộn cổ xuống ao. . . .*" Oh ah, the crane seeking food at night, it perches on too weak of a branch and plunges headfirst into the pond. . . .

You know this song, too? Yes, of course. Your mother used to sing it to you.

That night, I sang softly until the children's breathing became regular. It was quiet, perhaps Heaven could hear me. Bringing my hands to my chest, I prayed for Minh to be safe, for Công's soul to reach Heaven, for Auntie Tú to suffer no harm, for Mr. Hải and his family to face no risk. I prayed for the woman we'd met on the road; her shirt was warm against my skin, giving me comfort and strength.

I wondered if I could ever find Minh. In his message, Mr. Hải didn't say where Minh was heading or how to find him. I wished I could go back to our village and ask.

Ngọc's fever hadn't gone down. Her body was burning like a hot coal. I fumbled my way to the ditch between our path and the rice paddies. It was filled with rainwater, water that I drew into my mouth and fed Ngọc, water that I used to cool her body.

LATER, ĐẠT'S SOBS woke me.

I kissed his face, tasting the saltiness of his sorrow.

"I dreamed about Brother Minh, Mama, that they caught him."

"Your brother is as quick as a cat. He's fine, trust me."

"I miss him, Mama."

"We'll find him, I promise."

"I miss Uncle Công and Papa." Đạt's tears burnt my face. "Why does bad stuff keep happening to our family?"

"I don't know, but we're not the only ones who've suffered. *Trời có mắt*—Heaven has eyes, Darling. Heaven will punish people who do bad things."

"Are you sure we'll be safe in Hà Nội, Mama?"

"I hope so." I caressed Đạt's hair. "Remember when you and Minh found a bird nest in the eave of our house? Together you watched the eggs hatch."

"We fed the baby birds with insects, until they were big enough to fly away."

"One day we'll be back to our home, Son. We'll be back and birds from all over the world can come and nest with us. . . ."

After Đạt had fallen back to sleep, I tossed and turned. Darkness was thinning, the shadows of villages that bordered the horizon looked like women whose backs were bent with the burdens of life. My mother had had to bear hers, and it was now my turn.

As the sky became a rosy glow, I washed my face by the ditch. The water only made my stomach feel emptier. I searched but found nothing to eat. Squatting down next to a paddy field, I ran my hands over the rice plants, hoping to find a rice flower. But the plants here were much too young.

It was my father who'd carried me out to the rice field when I was a child. He'd picked a thick rice stalk, peeled it, and given me a milky rice flower. I remembered the fragrant sweetness in my mouth, and how long I'd laughed as he carried me on his back, galloping like a horse on the rice field's bank.

I cast my eyes at the national highway. On this road my father had been beheaded, his blood trampled on by people and animals, rolled over by vehicles, washed away by storms and rain. He had been the one who let me drive the buffalo cart, as a way of telling me that women could be in charge. He had believed in me so that I had faith: I could save myself as well as my children. I heard his voice urging me on.

I leaned over and uprooted a couple of rice plants. Stripping away their roots and leaves, I stuffed the skinny stems into my mouth. It didn't taste as bad as I thought. My hands worked furiously.

When I woke the children, giving them the stems, Ngọc refused to eat. Her fever had gone up even higher. Her eyes were swollen, her face bright red.

"We need help." I eyed the village closest to us. We couldn't run away from humans anymore.

"Isn't it dangerous?" Đạt glanced toward the clusters of trees where shouts and drumrolls were rising into the first sunrays.

"We need food and clean water, Son."

"There'll be angry people." Ngọc's lips quivered.

"They'll tie you up again," Hạnh said.

"They'll shout at us." Thuận's face twisted.

"We'll be careful." I studied our clothes, which looked like rags since we'd ripped them. Under my brown outer shirt, though, my silk blouse was still intact. I needed to hold on to my brother's gift—my last memory of him.

"I have an idea," said Đạt. "Why don't you all wait here? Let me go alone. It's safer. I can—"

"No! I can't let another child out of my sight."

"I'll be careful, Mama."

I shook my head. "Let's stay together. We're a team."

We made our way toward the village, like a group of beaten animals. My legs weakened at the sounds of violent shouts and drumrolls that rang louder as we approached.

"Mama, I'm scared." Ngọc clutched my arm.

WE WENT DOWN a dirt path. Thick clusters of bamboo soared over us, leaves rustling in the wind. A pair of brick towers covered by green moss framed the village gate.

My eyes caught sight of the first house, roofed and walled by rice straw. I put my finger to my lips. The children were silent as clams.

Thankfully, Sáng was sleeping on my back. We tiptoed closer to the house fence. Behind it stood a papaya tree laden with green and golden fruit.

My mouth watered, ready to welcome a piece of soft, sweet papaya. I saw myself climbing over the fence, dashing across the garden.

Violent barks. A dog darted out of the house. In a flash, it leaped up, launching itself at my face. The fence shook. We jumped back.

"Bad dog, bad dog." A shout sprang up from a neighboring house. An elderly lady emerged, waving her broom toward the dog. Time had carved deep lines onto her face and bleached her hair silver white. She looked kind. She must be kind.

Leading the children, I approached her. "Thank you, Auntie." I smiled. "Would you spare us some leftover rice? My kids are sick. Please, Auntie . . ."

She looked us up and down then grimaced. "You beggars bring bad luck. I haven't even started my day. Go away." She hurried inside, through her gate.

Instead of being miserable, I was laughing. "That's good, isn't it? No one can recognize us now."

"Down with wicked landowners!" The shouts, echoing from a close distance, made me shut my mouth.

"Is she going to the market, Mama?" Hạnh pointed ahead. A woman had just appeared from a lane that cut into our path, walking swiftly forward with a bamboo pole braced across her shoulder. At each end of the pole dangled a bamboo basket piled with green vegetables.

"Market, lots of food. Market," Đạt whispered. "Let's follow her."

We passed lush gardens but didn't dare get closer to any of them. Without being told, the children bent their heads, hiding their faces.

The woman disappeared into a lane. We caught up and found

ourselves in an open area, bursting with noise and colors. The village's morning market.

Rows of sellers sat behind baskets filled with all types of uncooked food: vegetables, rice, beans, fish, and meat. The air no longer smelled of fear, but of happiness and excitement.

Đạt pulled my arm, and I looked to my left. Wisps of smoke twirled from a huge pot mounted on a coal-lit stove. Behind the pot stood a woman, stirring the contents. The appetizing aroma of phở floated up to me. "Beef noodle soup, freshly-cooked beef noodle soup," the woman sang.

We inched closer. The children licked their lips, staring at large bowls placed on tables set in an open area where men, women, and children sat, their faces submerged in rising curtains of steam, their slurping irresistible.

"Beggars," the seller suddenly shouted. "Go away." She flicked her chopsticks at us. "It's too early. Don't you dare bring me bad luck."

I pulled the children back.

"Lazy beggars, go work to earn your living. Go work like us!"

We dragged ourselves away.

We passed a rubbish dump where clouds of flies scattered. We searched for something edible, but the stench told me anything there would harbor sickness. The children found something useful, though: a tattered nón lá, which I put onto my head to conceal my face.

We reached the market entrance where people streamed through. We needed food.

There was only one thing left for us to do.

I asked the children to kneel down.

They objected but I was on my knees, stretching out my palms. "Sir, Madam, we beg you. Have pity on us. We're hungry," I said, fearing my own voice.

Sáng woke up. His cries throbbed against my temples.

The children lowered themselves down next to me. "Sir, Madam, we beg you. Have pity on us. We're hungry," they repeated after me.

I lifted my blouse. I had no more milk. Sáng continued to fuss.

Around us, people were talking, laughing, bargaining, arguing. I smelled the soup. I watched feet striding past us. I thought about the happy meals our family had shared, about plates heaped with food, fields full of rice and manioc.

"Sir, Madam, please help, we're hungry." The voices of the children trembled. But it seemed we had become invisible. No one stopped. No one.

WE SAT THERE for a long time, begging. Sáng was exhausted; he could only manage occasional sobs.

At last, somebody paused. Coins clinked happily as they were dropped into Hạnh's palms. "Here you go," a woman's voice said.

"Thank you, Grandma," the children shrilled.

I turned to see a slender lady, her hair long and black, her face smiling. My eyes followed her as she walked to a vegetable stall and held up a bunch of water spinach. I saw my mother in her grace.

"Sir and Madam, look into your heart, show your sympathy." The children seemed to gain new energy, their voices more determined, their palms cutting into the flow of people walking past us.

As I grew desperate, Thuận's voice sprang up. A man had bent down, placing a few coins into his palms. Our thankful words followed him until he disappeared into the market.

A whipping sound rent the air. I jumped, pulling my children toward me.

A man confronted us, a bamboo rod in his hand, anger reddening his face. "No beggars allowed in this village. Leave now."

"Sorry, Sir, we didn't know." I bent, hiding myself under the hat. The children clutched the hem of my shirt. We hurried away.

"Don't come back here, do you hear me? Don't you dare come back." His angry voice chased us. We arrived under a large tree a short distance away from the phở shop. Its cool shadow soothed my nerves.

Ngọc rested against the tree as the children counted the coins together.

"Twelve cents, Mama." Đạt showed me his broad smile.

I handed Sáng to him and took the coins.

The phở shop was buzzing with customers. The seller was busy dropping white strings of noodles into bowls, topping them with slices of beef, spring onions, and coriander. She shouted at a young boy who was trying to navigate his way around the tables, steaming bowls in his hands.

"Madam, how much is each?" I asked as the woman started ladling boiling soup into the bowls.

"Five cents." She eyed me, a deep line creasing between her eyebrows.

"Please, one bowl." I hesitated, the coins dampening in my palms. "No . . . I'll take two."

"Show me your money." Glancing at the coins, her eyes softened. "Take a seat."

The children jumped up and down when I said our food was coming.

We sat around a table, our stomachs groaning. After emptying a large jug of water, we asked for more. The boy helper was too slow. The seller's complaints only made him more confused and deliver food to the wrong tables.

I stood up. Đạt pushed his chair aside, joining me.

"Money for two bowls." I placed a stack of coins next to the seller. "Please, could we have our soup now? My children are starving."

"Did your hunger eat away your patience?" Her gaze lingered on Đạt. "Ah, you've got a strong-looking boy. Why beg when he can work?"

"Work where, Madam?" Đạt's face lit up.

"I need another helper. That slow snail has to go." She raised her chin toward the boy helper.

"Can I work for you instead?" I hurried to say. "I can help you cook—"

"You think I'm stupid? How many children do you have? Five? Now get lost." She pushed two steaming bowls over to us.

The children dove into the food. I fed Sáng. He clapped his hands, opening his mouth like a bird. I didn't remember food ever being this delicious.

"Mama, can I work here?" Đạt looked up from his spoon.

"No. We leave today for Hà Nội. Our destination, remember?"

"Mama." Ngọc begged me with her eyes. "It's horrible to walk so far. I thought I'd die. Let's stay here. Let's look for a job."

"Can't you hear the drums?" I lowered my voice. "It's not safe for us here."

"Nobody knows who we are." Đạt chuckled. "They all think we're pitiful beggars."

"Have no fear, Mama," said Ngọc.

"No, it's dangerous—"

"I need to pee." Đạt stood up, heading for the rubbish dump. Halfway there though, he turned and quickened his pace toward the phở seller.

"Đạt, don't—" I stood up.

"Let him." Ngọc made me sit down.

Đạt was talking to the seller now. She told him something and swung her arm, pointing at the tin-roofed shack behind her back. Đạt disappeared into its dark mouth and came out a new person. His hair was combed, and he had a clean shirt on. The children giggled, watching him pick up steaming bowls and carry them to customers.

"Look at Brother Đạt, he's so fast," Ngọc said.

"Those customers, they're smiling at him," whispered Hạnh.

Believe me, Guava, your Uncle Đạt was a charming boy.

Thuận picked up my bowl, slurping down the last droplets of soup. He smacked his lips so loud, everyone had to laugh.

We moved back into the tree's shadow. Sitting there, I hoped we wouldn't run into trouble. The man with the bamboo rod was browsing the market. He'd chased away a couple of other beggars, not just by his words; his rod had rained blows down onto them.

Holding Sáng, I leaned my back against the tree, my legs pillows for the children who had lain down. I looked up at the tree trunk, at its hundreds of hanging roots, and realized it was a Bodhi tree. Buddha had meditated and became enlightened under the Bodhi tree. I felt his blessing on a cool wind that caressed my face.

My eyes were heavy as lead. I told myself to stay awake to watch over the children, but sleep drifted me away.

A delicious smell woke me up. Đạt had squatted down, a bowl in his hand. As his siblings shared the soup, he told me he'd gotten the job.

"How much will she pay you, Son?" I asked.

"Ten cents each day."

"That's only two bowls of phở. That's pure exploitation!"

"But it can buy us food." Đạt pulled bits of dry leaves from Thuận and Hạnh's hair. "Mama, we need a short rest. Let me give this a try. We'll see in a couple of days."

The children begged me with their eyes. My aching body begged me, too. I nodded.

"I have some bad news, though," said Đạt. "Even though I tried, she only wants to take me. And she allows only me to sleep in her shop."

"What about us?" Ngọc looked at me. She shrugged. "I guess there're plenty of bushes around."

"Đạt, are you coming or what?" an angry voice boomed. The phở seller arrived under the tree, looking down at us, her hands on her hips, her lips smeared with the red juice of the betel quid she was chewing.

"Madam." I stood up. "Please . . . I can help you better than my son. The kids can look after themselves—"

"Stupid woman." The seller rolled her eyes, spitting a mouthful of red liquid onto the ground. "Haven't you heard about the Land Reform? You think I'm so dumb?" She edged closer to me, her breath pungent. "I might be a fool but not foolish enough to employ a grownup. They'd execute me for being a rich person, an exploiter, a member of the bourgeoisie." She chuckled. "I'm not hiring your son, understand? He's the son of my faraway brother, and he's just helping out."

"Let's go." She pulled Đạt up. "Bring that bowl with you. Plenty of dishes to wash." She turned to me. "Take your children and leave. You can't hang around here. He's trouble." She glanced at the man with the bamboo rod as she strode away.

"Mama." Đạt leaned toward me, whispering, "Where do we meet tonight? I'll bring you some food and water."

"Outside the village gate. Behind the bamboo grove." Tears welled in my eyes.

"Be careful, don't let people recognize you, Son."

"Plenty of soot over there." Đạt grinned, signaling toward the phở pot. "A black mustache would suit me fine, don't you think?" He winked then dashed away.

THE NIGHT WAS hot and thick, swollen with buzzing insects. Sáng slept like an angel in my arms. The phở had brought back some of my milk. Ngọc fanned the mosquitoes away with my hat. She'd just woken from another deep sleep and her fever had eased.

A flickering dot appeared at the end of the dark road. Gradually the dot turned into a flame that floated midair.

"It's him. Brother Đạt."

"Quiet, it could be somebody else."

"It's him, I know." Thuận's voice drifted away from us.

"Thuận, come back," I hissed.

"Over here, Brother Đạt, over here," Thuận cheered.

The flame wobbled and disappeared. We sank again into darkness.

I heard my own heartbeat, then footsteps on dry leaves, and Thuận's laugh. "I knew it was you, Brother Đạt."

I held Đạt in my arms. My beloved son. I kissed his hair. He smelled like home.

"Brother Đạt, Brother Đạt." Ngọc and Hạnh clapped their hands.

"*Shhh.*" Đạt chuckled. "You guys hungry? I brought something."

"Where? Where?"

We fumbled and squatted on the ground. Đạt placed a package into my hands. I felt the smoothness of fresh banana leaves and inhaled the fragrance of boiled sweet potatoes and maniocs.

I distributed the food to the children.

"Water, Mama." Đạt gave me a bottle. He reached for my face. "Don't cry. It's not bad to work there. Much better than in the rice field."

"How's the woman treating you?"

"She's okay, Mama."

"I'm so glad to see you, Brother Đạt," said Hạnh.

"No, I miss him more," said Thuận.

"*Shhh,* quiet." Đạt laughed.

OH, GUAVA, THAT was a special night. It was too dark for us to see each other's faces. Mosquitoes punctured our skin. Threatening drumrolls and shouts of vicious slogans rang from afar, but I felt as if the rustling bamboo had built a fortress around us.

When it was time for Đạt to leave, he promised to come back the next night. I walked with him to the phở shop. After he'd hugged me good-bye, I stood hiding in the cloak of the night, telling myself that I had to love him more.

The children were sound asleep when I returned. I lay down and let the rustling of the bamboo carry me away.

I woke to the sound of people talking. Soft light was scattering from the sky. Morning dew had dampened my clothes, soaking the layer of fallen leaves on which we slept.

Through small gaps between the large bamboo trunks, I saw three men across the dirt path, their backs toward me, an ox-cart next to them. Sounds of zippers being pulled down. Noises of water hitting the ground.

"That bitch and her son, where the hell could they be?" one man spat out his words.

The man's voice terrified me. I knew him. I flattened myself on the ground, my eyes fixed on Sáng. What would I do if he cried?

"Damn it. The tribunal will take place soon. We'll look like a bunch of idiots," another voice said.

"They can't be too far away. We'll comb all the villages till we find them," the first man said.

Another voice chuckled. "She can't run far, that bitch. Can't run far with so many children hanging onto her shirt hem."

I held my breath as the men got back into their cart. As soon as they disappeared behind the mossy village gate, I shook Ngọc, Thuận, and Hạnh awake.

"We must leave. Those vicious people are here, looking for me."

"How about Brother Đạt?" Thuận rubbed tiredness from his eyes.

"We'll meet him at the next village. Hurry!" The lie tasted bitter in my mouth. Đạt was smart. He could earn his food and should be safe.

With Sáng on my back, we scurried away. If I let those people catch me, I'd surely face a death sentence.

My heart ached with each footstep that pulled me away from Đạt. What type of mother was I, to abandon my son to a stranger? Yet it would be better for him to stay put and wait for me to come back. He knew how to disguise himself. He had food and a roof over his head. He'd taken a new identity as a nephew of the phở seller. But I dreaded the moment Đạt returned to the bamboo grove, looking for us and finding no one there. Can you imagine how desperate he must have been?

YEARS HAVE PASSED since the day I left Đạt behind, but I still question my decision, and the ones I'd make next. We've talked about this as a family many times, but my guilt is still too overwhelming for me to feel that I'm good enough as a mother. That's why I'm still trying every day, Guava. Being a mother is never easy, though. It's about failing, learning, and then failing again.

YOUR MOTHER SCREAMED when she realized Đạt wasn't going to be at the next village. She begged me to go back and get him, but I couldn't. It would have been too dangerous, you see.

Watching how Ngọc dragged her feet behind me, and listening to her sobs, I feared she was never going to forgive me.

It was Đạt who saved us during the next days of our walk. The yams and sweet potatoes, the water, and a box of matchsticks kept us alive. We were able to make a small fire here and there, grilling a snail or crab.

We made good progress toward Hà Nội, until Hạnh got food

poisoning. She threw up violently, then had diarrhea. She was severely dehydrated, drooping like a withered leaf. I no longer dared to feed her the water I found along the way, knowing she'd only get worse.

"Wait here with Thuận and Sáng," I told Ngọc. "If we go in there as a group, we'll face danger." We'd stopped under a shady bush that looked across streams of fast-running currents and patches of emerald rice fields, toward a village.

"Where are you bringing her?" Ngọc clutched Hạnh tighter in her arms.

"She needs medicine."

I walked, Hạnh on my back, my feet stiff with terror as I approached the village. Avoiding the main entrance, I turned into a small lane. Spotting a secluded house, I edged close to its gate. I saw her immediately—a woman around my age. She was washing some kind of vegetable by the bank of her house's pond. Yellow *mướp* flowers lit up like a flock of butterflies above her head.

"Sister, help us," I called softly.

The woman looked up, gasping at the sight of Hạnh's head slouching over my shoulder. Unlatching the gate, she took Hạnh into her arms and scolded me for not seeking help sooner. Inside her cool house, we placed Hạnh down onto a bamboo bed.

Hạnh opened her mouth to receive water, but her eyes remained shut.

Using wet cloths, we cooled Hạnh's fever. The woman sucked her teeth, as if she herself were in pain. She caressed Hạnh's face. "Where does it hurt, Sweetheart?"

Hạnh put her hands on her stomach, opened her eyes, and smiled weakly.

"My daughter has food poisoning, Sister."

"Ginger. Ginger tea." The woman rushed outside.

"We're lucky today, and you'll be fine soon." I kissed Hạnh's fore-head. The woman could've shooed us away, us with our uncombed hair and ragged clothes, us with our hungry eyes and bodies that stank like rotten fish.

I fed Hạnh some more water. "Sleep, baby." A lullaby warmed my lips.

On the wall of the room I noticed a faded wedding photo of the woman and her husband; next to it was a more recent picture of the two of them. Several certificates told me the woman's name was Thảo, that she was a kindergarten teacher and her husband a government official.

Mrs. Thảo came back with a handful of fresh ginger. I followed her into a cozy kitchen. Soot-blackened pots and pans dangled on the mud wall, above a pile of rice straw and stoves built of dried mud. Everything said its owner was tidy and knew how to take care of the household.

We peeled and sliced the ginger. Mrs. Thảo lit a stove, fed the fire with rice straw, and boiled a pot of water, into which she poured some leftover rice. "Porridge . . . Hạnh needs it." She shook her head. "You beggars only care for money." She lit the second stove for me to roast the ginger.

"Some mothers don't know how lucky they are." Mrs. Thảo's eyes were fixed on the glowing fires. "For years, I've traveled to pagodas and temples, even to the famed Perfume Pagoda near Hà Nội. . . . I'm still waiting for my blessing."

Thoughts swirled in my mind. I knew I couldn't manage to bring all four children to Hà Nội. Mrs. Thảo seemed kind. But how could I leave another child to another stranger?

The ginger glided back and forth on the frying pan, its intense smell making my eyes weep.

"Sister," I mumbled, "I left our bag of clothes at the market. No one's looking out for it. I was in such a hurry—"

"Go get it then."

It was terrible that I lied to such a kind woman. But how could I tell her the truth? Her husband was an official, after all.

"Sister, please take care of my daughter when I'm gone."

"You silly woman," laughed Mrs. Thảo. "Hạnh isn't allowed to go anywhere until she's drunk my tea and eaten my porridge."

Out in the front room, Hạnh was sleeping. She was my eight-year-old angel. I carved her features into my memory: her beautiful oval face, her long eyelashes, her blushed cheeks. I drew her breath into my lungs. "Good-bye my love, I'll come back for you."

The gate banged shut behind me. Standing behind a bush, I studied the house so I could remember it. I had to come back and get my child. I didn't know when, and that was the hardest part.

Oh, Guava, your mother was sobbing when I got back. She'd managed to put both Sáng and Thuận to sleep under the shade.

"So you're really doing this!" she hissed. "You're throwing us away, one by one."

The truth in her words cut into me like sharp knives.

"I'll come back for Đạt and Hạnh when it's safer. You saw how sick Hạnh was. She needs help. There's no way she can last until Hà Nội."

"Where did you abandon her?"

"Abandon?" I shuddered. "She's in good hands, Ngọc. A teacher with no child—"

"How long did you tell Hạnh you'd be gone for?"

I couldn't answer that question.

"See, you're throwing us away. You're giving us to strangers." Ngọc bent her head, her shoulders quivering. When she looked up at me, anger had filled her eyes.

"I will never forgive you, Mama. I will never forgive you for doing this to us. Never, ever."

Ngọc didn't talk to me for days and nights. Now there were only four of us left, but things didn't get any easier. We ran out of matches and could no longer light a fire. Hunger and exhaustion were our constant companions.

One night, I left the children sleeping and ventured close to a village. The full moon had come out to light my way. The moon witnessed my theft. I found rows of peanut plants and hurried to uproot them.

I woke the children and scurried away at the first sound of a rooster. The sun was high above our heads before I agreed to stop. Thuận and Ngọc looked stunned when I pulled peanut shells out of my pockets.

"Where did you get these?" Ngọc asked. Her voice was music to the new day.

"Stole them last night." I smiled.

She turned away, breaking the shells, giving the peanuts to Thuận.

"Mama, where are Brother Đạt and Sister Hạnh?" Thuận asked.

"We're going to see them soon. They're staying with my friends."

"I want to stay with them!" cried Thuận.

"Hush. We'll see them soon." I pulled him forward.

I was becoming a bad mother and a good liar, Guava. I saw the fierceness of your mother's glance. I absorbed it. I deserved all the blame, for what I was doing to my children. But I had to save them.

We stopped for the night. Ngọc ate her peanuts quietly, sitting away from us. I couldn't beg for her forgiveness anymore. I knew she wouldn't change her mind.

At another village I stole some cassava, but without a fire, we had to eat them raw, which made us ill.

From then on, we tried to survive on water and tiny wild fruits that we found occasionally along the way. We ate young rice plants and grass. We could make it together to Hà Nội, I told myself. I was determined as ever, you know.

Everything changed when Thuận fell sick.

It was not diarrhea this time but some other illness. A blanket of red dots covered him from head to toe.

"Mama, I'm dizzy," he said. "Sister Ngọc, help me. My legs, oh they hurt!"

I tried to relieve the fever with water. It didn't help.

I remember sitting there in the middle of nowhere, Thuận in my arms. He was shivering, his body burning up.

When I asked your mother to look after Sáng and wait for me to come back, she didn't protest. Instead she came over to me, took Thuận from my arms, held him close, and told him she loved him. She let me go.

Thuận was as light as a feather as I carried him, running for the nearest village. Would I be able to find a healer? Would the healer help him in exchange for the two cents I still had?

The village was bare of trees and bushes. Nowhere for me to hide. Entering through a dirt road, I found a chaotic scene packed with loud cheers, drumbeats, and threatening shouts. People were rushing about. The Land Reform was very much alive here.

I hid my face under the wrecked *nón lá*, scuttling deeper into the village. My heart pounded when I confronted an approaching crowd. Catching a glimpse of large sticks in their hands, I squatted on the roadside. Letting Thuận lean against me, I opened my palms. "Sir, Madam, take pity on us. We're hungry."

Glancing up from under the rim of my hat, I saw a woman with a large protruding forehead and teeth that looked like those of a rabbit. The butcher-woman! I couldn't believe that she was still out looking for me. Much later, I found out that our village had been chosen as a model for the Land Reform implementation. Important officials were going to travel all the way from Hà Nội to our village to oversee the tribunal. The local authorities would be in trouble if they couldn't find Minh and me. So they had sent many groups of people hunting for us.

Together with angry men and women, the butcher-woman marched, studying the faces of those who passed. She didn't expect that I—a rich landowner who had sat in cool shadows and eaten from golden bowls—had been reduced to pitiful begging, squatting with a very sick boy, instead of six healthy children.

As soon as the crowd moved past, I got to my feet. Turning into a lane to avoid flocks of people, I found an old, stooping woman. Her back was so bent that the upper part of her body was parallel to the road. She was inching forward with the help of a bamboo cane.

"Grandma," I called. "Please, my son is sick. Would you know a healer?"

The lady turned her face sideways and looked up at me. "What's wrong with your boy?" she asked.

"I don't know, Grandma. Bad fever and terrible rash."

I lowered Thuận. The lady's wrinkled hand stayed awhile on his forehead.

"He's really ill." She grimaced. "But I'm afraid our village no longer has a healer. He was condemned as a rich landlord and executed. Shot in the head. The kind man, poor him." She sighed and turned back to the road. The cane clicked as she moved forward.

Sensing sympathy in her voice, I followed her. Finally, she stopped and looked sideways at me again. "Go to the end of this lane, turn left, then right. The village pagoda behind the Bodhi tree . . . The nun there is kind."

I thanked her and hurried away.

The pagoda looked like another old and stooping person. With a roof laden with moss, it stood almost hidden behind the hundreds of roots hanging from a gigantic Bodhi tree. Stepping closer, I was enveloped by a fragrant wreath of incense smoke.

The chatter of young children met me. Some of them were sitting on the floor, playing with stones and sticks; some were munching on green guavas; others were kicking a featherball high.

Through the open doorway, I saw a nun kneeling in front of a large Buddha. Her murmurs and the rhythmic sounds of her wooden bell rippled calmness into the air. I gazed at Buddha's earlobes, so long they touched his shoulders. My mother had told me that with those ears, Buddha could hear our cries of suffering. Perhaps today he would hear mine. With Thuận in my arms, I knelt down.

The children had dropped whatever they were doing. They stood behind my back, whispering. Inside the pagoda, the nun reached up to clink a metal bell. She bowed to Buddha, her forehead touching the floor.

"Nun Hiền, someone's looking for you," a child called as soon as she stood up.

The nun made her way to us.

"*Nam Mô A Di Đà Phật,*" she said, a Buddhist prayer in place of a greeting.

"*Nam Mô A Di Đà Phật,*" I answered as she studied my face and Thuận's.

She turned to the children. "Go back to your games, Darlings."

"Come, come with me." She pulled my arm and hurried to the side of the building. Passing a garden filled with vegetables and flowers, she took me into a room. She closed the door and gestured toward a bed. I laid Thuận down. He writhed in pain.

Nun Hiền listened to what I had to say about how Thuận got ill. She examined him. "It's dengue fever," she said. "Dangerous if the patient doesn't drink enough. Plenty of good rest and good nutrition will do him good."

I recalled a dengue outbreak in my village many years before. Some children had died. But I didn't have any experience with this type of illness. We'd always been careful with mosquitoes.

"I'll get him something to drink." The nun stood up, closing the door behind her.

I massaged Thuận's legs and arms, soothing him with my voice.

Nun Hiền came back, but she wasn't alone. A boy was with her. She pointed at the bowl of brown liquid he was holding. "Juice made from roasted rice grains," she told me. "I've added some salt. Lộc will feed your boy."

As I was mumbling my thanks, Nun Hiền pulled me into the darkest corner of the room. "You are Diệu Lan, aren't you?" she asked.

My heart jumped to my mouth.

"Some people were here looking for you. Said you exploited poor farmers and have to pay for it with your blood."

"But Madam . . . how did you know it's me?" My words tumbled out unbidden.

"Ha!" The nun's eyes flickered. "It's not difficult. Middle-region accent. Long hair. White teeth. Running away with children."

Then she said something else that made me even more afraid: "Diệu Lan, where are the rest of your children? Where are they?"

A voice answered, startling me. "Here I am. I'm her daughter."

I turned and saw your mother, Guava. With Sáng in her arms, she was standing in the doorway, her skinny figure silhouetted against the afternoon sun.

"Ngọc, what're you doing here?" I stepped toward her.

"I had to find my brother." She headed for the bed. "I'm here, Thuận. I won't abandon you." ❦

Sáng cried for me. I reached for him, clutching him to my chest. What was the nun going to do? Would she have us arrested?

"Lộc, you're wonderful, thank you," Nun Hiền told the boy. "Go sit under the Bodhi tree. If those angry people come again, run in here quick and tell me, okay?"

Lộc bowed and left the room.

Sáng latched onto my breast. I winced at the sharpness of his new teeth.

Shutting the door, the nun turned to me. "Listen. I'm sorry, but you have to leave."

"Madam, what those people said is a lie. We've suffered from injustice, please believe me. My brother and I worked so hard. We gave farmers jobs, well-paid jobs. I don't understand why we're being punished."

The nun sighed. "Terrible things have happened at this village, too, but I can't help you. You'd bring harm to the children here."

"Yes, Madam, I know. . . ."

Ngọc had picked up the bowl, feeding Thuận the liquid.

"Sister," Thuận said. "Do you have something to eat? I'm hungry."

"Sorry, Brother," Ngọc said.

The nun stared at me.

"Madam," I begged her. "It was twenty-one days ago when the Land Reform hit our family. My brother was killed, my eldest son captured. We had no choice but to escape. We have no money, no food."

The nun closed her eyes. She sighed again. "I might have some left-over soup."

IT TURNED OUT Nun Hiền had more than soup. She brought us rice and fish sauce as well. As Ngọc, Thuận, and Sáng devoured the meal, I stood with her watching the road that led to the pagoda, through the door's crack.

"Madam, may I ask you something before I leave?" I whispered.

"Go ahead."

"Everything that has happened to me . . . is it fate? I didn't believe in it, but once a fortune-teller predicted I'd be a beggar wandering in a faraway city."

Nun Hiền held up my hands, studying my palms. She nodded. "You need to get to a big city to change your destiny. But the star that predicts your fortune has shifted a little, so you'll find a way to earn your living. You'll no longer need to beg but . . . but I don't know how you can go far with these three." She looked at the children. "Any big city is a long way from here. Besides, many more challenges still lie ahead of you, Diệu Lan. You need to be careful."

"Madam . . . Thuận's dengue, do you think he'll be all right?"

"With good rest and adequate food, he'll be up on his feet in a few days."

I closed my eyes, taking a deep breath. My words struggled to come out. "The kids in the front yard . . . are you caring for them, Madam?"

"Yes, they're orphans or have been abandoned by their parents. Thanks to them, our pagoda has been spared from being burned."

"Madam, could Thuận—"

"Oh no, I already have too many mouths to feed. You should get moving before . . ." The nun bent her head. When she looked up, she had a question for me. "I guess Thuận is younger than ten?"

"He's eight this year, Madam."

"All right then, he can stay. After all, we Buddhists are here to help the helpless."

"Madam, could I stay too?" Ngọc stood up. "I can do anything you ask. I can help you take care of the little ones."

"Oh no, you can't." Nun Hiền threw her hands into the air. "No helper allowed. No child older than ten. They would close down this place. . . ."

I came to Thuận. He was opening his eyes wide. Tears were running down his gaunt cheeks.

"Mama, is that what you did to Brother Đạt and Hạnh? You left them behind?" Finally, he understood.

I held him against me. "Son, it's a turbulent world out there. You'll be safe here. I need to go and find a home for us. I'll be back as soon as I can, and I'll bring you with me, I promise."

"Thuận, be a good boy and let your mama go. You'll have food and plenty of friends to play with here," said Nun Hiền.

"Sister, will you come back for me?" Thuận held on to Ngọc's hands.

"Yes, I swear." She bent down to hug him.

With Sáng in my arms, I bowed to Nun Hiền. "I owe you my life."

"Take good care. Come back when it's safe."

"I will, Madam, I will."

WE WERE OUT on the road again, Sáng asleep in my arms, Ngọc dragging her feet behind me.

"Go ahead. You don't need me," Ngọc said as I stopped to wait for her.

"Please, Daughter. We can make it to Hà Nội together."

"Why should I trust you? You said you wouldn't let us out of your sight, but you've been doing the opposite."

"I'm sorry," I whispered. "I have no choice."

"Yes, you do." She stomped her feet. "Every mother has a choice. Every mother has to take care of her children."

Tears blurred my eyesight. "Yes, I failed. But I'll make it up to all of you. In Hà Nội, I'll be one in tens of thousands. There we can start a new life."

"Then just go ahead." Ngọc skirted around me, staggering forward.

"Wait. Tell me what to do?"

"You're smart. You always know what to do, Mama."

After these words, she left me.

I followed her from one lane to the next. I searched among my knotted thoughts for words of apology to say to my daughter but found none. The truth had sunk deep into my bones, that I had indeed, by abandoning my children one by one, become the worst mother. I didn't know what would happen to us, but I knew one thing: my children might never forgive me.

After a while, Ngọc turned and disappeared behind a thick fence of leafy plants. Peeking through, I saw her kneeling on a front yard's dirt surface. There, five or six children were playing, tossing pebbles and catching them while holding a pair of chopsticks in the same hand. Do you remember, Guava, how good your mother was with that game? She'd been an expert since a very young age. Now she was enchanting the children with her skills.

Behind Ngọc stood a house, walled by thin bamboo slats and roofed with dry rice stalks. It was a typical home of a farmer, someone who was not rich, but not too poor. A woman appeared in the open doorway, a baby clutched at her waist.

I ducked so she wouldn't see me.

"Mama," the children called. "We got a new friend. She's so good at this."

I heard Ngọc's polite greeting and the *click-clack* sounds of pebbles being tossed and caught mid-air. The children cheered and clapped.

"Where do you come from?" the woman asked.

"My parents died last year, Auntie. I've been wandering, looking for a job."

"Poor you. Does it mean you have no home?" a girl's voice said.

"I have none for now."

"Mama, could she stay with us? Please, Mama," said a boy.

"Don't you even suggest that, Son," the woman said. "We have too little to eat ourselves. We can't hire anybody."

"I can share my rice with her," said a girl.

"Me, too. Me, too." Other voices followed.

"I could be your faraway relative coming for a visit," said Ngọc. "Please, Auntie. I'm honest and hard-working. Let me help look after your kids. I can cook and keep the house clean. I'm good at planting rice. I'll do anything you ask. All I need is food and somewhere to sleep."

"Uhm, I'm not sure. . . . I have to ask my husband first."

"Daddy will agree. He always complains about too much work," said a boy.

"I can teach your children how to read and write," said Ngọc. "My parents used to send me to the best school. I even had a private teacher." This part was true and as she said it, Ngọc began to cry.

"Mama, Mama, please, let her stay," the children begged.

When I lifted my head and peered through the fence, I no longer saw my daughter. Everyone was gone, leaving behind nothing but an empty yard.

My Mother's Secret

Hà Nội—1975–1976

Sitting next to Uncle Đạt and listening to his story that night, I realized that war was monstrous. If it didn't kill those it touched, it took away a piece of their souls, so they could never be whole again.

A sob. Grandma emerged from the darkness, tears glistening on her face. She opened her arms, wrapping them around Uncle Đạt. "What a journey you had to go through. I'm sorry, Son."

"I'm sorry, too, Mama . . . for taking so long to come back."

"It doesn't matter anymore. You're here now."

The *bàng* tree stirred, its branches rustling against our roof. I'd seen a pair of brown birds building their nest on a high branch. Now I heard them call each other. The sun was yet to rise, but I saw light ahead of me: with Uncle Đạt home, for sure my mother would return.

"Tea?" I asked.

Grandma put on her jacket. "Go back to bed, both of you." She reached for the bicycle's handle, then swirled around, smiling at Uncle Đạt. "Ngọc and Sáng will be so happy to see you."

I was pouring water into the kettle when Uncle Đạt cleared his voice. "Hương, I need a favor."

"Sure." I nodded, expecting him to ask me to go get him more liquor.

"I hope Nhung doesn't come back. If she does, tell her I'm not home."

"But why, Uncle?"

"Well . . . things change. People change."

I bit my lip. Miss Nhung looked so wretched last night. "I'm sorry, Uncle, but I can't lie. Miss Nhung has been kinder to Grandma than Uncle Sáng's wife. She is one of the few people who still visits our home, despite Grandma's job."

"It's over between us, Hương."

"She taught me how to ride a bicycle—"

"I don't care, and I don't want to talk about her anymore. Okay?"

I turned away at the harshness of his voice.

AFTER FINISHING BREAKFAST, I was about to feed the squealing pigs when my mother called at the door. Pulling it open, I met her face, wet with tears.

"Hương, where's your uncle?"

Uncle Đạt was sitting with his back in our direction. He was as still as a statue frozen by time.

"Đạt!" My mother stumbled toward him.

My uncle remained motionless until his shoulders shook. He grabbed his chair's wheels, turning around. His body was bathed in morning light, his chest sunken under his shirt, his face gaunt under the sprouting beard. The stumps of his legs. Their horrendous scars.

"Sister Ngọc." His face twisted into a smile.

My mother held my uncle, her cries muffled.

"You made it home." She knelt down, touching the stumps. "Your legs . . . I'm sorry."

"Mama told me you went to the battlefields. I'm glad you got out alive."

"Brother, I wish they'd taken my arms and legs instead."

"Why say that, Sister? What happened?"

My mother didn't answer. Her back hunched, as if she had to carry a burden larger than herself.

"Sister, something bad happened to you? Tell me." Uncle Đạt dried her tears. "No secrets between us, remember?"

The look on my mother's face told me she wanted some private moments. She had a secret she didn't want me to know.

The pigs' squealing had risen into a high-pitched screeching. "These awful animals," I mumbled. "Let me go feed them."

Hurrying over to the animals, I prepared their food, dumping it into their trough. In the living room, my mother was pouring tea into cups. Wiping my hands against my pants, I sneaked into my room. Keeping the door slightly ajar, I stood eavesdropping. For once, I was grateful that our house was small and the distance between me and the kitchen was short.

"Mama told me you saw Hoàng," my mother said.

"We underwent the same training in Ba Vì with Thuận, Sister. Unfortunately, all of us were separated before going south. I saw him weeks later, when I was struck down with malaria and had to camp by the roadside."

"How was he? How much time did you have together?"

"He was in good spirits, and in good health. During the one day that we had together, I laughed more than I did during the many previous months. Hoàng couldn't stop talking about you. He told me how he'd torn up his outer shirt to win your heart—"

"You know where he was going? Did you see him again?"

My mother's questions told me she didn't want to talk about the happy memories with my father.

"I didn't see Hoàng again, no. . . . ," said my uncle. "He was heading south but didn't know exactly where. He told me he'd do all he could to survive, to come back to you."

"Brother, I don't deserve him." My mother's words were not knives but they would leave me bleeding for years to come.

"Sister, why did you say that? What happened?"

"I can't tell you."

"Why not?"

"Because I'm ashamed of myself. I did a very bad thing. I'm a bad, bad person."

My palms were sweaty. So my suspicion was true. My mother had killed people on the battlefield. Innocent people.

"Listen to me, Sister Ngọc. Look at me. I won't judge you. Trust me."

Silence. The shuffling of my mother's feet. Was she leaving? I reached for the door's handle, ready to rush out to stop her.

"Sister Ngọc, we all had to fight against the enemy to be able to survive. Don't feel guilty—"

"It's not about that, Brother. It's worse."

"Tell me. I've seen enough horror to understand."

Silence.

"Sister, if you can't talk to me, confide in Mama. She can help you."

"No, Brother . . . I can't burden Mama. Besides, I feel filthy. I don't deserve her. I don't deserve Hương, either."

I cupped my mouth with my hands.

"I don't know what happened to you, Sister, but the fact you risked your life looking for Hoàng is very honorable. And you must have saved many patients along the way."

Silence.

"Sister, why don't you move back home? Hương needs you. I've seen the sadness in her eyes."

"I have nothing to offer her. My misery will only drag her down. I'm not ready yet."

"When will you be ready? Look at me, Sister. . . . I can't cope without you here. There're even two beds in my room. Come home and be my legs. Do this for me, please?"

DESPITE UNCLE ĐẠT's best efforts, it was more than another week before my mother came home. Grandma acted as if they hadn't fought; she prepared a big welcome-back meal. But my mother hardly ate; she didn't talk at all. While we were still at the table, she retreated into the bedroom.

I got up early the next day, excited to share breakfast with my mother, but she'd already left for the factory. Returning home, she had dinner in silence. And in silence she helped Uncle Đạt wash. Watching them, a lump of envy filled my throat. Perhaps I had to make myself injured so she would touch me?

"What's going on with her?" I asked Uncle Đạt the following day after my mother and Grandma had gone to work. He was sitting at the table, going through the pile of books Grandma had selected from our bookshelf.

"I have no idea." He flipped through the pages of a book. "She doesn't want to talk yet. Give her time."

"Everybody tells me to give her time. How much longer does she need?"

"I don't know." He dropped the book, picking up another one. "Many of my friends aren't able to speak, either. Everyone is trying to cope in their own way."

I shook my head. What more could I have done to deserve my mother's trust?

My uncle pushed the books away. "These are all so boring, don't you have an interesting one?"

"I think my mother killed somebody. A baby. That's why she doesn't want us to know." Words blurted out of my mouth.

Uncle Đạt stared at me.

"I heard her say it. In her sleep."

"Don't mention such a thing! Whatever happened, I know your mother didn't intentionally kill an innocent person."

I picked up my school bag, heading for the door. I didn't say good-bye to my uncle. I'd expected him to help me, but there he was, telling me off.

SEVERAL DAYS PASSED. I tried to listen to whatever my mother said to Uncle Đạt, but heard nothing new. She remained cold and distant. A stranger among us.

And why didn't Grandma do more? Whenever she was home, she buried her nose in her cooking, cleaning, and washing. As if all those chores could heal my mother.

I dreamed of leaving, of abandoning the stuffiness of our home, the secrets, the dark history. I knew where Grandma hid her money and I could take some, to buy a bus or a train ticket and food for the road. I'd go from North to South by myself, and I'd search for my father along the way. I could find him, and if not, *đi một ngày đàng học một sàng khôn*—Each day of travel earns one basketful of wisdom. Once tired of traveling, I'd stay in Sài Gòn with Auntie Hạnh. Perhaps under the light of my aunt's lucky star, I could be free from the bad omens that seemed to cling on to our family.

But the thoughts of leaving vanished as soon as I saw how deep the wrinkles were on Grandma's face. It was as if each of her children's returns had given her nothing but those wrinkles. She was the one who'd shielded me from the bombs, and perhaps it was now my turn to help her survive those weapons' impact, years after the moments they were dropped onto our lives.

So I didn't leave. And I tried to find ways to get to know my mother again. Still, she'd closed all the doors into her world and refused to hear me knocking.

The week after my mother's return, I headed to her room to tell her dinner was ready. Pushing against the door, I saw her on the bed, her head bent over a notebook, the pen in her hand scribbling across the page.

As she looked up, her mouth opened. She hid the notebook behind her. "You should have knocked."

"Come and eat." I turned away.

From then on, whenever my mother was out of the house, a fire was ignited in my stomach. I found myself passing her bedroom often, but Uncle Đạt was there all the time. I tried to appear helpful. As I brought him another glass of water, some more liquor, a bowl of peanuts, or another book, I looked around. My mother's bag was on the floor. A bamboo cabinet stood, the lips of its mouth—its two doors—tightly closed.

I wished Uncle Đạt would go out. He'd been an engineering student before he was drafted. Without any work experience, a degree, or his legs, nobody wanted to hire him. Grandma had talked to countless people about him, but it was all in vain.

"I'm going to clean your room, too dusty," I told Uncle Đạt two days later, when he was by the dining table, listening to his portable radio.

Inside the room, I reached for my mother's bag. She hadn't unpacked her clothes, as if she needed to be ready to depart any day. No notebook. I opened the cabinet, my hands running frantically among Uncle Đạt's belongings. I looked under the two beds. Nothing.

How stupid of me to have hoped. The notebook was small, my mother could have brought it with her.

Days passed, bringing me only frustration.

One afternoon, I returned home to see Uncle Đạt's message on the table. His friends had come by, bringing him to the funeral of a former teacher. I raced to the front door. The lock was secured, yet there was no inside latch. My mother and Grandma could come in at any time with their key. I pushed a chair against the door, piling another chair on top. Should someone enter, the crashing sound would be my alarm.

I searched my mother's bag. This time, it contained a worn-out notebook. I held my breath as my fingers opened the pages. Rows and rows of my mother's handwriting, not as neat as I remembered, but tottering, as if the words were rice plants bashed by a storm.

Names of trees and herbs and detailed notes on their medicinal qualities. Pages and pages of them. Recipes for treating different ailments. Many plants bore strange names, and my mother even sketched their trunks, branches, and leaves.

I flipped to the last page, which contained more notes on herbal medicine. Some of the words had been smeared with drops of water. They'd been written a while ago, perhaps in the jungle. But from whom had she learned these herbal treatments? I didn't remember her having anything to do with our traditional medicine.

I closed the notebook. For sure she was recording something else the other night, something she wanted to hide from me. On another notebook, smaller than this.

I was tired of not knowing. Perhaps my mother had met my father on the battlefield and something terrible had happened between them.

Pressing my stomach onto the floor, I looked under the beds. Dust had gathered into a thin layer. Sneezing, I stood up. Putting aside my mother's pillow, I peeled her straw mat away, searching among the bamboo slats that made up the bed's frame. Nothing.

I eyed the pillow. It looked a little crooked. I picked it up, squeezing it. My heart dipped as my hands made out something hard. Here it was, the smaller notebook, hidden inside the soft cotton. It was rather new, bound with a rubber string. I opened the first page. My mother's handwriting. As tottering as I'd seen on the other notebook.

16/5/1975

My son,

Would you ever forgive me? There've been countless nights when I dreamed about you. I dreamed about your blue face. The blue face that is now buried under the earth. Oh my baby, please forgive me. Forgive me. . . .

The diary left my hand, falling onto the bed. My mother had a son. With whom? I stood up, pacing back and forth. I wanted to continue reading, but feared that what I learned would tear my family apart. My mother had started writing down her thoughts recently, after she'd moved to Auntie Duyên's home.

I almost laughed at myself. Here I was, thinking that I'd found the key to my mother's secret, yet once I opened her door, I wanted to lock it and throw the key away. Sometimes something is so terrible that you need to pretend it doesn't exist.

The wall clock struck five times. My mother, Grandma, and Uncle Đạt could be home anytime. I eyed the diary's cover. I had caught a glimpse of my mother's sorrow, I had to see what type of a monster it was. Besides, my world had already been shattered, ignorance couldn't save it now.

I turned to the second page.

18/5/1975

Hoàng, my darling husband, where are you? Now the war has ended, many soldiers are returning home. Why haven't we heard from you?

Oh my darling, I used to believe that my love for you would be strong enough to help me overcome the bombs and bullets, so that I could find you, to tell you how sorry I am. I'm so sorry. I was a coward for pushing you to go to war. Only when you left did I learn you were my life. The jungles I passed, the rivers I crossed, did you ever set foot there? I desperately hunted for news about you. Oh my love, don't stay away from me. Please come home. Please forgive me. I beg you to forgive me. Last night in my dream, you looked at me sternly. Your eyes told me I'm no longer worthy to be your wife. I'm sorry . . . I'm so sorry.

21/5/1975

Last night Duyên shook me awake. The night was cool, but my whole body was soaked with sweat. My throat burned. Duyên told me that I'd been screaming. I nodded, saying that it was only a nightmare. When she fell asleep again, I sat there, curled against darkness. I feared sleep. I feared darkness. Whenever sleep or darkness approached, they rushed at me. They pinned me to the jungle floor, their hands choking my throat. Other pairs of hands pressed me against the earth, against rocks and tree roots. Their mouths were red as fire as they laughed. Pain, hot as burning coals, pierced my body. I was being torn into a million pieces. Where are they now, those monsters? I hope that they rot in jungles and valleys, that their souls will never be able to come home.

I read the entry again. What was that all about? Who were they?

30/5/1975

I shouldn't have ventured out, but Duyên said a walk would do me good, fresh air from the river would make me feel better. We hadn't gone far from Duyên's house when a hut came into view. Unlike other homes, its roof was covered with leaves and twigs, just like our medical stations in the jungle. Without thinking, I crouched down low. Next to me was no longer Duyên, nor Hà Nội, nor the peaceful Red River. I was back inside my hut in Trường Sơn, a young soldier, his head white with bandages, moaning under my hands. Distant sounds of gunfire, sounds of hand grenades exploding. Nurse Hòa ran in. "Sister, the enemy is coming!" she said. Hòa and I hurried to carry the soldiers out of the hut's back entrance, into the jungle, and down into the secret shelter. Those who could walk helped us. We ran, panted, and ran. Explosions drew closer, forcing us to cover our tracks. I returned to the hut to see injured soldiers still stuck on the bamboo slats that served as their beds.

"Into fighting position," I screamed at Hòa, then ran to a corner of the hut, picking up my rifle. An explosion shook the ground. Hollers from the hut next door. Shouts in the Southern Vietnamese dialect.

A man darted past our open door, throwing something inside. I don't remember pulling the trigger, just the butt of my

AK slamming repeatedly against my shoulder. The man stopped running. He clutched his chest, sank to his knees, collapsing to the ground. The hand grenade he'd thrown was rolling on the dirt floor. I ducked. A powerful blast. My world became blank.

Duyên's voice called me. I blinked to see myself on the Red River's bank, surrounded by men, women, children. They were staring at me, whispering. I wanted to disappear, crawl into a crack of dirt. In people's eyes, I've become mad, possessed by ghosts. One of the women was telling Duyên she should seek a shaman and make an offering, to chase away the dead spirits who'd stolen my soul.

3/6/1975

These days I spend my time indoors, not daring to come out. This morning a young man passed by my window. He'd lost both arms. Such a handsome man. The men I'd journeyed south with were handsome, too. They had hope in their eyes, songs on their lips, laughter in their hearts. But at the clinics where I was stationed, the men who came to me were no longer singing. Some had their insides spilling out from torn stomachs, some had dangling arms or legs, others had half of their faces blown off. Did they hate me when I had to operate on them without the help of anesthesia? As they were tied down onto makeshift operating tables, I cut into them. Should I have tried harder to keep their limbs?

And the two men who'd been roasted alive by napalm, my tears couldn't extinguish the smoke rising from their flesh. Could I have done more to save them?

15/6/1975

I was cooking when terrifying noises came from a neighbor's house. A man was kicking and screaming at his dog. I heard the dog's howls and saw myself lying on the jungle floor, my hands tied behind my back. Pain sprang up from my legs, which were bleeding.

"Fuck your mother!" A man kicked me hard in the stomach. "You killed my friend."

I curled into a ball after the kick, telling myself not to bawl. If I did, I'd give the enemy satisfaction. I glanced around. The hut of my clinic was a short distance away, columns of dark smoke twisting above its roof. My stomach wrenched. What had happened to those who remained in the hut?

Another man grabbed me by the hair. "Show us the place where you hid your comrades!" He pulled my head up and around so I could see in all directions. "Where the hell is it?" he screamed. "Point it out to us and we'll spare your life."

I closed my eyes, not believing in the enemy's promise. I'd be a fool to trust them. The shelter, luckily, was far away, on the other side of the hut. Among the patients in hiding was a high-ranking officer whom the enemy must be after. His personal guard was in charge of protecting the shelter, but if the enemy found it, the guard's fighting would be an egg thrown against boulders.

"Tell us now, you Communist bitch with your thick cunt!" A kick landed on my ribs. Another on my face. I couldn't help but howl.

Duyên's children came, asking me what was wrong. Everything is wrong with me. Perhaps it's true that the ghosts have possessed me. Perhaps they've taken my soul, so that I'm just an empty shell.

I pressed the diary against my chest, every cell of my body aching for my mother. I'd tried to imagine the horror she'd had to face, but it was even worse than that. How lucky that my mother had slipped through the grasp of death to come back to me. How courageous of her to have stood up for her comrades. I couldn't wait to tell her how proud I was to be her daughter.

I cocked my head. No noise at the door. I eyed the clock once more. Time was running away from me. I lifted the diary with both hands, flipping the page as gently as I could.

17/6/1975

Last night, enemy planes roared into my dreams. Explosions shook the jungle. Smoke burned my eyes. The air stank of burnt flesh. A pillar of our clinic had collapsed onto Dương's stomach, the stomach that I'd sewn up the day before. Next to Dương were the scattered body parts of Nurse Sánh. I knew I should be rushing patients down to our shelter, but I found myself running out of the clinic, into the open air. I held my face to the sky, yelling at the coward enemy who sat high in those airplanes.

I woke up again with my cries choking my throat. Every night this happens. My head throbbed. I needed some water, but couldn't get up. My hands were sticky, as sticky as Nurse Sánh's blood.

I want to meet the pilot who launched the rocket that killed Sánh. I want to rub her blood onto his face, so he could taste her suffering.

20/6/1975

Duyên told me there was a job opening at her factory and that she'd talked to her supervisor about me. I could take the job if I wanted to. Not much skill is required, she said. I would need to iron newly made clothes, fold them, and put them into boxes. First I shook my head, but she said manual work would be good for me; it'd stop my mind from running wild. "Besides, you can't live on your mother's labor forever," she said. I let those words sink deep into me. She was right. I had become a burden for Mama, for Hương, for her, for everyone.

I asked if I could think about it for a couple of days. I know I must work. But I fear meeting people. I fear their questions. At least Duyên hasn't questioned me much. I'd told her everything about my trip South, but not the fact that my body had been soiled. Not about the baby.

She can't know, otherwise she'll tell Hoàng when he comes back. And if he knows, he won't touch me anymore. Who would want to touch a woman who had been trampled by other men?

Today I rubbed my body until it bled. I want to wash the filth from my skin, but it's too late.

21/6/1975

Hương visited me. She's taller than me now, more beautiful than I could ever imagine my daughter to be. Her skin glows its youthfulness, her eyes lit up with the light of innocence. Watching her, I saw the best of Hoàng and me. I saw determination and love for life.

She seemed very happy today. I took in her gentle voice as she read the letter from her admirer to me. I wish I could tell her that I am her admirer, too, that I love her so much. How come I can't tell her that I love her, my own daughter? In our family, love is something that we show, not something we speak about. Mama has never said that she loves me, but she shows it by caring and cooking for me. Now that I'm incapable of taking care of Hương and cooking for her, I wish I had the courage to tell her how much I love her.

But Hương must hate me now. She must hate me for being stupid. I'm stupid for telling her the truth about me encouraging her father to go to war. I'm stupid, stupid, stupid!

1/7/1975

Mama came by. Seeing the bones that protruded from her shoulders, I remembered lines from an old folk poem: "My elderly mother is a ripe banana clinging onto the tree, the wind could rattle her to fall, leaving me an orphan."

Mama is not yet old, just fifty-five this year, but she doesn't look young. I fear that she could fall anytime, my heavy burden on her back. I'm a terrible daughter, for having been angry at her, for blaming her. I wish I could take back the words I'd flung at her, but words are like water: once they have escaped one's mouth, they're spilled onto the floor. Words are like knives, leaving invisible wounds that continue to bleed.

But Mama didn't visit to talk about our fight. She insisted that I come to town with her. She said she'd asked a well-known healer to help me. Sitting on her bike's back saddle, I rested my face against her shirt. She smelled so clean, so fresh. Fresh like the rice fields of our village in my faraway childhood. Fresh like the laughter of my brothers and sister. With my eyes closed, I saw the smiling faces of Thuận, Đạt, and Minh. They can't be dead. They must come back to me.

I lifted my head once we entered the Old Quarter. Our bike passed small lanes. Lanes that were covered with the footsteps of Hoàng and me. Over there, under the curving roof of Bạch Mã Temple, Hoàng had told me he wanted to marry me, his kiss still hot on my lips. When will he come back? Will he ever kiss me again?

Will I ever have one single day when I can forgive myself?

When the bike approached Traditional Medicine Street, the smell of herbal plants flooded into my nose. I shuddered. I was back in Trường Sơn, in front of my eyes was Mrs. Ninô, brewing jungle medicine in her clay pot. She poured the condensed liquid into a bowl and set it in front of me. She asked if I was sure. Instead of answering her, I looked down at my stomach. A tiny body was nesting inside of me. My flesh and blood, my own child. Tears blinded me as I gulped down the bitter liquid. I was killing my baby. My own baby.

"Hương, what are you doing?" I started, and looked up to see my mother. She snatched the diary from my hands. "How dare you?"

"Mama . . ."

She brought her diary to her face and screamed so loud that I jumped away from her.

I was thinking of what to say when she picked up her sandals, flinging them at me. I ducked and the sandals hit the wall behind me with a big thump.

"My thoughts are private, for me to keep!" she hollered.

I stared at the woman in front of me, her face red, her hair unkempt. I'd searched for the mother I knew, and I thought I'd seen a glimpse of her in the diary, only to end up confronting a stranger. Only a stranger would want to hit me. Only a stranger would have a child with another man and abort her pregnancy to conceal her sins. "You're a baby killer," I heard myself say. "You betrayed Papa! Wait until I tell him."

"Fine. Go and find him. Tell him. Tell him!"

Slamming the front door behind me, I ran. I didn't know where to go, but I had to get away from my mother. I no longer wanted to see her face.

Cries choked my breath and I slowed down. I had run all the way to the Long Biên Bridge, its body arching like a skeleton across the Red River. Perhaps my father had died. Perhaps the river could take me to him.

Closing my eyes, I saw Grandma as a young child, being cursed by the fortune-teller, I saw my mother in the jungle, drinking herbal medicine to abort her baby. We had all been cursed, generations of the Trần family. I had to end it now. I pushed myself ahead.

The river curled its red in front of me. I looked down at its fast current. Thủy and I had been here, dipping our feet into the water, our laughter still singing in my ears. I had no more friends. No more family who cared about me.

"Hương." Someone snatched my hand, pulling me back. "I'm so sorry."

I shoved my mother away and kept walking. No words could take back what she'd done to me.

She ran, blocking my path. "You've discovered the root of my sorrow, yet it's only half of the truth. Please . . . give me the chance to explain."

WE SAT IN a corner of a tea shop. My mother had ordered a glass of soybean milk for me, but I left it there, untouched.

"You'll answer all of my questions?" I asked.

She nodded, glancing around, even though the shop was empty; the owner was out on the street, talking to her neighbors.

"Who's the father of the baby?"

She squeezed her cup of tea, her knuckles white. "I . . . I don't know."

"What do you mean you don't know?" Something that felt like vomit rose to my throat.

My mother bent her head. Her mouth was closed, as tight as a clam.

"See? You said you'd tell me everything, but you can't. You can't because you betrayed Pa—"

"Please . . ." My mother raised her hands. "The truth would only hurt you more."

"Hurt me? Nothing is worse than knowing you had a child with another man."

My mother's face scrunched up. She opened her mouth, but instead of words, delirious laughter spilled out from her lips. "Would it be worse if the father of my child is the enemy?"

I stared at her. She couldn't be sane.

"You're right." She nodded. "I betrayed your father since I wasn't strong enough to fight them."

"What do you mean? Who are they?"

Clutching my shirt's collar, she pulled me to her. "The enemy . . . a group of men . . . they captured me . . . they did horrible things to me. One of them . . . fathered the baby."

I shook my head. I couldn't accept what she'd just said.

My mother released me. She covered her face with her hands. "If you must know, the men were Vietnamese. They spoke the Southern dialect."

I shut my eyes. I wanted everything to turn dark, get smaller, and disappear. Disappear and take me with it.

To this very day, I still wish I could go back to the moment my mother found me with her diary. I should have been able to figure out her reasons for aborting the baby from what I'd read. On the other hand, I was just a fifteen-year-old girl who hadn't experienced her first kiss, who had had no idea, really, how babies were made.

"Hương, I'm sorry you had to find out this way," whispered my mother.

"I'm the one who's sorry, Mama. I'm terrible . . . for doubting you. . . ." I gripped her hand. "Mama, in your diary, you said that you love me. I love you, too. And I need you."

"Oh, my darling. You are my everything."

We hugged each other, our tears flowing onto each other's face.

"Mama, I need to understand. I want you to get better, so that we can be a family again. How long were you captured? And how did you escape?"

"Those monsters . . . they had me for a couple of days. I thought they'd kill me, but a soldier on their side took pity on me and helped me get away."

"A soldier on their side?"

"Yes . . . a Southern Vietnamese soldier. During the night, he unbound me and led me into the jungle. He said he'd seen my diary, with your picture among the pages. He had a daughter of the same age."

"What happened after he let you go?"

"I wandered among the trees, lost. I wanted to take my own life, but your voice and Grandma's held me back. I don't remember where I fainted, but when I came to, I was in a cave, surrounded by local people, who'd abandoned their village for the cave because of the bombings. One of them was a traditional healer. She cured my injuries with medicinal plants. During the month that I was there, she taught me many things about jungle medicine. When my physical injuries had been healed, I left the cave to join another medical unit."

"Your pregnancy . . . when did you find out?"

"When I'd spent a few weeks at a new clinic. . . . At first I didn't think about it when my bleeding didn't come. When I noticed the changes in my body . . ."

I twirled the glass in my hand.

"When I was sure I was pregnant, I had to find my way back to the healer. I couldn't bring the baby here. I couldn't raise the child of our enemy. I didn't want you, your father, or Grandma to find out."

I bent my head, the baby's blue face filling my vision, his faint cries throbbing in my chest. What would it feel like to hold him?

My mother swallowed hard. "The decision to terminate the pregnancy . . . it was the hardest I'd ever made. When I staggered out of the cave, I wanted to continue my mission, to find your father, Hương . . . but I no longer had any strength. I realized that I'd been a fool, for thinking that I could brave the war and find him. During my long walk to return to Hà Nội, I wasn't afraid of the bombs, but I was fearful that he would discover about my body being soiled, and that I'd killed an innocent soul. . . ."

I hugged my mother's shoulders, unable to find a single word to console her.

"Sometimes I think your father doesn't come back because he knows," she sighed.

ARRIVING HOME, WE found a crowd of people in our living room. Grandma was wailing. She'd returned from work to see the front door wide open and chairs strewn across the floor.

Seeing Mama and me, she laughed and cried. She hugged me so tight, I struggled to breathe.

The next evening, I made Grandma and my mother go out with each other. They came back, their faces red, their eyes swollen.

Grandma held a large oil lamp, which she'd just bought. She filled the lamp with oil, lit it, and placed it on a chair next to my mother's bed. That night, and during years later, my mother would sleep with the lamp burning bright next to her.

But now she was no longer alone. She began talking to Uncle Đạt, too. I heard their murmurs whenever I walked past their room in the evenings.

I often found myself wondering about the baby. Would I have been able to love him the way a sister was supposed to love her brother, or would I hate him because half of his blood had come from the man who had attempted to kill my mother's soul?

Nightmares still tortured my mother, but she no longer kept herself isolated from us. After coming home from her factory, she cooked. She asked me about school and Grandma about life in the Old Quarter. She wheeled my uncle out for a walk and helped him exercise. One day, she brought packages of dried plants home. As she brewed a pot of those sliced roots, stems, flowers, and seeds, her tears fell. But she told me she had to conquer her demons: the medicine was for Uncle Đạt, who'd told her his disability went beyond what the eyes could see, that he could no longer make a woman happy. My mother hoped the brew would help him; her recipe for treatment was among the many she'd learnt from her healer and recorded in her notebook.

Two weeks after my mother had laid bare her soul to me, the *bàng* tree provided shade for us to wash our hair, and the oil lamp gave light for my mother to help me with my homework. She showed me different ways to answer the most difficult math questions, and I was amazed.

Bit by bit, Miss Nhung found small ways back into my uncle's life. She visited occasionally, bringing with her one time a cassette full of songs that Uncle Đạt ended up listening to every day, and another time a book that Uncle Đạt stayed up the whole night reading. My mother told me that when Uncle Đạt returned, he still loved Miss Nhung, but he believed she would be better off with another man.

The only one who hadn't turned around was Uncle Sáng, so one day, when my mother told me she needed to pay him a visit, I joined her. My uncle hadn't been to our house at all, but he and his wife kept eating Grandma's food. Twice a week, Grandma had been preparing different dishes, and I had to deliver them.

It was night when we lugged the bike up to Uncle Sáng's apartment. My uncle poked his head out of the door's crack. "Sister Ngọc . . . Hương." He glanced down to my empty hands. A look of disappointment crossed his thin face.

"How are you, Brother?" My mother pushed the bike inside.

Uncle Sáng closed the door behind us. "Fine, Sister."

"I thought you were sick, terribly sick! Too sick to come see your Brother Đạt."

"*Shhh*. Keep your voice low, won't you? Hoa is already sleeping." Uncle Sáng grabbed my mother's hand, pulling her deeper into the gloomy apartment. "Sit down, Sister. You, too, Hương." He gestured toward the reed mat on the floor.

"We don't have to sit." My mother's voice was icy. "Why haven't you been home to see Đạt?"

"Things are complicated." My uncle wrinkled his forehead. "I'm leading a campaign to wipe out capitalists, bourgeoisie, and traders. And Mama . . . as you know, is a *con buôn*."

"So that's the way you two treat Mama? You despise her in front of others but you use her as your slave?"

"No. No. You're getting me all wrong here."

"Tell me in what way I'm wrong."

"Lower your voice." Uncle Sáng knitted his brows. "I'm thankful to Mama, but I have to abide by the Party rules. We need to rebuild our country with the hard work of laborers and farmers. No association with capitalists, bourgeoisie, and traders."

"Capitalists, bourgeoisie, traders? Sáng, Mama labors so hard out there to earn every single cent. She's a worker, not a bourgeois."

"I have to abide by the Party rules. 'No association with capitalists, bourgeois, and traders,'" my uncle repeated.

"So the Party is your God, is that it?"

"Sister, we fought so hard to regain peace for our country. We sacrificed our lives to chase away the capitalists, the exploiting class—"

"Exploiting class? Don't let them brainwash you, Sáng. You know what happened to us during the Land Reform. They condemned our family wrongly. They called us exploiters. They killed—"

"Shut up," Uncle Sáng hissed. "I have no connection with landlords."

"I know. You faked your papers. You erased your family roots so that you could become a Party member. How sad. But don't forget, Sáng, how our father died."

"Don't you dare make things up. Get out of my house."

"Sáng, I'm not here to argue with you. Please come home and see your Brother Đạt."

"I told you I can't, but he can visit me."

"He lost his legs, Sáng. He lost his fucking legs and can't walk."

"He has a wheelchair and—"

Whap. A smacking sound. My mother had slapped Uncle Sáng across his cheek.

"What kind of brother are you?" she screamed. "Don't sell your family so cheap for some political ideology!"

My uncle's hand reached up to his cheek. His face twisted into a look of disgust.

"You crazy woman!" he hollered. "Get out of here, or I'll have you arrested."

"Arrest me then. Arrest me!" My mother beat her fists against her chest.

"*Mẹ ơi!*" I reached out for her. "Let's go."

My mother looked at me, tears filling her eyes. "Just a minute, Hương." She straightened her back and faced my uncle. "I know you've climbed up the ladder, Sáng, but don't think you're too high up. You're still my younger brother. Without Brother Minh here, I'm the eldest in the family. I have the responsibility to teach you."

"I don't need anyone's teaching. Get out of my house."

My mother coughed and spat on the floor. "From now on, you're no longer my family. I hope your children will do better than you and remember their roots."

We walked out.

I felt proud that my mother had stood up for Grandma, but somehow I also found myself mourning for the youngest uncle of my childhood—someone who had laughed with me as he slivered bamboo, creating colorful lanterns that came alive under moonlight of the Mid-Autumn Festival.

I RAN UP the staircase leading to my class, my stomach empty since I hadn't had time for breakfast. All was quiet around me.

On the third floor, I turned into a long corridor.

Teachers had started their lessons inside the classrooms I passed. Some boys were stealing glances at me through the open windows. I tried to make myself smaller, embarrassed at the sounds my sandals were making.

The bursting noise of my class welcomed me in. No sign of a teacher. Good. I hurried to my seat.

"What happened? Why are you late?" Trân rushed toward me.

"I overslept." I smiled at her. She was one of the girls most friendly with me. I wondered if she'd visit my home some time.

"Watch out," voices rang from behind my back, then roaring laughter. I didn't have to turn to know the boys were playing some stupid games again.

Trân took something out of my hair. A paper plane with my name scribbled on its wings. "From Nam. He really likes you."

"Well, I don't like him." I opened my bag, pulling out my notebook.

"I see Teacher Định," someone called out. My classmates shouldered each other, scrambling to their desks. Our history teacher appeared, but he wasn't alone. Next to him was a tall boy; unlike those in my class, his skin was as dark as a farmer's.

We stood up in unison to greet our teacher, who smiled and nodded for us to sit down.

"Tâm, your new classmate." Teacher Định gestured toward the boy. "Help him get settled and don't give him a hard time, is that clear?"

"Yes, Teacher," we chorused.

"Come see me if you have any problems," Teacher Định told Tâm. "And to help you get familiar with things, Thiết, our class president, will take you on a tour when school finishes today."

"Thiết is sick, Teacher," someone said.

Teacher Định looked around the room. "Someone else will give you a tour then." His eyes found me. "Hương, okay?"

"Yes, Teacher," I mumbled, though all I could think about was how I wished I could skip the entire day, to be home, to have a long chat with Uncle Đạt. I needed to say sorry. There had been moments when I considered him a burden, even though I'd promised to help him when he first returned.

At the sounds of drumbeats, my classmates spilled out of the room like bees fleeing their hive.

"Need help with guiding the new cutie?" Trân came to me, giggling.

"Thanks, but it'll be a quick tour." I stuffed my notebook into my bag. How could Trân even think that the new boy was handsome? What was his name again?

Trân glanced toward the back of our classroom. I followed her gaze. The new boy was at his desk, his head bent over a book. I wondered what he was reading.

"Hi, Hương," someone called out. Nam. He smiled nervously at me. "Can I invite you for—"

I dropped the paper plane into his half-open bag. "I'm on duty today, the introduction tour."

"Oh." He scratched his head.

"Want to invite me instead?" Trân pulled Nam's arm. When they were nearly out of the classroom, Trân turned her head. "Have fun," she mouthed.

I cleared my desk. I remembered the boy's name now. Tâm. His name meant "Good Conscience."

Tâm was still reading when I got to him. "Ready to go?"

He lifted his face. His eyes were deep brown, framed by long lashes. "Go where?"

His heavy middle-region accent surprised me. Grandma spoke this accent, but only at home. Why did Tâm leave the middle region to come here?

"The tour, remember?" I mumbled. I wished I'd asked Trân to take over the duty, but no student would dare disobey the teachers. If we wanted to pass our grade, our mark for the "Good Behavior" subject had to be adequate.

"Oh." Tâm stood up. "Thanks for doing this."

We left the classroom. The corridor was empty. Gray clouds had gathered in the sky, sprinkling a drizzle onto the yard. We stood on the balcony, gazing down at the wetness beneath.

"We have around five hundred students here." I zipped up my jacket. "School starts at seven-thirty every morning except for Monday, when we arrive one hour earlier to sing the national anthem and greet the national flag. Behind that tree is the canteen, the soccer field is at the back of that building."

"Is there a library?"

"Yes, but it doesn't have many interesting titles, to be honest. The book you're reading, is it good?"

"It's too good. I can't stop." Tâm showed me the cover. *The Hunchback of Notre Dame.*

"Ah, Victor Hugo is an incredible writer." I smiled. "I adore his poetry. I read this last year and dreamt about visiting France to see that magnificent cathedral."

"I know." Tâm returned the book to his bag. "I'd love to visit Paris one day, too. . . . And I was hoping our library would have a great collection. I've left most of my books at my village, for my sister."

"That's nice of you. . . . I have a few books and could lend you some."

"Really?" Tâm's eyes brightened. "That'd be great. Thanks." He pulled up the collar of his jacket. "Do you live far away from here?"

"I'm on Khâm Thiên Street. Where's your home village?"

"In Hà Tĩnh Province. Uhm . . . your neighborhood, Khâm Thiên, was heavily bombed, wasn't it? I'm sorry."

I nodded and stared at the branches of a *phượng* tree. They were barren, shivering in the wind, like Grandma and I had during our walk to Hòa Bình. I pointed out the brown lids scattered around the schoolyard. "Bomb shelters. The largest one is in front of the canteen. You should know where to run if the bombs come back."

"I hope they never do. In fact, I wish there would never be another war on the face of this earth."

I turned to Tâm. I'd never heard any boy talk like him. "You have a relative who fought?"

"My father . . . he came back miserable. We are lucky, though. Many men of my village never returned. How about your relatives?"

"My Uncle Thuận died. Uncle Đạt lost both of his legs. We're still waiting for my father." I felt the heat behind my eyelids and bit my lip hard to stop myself from crying in front of a boy I barely knew.

"I'm sorry. . . . How long has your father been gone? Have you heard from him at all?"

"Seven years, nine months and twenty-five days." I lifted the Sơn ca from my pocket. "My Papa carved this for me in the jungle." I could no longer hold back the tears.

"*Shhh.*" Tâm put a finger on his lips. He brought the bird to his ear. "*Uhm huhm.*" He nodded. "*Uhm huhm,* thank you, Birdie." He arched his brow. "Oh, you want to talk to her now, Birdie? Okay, here she is."

He placed the Sơn ca next to my ear. "Do you hear him?"

I shook my head, smiled, and wiped my tears.

"He said you're a special girl, a princess, and you shouldn't hang out with me."

"Oh. Why not?"

"Because I'm a *nhà quê.*" Tâm called himself a country bumpkin. He dropped his bag, stepping away from me. He bent low, pretending to hoe his field. He thumped his back with his fist, wiping the invisible droplets of sweat from his face, and resuming his hoeing again. He looked so funny that I had to laugh.

CYCLING HOME, I couldn't get Tâm out of my mind. His smiling eyes and his warm voice made me giddy. I told myself to stop thinking about him. Men could be evil, like those who'd harmed my mother. I had no idea what type of a person Tâm was. I shouldn't trust him so easily.

I arrived home to find Uncle Đạt on the floor, whistling. He was working on a new trough for the pigs.

My mother was busy in the kitchen, delicious smells twirling up from her hands.

She looked at me over her shoulder. "Feed the animals, they're driving me crazy."

"Sure." I laughed. "What're you cooking?"

"Tofu in tomato sauce and coriander."

My stomach cheered. I hadn't had it for such a long time. My mother cooked it the best.

"Will lunch be ready soon?" Uncle Đạt glanced up at the clock. "Nhung will be here in a minute."

"I'm excited to see her, too." My mother tossed a bunch of green spinach into a sizzling pan.

When I finished feeding the pigs, the food was on the table. Miss Nhung distributed the chopsticks. She was so thin that I could see the blue veins on the back of her hands. I hoped Uncle Đạt would take care of her, but how could he, without a job?

"How do you like your new school, Hương?" Miss Nhung smiled at me.

"It's not so new anymore, but it's great, Auntie." I thought again about Tâm.

"What do you want to study later when you go to the university?"

University sounded grand. I hoped I could make it. I sucked in a breath. "I don't know yet, Auntie." I found words beautiful, but didn't know whether I'd be brave enough to be a writer. I'd been reading books by Phùng Quán, Trần Dần, Hoàng Cầm, and Lê Đạt—writers who'd been imprisoned in the *Nhân Văn Giai Phẩm* movement. Their work during the mid-1950s called for freedom of speech and human rights, bringing me closer to my grandpa, who lived at the same time and held the same liberal ideas. Yet such work also highlighted to me the risks that writers faced, with a government that censored everything. "A circus rope walker balances breath-taking difficulties," the poet Phùng Quán wrote. "Yet tougher still to be a writer enduring a lifetime on the path of truth."

I knew that, like Phùng Quán, if I wrote, it could only be the truth as I saw it. I couldn't twist my words to please the ears of those in power.

"I hope you'll become a doctor, Hương," said Uncle Đạt. "Your mother can teach you a few things about herbal medicine. It has magical powers." He winked at Miss Nhung, who blushed.

My mother smiled, scooping tofu into Uncle Đạt's bowl. "When do we need to leave?"

"In half an hour."

"I have oranges and incense for Thành's altar," Miss Nhung said.

My mother nodded. "I've prepared a small bag of rice for his parents."

"You two are wonderful," Uncle Đạt whispered, and I felt glad that my mother and Miss Nhung had taken the afternoon off work to accompany him. His friend died in the bamboo forest on this day three years ago, and Uncle Đạt needed to burn incense for him. But it would be hard for my uncle to tell the grieving family about their son's final moments as his life was extinguished by the B-52 bombs.

Uncle Đạt shifted in his chair. He'd turned to look at the kitchen cabinet several times. There was a glass of water in front of him, and he kept staring at it.

"You okay?" Miss Nhung reached for his hand.

He shook his head. "Sister Ngọc . . . would you mind getting me some liquor?"

He turned to Miss Nhung. "If you haven't heard, *em*, I've had problems."

She put down her chopsticks. "Yes, your mother told me, *anh*. It won't be easy to give up alcohol, but I hope you'll try."

My mother went to the kitchen and fetched the bottle.

"Don't put the whole thing in front of me, Sister," said my uncle. "One small glass will do for now."

Receiving the glass from my mother, Uncle Đạt sniffed it. He finished it in one go and closed his eyes.

Destination

Thanh Hóa–Hà Nội, 1955–1956

Guava, that day outside the house with the thick fence of leafy plants, I waited for your mother, Sáng sleeping in my arm. To disguise myself, I squatted under a tree opposite the house, spreading out my palm. I was a beggar, begging for hope.

It was a long while before Ngọc emerged, holding hands with a little girl. They were both running and crouching down low.

"Older Sister, aren't we supposed to hide inside?" The girl giggled as they approached me.

"Nobody said so." Ngọc glanced at me. Her hair had been washed and flowed in a smooth stream down her back. Her face, now cleared of dust and tear stains, glowed. Wearing clean pants and a shirt, she looked as fresh and pretty as a jasmine flower.

"Quick, Younger Sister. Behind that tree." Ngọc pointed past me. As the girl rushed forward, Ngọc lagged behind, her hands reaching for her waistband. Something white gleamed in her fingers.

"I got a job, Mama." She dropped two tightly pressed balls of cooked rice into my open palm. "You go. I'll be fine. I'll check for Thuận when I can."

"Are you sure, Ngọc?" There was no answer. Ngọc had already run away from me to join her new sister.

So, with Sáng on my waist, I continued my long journey toward Hà Nội. Now that I'd shed four children along the way, I was a butterfly who'd lost its wings, a tree who'd forsaken all of its leaves and branches. My mind was dull with guilt, but my legs had to push on. I punished myself by walking day and night. To stay alive, I ate grass, rice plants, and things I could steal from the fields. Sáng survived on my milk and the little food I gave him. The air was getting colder, and I bundled him in Mrs. Tú's carrying cloth; its scent made me weep. Yet I knew I couldn't waste my energy on even a single teardrop: I had to hurry if I wanted to see Minh, Ngọc, Đạt, Hạnh, and Thuận again.

We were moving faster, but not fast enough. The national highway was the shortest route to Hà Nội. One early morning, I'd ventured onto it again and asked for a ride. There weren't a lot of vehicles at that time, just the occasional car or buffalo cart. Very few people stopped when I waved and called, but they all turned down my plea for help. There were checkpoints along the highway, and nobody dared to assist a woman without a travel permit.

I resumed walking on the dirt path parallel to the highway. Then I remembered something. Can you believe it? In my crazy mind, I'd forgotten I was wearing something quite valuable.

I went behind a bush and took off the brown outer shirt. Holding my breath, I peeled the silk blouse away from my skin. It was sweaty and dirty but wasn't ruined. My brother had chosen the best material, and the outer shirt had protected it.

I put my face into the blouse; Công's tender face and his smile were alive in my mind. I hoped Mr. Hải had managed to recover his body and bury him. I imagined my brother's death and felt his pain. Never could I have thought that so much violence would crash down onto our family. On the other hand, everyone I knew had lost family members to violent deaths. I wondered when the circle of violence would end.

I found a stream and dipped the blouse into the rolling current, washing it. Sunlight glistened on the exquisite green fabric, lighting up the countless ancient words of *Phúc*—Blessings. Holding the blouse in one arm, I walked with Sáng on my other arm. *Cái khó ló cái khôn*—Difficulty gives light to wisdom. The shirt could be a ticket to help us get to Hà Nội.

Your Uncle Sáng was such a good boy. He babbled and pointed at flowers and butterflies, at cars and carts crawling like bugs on the national highway. Then he pointed at a tree by the roadside. When we came closer, he pointed at a pair of bamboo baskets lying there. Inside the baskets sat small piles of guavas and oranges, some areca nuts, and betel leaves. Beside the baskets were ropes that connected them to a bamboo pole. The owner of the baskets was squatting on the ground, leaning against the tree trunk, fanning herself with her hat.

"Hello, Sister." I lowered myself down next to her. Sáng crawled out of my hands, toward the fruit.

"Don't touch." I held him back.

"He can have one." The woman picked up a golden guava. She checked for its softness and gave it to Sáng.

"*Ổi, ổi.*" Sáng babbled, clapping his hands. He sank his baby teeth into the fruit.

"Oh, you're so cute." She pinched his cheek.

"Did you just return from the market, Sister?" I asked.

"It was a market all right . . . but nobody wanted to buy. Everyone tried to sell what they got from their own fields and gardens."

"Sister, may I make an offer?" I held out the blouse. "This is silk, woven at Vạn Phúc Village." I rubbed the fabric against her cheek.

"So soft." She grinned. "I heard about silk and always wondered."

"It's my brother's precious gift to me." I choked, not wanting to part with my last memory of Công, but knowing I had no other choice. I put the blouse into the woman's hand. "It'd look great on you. Try it on."

"No." She pushed it back, eyeing me up and down.

"Sister . . . I didn't steal this, I swear. My brother paid a high price for it."

"Why would you want to give it to me then?"

"Would you accept this in exchange for your baskets and carrying pole?"

The woman stared at me.

I held her gaze. "Sister, I need a job. I want to earn my living with these baskets and carrying pole." I gave her the two cents. "This and the blouse?"

I pulled her up and made her put the blouse on.

"*Đẹp quá.*" Sáng clapped his hands, praising how beautiful the woman looked.

The woman twirled around, laughing. Seeing how her eyes lit up, I knew the deal was done.

"Ah, *vui, vui.*" Sáng babbled about being happy as he sat in the front basket, bouncing up and down together with the rhythms of my footsteps. At my back, another basket bounced up and down, half-filled with guavas and oranges. "Sit still," I told him, going slowly at first, then faster, as Sáng clutched the ropes with both hands, sitting like a Buddha. He lifted his head, chuckling, eyeing a flock of birds speeding a large V shape across the deep blue sky.

"You're a good boy, Sáng. Sit still and we'll be in Hà Nội in no time." I pressed on harder toward the national highway. Now with the baskets and bamboo pole, I'd have a reason to travel on the road: to get to the next town's market. I hoped nobody would make trouble for a poor saleswoman who carried a baby, traveling through winter.

"*Ai mua ổi đây, cam đây?*" I sang out loud, red juice oozing from my mouth. I was chewing a betel quid, to discolor my white teeth. In exchange for the blouse and money, the woman had given me all the contents of her baskets. The sale of these oranges and guavas would make the capital for my business.

"*Ai mua ổi 'ây, cam 'ây,*" Sáng babbled, enjoying the new way of traveling. He couldn't pronounce the *đ* yet and sounded hilarious.

"Get out of the way!" Shouts rang out from behind my back. I turned to see a man and several women on a buffalo cart.

"Sisters, Brother . . . my guavas are homegrown . . . sugar sweet," I called out to them.

"*Ai mua ổi 'ây, cam 'ây,*" Sáng chanted, and clapped his hands.

"Oh, that baby's so cute," a woman said and the rest of them burst out laughing.

The cart pulled to a stop. The women hopped down, approaching us.

But I could no longer see them. The panting buffaloes had caught my eyes. My father was standing by the cart, smiling at me. *Papa!*

"Sister, how much for one? Didn't you hear me?" A woman was pulling my shirtsleeve.

I blinked and the image of my father disappeared.

As the woman tugged my arm again, I turned to her. "Sorry. Two cents each."

"That's expensive!" snapped another woman.

"It's a long way to bring them here, Sister. They're tender and juicy."

The women shook their heads. It was Sáng who rescued me. *"Ai mua ổi 'ây, cam 'ây."* He clapped his hands, dimples flowering onto his cheeks.

The women burst out laughing again.

"All right, give us three oranges and two guavas. We're only buying because of this cutie." A woman giggled, unhooking the safety pin that secured her pocket. She pulled out a stack of coins.

"You did it!" I dropped to my knees, hugging Sáng as the cart crawled out of earshot. "We earned two bowls of phở in just a few minutes."

Sáng and I sold everything we had that afternoon. The money we earned that day, Guava, it was enough for us to buy twenty bowls of phở.

For weeks, I journeyed, trying to make as much money as I could. At checkpoints on the highway, the guards always stopped us. I bribed them with money or fruit, and managed to convince them that I was truly heading to the next town's market. And Sáng did such a great job in charming those guards. Yes, Guava . . . I know your uncle has become quite a serious young man, but he was my cute and cheerful helper then.

To get new supplies, we had to travel to nearby villages. Arriving at a market before sunrise, we could buy the best fruits at the cheapest price. By then, my teeth were colored red by betel nuts and my skin dark. I'd also become very thin. I knew my hunters wouldn't recognize me so easily anymore. Still, dangers were sharp thorns that surrounded me. Coming closer to Hà Nội, my middle-region accent made me stand out from everyone else.

I tried to imitate the Northern accent and speak as little as I could.

With our profit, I bought us sandals, some warmer clothes, and a *nón lá* for Sáng. Now that your uncle sat all day in the sun or rain, he needed a hat. But he almost always tilted his hat backward to seduce customers. He was the one who made everybody want to buy our fruits. As for my hat, I had to keep it. The children had found it for me and, as I wore it, I heard them urging me on. By then, I'd had enough time to think, and I still believed that the only one who could help us would be Master Thịnh. My father had been so close to my former teacher that he used to stay with him, his wife, and their two children in Hà Nội.

With hope being my guiding light, I journeyed on. Sometimes when I allowed myself a good sleep, I'd go into a village and ask people to let us stay the night. I paid for it. There were plenty of thieves around, true, but many country people opened their doors to us. We slept on dirt floors, or, if we were lucky, in a nest made out of straw. Thinking back to those days, I miss the smell of dry rice straw. It was like perfume, the perfume of my sleep.

So I walked, and walked, and walked. I looked for Minh wherever I was, but there was never any sign of him.

I was exhausted at the end of each day. I experienced many moments of despair. Even now, sometimes in my dreams, I find myself marching with the bamboo pole braced across my shoulder, my baskets heavy, the road in front of me stretching until eternity. I wake with sweat dampening my back.

Once, on the way to a village, I broke down crying. Around me, rice plants began rustling their tiny, green hands. They were offering me their most soothing rice lullaby. I realized that whenever humans failed us, it was nature who could help save us.

I willed myself to be like nature, so I found myself singing, just like the rice plants. I sang to Sáng and to myself. I sang out loud and in silence. I was determined to sing on. I learned then that as long as I have my voice, I am still alive.

IT WAS DECEMBER 1955, two months after running away from my village, that I carried Sáng into the winter of Hà Nội. A drizzle blanketed the city. Everything was shrouded in a mysterious mist. I'd bought us each a thick winter jacket and a woolen scarf, but still, I was shivering.

Wrapping Mrs. Tú's cloth around my head, I felt the warmth of her love. I hoped our escape hadn't brought her trouble.

It was late in the afternoon when we arrived at a paved road edged with tall trees. A few houses stood desolate. Not a soul was in sight. How could I ask for directions to Silver Street, where Master Thịnh lived?

I looked up at the darkened sky. I'd covered Sáng's basket. He sat inside, bundled in warm clothes, poking his little head out.

"*Lửa.*" Sáng babbled, pointing toward a street corner, which had just come into view. Behind a tree, a circle of people huddled around a large bonfire. The fire crackled, raging against the wind and rain. I had to be that fire, raging against all odds.

I pressed forward, calling out my greeting to the group. As they turned, I halted in my steps. They were all men, all looking vicious. Anger and hunger glinted in their eyes.

Clutching the ropes that bound the baskets, I hurried away, my eyes on the slippery road. "Sit still," I told Sáng. I sensed that I had *tránh vỏ dưa gặp vỏ dừa*—dodged melon skin only to stumble on coconut shell.

"Hey, why are you leaving us so fast, Sister?" someone shouted. A chorus of laughter exploded. Not the friendly type of laughter.

Several men leaped onto the road, blocking my path. "I asked why you're leaving us," grunted a voice.

A man faced me. His eyes were hollow, his cheeks sunken, thin hair sticking to his skull. The stench of liquor rose from his filthy clothes.

He snatched the *nón lá* from my head. "Show me that beautiful face of yours." Mrs. Tú's carrying cloth fluttered onto the road.

I stepped back, clutching the ropes tighter, glancing down at Sáng. I had to protect my baby, no matter what. "Please . . . let me go. My husband and his friends are waiting for us."

"Oh, what a cute middle-region accent."

A yellow-toothed man leaned over at me. His bloodshot eyes pierced into mine. "Husband? Where? Where's the lucky bastard?"

I pointed straight ahead. My hand was shaking. I couldn't help it.

The men threw back their heads, laughing.

"She's afraid of you, Brother." A man with a mustache elbowed the yellow-toothed man.

"She's lying. Teach her a lesson," said another man. Cheers followed his voice.

Sáng started to cry. Someone had snatched away his hat. I picked my baby up, holding him against my chest. I rocked and hummed to him, but he was so frightened, he kept screaming.

"Brothers, please." Tears blurred my eyes. "You're scaring my son. Please, let us go."

"Tell him to shut up," someone snapped.

I rubbed Sáng's back. I tried to rest his face against my shoulder, but he turned away. His fearful cries rose higher.

Whap. A smacking noise. The yellow-toothed man had slapped Sáng. "Shut up, little monster!" he hissed.

I shielded my son with my bare hand. "You're a monster yourself to hit a child!" I screamed.

"Ah, a tigress," laughed a man. Something glimmered in his hand. A knife. Its tip glided under my scarf, pressing against my neck.

"Stop making a scene, or else," the man growled, his palm over my mouth.

Sáng quivered in my arms. I held him tight. As the men searched my clothes, I gritted my teeth. If I moved, they could harm my baby.

"Shit, this bitch is rich." They chuckled.

"Drop everything into these hats, idiot. It's not just for you," a voice barked.

Coins and notes were pulled out of my pockets. The coins and notes soaked with the sweat of my hard work and sorrow, the coins and notes that would bring me back to my children.

"This money is my life," I shouted, but my voice was a gurgle inside my throat.

"Stand still, bitch." The knife pressed hard against my neck. A sharp pain cut into me. "Stand still, or I'll slice your throat."

"Someone's coming," a voice whispered. "Hurry up, you idiots."

The mob snatched my bamboo pole and baskets. They started running away.

"Robbers. Help. Somebody help!" I hollered, but the men were disappearing into the mist. They even took Mrs. Tú's cloth with them.

Sáng was shaken but uninjured. I held him, sobbing into his chest.

Sounds of running footsteps. A group of women rushed toward us, each carrying a pair of baskets on a bamboo pole.

"Are you all right, Sister?"

"What happened?"

I searched my body but only emptiness met my fingers. "The robbers, they took all my money."

"I knew it." A woman thumped one end of her carrying pole onto the road.

"Hà Nội can be a dangerous place, Sister," another woman said. "Don't walk around on your own when it's getting dark."

I stood with Sáng on my waist, feeling like a tree without its roots. I was stupid beyond belief. I'd wasted all that time buying and selling, for all the earnings to be robbed. What would I do in this city, without any money?

Someone peeled a sweet potato and gave it to Sáng. He stopped crying, munching on it. My poor boy, he was hungry again.

There must have been fifteen women around us now. Sheets covered their baskets, from which the sweet smell of boiled yam, potatoes, and maniocs rose.

"I was selling fruits," I told the women. "The mob took away my baskets and pole."

"How terrible! What're you going to do?"

"I have to get to the Old Quarter, Sisters, to find Silver Street."

"But it's a long walk, and it's getting dark."

More mist had settled around us, concealing the road ahead. Drizzle cut across the cold air.

"Sisters, I need to get there tonight," I insisted. "Please, could you show us the way?"

The women stepped aside, putting their heads together. One of them came to me.

"We've decided to change our route. We'll take you to Silver Street."

"Are you . . . are you sure?"

"It's not a bad idea for us to try and sell there."

Life is great, Guava, because whenever I was put down, there were always kind people who picked me up.

IT WAS DARK when we got to the Old Quarter, a maze of lanes woven along old, slanting houses. I gazed up at bright streetlights atop metal poles. It was much busier here. Life spilled onto the pavement. People were cooking, washing, and drinking tea outside their homes, their voices soft whispers against the wind.

"Here you are. Silver Street. Good luck." One of the women pushed a bag into my hands. "Something from all of us. Just cheap sweet potatoes."

A knot expanded in my throat. Human kindness never ceased to amaze me.

Sáng waved his little hands. "Thank you, Aunties," I said on his behalf.

"Thank you, Aunties," repeated Sáng. The women waved back, giggling.

I took a deep breath. In front of me stood Silver Street and its hundreds of houses. Where could Master Thịnh's be?

I didn't know the address of my teacher's home. His parents used to be silversmiths, so his house had to have a silver shop. I stood in the middle of the road, looked both ways and decided to head in the direction where more lights were glowing.

"*Đẹp quá*—Oooh, pretty." Sáng pointed at magnificently lit doors and windows. Shops lined our path. Silver and gold jewelry glimmered under long glass counters. A few people were browsing, their bodies huddled inside thick winter jackets.

I stepped into a shop where a man sat behind a counter, working on a gold bracelet. He lowered his glasses, looking up at me.

"*Chào chú.*" I bowed in greeting. "I'm looking for my childhood teacher. Master Thịnh. Do you know him? His family lives here, on Silver Street."

"Master Thịnh?" The goldsmith wrinkled his already-creased forehead. "Didn't he leave Hà Nội for a while and teach in Nghệ An?"

"Yes, that's him! I'm his student from Nghệ An, Uncle."

"He used to be my elder brother's classmate." The goldsmith pulled the glasses away from his face. "But Master Thịnh . . . he died many years ago."

A cry escaped from deep inside my chest. So I would never have the chance to see my teacher again. Upon his leaving, he'd given Công and me half of his books. "You have a fierce will to learn. Keep it burning inside of you," he'd told us.

I begged the goldsmith with my eyes. "Uncle, I'd like to talk to Master Thịnh's family."

"They're no longer here. His wife and children moved south. They followed the French." He studied Sáng's face. "Are you looking for him to say hello, or is there something else?"

"Does he have relatives who still live around here, Uncle?"

"I don't know." He lowered his voice. "We're not supposed to keep in touch with those who migrated south, you know. They're our enemies now." He put back his glasses and resumed his work.

The news emptied my body of hope, and I thought I would crumble. I had made no alternative plans, how stupid. At that moment, my mother's voice echoed in my mind: *"Còn nước còn tát."* While there's still water, we will scoop.

"Uncle . . . do you think I can talk to the people who live at his house?" I asked.

"Well, good luck. It's four houses away from here, on this side of the street, the shop that has the *bàng* tree in front."

Out on the road, winter seeped back into my bones. I wrapped Sáng's scarf tighter around his neck. Whatever obstacles lay ahead, I needed to fight them to see my children again.

There it was, the shop that occupied the ground floor of Master Thịnh's house. I stood outside, dazzled by its bright glow.

Inside, a middle-aged woman emerged from a wooden staircase. "Hello, Sister," she called cheerfully. "Come on in. What are you looking for? A ring, bracelet, or necklace?"

I stepped forward, conscious of my broken sandals and my blistered feet on the spotless floor. Behind the counter, the woman smiled. Gold jewelry dangled from her ears and clattered on her wrists.

"Madam." I took a deep breath, "I used to be Master Thịnh's student. . . ."

The smile on the woman's face dropped. She scanned me from head to toe. "Master Thịnh died many years ago. Why are you looking for him?"

"Are you his relative, Madam?"

"That's none of your business!"

"Sorry, I didn't mean to pry. It's just . . . I can only discuss this with the relatives of my master."

"Spit it out then. I'm his niece." The woman picked up a cloth, flicking it against the glass counter, as if wanting to chase away bad luck.

"Madam, Master Thịnh was my teacher. He taught my brother and me for five years. He was my father's best friend. He lived with my family in Vĩnh Phúc Village—"

"So what? What do you want?" The woman knitted her brow. Her gaze shifted to Sáng, who was clinging to me, watching a large clock in the shape of a cat with a swaying tail on the wall.

"I beg you for a job, Madam. We had trouble with our business and lost our home. Master Thịnh would want his family to help. He was an uncle to us—"

"Uncle? Help?" The woman laughed. "How ridiculous! I'm not even sure you knew him."

"Is there a problem, Châu?" A man asked, coming down the stairs. His bushy eyebrows and bright eyes reminded me of my master.

"Hello, Sir." I bowed my head. "I used to be Master Thịnh's student in Nghệ An—"

"Trust no one these days, *anh* Toàn." The woman flicked her cloth. "Too many thieves around."

"But she does have the middle-region accent." The man stepped closer. "Uncle Thịnh used to tell me about Nghệ An. What's your name?"

"Diệu Lan." I was breathless. "My brother was Trần Minh Công and my parents Trần Văn Lương and Lê Thị Mận. Master Thịnh taught us from 1930 till 1935. He stayed with our family then. He could speak and write Chinese and French. He taught me the Nôm language. His full name was Đinh Văn Thịnh, he was born in the Year of the Dragon. He was an expert in playing the *đàn nhị* musical instrument."

"Yes, that's my uncle, the scholar." The man smiled.

I recalled what my master had said and remembered that his name, when put together with his younger brother's, meant prosperity. "Master Thịnh told us he had a younger brother named Vượng who continued the family tradition of making silver so he could teach."

"That's my father. You're truly Diệu Lan then." The man clasped his hands. "When did you get to Hà Nội, Sister?"

"Sister this and Sister that," said the woman. "We can't afford to give charity to everyone Uncle Thịnh knew."

The man ignored the woman. He pulled up a chair for me to sit down. "Diệu Lan, your father used to come here with his buffalo cart. Wasn't it 1942 when he didn't come anymore? My uncle was very much saddened."

"Yes, it was 1942. . . . My father was traveling to Hà Nội, he planned to see Master Thịnh but . . . but an accident killed him. Since then, terrible things have happened to us. I lost my mother, brother, and husband." I hated to cry, but my tears flowed, warming my cheeks. "Please, I beg you for a job. I can clean, cook, wash, help with any household chore."

The man closed his eyes for a moment then turned to the woman.

"Châu . . . you've been so stressed with the children. It'd be good to have some help."

"Help? How could she help with such a young son clinging to her shirt hẻm? Hire her and we'll have extra burdens."

"Madam, I'll find someone to care for my son." I didn't know whom but there should be a way. "I can do all types of housework. I'm good with children."

"I don't trust strangers," the woman said.

The man shook his head. "Diệu Lan, my apologies. I need to talk to my wife about this. Come back tomorrow afternoon, and I'll let you know."

"There's nothing to talk about," hissed the woman. "Haven't you heard about the Land Reform? She might be a rich landlord running away. Assist her and we'll be in trouble."

"Shut up," the man snapped. "Don't let evil people poison your mind."

I stood up to leave but didn't know where to go. Through the door, darkness looked like it harbored the men who'd just robbed me. In the hope that Master Thịnh's nephew would ask where I'd sleep, I sat down again, placing Sáng on my lap. I took off my scarf, wrapping it around his head. If we were to choose the pavement as our home, my baby had to stay warm.

"Hold on," the man exclaimed. "What happened to your neck, Diệu Lan? It's bleeding."

My hand crept up to my neck. I'd been too dazed by the robbery to notice the pain, which now sprang up under my touch. My fingers groped at a sticky liquid. Blood. Quite a lot of it. My scarf had concealed it from the women sellers and Mrs. Châu, but now, it must be quite a sight.

"*Ew,*" said the woman. "You didn't believe me, but can't you see, *anh* Toàn? She's indeed bringing us bad luck."

"You need to see Mr. Văn the healer. I'll take you," the man told me.

"No, you won't," said the woman. "Mrs. Chinh is picking up her earrings and they aren't ready yet."

"Madam is right, I can find my own way to Mr. Văn, Sir." I bowed to the man.

"He's a few hundred meters away from here." The man sighed and pointed to his right. "If you ask our neighbors, they'll show you the way to Kim Ngân Temple. He's the keeper there."

I headed for the door, dizzy. Even if I found the healer, would he treat me without any money?

I wandered through Silver Street, passing homes and shops filled with people and their happiness. My heart sobbed for my children. What a terrible mistake I'd made, walking to Hà Nội, to become a bird without its nest, a tree without its root.

When I found the temple, I went through the antique wooden doors of its entrance, through a spacious yard, and saw a man with white, long hair. His beard was also white, reaching his chest. Sitting cross-legged on the veranda, he was motionless; his eyes were closed, his back straight, his hands on his lap.

Sáng stayed in my arms, watching. After a long while, the man took a few deep breaths and opened his eyes. I came to him, my head bowed low. He nodded his greeting. His calmness reminded me of the wise men who always appeared in our fairy tales, to bring blessings to the unfortunate. My instincts told me he must be Mr. Văn.

"Uncle, I'm told you're a healer, but I don't have any money." When the words escaped my mouth, the shame made me feel as small as an ant.

"How can I help you, my child?"

I knelt, showing him my neck.

"That's a deep wound." Mr. Văn winced. He brought out his box of medicine and treated my injury. "Somebody cut you with a knife? What happened?"

"Robbers, Uncle, earlier today."

"You're lucky they caused you no other harm." He shook his head. "A young woman like you should know how to protect herself during these chaotic times."

WE SPENT THE night on the street. The air was cold but I was warm. Mr. Văn hadn't charged me for the treatment. I'd asked whether he knew someone who could babysit, and he'd taken me to the house of Mrs. Thự, one of his neighbors. She was an artisan, skilled at making paper animals. She agreed to look after Sáng in exchange for me cleaning her home and washing her clothes. Our agreement had to be kept a secret, of course.

It was barely after lunchtime when I arrived back at the shop, which looked even bigger and brighter than the night before. Master Thịnh's nephew was behind the counter.

"Hello, Sir," I greeted him.

He looked up. "Call me Toàn, please." He glanced toward the entrance, then lowered his voice. "My wife agreed for you to help, but please, stay out of sight when you're here. Don't come out unless you have to. If someone asks, pretend to be my cousin who visits for a few days. And if there's any hint of trouble . . ."

"Then I'll leave."

That afternoon, under the watchful eyes of Mrs. Châu, I cleaned the house, washed buckets of clothes, cooked dinner, and bathed the children who came home from school. I tried to keep a cheerful face, but Guava, darkness overwhelmed my every cell. Here I was, taking care of other people's children while I'd abandoned my own.

I worked twelve hours a day, every day of the week, except for half a day on Sunday. Mrs. Châu might have agreed to hire me at her husband's request, but she seemed to enjoy having me as *nô lệ*—a slave to boss around. And my salary was so small that I didn't have anything left after paying for a place to sleep at the back of the artisan's house, and after buying meager food for Sáng and me.

How could I ever set up a home and bring my children to Hà Nội?

I looked for a better job, but there were many unemployed people sitting on street corners, offering their labor for next to nothing. I tried to please my employers, hoping for a salary raise, but all I got from Mrs. Châu were complaints. I wanted to ask Mr. Toàn for help but didn't dare. News about the punishment of landlords was flooding into Hà Nội. Each village, each hamlet, and each town had been given a quota of how many rich landowners to denounce, beat, or execute. In poorer villages, even farmers with tiny pieces of land had been killed and their property taken away.

I wondered whether Mr. Toàn knew. Not once did he ask any questions. I think he was afraid of knowing the truth. I didn't blame him.

So, the days passed. As I did the chores, sang for and laughed with my employers' children, I ached. Sleep no longer came when the night arrived. I just lay there in darkness, thinking about Minh, Ngọc, Đạt, Thuận, and Hạnh, praying that they were okay, and that they were surviving. Fearful that I wouldn't be able to find my children again, I mapped out the locations where I'd left them on a piece of paper. I learned the map by heart and talked to Sáng every night about it, so maybe one day he could find his brothers and sisters if something happened to me.

Whenever I could, I wandered Hà Nội, looking for Minh. There were many times I ran after men on the street because they looked like him from behind. But my search only brought me sadness. If Minh wasn't here in Hà Nội, how could I ever find him again?

"Stay calm. Your fate will change. Be patient," I told myself, recalling what Nun Hiền had said. The star that predicted my fortune had been shifting, and soon I'd find a way.

When I returned to Kim Ngân Temple to thank Mr. Văn, I found out that he taught a self-defense class, for free.

I must tell you, Guava, that I detest violence. But life taught me that I must build up my inner strength and physical skills to defend not just myself, but also those around me.

So every Sunday afternoon I walked with Sáng to the temple, my baby practicing his steps along the way. Arriving at the temple yard, where the perfume of plumeria flowers lingered, I'd devote my full attention to being a student. Sáng would play happily on the verandah with the children of my classmates, or under the shades of tall plumeria trees.

My self-defense class turned out to be a great blessing. Having won many martial arts contests, Master Văn had developed a method of self-defense called Kick-Poke-Chop. The main idea is that when a man tries to punch you and harm you seriously, you back away, block his punches with your arms, gather your momentum, and then kick him straight in his groin. While he crouches down in pain, you grab his hair, knee him in his face, then use your arm to deliver a thundering chop to his neck.

Guava, here, let me show you. Yes, kick like that, but it has to be hard. Harder. Straight. Use the balls of your feet. There, good. Don't laugh. Do it again. Good! Now I'm crouching down in pain, what do you do? Yes, yes, grab my hair, pull my head down, and chop my neck. Like that. Yes, but it has to be hard. Let me teach you later properly, okay?

Master Văn's class helped my classmates and me toughen our arm muscles. We hit our arms against each other's repeatedly, and against tree trunks. We meditated to improve our ability to focus and stay calm during emergencies. We learned to think and act quickly.

Master Văn also taught us ways to deal with situations when our attackers had weapons. He showed us how to disarm those attackers and bring them to the ground. He made us practice so hard, we sweated furiously, our muscles screaming with pain. When he was confident I was good enough, he asked the men in my class to attack me with real knives and mock guns.

My mother used to say, "Good luck hides inside bad luck." That is so true. The robbers had stolen all my money, but it was the injury they caused that led me to Master Văn, and it was Master Văn who would help change my fate.

IT HAPPENED AROUND the end of February, 1956, nearly three months after my arrival in Hà Nội. I was cleaning the house of Mr. Toàn and Mrs. Châu. It was lunchtime, and the street was quiet. Coming out into the shop to sweep the floor, I saw a bulky man with his back to me. He was holding Mrs. Châu with one hand, his other hand pressing a knife against her neck.

"All your gold and silver. Into the bag. Quick! Make a noise and I'll slice her throat."

Behind the counter, Mr. Toàn looked as pale as a ghost.

"Fill the bag, hurry." The man pressed the knife harder against Mrs. Châu's neck. She screeched, but he brought his hand to her mouth. "Want to die, bitch?"

A brown bag had been left on the counter. Mr. Toàn started shoving jewelry into it.

As quiet as a cat, I moved to the robber's side. My fingers became powerful claws that clutched the robber's wrist, pulling it away from Mrs. Châu's neck, twisting it hard. My hours of training had given me tremendous power. The knife clattered to the floor.

The robber turned around to face me, just in time for me to poke my fingers into his eyes. Howling, he released Mrs. Châu, who ran to her husband. As the robber brought his hands to his face, I kicked straight into his groin, grabbed his hair, and delivered a thundering chop to his neck, sending him crashing to the floor.

Mrs. Châu was hysterical while I held the robber's hands behind his back, my knee pinning him down. I shouted for Mr. Toàn to find some rope. Blood had drained from the robber's face. He was lucky I hadn't used my full force to attack his eyes. I knew they hurt, but he wouldn't lose them.

The neighbors called the police, who took the robber away. Mr. Toàn and Mrs. Châu were so shocked, they closed their shop for the rest of the day. The next morning, when I came back to work, Mrs. Châu called me into her bedroom.

"Close the door," she told me. "Where did you learn to fight like that?"

"From Master Văn, the temple keeper, Madam."

"I see." She studied my face. "You're quite a fighter, Diệu Lan. There's no telling what somebody with your skills might be capable of. If you can bring down a big man like that, who's to say that you might not think of overpowering me in the same way? If you took it into your head to do it, you could probably beat me senseless."

I was stunned. "But . . . I rescued you. I saved your fortune."

"Yes, but saved for what? Who knows if you're planning to take it yourself. My husband is a very successful man. He'd be a fine catch for any woman. Especially for a poor destitute woman, down on her luck."

"That's not true, Madam." I remained polite but was very angry.

"Oh, come on, you think I'm stupid? I've seen the way he looks at you . . . and who can blame him? Those big eyes of yours, the smooth skin and long legs, those large breasts. I've also seen the way you flaunt yourself at him."

"That's ridiculous!"

"Oh yes, of course. Innocent little Diệu Lan. Wouldn't hurt a fly.

But I've seen the way he looks at you. I'm sure you know the old saying, *'Nuôi ong tay áo.'* I can't raise bees in my shirtsleeve. So, Diệu Lan, I have to let you go."

"You're firing me?"

"Let's just say I'm taking care of my family. Here's your final salary. Take it and never come back, or else I'll make your life miserable."

She threw a tiny cloth bag onto her bed. I bent to pick it up. It was light. What would I do with the few coins she'd given me?

Mr. Toàn was downstairs serving a customer when I quietly walked past him. I didn't say good-bye, to avoid more trouble with Mrs. Châu. She was a Hà Đông lion, a woman who's unreasonably jealous.

Back at my living quarters, I sat with Sáng on our straw mat. What would I do now, without a job? When would I be able to gather my children into my arms?

Sáng wriggled away, crawling toward the cloth bag, which I'd thrown onto the mat without any thought. As he pulled it open, some glittering metal coins fell out.

I held them up, gasping.

Mr. Giáp the goldsmith stared at me, his face full of questions after I'd showed him the coins. "Where did you get these?"

"Master Thịnh's relatives gave them to me, Uncle. Are they real?"

He narrowed his eyes at me. After asking his wife to look after the shop, he told me to wait outside, picked up the bag, and left in a hurry. I had no idea where he was going, but the furious look on his face stopped me from asking any question.

Out on the pavement, my insides felt like they were being roasted. If the coins were real gold and silver, my fate would be changed. But what if Mrs. Châu was playing games with me? I looked around. No sight of Mr. Giáp. It was a busy time of the day, people hurrying about.

Sáng reached for my face. "Mama, Mama," he babbled.

The Country Bumpkin Boy

Hà Nội, 1976

The shrill of cicadas rolled through the sky. The air swelled with summer blaze. Sweat streamed down my face. My schoolbag was a boulder on my back. I leaned forward, pedaling. I had to get home quick, to avoid the midday heat.

Grinding noises rang up from under my feet. I pushed against the pedals. An ominous snapping sound.

I led the bike up onto the pavement, leaning it against a tree. The chain had fallen away from both cogs, exposing jagged metal teeth.

I wriggled my hands through the frame, reaching for the chain, trying to lift it up. It refused to budge. Black oil clung to my skin. The sun beat relentlessly down on me. I pulled harder. Nothing happened.

"Need help?" I looked up to see Tâm, his face framed by a red canopy of flamboyant *phượng* flowers above him. I hadn't talked to him for months. My heart pounded.

I hid my black hands behind my back and mumbled my hello.

"Oh, I see. The chain." Tâm squatted down next to me and studied the bike.

Men are bad, a voice in my head said. *Don't let yourself fall for Tâm.*

You can like him, argued another voice. *He's as kind and generous as your father, Uncle Đạt, and Uncle Thuận.*

I stayed glued to the pavement as Tâm stood up, walked away, and came back with a twig. He broke it into two. "Try not to use your fingers next time." A smile lingered in his eyes. "This oil is hard to get rid of."

He rolled up the sleeves of his shirt. I found myself gazing at the muscles of his arms. I wondered if he'd gained his muscles by hoeing in the ricefields. In a swift movement, Tâm flipped the bike upside down and lifted the chain with the two halves of the twig. He released the part that was stuck, slipping the chain back onto its cogs.

"I fix bikes with my uncle in the afternoon." Tâm spun the pedal. "This chain is much too loose. It'll give you trouble again."

"Happened twice this week." Heat rushed into my face. The girls in my class had been whispering about Tâm. Quite a few of them had a crush on him. I wondered if he knew.

Tâm returned the bike to its wheels. "Let's get it fixed then." He looked straight ahead, his face suddenly brightened. "See over there?"

Squinting, I saw a man a distance away from us. He was squatting on the pavement, hunching over something that looked like a tin basin. "A bicycle repairman?"

Tâm grinned and nodded. He pushed my bike. We walked side by side. A cool breeze rushed at us, unfolding a sweet fragrance. Across the road, giant leaves and pink flowers brimmed a pond. Lotus. Why hadn't I noticed them before?

"You seem to have settled down well." I tucked a hair lock behind my ear, hating myself for trying to charm Tâm.

"I really like it here. Can't believe it's already five months."

Five months. It'd been that long since I guided him around our school. We may not have talked but I'd seen him watching me.

"I'm glad your mother returned to her job as a doctor at Bạch Mai, and your Uncle Đạt is getting better," Tâm said.

"But how . . . how do you know?"

"I've been asking about you, of course. Any news from your father?"

I shook my head.

"You know . . . I was hoping to run into you, so we could talk."

"About what?"

"Well, you don't remember the many things we talked about?"

I turned away, hiding my smile. I couldn't tell him that everything we'd said to each other was like a song that kept rolling over and over in my mind.

The repairman was an elderly person whose hair looked like a puff of cloud that had fallen down from the sky. He was holding the pumped-up inner tube of a bicycle tire, dipping it into a water basin. A lady sat next to him, watching. She gasped when a stream of bubbles popped up from the tube, rising to the surface.

"That's a big hole, no wonder you got a flat tire," the man told the lady. He pushed a toothpick against the bubbles and into the tube. "I'm just marking the hole and will fix it later. Let's see if there's another one."

I'd expected to wait for the repairman, but Tâm asked whether he could borrow some of his tools.

"Help yourself." The man gestured toward a metal box.

Tâm dropped his school bag onto the pavement. Sweat rolled down his face as he peeled the chain away, shortened it, and put it back. He turned the pedal, listening to the smooth sound the bike now made, his head nodding. He tightened the brakes, checked the tires and gave them some air with a hand pump.

"He looks like an expert. Where did you find him?" the repairman asked me. He'd started a fire and was using a pair of metal chopsticks to heat up a piece of rubber.

"Tâm is my classmate." I felt my face getting redder.

"You two look like a fine couple." The lady winked.

"Couldn't agree more," the repairman said as he placed the tube, which was now empty of air, onto a wooden board. He removed the toothpick, sealing the hole with the heated rubber patch. Placing a piece of flat metal on top, he hammered it down a few times before dipping the tube into the basin. The water sizzled, sending a curl of smoke and steam upward.

I pretended to watch him, hoping Tâm hadn't heard what the lady had said about us being a couple.

"Done." Tâm let my bike rest on its kickstand. He returned the tools to the repairman and helped him put the tire back on the lady's bicycle.

"Thank you, young man." The repairman looked impressed.

"What a nice boy." The lady leaned toward me. "Don't let him out of your sight."

The repairman lifted his water can, but it appeared to be empty. "Over there." He gestured toward the lotus pond. "Plenty of water to wash your hands."

I wished I could pick up Tâm's bag. With my black hands, I stood there like an idiot as the lady looped the bag strap around his shoulder. He thanked her and turned to me. "Shall we?"

With Tâm leading my bike, we crossed the road to reach the pond's bank. A distance away from us, behind a ring of rippling water, the lotus stretched out, their flowers opening to the wind.

Tâm leaned my bike against an ancient tree. Dropping his bag onto the grass, he squatted on the bank, which rose high above the pond's surface. He bent forward, scooping up some water to wash his hands.

I let go of my bag, too, wishing I could follow Tâm but fearing I'd fall into the pond. It looked deep, and I didn't know how to swim.

"Come, wash your hands," Tâm said. Before I could answer, he splashed a handful of water at me.

I took a few steps back. "Don't . . ."

Tâm chuckled, bent down and scooped up another handful. I ran—and tripped on a large, protruding tree root.

"Hương!" Tâm cried. He rushed to me. "Are you hurt?"

I giggled, trying to get back to my feet. Tâm held out his hands and pulled me up. His strength caused me to almost crash into him. His scent made my heart miss a beat. We were so close now. I could feel his breath on my face.

"It's my turn," I said. Tâm's eyes flew open as my hands smeared the oil onto his cheeks. I swirled around and started running. Tâm caught me by my waist, holding me back.

I laughed. Tâm pulled me toward him, his chest brushing against my back.

We faced each other. I lowered my gaze to avoid his eyes. A new and powerful sensation swept through me. We stood in silence, the wind above our heads.

"I . . . I have to go." I pulled myself away from him, my whole body tingling. "It must be late and I must . . ."

"Come wash your hands." Tâm took my arm, leading me back to

the pond. There, he scooped up water and rubbed the oil away from my skin. When he was done, I bent, dipping my handkerchief into the water. With Tâm next to me, I was no longer afraid of falling.

Tâm closed his eyes as I brought the handkerchief to his face. Tenderly, I wiped away the black marks.

He opened one eye to look at me, his mouth lifting into a radiant smile. "Help me with something?"

"What?" I tried to avoid staring at his long eyelashes and his full lips.

"Hold my hand?"

"Huh?"

He pointed at a lotus flower just away from our reach. Then he gestured at the protruding root of the ancient tree. "And hold on to that?"

"But . . . are you sure it's allowed?"

He shrugged, smiled, and gave me his hand.

I grabbed the root. My other hand clutched Tâm's hand. "Be careful."

Holding tight to me, Tâm stretched his body out to the water. I closed my eyes, not wanting to see him fall. I didn't think he could reach the flower, but when I sneaked a look, the pink petals were trembling against his chest.

He offered the flower to me. "For the most charming and most intelligent girl."

I hid my smile behind the lotus, its fragrance stealing my breath.

"Hey. You thieves!" Angry shouts sprang up somewhere out on the water. I turned to see a man in frantic motions. He was rowing a sampan toward us. "My flowers!"

"Oops." Tâm pulled me up. As I hurried to grab our bags, slinging them over my shoulder, Tâm picked up my handkerchief. He rushed my bike across the grass and onto the road.

"Sorry, Uncle," Tâm called over to the boatman. "This flower, it's the first one I ever picked for a girl. Forgive me, please."

I wasn't sure if the boatman heard Tâm. He was still rowing furiously, shouting along the way. Tâm hopped onto my bike. I jumped on behind him.

Holding on to his waist, my fingers burned as they felt the muscles through his shirt. Tâm raced us through the streets, navigating through traffic. "You alright?"

"Sure." I giggled, the flower nesting against my chest.

Our laughter rose up together. Around me, summer was in full bloom. Something blossomed inside me, too.

"So now . . . where to?" Tâm asked.

"Oh, no! What time is it?" How could I have forgotten that Uncle Đạt was alone and needed my help? "I should hurry home."

"I'll take you there."

Tâm already knew the maze that made up the roads of Hà Nội. He found a shortcut that took us to Khâm Thiên.

It had been a long time since a friend visited my home. Wanting to show Tâm off to Thủy, I looked hard when we passed her house. No sight of her. She'd dropped out of school and taken a job stringing bamboo curtains for a cooperative.

I opened our door to see Grandma standing there. "Where have you been?" Wrinkles deepened on her face.

"Chào bà." Tâm bowed his greeting.

She nodded, eyeing him, not a single word escaping her lips.

Tâm turned to me. "See you tomorrow."

"Who's that?" Grandma asked as I pushed my bike inside.

"I wish you were more friendly, Grandma. Couldn't you have invited him in?"

"I don't know who he is. And where did you go?"

"Can't I have friends?" I threw my schoolbag onto the floor, holding on to the lotus. For sure Tâm disliked me now.

"Hương is right, Mama," Uncle Đạt said from his wheelchair. "She's a big girl. Give her some freedom." He smiled at me. "That's a nice flower."

"Glad someone noticed." I gave it to him.

He gestured at the table. "Eat, the food's getting cold."

I dived into the plates and bowls, knowing that I should wash my hands first. But Tâm's touch still felt soft on my skin; I wanted it to stay.

Grandma rummaged the cupboard for a vase. "A female friend would be better for your age, Hương."

"He's a classmate, Grandma." I rolled my eyes.

"How come I haven't seen him before? And that middle-region accent of his . . ."

"He moved a couple of months ago from Hà Tĩnh Province."

"That's not too far from our home village." Uncle Đạt inhaled the lotus's perfume. "Men from Hà Tĩnh are known to be honest and hard-working."

I smiled at my uncle, glad that he was on my side.

"We'll see about that." Grandma put the vase and the lotus onto the table. She poured me a glass of water. "As I was saying, Đạt, I asked Hạnh to rerun the search notice in the newspapers. Hopefully your brother Minh will see it."

"You think he's in the South, Mama?"

"I'm sure." Grandma turned to me. "Your aunt ran search notices for your father, too. She'll let us know as soon as there's any news."

I nodded, reminding myself to write more often to my aunt. Our proverb said "*Xa mặt cách lòng*—Distant faces, faded hearts," but Auntie Hạnh had stayed close despite more than a thousand kilometers between us.

After I'd cleared away the plates and bowls, Grandma put a large basket onto the table, unloading pieces of flattened rubber tires.

Uncle Đạt struggled but managed to swing himself into a dining chair. For months he'd been training his arms, lifting heavy weights. I wished the artificial legs would arrive soon. Grandma had sold the piglets and gathered all her savings, as well as money from Auntie Hạnh and my mother. My uncle had gone to have his stumps measured, but it was taking longer than we'd hoped for the legs to be ready. With so many injured soldiers, the demand for artificial limbs was too high.

We pushed the chair closer to the table. Uncle Đạt leaned his upper body forward, reaching into the basket. He held up a pair of large scissors. Grandma picked up a cardboard piece in the shape of a sandal's base, placing it on top of a rubber chunk.

"Oh yeah." Uncle Đạt started cutting.

"What's all this?" I asked.

"Your old uncle got a job." Uncle Đạt grinned. "Making sandals. Cool, right?"

"For the Thuận Việt Cooperative," Grandma added, and I understood. Uncle Đạt's only pair of rubber sandals had survived his tough six-month walk through the jungles. These sandals were sturdy, cheap, and getting more and more popular.

"As easy as eating porridge," he said. "I used to fix them all the time."

Uncle Đạt's breath no longer stank of liquor. Giving it up was not easy for him, though. He'd told us to throw out all of the liquor, only to search the kitchen, screaming when he found none. There had been days when he stayed in bed, refusing to talk. Luckily, Miss Nhung had been there whenever he needed her most. They spent a long time together in his room, and Grandma told me not to disturb them.

Sometimes I heard soft moans coming through the closed door and felt myself blushing. I imagined Uncle Đạt and Miss Nhung kissing, the way I wanted to kiss Tâm.

Thinking about Tâm, my body grew hot. When would I get to talk to him again? I'd had doubts about him, but Uncle Đạt had said that men from Hà Tĩnh were honest. Honesty was what I needed most in a friend.

"I must get back to work," said Grandma. "If you make a mistake, Đạt, don't worry. These tires are cheap."

"My sandals will be better than theirs, let me assure you." Uncle Đạt's eyes stayed fixed to the scissors.

"Be careful on the road, Grandma." I pushed her bike out to the lane. I didn't like how bossy she was but knew she was watching out for me.

"I'll be back late. There's not much food left, but we still have some dry fish."

I tested the bike's brake. "Dry fish is perfect, Grandma. I'll cook tonight."

A SHOWER BLANKETED the afternoon. My mother came home, a trembling leaf. I pulled her into our room, where her bed lay next to mine and Grandma's. I helped dry her and urged her to change; my throat tightened as I watched how her ribs protruded. Her nightmares had come roaring back. During the night, Grandma and I took turns staying by her side, holding her as she shook violently, screaming.

And I wished I could hug her so hard, to squeeze out all the terrible memories.

But my mother didn't let me pity her. As soon as she was dressed, she picked up my comb, untangling my hair. She asked me about school and told me about her day. She was glad to feel useful again. Her hospital was struggling with too many patients, few doctors, and even less medicine. There was much to do, and she regretted all the months she'd wasted by staying home, getting angry with everyone, and blaming herself.

In the evening, Miss Nhung came and sat with Uncle Đạt at the dining table. He convinced her to join him in making rubber sandals, for extra income for herself. When I took a break from my studies and went to the kitchen, I saw a pair of brand-new sandals in front of them. They were working on another pair now, he talked and she listened, laughing softly.

I went back to my books, back to the lotus flower, whose petals glowed like Tâm's face.

My mother was on her bed, sorting out different types of dried roots, fruits, barks, flowers, stems. She put them into bags, labeling them.

I brought her a glass of water.

"These just arrived from the Institute of Traditional Medicine." She indicated the bags. "I've been studying about them and need to get licensed."

"Licensed for what, Mama?"

"For practicing herbal medicine." She drank the water.

"You're already a brilliant doctor. For sure your knowledge of Western medicine will help?"

"Yes, once we know how the human organs function, we can better cure them with medicinal plants."

I nodded, picked up a root, sniffing it. A sweet scent lingered in my nostrils, but I knew it'd taste unpleasant. A few weeks earlier, I'd had a bad flu, and my mother brewed me a pot of herbal remedy. I recovered fast but would never want to drink a sip of that black liquid again. I shuddered at the memory of its taste.

"Somehow you look quite different today." My mother grinned, her dimples deepening on her cheeks. "Your face glows. . . . Is there something you'd like to tell me?"

"Oh, Mama," I moaned in embarrassment.

"You don't have to say anything." She lifted a tiny scale, weighing some brown bark, putting it into a bag. "You just look so happy, I thought I should ask."

I nodded. "I'm very happy. The happiest in a long time, Mama."

"Good."

"I'm happy because you're home, and Uncle Đạt is getting better."

"And because of some boy?" My mother continued to smile.

I thumped her back with my fist, hiding my face behind my palms. "Is it written all over my face?"

"Yes, it is." She giggled. "I was your age once, remember?"

"He . . ." I hesitated. "He's the one who gave me the lotus flower."

"He did?"

"He repaired my bike, Mama."

"Ah. A handyman, like your father."

"That's why I like him, I think. Just like Papa, he knows how to make me laugh."

"Tell me more about him then."

"Well . . . he's the same age as me. Sixteen. His name is Tâm." I liked how Tâm's name sounded on my lips. "Mama, please, don't tell anyone."

"Sure, I promise." My mother pulled me into her arms. "It's a wonderful secret. I'm so glad you told me."

WHEN I WENT to school the next day, I was hoping to talk to Tâm, but some of my classmates had seen him helping me with the bike, and everyone was making fun of us.

"Tâm and Hương are a couple. Hương and Tâm are a couple," they chanted. They whispered and laughed. I felt awkward. Tâm must have been embarrassed, too. After class, he walked home with a group of boys. For several days, I cycled past them, longing to stop and talk to him but didn't dare to.

I tried to focus on my end-of-year exams. No matter what I did, Tâm's face still appeared in my mind; so did his deep voice and his laughter. I realized that I missed him. As the days dragged on, I resented him, for making my mind wander, for creating this big hole of emptiness inside of me, the hole I didn't know how to fill.

Time crawled by. A week passed; the lotus flower had withered; I gathered the fallen petals, dumping them into the trash. I changed my route going home, to avoid seeing Tâm and his friends.

Tonight, at my desk, I opened my notebook. In front of me was a difficult math question I had to crack.

A knock at the door. Miss Nhung came in. "Hương, a boy is here to see you. Said his name is Tâm."

"Oh." I jumped to my feet. "Tell him to wait, Auntie."

I leaned against the door, dizzy. Hurrying to my closet, I pulled out my favorite shirts. I picked one up, tossed it aside and chose another one. I put it on, only to change my mind.

I went out to the living room. Tâm wasn't there. Perhaps I'd taken such a long time that he left? Uncle Đạt and Miss Nhung sat in our oil lamp's light, talking and working on the sandals, looking like lovebirds.

Grandma came to me. "He's outside."

"Did you give him a hard time?" I stared at her.

"No, but please—"

I raised my hand and headed for the door.

Under the *bàng* tree, Tâm stood, his hands behind his back. He was tall, taller than I'd remembered. Moonlight scattered around him, glowing on his face.

"Hi, Hương," he said.

"Hello." I stepped toward him, my arms and legs too clumsy, I didn't quite know what to do with them.

"Yours." On his palm was my handkerchief, clean and folded into a rectangle. "It still smells like the lotus . . ."

"Keep it if you like," I said, surprised at my offer.

"A gift?" Tâm grinned. "Then in return, I need to give you something." He drew his other hand out from behind his back. Lotus flowers. A bunch of them, magnificent and half-opened. "Had to go back to the boatman. Bought these in exchange for his forgiveness."

"You're incredible." I laughed. The lotus nestled their budding promises against me. I forgave Tâm, too, for not talking to me during the entire week.

We stood in silence. I looked down at the flowers, admiring them.

"You said I could borrow some books." Tâm smiled at me.

I nodded, glad that he remembered. The more he borrowed, the more reasons I'd have to talk to him again. "Come inside. I have quite a few for you to choose from."

"If you don't mind, I'll just wait out here. . . . How about lending me three of your favorites?"

"What if you've read them before?"

"Then I'll read them again."

Indoors, I handed Grandma the lotus. "He gave me these so I'd loan him some books. You may not know him, but he's an avid reader."

She arched her eyebrows.

I ran to the bookshelf.

"*War and Peace* by Leo Tolstoy?" Tâm said when I gave him the first. "I've heard so much about this."

"Tell me what you think when you finish reading. It's long." I showed him the other two. "Not sure you'll like these though."

"Oh, love poems by Xuân Quỳnh and Nguyễn Bính? They're my favorite poets."

"Now . . . don't try so hard to be nice. Not everybody likes poetry, I know. I can change them for fiction if you want."

"No, no." Tâm's eyes were sincere. "I like poetry, really. Love poems suit my mood for now."

"Oh." Heat rushed to my face, and I had to look away.

"Sorry, Hương," Tâm whispered. "Our classmates . . . I want to talk to you every day in class but don't want to embarrass you."

"You won't embarrass me." I gazed up at him, dazed. "I'm glad you're my friend."

"Me, too." Tâm smiled.

"I think you should know something." I bit my lip. "My grandma is a trader."

"So our classmates said."

"Did they warn you against visiting me, too?" Bitterness rose up in my throat.

"Well, I don't care," he said firmly. "People have the right to trade."

I'd heard no one talk like Tâm. During class time, my teachers had been denouncing traders and capitalists, saying that they were *cặn bã của xã hội*—dregs of society that had to be mopped away.

We walked side by side on the neighborhood lane, he carried the novel and I the two poetry books. The sky had absorbed the sun's heat and released its stars. A full moon spilled light onto our path.

"Where do you live, Tâm?"

"In Đống Đa Quarter."

"That's far away."

"Not too far, and walking does me good."

Several kids ran up to us, dashing through the narrow gap between Tâm and me. They galloped away, dragging their laughter with them.

I smiled, shaking my head. I used to do the same, making fun of couples.

"I've been thinking about your father," Tâm said, "and about the bird he carved for you. He must be a very special person."

I nodded and told Tâm how dear my father was to me. I talked about Uncle Đạt's journey through the war and how he'd brought the Sơn ca back to me. I talked about Uncle Thuận's death, my mother returning from the war, Grandma's job, and Uncle Sáng's strange behavior.

"I'm sorry," Tâm told me. "It's even more incredible to me now, how good you are at school despite all of that."

"I'm not that good. I should study harder."

"Don't you believe it." Tâm's shoulder pushed playfully against mine. "The math test yesterday, you're the only one who got a perfect mark."

"You didn't do too badly yourself. You got ninety-eight percent."

"I wish our teachers would stop reading our marks aloud." Tâm sighed. "They embarrass those who don't do so well."

"I know."

"Want to know something else, Hương?"

"What?"

"The boys in our class say you intimidate them by your good grades."

"That can't be true."

"Yeah, that's what they say. But I think they're wrong. You're not intimidating at all, on the contrary. . ." Tâm left his words hanging in mid-air.

We'd turned back, and now I found us standing under the *bàng* tree. Some minutes of silence passed.

"You should go in," said Tâm. "We don't want your grandma to worry."

I nodded and gave him the books. His fingers brushed against mine.

"Good night," he whispered. "Sweet dreams."

The look on his face was so tender that I turned and fled.

Grandma asked countless questions about Tâm, and when I said he was very good at math, she softened a bit. Still, she told me not to go any place where the two of us could be alone.

"You think I'll let bad things happen to me, the way they've happened to my mother, Grandma?" I fumed.

"Oh Hương, you're young and the world is complicated. Just be careful, please."

"I *am* careful. And you need to trust me, Grandma."

"Darling, I trust you, but other people have to earn my trust."

GRANDMA HAD LEARNED about my mother and Uncle Sáng's fight. She'd stopped sending food for a while, but as Auntie Hoa's pregnancy advanced, she didn't want the baby to go hungry.

Two evenings a week, when my mother was on her night shift, I was on duty, bringing food to Uncle Sáng's apartment. Though my uncle knew Grandma was sometimes waiting downstairs, he never invited her up. He acted as if it was our responsibility to supply him food. He never asked about Uncle Đạt, whom he'd only seen once at a tea stall. Miss Nhung had arranged the meeting, from which Uncle Đạt came back seething. He said Uncle Sáng was stuffed with propaganda rubbish.

It seemed that among the siblings, Uncle Sáng was the luckiest.

He'd emerged from the war okay. When Grandma escaped from her village, she hadn't had to leave him behind.

"Mama spoiled Sáng," Uncle Đạt told my mother. "If you think about it, she always had a soft spot for him, her youngest son."

Uncle Đạt was right. Uncle Sáng had had plenty of time to bond with Grandma on her long walk to Hà Nội, and he used that bond to manipulate Grandma.

I disliked seeing Uncle Sáng and felt relieved when Tâm started to accompany me on the food-delivery trips. His uncle had bought him an old bicycle, and he overhauled it, fixing a soft cushion onto its back. I got to sit behind him as he rode his bike into the evenings. We chatted along the way, and I learned about his family. His parents were farmers. They worked hard to send him to Hà Nội to live with his uncle so he could prepare himself better for university. Tâm had a younger sister who wanted to outdo him in everything. Of his grandparents, only his mother's father was still around. He was a difficult man, who was ill and preferred to be alone, in his room. Tâm wondered whether his grandfather was crazy. Sometimes he'd overheard the old man weeping and mumbling to himself.

"Perhaps something bad happened to him? Did you try to talk to him?" I said, thinking about my mother after her return.

"I did, but he called me by all types of names. He even tried to beat me up."

"How terrible! Did you ask your mother why he's so unhappy?"

"She doesn't have much to tell. He's never let her get close to him. It's hard to believe she's come from such a man. She's totally the opposite."

Tâm went on to say he missed his parents and sister but felt lucky to be living with his uncle. His uncle's wife had died several years ago, and the kind man had never looked at another woman since.

"My uncle told me true love only happens once in your life," Tâm said.

I thought about Uncle Đạt and Miss Nhung and the blossoming of their love. The artificial legs had finally arrived. Uncle Đạt had hated them at first, but with Miss Nhung's help, he learned how to use them.

"Uncle Đạt doesn't drink anymore," I told Tâm. "Miss Nhung visits him every night to make sandals and talk."

"They're a good team, just like us, don't you think?"

"I don't know." I thumped his back, blushing.

"TAY EM TÊM trầu, lá trầu cay xứ Nghệ . . ." Grandma's singing voice filled the kitchen with light. This folk song, about a girl inviting her visitors to eat betel quid, used to be my mother's favorite. I stole a glance at my mother, hoping she'd at least hum along. No sound escaped her lips. It seemed her silky voice had been robbed from her.

Uncle Đạt walked to the dining table, looking tall and manly. The gauntness on his face had disappeared, replaced by a healthy glow.

"Looking good." Grandma poured steaming vegetables into a big bowl set on the table. "You're doing well, Son. Just in time for the engagement party."

"What?" I gasped.

"Haven't you heard, Hương?" My mother lowered the rice pot onto the table. "Đạt and Nhung are getting engaged."

I rushed to my uncle, embracing him.

"Hey, easy, easy." My uncle laughed, putting his hands on my shoulders to keep his balance. "I'm very happy, and so thankful."

My mother pulled up a chair and helped my uncle sit down.

"To be honest, I was afraid Nhung's parents would say no." Grandma distributed the chopsticks. "Turned out the girl had done lots of convincing. We have our ancestors' blessings." She looked up at our family altar, where incense sticks were smoldering, spreading fragrance around the room.

"Still can't believe my luck," my uncle said. "For so long, I didn't dare to think Nhung would want to see my face again."

"You underestimated her, Son." Grandma ladled rice into our bowls.

"I guess I did," my uncle said, nodding. "Do you think Sister Hạnh will be able to come to the party, Mama?"

"I need to write her. I know she wants to see you and celebrate with us."

I wondered when we'd be able to visit my aunt in Sài Gòn. Her family was doing well; Uncle Tuấn had become a senior army officer.

"I hope Tuấn isn't involved in those reeducation camps or in punishing Southerners." Grandma sighed. "Northerners or Southerners, we're all Vietnamese. I wish that everyone could now live in peace."

"You think," whispered Uncle Đạt, "that Brother Minh might be in one of those camps? If he went to the South, he might have fought alongside the Americans."

"I'm sure he didn't." My mother put fried spinach into my bowl. "He knew we would be drafted. He wouldn't want to fight against us."

"What if he was drafted himself? What if he had no choice but to fight?"

"I don't care what Minh did," said Grandma. "I don't care, as long as he's alive. But I have to find him, otherwise I won't be able to close my eyes when death comes and takes me."

"We'll find him, Mama," said Uncle Đạt. "And now the war has ended, he'll look for us."

"I just telexed Mr. Hải again, he'll let us know once Minh sends any news to our village," said Grandma.

Uncle Đạt turned to me. "Someone looks very happy these days. Something wonderful is definitely blossoming."

I swallowed my rice, not knowing what to say.

"Tell Tâm to come in," said Grandma. "You two can talk here, you don't have to wander around the streets."

"You mean it, Grandma?" I grabbed her hand.

"What choice do I have?" She shrugged. "When your granddaughter is *ngang như cua*, you have to give in."

I grinned. "Yes, you're right, Grandma. I'm stubborn as a sideways-walking crab, but I learned it from someone."

My mother burst out laughing.

"Plenty of stubborn crabs in this family." My uncle chuckled.

GRANDMA LOOKED NERVOUS. She was pacing back and forth in front of the National Hospital of Obstetrics, sweat drenching the back of her shirt.

"How is she? How's the baby?" she asked as soon as she saw me.

"Auntie Hoa is still in labor. I haven't been able to see her yet." I handed the empty tin containers back to her. How cruel that Uncle Sáng forbade Grandma to come up. He'd said that his colleagues would be visiting and he'd risk losing his job. How ridiculous.

"Still in labor? But it's been ages. Do you think she's all right?"

I shrugged. Only Uncle Sáng could talk to the doctors. I hadn't seen him. It was his assistant who'd returned the tin boxes, telling me to bring more of Grandma's porridge.

"This is insane!" Grandma's shout startled me. She lifted the containers. My eyes popped open as she flung her arms in the air, sending the boxes crashing down onto the pavement. "I can't stand this a minute more." She walked away.

"Where're you going, Grandma?"

"To see Hoa, and to tell Sáng enough is enough."

The corridor was filled with people. No sign of my uncle or his assistant. Grandma stopped a hurrying nurse. "My daughter-in-law is giving birth. Nguyễn Thị Hoa. Where is she, please?"

"Nguyễn . . . Thị . . . Hoa?" The nurse went through her list. "In the operating room." She pointed toward the end of the corridor.

"Operating room? Is there something wrong?" Grandma's words came out as a yell.

"It's an emergency." The nurse hurried past us.

I pulled Grandma's arm. Racing past people who lay and sat in the corridor, we arrived in front of the operating room as three men dressed in white medical gowns emerged. They looked tense, whispering to each other.

Grandma dashed past the men, toward the closing door.

"Hey, where do you think you're going?" someone shouted.

"I'm her mother-in-law." Grandma pushed against the door, charging in. I followed her.

The strong stench of medicine hit my nostrils. Auntie Hoa was on a bed, her hands on her face. Uncle Sáng was standing beside her, his back to us.

At the sound of our footsteps, my uncle turned. I'd expected him to scorn Grandma, but his face was twisting. "Oh, Mama!" he cried.

"Is the baby all right?" Grandma ran to the bed.

Arriving at her side, I cupped my mouth with my hand. Was that a baby next to Auntie Hoa? Its head was at least three times the size of its chest. Its forehead bulged out. It had no arms or legs.

"No. No. *No!*" Grandma picked the baby up, holding it against her chest. The baby didn't move or make a sound. It was lifeless.

Uncle Sáng wrapped Grandma in his arms. He buried his head in her hair, his muffled cries cutting through my heart.

I knelt down next to Auntie Hoa. She looked terrified. I took her hand into mine. I wanted to hug her, but she quietly turned away from me.

LATER, IN AN office where piles of documents were stacked on top of a cluttered desk, an old doctor told Grandma and Uncle Sáng that he was sorry.

"Where did you fight during the war, Comrade?" he asked my uncle.

"Mainly in Quảng Trị. Why, Doctor?"

"Quảng Trị, I see. Were you exposed to Agent Orange?"

Uncle Sáng stood up, walking to a wall. His shoulders began to shake. Grandma ran to him. When my uncle turned back to the doctor, his face was white.

"Agent Orange? I felt it many times on my face. It drenched my clothes. That chemical, wasn't it meant to destroy the trees?"

The doctor rose up from his chair. "We're not sure yet how Agent Orange affects people. But many veterans who were exposed to it have had dead or deformed children."

Uncle Sáng beat his fists against the wall. Grandma reached for his hands, pulling them back.

This couldn't be happening to our family. What about Uncle Đạt and Auntie Nhung? What would happen to their children?

A FEW DAYS later, we sat around the dining table. Uncle Sáng looked haggard, a bag of clothes in front of him.

"Can't believe she asked you to move out," said Uncle Đạt.

"Things hadn't been going too well between us. And now, whenever she looks at me, she sees the Agent Orange Devil, you know. . . ."

The *bàng* scratched its branches against our roof. Would the ghosts of war ever release us from their grip?

"The areas where I fought were heavily sprayed." Uncle Đạt sounded like he was about to cry.

Auntie Nhung reached for his hands, bringing them to her lips. Tears glimmered in her eyes. "We'll raise our child, regardless of what happens."

"Don't worry, Đạt," said my mother. "People react to chemical exposure very differently. Many war veterans have had normal, healthy children." She shifted her gaze to Auntie Nhung. "My hospital is going to import an ultrasound machine. It can let us know about problems before the baby is born."

Auntie Nhung took Uncle Đạt's face into her hands. "Have you heard Sister Ngọc? We're going to be fine. Whatever happens, we'll deal with it together, okay?"

Tears rolled down Uncle Đạt's cheeks.

Grandma blew her nose. "Sáng, I'm glad to have you home."

"I'll only trouble you with this one night, Mama. Tomorrow I'll find somewhere else to stay."

"This is your home, Sáng! It's warmer with you here. You don't need to go anywhere else."

Uncle Sáng cast his eyes around the room. He looked *căng như dây đàn*—stressed like taut guitar strings. "This lavish lifestyle . . . I can't." He lowered his voice. "Please, don't tell anyone I'm staying here tonight. I'll leave before dawn tomorrow."

My mother shook her head. I'd seen her grieve for Uncle Sáng's baby, but she hadn't spoken to him since the argument. She was so right about him: he'd sold us for some political ideology.

"Fine." Grandma sighed. "Can I ask you for just one thing, Sáng? You have many connections in the South. Could you use them to find your brother Minh?"

"There's no proof that he's gone south."

"If he were still here, he'd have come back to our village by now. Please, do it for me."

"Looking for him is like searching for a needle on the ocean's floor. I can't promise, but I'll see what I can do."

I no longer trusted Uncle Sáng. If Uncle Minh was found in the South, he would crash the career ladder Uncle Sáng was hoping to climb.

I WAS STUDYING when my mother came to my desk, with Uncle Đạt behind her. She combed my hair with her fingers. "Hương, I'd like to ask you something."

"Yes, Mama."

"It's been more than a year since the war ended. I've been asking around. There's just no news about your father. He'd be home now if . . . if he were still alive."

I stood up. "He's alive. I know he is."

"Hương, listen to me. Your father loved us too much to not come back. Even if he was injured, he would drag himself back here. Or write, he would at least write to us."

"He'll be home soon. His bird tells me every single day."

"I'd like to believe that, too, Darling. But it's not fair for your father if we don't call his soul home. Unless we burn incense for him, his soul won't find its way back."

"Mama, incense is for dead people!"

She gripped my shoulder. "We need to set up an altar for your father, Hương. We need to ask his soul to come home."

I pushed her away. "My father is not dead."

"Hương," Uncle Đạt broke in. "There's something I need to tell you." He looked at my mother, then back at me. "When I first returned, I told you I'd met your father in the jungle, that we bid good-byes, and two weeks later, the bombings hit. The truth is that . . . your father left not long . . . maybe just half an hour before the bombs arrived. I don't know how far he could have gotten, but . . ."

I put my face into my palms and screamed.

"I'm sorry, Hương. I wanted to go look for him, but I was so sick, I could only crawl. The bombing went on for days. Once I regained my strength, I left the cave to search for him, but vast jungles had been uprooted. I didn't find anybody among the burnt trees."

"You've lied to me all this time, Uncle? For what?"

"Because hope helps to keep us alive, Hương. I've tried to hope that your father survived, but now it's time—"

"What else did you lie about?" I shouted. "Are you happy to see how much I've suffered?"

"I'm so sorry I just couldn't bring myself to tell you any sooner." Tears ran down my uncle's face as he walked to me.

I skirted around him. I ran out of the house.

Streets blurred past me. The air that rushed by my ears sounded like the whizzing of bombs being dropped. The thumps of my footsteps on the ground sent tremors through my body like explosions. I saw my father in the jungle, roasted by flames, I heard him call my name as tongues of fire ate into him, disfigured him. I howled. Around me, people shouted, dashing out of my way. Vehicles beeped, whirling past me.

Cries choked my chest as I slumped down onto the pavement.

My mother arrived at my side. She knelt, opened her arms, and enfolded me into her. "I'm sorry, my darling daughter," she panted. "We won't set up the altar if you don't want to. I'm sorry. I'm so sorry. . . ."

She rubbed my back until my sobs eased, then pushed me gently away from her. She caressed my cheek. "Look at you. You're taller than me now. Smarter, more beautiful. Your father is proud of you."

"I miss him, Mama."

"He's right here with us. He's never far away." She put her hand on her heart.

LATER THAT NIGHT, Tâm rode me away on his bike. "Where would you like to go?" he asked.

"Wherever." I leaned my face against his back.

"To a lake where it's cool, okay?"

I closed my eyes and saw my father's face. He was smiling at me across the distance of eight years and sixty-five days.

Above us, the moon was floating on a dome of darkness, surrounded by glittering stars. If paradise was up there, perhaps my father was free from all the pain of this world.

Ngọc Khánh Lake unfurled itself in front of us. Oil lamps lit by tea sellers glowed on the water's surface, like floating lanterns. Tâm waited for me to get off the bike before leading it up to the pavement. We crossed a large patch of grass and arrived at the lakeside. Tiny waves rode on moonlight, rippling toward us.

"Thanks for being here, Tâm. I love my father too much to let him go."

"He lives on in you, Hương. He'll live on in your children and grandchildren."

He embraced me. The scent of his body sweetened the air around me, his heart beating inside my chest.

I raised my face to meet his. We kissed under the speechless sky.

The Way to Happiness

Hà Nội–Nghệ An–Hà Nội, 1956–1965

After Mr. Giáp the goldsmith had disappeared into the crowd, my stomach burned and flipped.

As I waited, I helped Sáng practice his baby steps on the pavement. When he was bored, I bought him an ice cream. Only when Sáng had finished eating it did Mr. Giáp come back. He apologized for thinking that I'd stolen the silver and gold from my employers. Mr. Toàn had explained to him that they would've gone bankrupt without my help, and the payment was just a gesture of gratitude.

Even today, I can't believe how those coins had changed my fate. Right away I bought a tiny hut in the outskirts of Hà Nội and a travel permit. Master Văn helped me rent a car and a driver—someone he knew and I could trust.

But the happiest day of my life was also the most frightening. It was the third of March, 1956, when I left Hà Nội to look for Minh, Đạt, Ngọc, Thuận, and Hạnh. It had been nearly five months since I last saw them, and time was a bird wrestling to flee from me, taking on its wings the possibility that I'd never see my children again.

"*Trâu.*" Sáng pointed out a water buffalo that rose like a hillock above a patch of grass. Beyond, the sun was spreading its blaze across rice fields.

"Water buffalo," I echoed Sáng's voice, holding him against me.

The driver had rolled down the windows, and the scent of lush countryside filled my nostrils. I stared at every face that came into view, hoping to see Minh.

It was midday when our car approached Kỳ Đồng Village, Thanh Hóa Province. I asked the driver to wait a distance away from the village as I carried Sáng, venturing inside. The car made me look rich, hence trouble.

I'd come back to this village many times in my mind. Now, memory led us through winding lanes. Arriving under a tree, I looked across to a house with a thick fence made of leafy plants. Do you know where I was, Guava?

Yes . . . I was in front of the house where your mother had stayed.

I listened but heard no noise. I waited, but no one came out. There seemed to be thousands of ants biting my skin.

"*Ngọc ơi?*" I called.

"Ngọc," Sáng babbled.

No answer. I walked through the open gate and into the yard.

An unhappy grunt made me jump. A rough-looking man appeared behind the door's frame. He reminded me of the robbers I'd encountered in Hà Nội.

"What do you want?" he barked, holding his palm above his eyes.

"My daughter Ngọc . . . Is she here?"

"Why would she be in my home?" He bared his crooked teeth. "You crazy woman, get out."

I stepped closer. "Sir, a few months ago a fifteen-year-old girl came here, looking for a job. I believe—"

Just then, the little girl who'd played hide and seek with Ngọc emerged behind the man, mouthing something, her hand waving frantically to one side.

The man turned. "What're you doing here, Stupid?"

She darted away.

"But she knows my daughter." I protested.

"You crazy woman. Get the hell out."

I was standing on the road, Sáng crying in my arms, the worries for Ngọc a ball of jumbled threads inside my head, when a small figure burst out from behind the thick fence. The little girl raced toward us. I met her halfway.

"Sister Ngọc ran away from Daddy," she said, breathless.

I gritted my teeth. "Do you know where she is?"

She started crying. "I saw her begging at the village market a few days ago. Please . . . please find Sister Ngọc." She dashed back to her house.

I hurried forward.

The market was empty. Everyone had gone home to avoid noon's heat. There was nothing left except a barren patch of earth.

And a ragged bundle. Lying under a desolate tree, it looked like a human figure, wrapped in a tattered blanket. Could it be my Ngọc?

I raced faster than my heartbeat toward the tree. Kneeling down, I lifted the blanket to find the face that had filled my dreams, the lips that had called my name, the feet that had taken their baby steps at my clapping.

"Ngọc, oh my darling daughter." I put Sáng down and scooped her up.

"Mama. Mama!" Ngọc buried her face in my chest, her quivering sending tremors through my heart.

We cried and laughed. Then we laughed and cried.

NGỌC INSISTED ON holding Sáng as we made our way to the pagoda. I had my arm around her waist, afraid this was only an illusion.

"How long have you been living out on the street, my darling?" I asked.

"A couple of weeks, Mama."

"I'm sorry. Did that man do something to you?"

"He tried. I didn't let him. I fought him and ran away."

I clenched my fists. I wanted to hurt the man, and I knew how. But that would surely put us in danger. And I trusted Heaven to punish him. *Không ai trốn khỏi lưới trời*—No evil act escapes Heaven's net.

I hugged Ngọc tighter, promising myself that I had to take better care of her and make up for what she'd been through.

We reached the pagoda, which looked like it had aged years, not months. The moss-laden roof was sagging; many tiles had fallen, revealing the roof's flimsy skeleton.

In the front yard, the children gathered around us, bones protruding from their bodies, their naked feet filthy. I searched their faces. Thuận wasn't among them.

"Over there, Auntie," one of them said, pointing toward the garden, which had become a brown, punctured patch of dirt. Two boys were squatting and digging.

"Thuận," I called, and a boy turned. His face was smeared with soil. His mouth opened and twisted. I stumbled over to him.

Thuận's body was warm against mine. My flesh and blood, my life. I held him to my heart. Kissing his tears away, I knew I would die any day for my son to live on.

Nun Hiền was inside the room, sitting beside a sick child, rubbing his back, humming a lullaby.

As I walked through the half-open door, her thin face lit up in the afternoon light. "Diệu Lan?"

Out in the yard, she apologized for the state of the children. The government had further tightened its control over religious beliefs. Most people had stopped coming to pagodas to pray. Without their donations, she and the children had to survive on begging.

I learned then that your mother had been bringing food to feed Thuận and the other children.

"I'm so thankful for your help." Nun Hiền squeezed Ngọc's hand. "I'm sorry you couldn't stay here with us."

I pulled Nun Hiền aside, giving her some money. "My small contribution, Madam." She tried to refuse, but I insisted that it was for the children.

"Then you must receive something in return." Nun Hiền led me into the pagoda. She burned incense, praying for my blessings.

I knelt next to her. "Madam, please read my future again."

Nun Hiền took my hands, only to cup my fingers into my palms. "It's senseless to know, my child. Our challenges are there for a purpose. Those who can overcome challenges and remain kind to others will be able to join Buddha in Nirvana. You're a strong woman, Diệu Lan. You'll triumph over whatever life throws at you." She smiled and gave me her wooden bell. "My gift to you. Buddha will hear your prayers. Let Him come to you and give you peace."

So now you know how precious my prayer bell is, Guava. It's a sacred token of compassion between strangers.

I wish I could visit Nun Hiền with you now. A few years ago, I went back to her pagoda and stood in front of nothingness. Bombs had leveled the entire building. Villagers there told me they'd found Nun Hiền under the rubble, bodies of the children in her arms. The bombs had burned them beyond recognition.

I pray for Nun Hiền often. Not only did she save my life, and Thuận's life, but she also rescued my soul. Inspired by her, I became a Buddhist. I've been practicing *Nhẫn*, the principle of patience, which teaches me how to love other human beings. Only through love can we drive away the darkness of evil from this earth.

NEXT, LEAVING THE car outside the village where streams of fast currents weaved through rice fields, Ngọc, Thuận, and I traveled by foot, Sáng in my arms. Here it was, Mrs. Thảo's home. The door was shut. The pond's surface twinkled with the floating petals of yellow *mướp* flowers.

I tapped at the gate. "Anyone home?"

"Hạnh, Hạnh ơi!" Ngọc called for her sister.

The door slid open. A face poked out. Hạnh. Guava, your Auntie Hạnh. We all called her name. All of us.

Hạnh ran, her long hair bobbing behind her, tears gleaming on her face. I was astonished by how tall she'd grown.

"Mama!" She rushed into my arms. My baby. My beautiful princess.

The house was cool and as welcoming as it'd been. It looked happier now, with colorful paintings adorning the walls.

"Is anyone else home, Darling?" I asked.

"Mama Thảo and Papa Tiến are at work." Hạnh talked about them as naturally as a child would refer to her own parents. Then she beamed, pointing at the drawings. "They're all mine. Mama Thảo helped me make them."

The paintings were gorgeous; they were about joyful families, flowers, birds, and animals. I knew Hạnh was talented at drawing but must admit that Mrs. Thảo had brought the best out of her. Hạnh seemed to be content and well cared for here. Would she want to come with us?

"*Hạnh ơi,*" a voice called. I looked out to the gate. A smile was on Mrs. Thảo's face as she reached her arm through a gap, opening the latch.

"*Mẹ Thảo.*" Hạnh dashed toward her new mother, who bent down, lifting her up, twirling her around.

Hạnh leaned forward and whispered something into the ear of her new mama, who turned back to the house. As her eyes met mine, she pulled Hạnh closer.

I walked out to the yard. "I'm sorry . . ."

Mrs. Thảo gripped Hạnh's hand and walked past me. Inside, she stood under her family altar, turned away from us, Hạnh beside her.

"My name is Diệu Lan," I said. "I'm sorry for leaving my daughter with you. I've managed to set up a new home and would like Hạnh to join us."

Silence. Hạnh edged closer to the kindergarten teacher. "Mama, Mama Thảo."

"Oh, my precious sweetheart." Mrs. Thảo knelt, gathering Hạnh into her arms. When she stood up, anger rose in her voice. "I don't know what to think! When you didn't come back, I was so sure you didn't want your daughter anymore. It's been so long."

"Sorry, Sister. I wish I could've explained my circumstances."

"Explain them now!"

The children were watching me with their big eyes. I couldn't lie anymore, but would that put us in danger? After all, Mrs. Thảo's husband was a government official. But I could see that she truly loved Hạnh.

"I was a hard-working farmer with six children," I explained. "When the Land Reform hit our village, I was wrongly accused of exploiting others. My only brother was killed and my eldest son taken away. To stay alive, I had to escape with my kids."

"They are all yours?" Mrs. Thảo gestured at Ngọc, Sáng, and Thuận.

I nodded. "We still have to find my son Đạt. As for my eldest son Minh, I don't know where he is."

Mrs. Thảo bent her head. "The Land Reform went too far. Too many people have suffered injustice. I asked Hạnh about your family. It was selfish of me, but I was hoping . . ."

She held Hạnh for a long while, then kissed her forehead. "I'll always love you, my baby. Now go and be a good daughter to your brave mother." She turned to me. "Take Hạnh now. Leave quickly or else my husband will stop you."

I HUMMED MY songs to Hạnh. She cried as hard as the rain when the car sped us away.

Over the years, Guava, I've taken your auntie back to Mrs. Thảo's home several times. The kindergarten teacher remains Hạnh's second mother, her love is still a fertile soil enriching Hạnh's life.

My heartbeat quickened that day as I saw the bamboo grove and the mossy brick towers again. On the winding dirt road, the children held my hands, pulling me into the village market. It was late in the afternoon, and we were surrounded by people.

My heart rejoiced at the sight of the phở shop, packed with customers.

Some people were standing, waiting for a table. Passing them, I saw a boy carrying bowls of steaming phở. He was skinny and dark. He was your Uncle Đạt, Guava. Your Uncle Đạt.

"Đạt!" I called.

"*Anh* Đạt, *anh* Đạt!" Ngọc, Thuận, and Hạnh jumped up and down.

Đạt lifted his face. For a moment, he stood frozen. The phở bowls slipped from his hands, shattering onto the floor.

I wept when he shuddered and took off, running for us. Everything around me blurred. It sharpened again when I held your uncle, my face buried in his thick hair, my lungs filled with his laughter.

"What's going on?" someone shouted.

The phở seller had arrived. She glared at Đạt. "Get back to work, you idiot!"

"No," I said. "He's coming with us."

"What do you think my shop is?" the woman roared. "A place for you to dump your son when you don't need him?"

"Please, lower your voice." I pushed a handful of banknotes into her palm. "This should cover the broken bowls and help you hire another person."

The woman squinted, counting the money. "Give me twice as much. This idiot has broken many more dishes."

"No way," said Đạt. "I haven't broken anything else, and you've made me work extra hours without pay."

"Don't ever come back here," the woman barked. "Don't ever—"

But we were already out of earshot.

In the car, the children laughed and cried as they talked about how they'd missed each other and how scared they'd been. Watching them, joy filled my every cell. I was a tree trunk growing new branches, a bird regaining some feathers on its wings. It seemed the lucky star was shining in my favor, and I was sure I'd soon be united with Minh, Mrs. Tú, and Mr. Hải.

Darkness was as thick as ink when we arrived in Nghệ An, my hometown. At a guesthouse tucked away behind a cluster of rustling bamboo, I stepped out onto the balcony after the children had fallen asleep.

The home of my heart was so near, yet so far away. I longed to rest my forehead on the walls built by my ancestors, stand in front of our family altar and inhale the presence of my parents, husband, brother, and sister-in-law. So many storms had ravaged our home, but the Trần family would continue to stand. I felt the weight of responsibility on my shoulders, and I carried it with pride.

The sun was yet to rise when the car drove away, the driver bringing my letters to Mr. Hải and Mrs. Tú.

Time moved forward as slowly as a snail. The morning passed, and it was noon. As the afternoon advanced, I became feverish. Why was it taking the driver so long? Had he run into some kind of trouble?

A knock at the door. Mr. Hải! I rushed into his arms—the arms of a farmer who labored all his life in the field, the same arms who provided shelter for sufferers of injustice.

"It's so good to see you, Diệu Lan," he told me. Out on the balcony, he eyed the children, who sat on the bed, sharing the candies I'd brought from Hà Nội.

"Uncle, have you heard from Minh? Where's Auntie Tú?"

"Minh . . . I was hoping you'd have news about him."

His words hit my ears like a clap of thunder.

"Don't worry, child. The good news is that he hasn't been caught. . . . Minh is smart and brave. I'm sure you'll find him soon."

"Where's Mrs. Tú, Uncle? Why didn't she come?"

"Let me tell you what happened."

After we ran away, he said, the village was thrown into chaos. The officials sent people out to look for us, confident that they'd catch us and bring us back.

Mrs. Tú fiercely defended our family by telling others we didn't exploit our workers. She tried to protect our home, but the mob beat her and threw her out. They took away her savings, saying that she'd stolen from us. They destroyed our family altar and looted the house of everything of value. Seven families, including the butcher-woman, were given permission to move in. They fought each other and put up walls inside the rooms. They argued about the division of the yard and garden.

In the five months I'd been gone, we lost our home and all our land. The Agricultural Reform Tribunal had divided our fields among landless farmers, who then battled each other for their share. Greed grew like a weed in our village.

My poor Auntie Tú. Alone, she moved to her plot of land. Mr. Hải and his son helped build a hut for her. She survived on the fruits that grew in her garden. She planted vegetables and sold them. She was determined to keep going.

Mr. Hải reached for my shoulder. "Diệu Lan, around two months after your escape, a farmer saw Mrs. Tú on his way to work. . . . Her body was hanging from a branch."

I stared at him. "Tell me I heard it wrong, Uncle. Tell me Auntie Tú is waiting for me to come back!"

"*Shh.*" He put a finger to his lips, glancing around us. "There was a suicide note in her hut. It said she couldn't go on anymore."

"Auntie Tú was illiterate, Uncle."

"She was murdered, I know." He shook his head. "I'm sorry I couldn't help her. Terrible things have happened in our village, and not just to your family, Diệu Lan. Please . . . stay away for now. Those evil people are still looking for you. I'll send news as soon as I hear from Minh."

BACK IN Hà Nội, I set up an altar with an additional incense bowl for Mrs. Tú. I'll never forget her love and her generosity, Guava. Without her, I wouldn't be alive today, I'm sure of it, and you wouldn't be here either.

Till this day, if you happen to listen to my heartbeat, you might hear the singing voice of my Auntie Tú. She nurtured my soul with songs so that I can sing on.

And those songs helped Ngọc, Đạt, Thuận, and Hạnh, who were traumatized by what they'd gone through. During their first week at our new home, they begged me not to leave their side. When I had to go out to get food, I brought all of them along. We slept in the same room, huddled on the same bed, yet they were still shaken awake by nightmares.

We talked about what had happened and tried to help each other. I paid Master Văn so that he came to our house once a week and ran a class just for us. His meditation exercises calmed the children. The self-defense practice enabled them to gain back their confidence.

Have you heard this saying, Guava? *Lửa thử vàng, gian nan thử sức*—Fire proves gold, adversity proves men. The challenges they'd faced made your mother, uncles, and auntie value life. They went back to school and excelled in their studies. They worked hard: cleaning people's homes, sweeping streets, selling newspapers. We saved every single cent and spent the minimum on food and clothes.

As the fire of war was kindled between North and South Việt Nam, inside our North, the socialist revolution was in full swing. Those who lived in cities now faced a government campaign called *Cải tạo tư sản*—Reform of Capitalists. In Hà Nội, homes and property were taken away, families shattered. The assets of my former employers— Mr. Toàn and Mrs. Châu—were confiscated. They had to travel to the mountains up north to undergo a reeducation program, which lasted more than a year.

I wished I could help them, but I bent my head in silence, and worked; anyone who questioned the government could go to jail. My job, as a fruit seller at Long Biên Market, didn't pay much, but I was determined not to let my children starve again. Once Ngọc, Đạt, Thuận, and Hạnh had settled down at their school, I attended evening classes, learning to be a teacher. We cared for each other, our love turning our hut into a cozy nest. Many years later, we sold that nest and bought our current house on Khâm Thiên Street.

In 1957, nearly two years after my arrival in Hà Nội, the government announced that there had been much wrongdoing during the Land Reform. They acknowledged that the idea to redistribute wealth was correct, but its implementation spiraled out of control. They said many things but did almost nothing to undo these mistakes.

At last, though, I was free to travel to my village. Mr. Hải took me to Nam Đàn Forest. He'd buried my brother Công and my auntie Tú next to my mother's grave. Standing before them, I shed bitter tears. I heard them whisper to me, on the wind that sang among the green canopies of leaves.

I tried to get back our house and our fields, but Guava, I was banging my head against a brick wall. We no longer have our ancestral home, nor the land our ancestors passed down to us.

We weren't the only ones who suffered great losses. Many innocent people had been beaten and humiliated in public. Some had been executed; some killed themselves. Others went crazy after they'd lost everything. Two years after the Land Reform, the woman who had accused her father of raping her 159 times committed suicide. She hanged herself from a tree that had grown tall next to her father's grave.

I CONTINUED TO look for Minh. Master Văn told me perhaps he had gone south.

Every day, I pray for the fire of war to be extinguished. Then, your eldest uncle will step over the ashes of our losses and come home. I'm sure he will.

My Uncle Minh

Nha Trang, June 1979

I held Grandma's hand as we turned into a narrow lane. For a moment, all I could hear were Grandma's hurrying footsteps. The footsteps of twenty-four years of longing.

Grandma, my mother, Uncle Đạt, and I had boarded a squeaky train and rattled about for two days and three nights to get here to Nha Trang, a Southern province hundreds of kilometers away from Hà Nội. Auntie Hạnh had arrived a short while after and met us at the station. Our years apart had transformed her into a Sài Gòn person: her hair cut above her shoulders and permed, her skin smoothed by face powder, her lips painted a rosy color. She smelled of luxury, of a dream I was afraid I'd never be able to reach.

I looked for the number I'd learned by heart: seventy-two. It could

be written on any of the battered shacks bordering the two open gut-
ters along our path. An intense stink swelled into the thick, hot air. A
woman sat on the steps of her home, beating her palms against soapy
clothes that filled a bucket. She shouted at some kids who were following us. They scattered like birds.

A group of men sat by one gutter, small cups of clear liquid, probably rice liquor, between them. Their Southern accents floated lazily on
the heat. They stopped talking as we went by. Lifting their faces, they
followed us with sleepy eyes.

We hurried past a noodle seller whose gigantic black pot and red-
coaled stove bulged into the lane. Droplets of sweat streamed down
Grandma's neck. Her hair had more white strands than black. She
held up a telegram, which contained the address we were looking for.
Arriving at our home three days earlier, the telegram's two simple lines
had caused Grandma to faint. When she came to, she insisted that we
leave Hà Nội immediately.

My mother walked in front, carrying a knapsack swollen with dried
medicinal plants. Four years after her return, she was still so thin, I
feared a strong wind could lift her up and blow her away. The search
for my father continued, and her nightmares continued. At least we'd
just heard from Uncle Minh, but the news might not be good.

Grandma broke away from me, rushing toward a shack. Rusted tin
sheets made up its roof and walls. Scrawled across its rickety door was
the number seventy-two.

We joined her in tapping on the door, calling out for Uncle Minh.

No sound came back, just the tin sheets crackling under the intense
heat.

"He's home. Just let yourselves in," the noodle seller called, standing in the middle of the lane, the children around her, like baby chicks
crowding close to a mother hen.

Uncle Đạt pushed against the door. It collapsed to one side as if about to fall apart, then creaked open. Light gushed into a room, barren of furniture except for a tattered bamboo bed. On its straw mat lay what looked like the skeleton of a man.

He was on his side, facing away from us. His head was bald and wrinkled. Yellowish skin clung to the bones of his naked back.

"*Minh con ơi!*" howled Grandma.

The man struggled and turned to face us. His cheeks were hollow, his eyes sunken sockets, his chapped lips swollen with sores.

"*Mẹ,*" he said. His bony hands reached out. "Mama. You're here."

Grandma stumbled toward him. She sobbed into his trembling shoulder.

"Brother, oh, Brother," said Uncle Đạt, embracing Uncle Minh across his chest.

My mother knelt beside the bed. Uncle Minh's telegram had told us he was sick, but this sick? He looked twice his forty-one years. The towel beside him was smeared with blood.

Tears rolled down his haggard face. "Mama, Ngọc, Hạnh, Đạt. I've missed you—" His voice was broken by an intense cough. Violent movements ripped through his body.

We sat him up. My mother patted his back. He shook uncontrollably. Blood oozed from his mouth.

Grandma dabbed his face with her handkerchief. She caressed him with tender words until the coughing eased. As Uncle Đạt leaned Uncle Minh against the pile of pillows and blankets we'd made for him, Auntie Hạnh stepped back. She turned to hide her face, but I saw her nose wrinkling. I didn't blame her for forgetting how poverty and sickness smelled; I was only used to it since I'd visited my mother often at her hospital.

Uncle Minh's tired eyes acknowledged me as I fed him some water.

I felt a silent cord that bound us. The cord of our ancestors' lullabies that once Grandma had sung to him, and then to me.

"Hương, my daughter," my mother introduced me, and my uncle's eyes lit up. He opened his mouth, but my mother begged him not to speak. She told us not to ask him questions for now. Holding his hand, turning the palm up, she pressed her fingers against his wrist, feeling for his pulse.

Grandma tried to relieve us from the scorching heat with a paper fan. It was just mid-morning, but the sticky air clung to our skin. The tin sheets continued to crackle as if ready to burst.

"You're in good hands, Son," said Grandma as my mother reached into her knapsack. "Ngọc is an excellent doctor. You'll be better in no time."

My uncle nodded, the corners of his lips lifting. He gripped Grandma's arm, as if never wanting to let her go.

My mother placed her stethoscope on Uncle Minh's chest. She closed her eyes, listening as if her life depended on it. She checked his eyes, nose, mouth, throat, and back. When she was done, her face bore no expression. Her fingers trembled slightly as she folded the stethoscope, returning it to her knapsack.

"You must be in terrible pain," she told Uncle Minh. "How about a shot to relieve you from it?"

He closed his eyes to say yes.

She wiped her hands with the alcohol she'd brought along and administered an injection to his thin arm. "Please . . . don't talk yet. I'll brew a pot of herbal remedy. It should clear the mucus in your lungs. But first, you need a good meal."

Uncle Minh nodded then shook his head.

"Wait." I rummaged my knapsack, fetching a pen and a notebook.

"Where are Thuận and Sáng?" Uncle Minh wrote.

"On their way," said Grandma. "Son . . . your sister the doctor says you need to eat. The phở out there smells delicious. Can we bring you a bowl?"

"I'll get it," said Auntie Hạnh. She grabbed her handbag and left.

Uncle Minh gave a wrinkled banknote to Uncle Đạt. "Ice seller down the lane. Buy some to cool the room?" he wrote.

Uncle Đạt pushed the money back. "Pay me later, once you and I have come home to Hà Nội . . . with tickets to a soccer match."

Uncle Minh smiled and nodded.

I wondered if my eldest uncle had a family. I studied the shack, but the only thing that told me about his past was the altar—a wooden shelf clinging to the rusty wall. On it stood a statue of a man nailed to a cross. My uncle had become a Christian?

I followed Grandma through the back door, which opened into an area shaded by a thatched roof and surrounded by the tin sheets of the neighbors' homes. A clay stove sat on the earthen floor, next to a pile of firewood. A large, brown jar stood in the corner, half filled with water.

"There're so many things I want to ask him." Grandma cried into her palms. "I don't understand why he hadn't sent us any news. He could've tried to let me know that he was alive. All these years . . ."

"He must have his reasons, Grandma. He'll be able to tell us soon."

Scooping water out of the jar, we washed our faces. I soaked my washcloth, using it to cool Grandma's back. It pained me to see her bones and the scars inflicted by Wicked Ghost.

Grandma filled a bucket with water. Carrying it inside, I saw my mother sitting next to Uncle Minh, going through a stack of papers. As Grandma entered, she quickly put the papers into her knapsack.

"Ready for a sponge bath?" Grandma asked. Uncle Minh smiled.

Suddenly his body jumped with bouts of coughing. Glancing at my mother, I read the worry in her eyes.

The coughing eased. The front door opened, but instead of Auntie Hạnh, a boy came in, carrying a steaming bowl. I thanked him and fanned the phở.

Grandma washed Uncle Minh. My mother unpacked parcels of herbs. She weighed different ingredients, pouring them into the clay pot she'd brought along.

Uncle Đạt came back with a tray full of ice, which he placed next to Uncle Minh. He took the fan from me, flicking it, sending coolness around the room.

At the back of the shack, I kindled a fire. My mother poured water into the clay pot.

"How is he, Mama?" I fed the fire pieces of wood.

She pulled me to her, her lips against my ear. "Don't tell Grandma yet. Your uncle Minh is dying. Those papers he showed me . . . cancer. It's spread to his lungs and liver. He was hospitalized for months, but the doctors sent him home, said they could no longer help."

"But you, Mama, your medicine can do magic."

"I'm afraid it's too late. The cancer is too advanced. The results of his tests . . ." She bit her lip. "I'll try, but I think I can only help to relieve the pain of his last days."

My chest hurt for Grandma. How could she cope with such awful news?

I turned to the fire. Human lives were short and fragile. Time and illnesses consumed us, like flames burning away these pieces of wood. But it didn't matter how long or short we lived. It mattered more how much light we were able to shed on those we loved and how many people we touched with our compassion.

I thought about Tâm and how his love had brightened my life.

Whenever I felt low from missing my father, he'd been there to make me laugh. I wished he were here now to hold me and tell me everything would be all right.

The medicine bubbled, its thick scent woven into the air. My mother reduced the heat.

Uncle Đạt came out, dousing his face in water.

"Is Hạnh back?" My mother squinted her eyes against the smoke.

"Not yet," my uncle whispered. "I saw her chatting out there with the neighbors. She must be asking them about Brother Minh."

Inside, Uncle Minh was once again Grandma's child, opening his mouth as she fed him the noodle soup. He chewed with difficulty and winced as he swallowed, but his eyes glowed.

While he ate, Grandma told him briefly about her walk to Hà Nội. We had a wonderful house, she said, and as soon as he was well enough, she'd bring him home.

She talked about Uncle Đạt, his happy marriage to Auntie Nhung, and their three-month-old baby who was chubby like the Laughing Buddha. She didn't tell him how much we'd feared the little boy would have problems. The first thing Grandma did after the baby's birth was to count his fingers and toes. When the doctors said the baby was perfectly healthy, Grandma brought her forehead to the hospital's floor, thanking all the Gods she'd prayed to. Uncle Đạt and Auntie Nhung named the baby Thống Nhất, which meant "Unification," a fiery wish of many Vietnamese from North to South throughout the war.

Grandma told Uncle Minh about my mother's well-respected positions at both the Bạch Mai Hospital and the Institute of Traditional Medicine. She didn't tell him, though, that my mother had taken Grandma and me on a trip. In front of my baby brother's grave, she wept as Grandma and I chanted prayers, blessing his soul with peace. It was Grandma's turn to sob when we arrived at Trường Sơn Cemetery, where Uncle Thuận had been laid to rest with thousands of other soldiers. Rows of graves stretched to the horizon, as far as our eyes could see. Many of those graves were marked "Unknown Soldier." I'd wondered that day whether one of them held my father's bones and his love for me, the love that I knew would not stop burning, even when buried under the cold earth.

Grandma told Uncle Minh about Uncle Sáng steadily climbing the Party ladder, that he was now an important official in the Central Propaganda Department. And about Auntie Hạnh and her family doing so well in Sài Gòn.

Uncle Đạt went out to get more phở for all of us, which I ate, sitting on a straw mat spread on the floor while listening to Grandma. She now went on and on about the good marks I'd gotten from my first year at university, and that local newspapers had published some of my poems. She talked about Tâm, who was working toward a degree in agriculture and had been my boyfriend for three years.

"I gave him a hard time at first, but he earned my trust," she told Uncle Minh. "You'll like him, surely. He comes from the middle region, like us."

Uncle Minh looked truly happy for me. Some color had returned to his face. He scribbled in the notebook.

"About me?" Grandma laughed and said she was doing fine, that she liked her job trading in the Old Quarter. She'd made many friends and had many more regular customers.

My uncle raised his arm, smoothing the wrinkles on Grandma's face. The hard work had made her look much older than her fifty-nine years of age, though she was still a graceful woman. Through the years, I'd seen men coming to our home. Grandma had sent all of them away with her indifference. I knew the river of her love for my grandpa had never stopped flowing, and I saw how I'd turn out like her and my mother, loyal to one man.

"I'm perfectly happy now, having found you." Grandma rested her face against her son's hand. She tilted the bowl, pouring the rest of the soup into the spoon. "Well done, my child. Finished."

Uncle Đạt and I insisted that Grandma eat. She joined us on the straw mat. I went to the bed, picking up the fan. My mother came out of the cooking area, asking Uncle Minh to take a nap. He shook his head and held up the pen. "Ngọc, tell me about Hương's father?"

My mother sat down and massaged Uncle Minh's legs. It was a story I had asked to hear many times. "I met Hoàng when I was eighteen, at the Mid-Autumn Festival," she began.

It was a magical night, the sky adorned by the full moon. Around the Lake of the Returned Sword, thousands of paper lanterns lit by candles gathered for a parade, their lights bobbing like scales of a dragon to the rhythms of songs and drumbeats. My mother, too old to carry a lantern, chased her friends, racing past the lit-up figures of stars, animals, flowers. As her friends disappeared from her sight, she ran faster and tripped on a sharp rock. She fell, blood gushing from her foot.

She cried out in pain, but her voice was swallowed by the songs and drums. No one seemed to notice her. As she grew desperate, a young man emerged from the mass of people. He knelt down, took off his outer shirt, tore it up, and bandaged her foot. He brought her home and on the way, he made her laugh so hard, she forgot about the pain. They'd been inseparable from then until the man—my father—joined the Army.

I showed Uncle Minh the Sơn ca. "My father carved this for me."

My uncle studied the bird. "It's beautiful. Where did your father fight?" he wrote.

"I don't know. We never got a letter from him."

"I gave up looking for Hoàng," said my mother, "but recently there was this story in the newspaper. A soldier had been injured in an explosion and lost his memory. At the beginning of this year, he listened to the radio and heard a poem about the river that runs through his village. The poem evoked such powerful emotions that he remembered his way home. His family had no news from him for nine years, and then he turned up. Can you imagine how happy they were?"

I thought about the work I'd published. I longed for my father to read it and find his way back to us.

Auntie Hạnh appeared. Uncle Đạt met her at the door. She told him something and he frowned. I was desperate to know what was going on, but didn't want Uncle Minh to see us whispering.

Grandma returned to the bed. "Get some sleep, Son. We'll talk more later."

Uncle Minh nodded, but the pen scribbled across the page, "Mama, how are Grandma Tú, Mr. Hải, and his son?"

"Mr. Hải and his family are fine. They can't wait to see you. As for my beloved Auntie Tú . . . I'm sorry, Son . . . she died by the time I could return to our village. People said she'd committed suicide, but I don't believe it."

Uncle Minh gripped the pen tight. "You think someone killed her?"

"Yes, to take over our land. She was defending it so fiercely."

"Those evil people, they'll rot in hell." The pen trembled in my uncle's hand.

"What about Brother Thuận, Mama?"

Grandma was distraught. As my mother held her, I talked about the bombings and the two soldiers who'd brought the news of my youngest uncle.

"Thuận, oh my little brother . . . ," Uncle Minh howled. He thumped himself in the chest. He reached for Grandma's hand, tears flowing down his cheeks. "Mama, I'm sorry. You've suffered so."

"But my life is filled with blessings, too," Grandma choked. "It was a great blessing when I received your telegram. How did you have my address, Son? And why didn't you contact me any sooner?"

Uncle Đạt and Auntie Hạnh stood beside me, anxious for the answers. Uncle Minh wrote something, only to blacken it with the ink. He flipped to a new page, only to hold the pen with his eyes closed.

I flinched when he threw the pen and the notebook onto the bed. He struggled to sit up, then crawled toward Grandma. He kowtowed to her, his head touching her feet. "Mama . . . forgive this useless son."

"Minh." Grandma reached for his shoulders, pulling him to sit up. "If someone is to blame, it's me. I failed to keep our family together."

"But I haven't—" Violent coughing interrupted my uncle. He clutched his chest as my mother patted his back. Once the coughing eased, she gave him some water.

My uncle nodded his thanks. He peeled away a corner of his straw mat. Underneath was a swollen envelope. With both hands, he gave it to Grandma.

I leaned forward, catching a glimpse. "*Gửi Mẹ Trần Diệu Lan, 173 Phố Khâm Thiên, Hà Nội.*" The envelope was addressed to Grandma. There was no sender's name.

Uncle Minh picked up the pen. "I wanted to send it by post, but feared it'd fall into the wrong hands. Please, read it together," he wrote.

"We'll do that as soon as you've drunk your medicine." My mother looked at her watch.

As Uncle Đạt adjusted the pillows behind Uncle Minh's back to help him sit up straighter, Grandma stared at the envelope without opening it.

My mother returned, in her hands a bowl of black liquid. I winced at its smell. She fanned the liquid to cool and brought it to Uncle Minh's lips. "It's bitter but it will help."

He took a sip, then shuddered. He drew his head back, sticking out his tongue, shaking his head.

"Brother, please, you have to drink all of it," said Uncle Đạt. "Ngọc's treatments did wonders for me. I drank at least fifty pots of her brew and look how strong I am." He flexed his upper arms, which bulged with muscles.

Uncle Minh chuckled, coughed, then took a deep breath. He pinched his nose, swallowing the medicine in small gulps. Finally, he finished the bowl. We clapped.

"Now, you must rest." My mother helped my uncle lie down. "Sleep. We'll talk when you feel better."

WE SAT IN a circle on the floor, far away from the bed. "Keep your voices low," my mother said.

The envelope stayed still in Grandma's hands. Auntie Hạnh reached for it. As she opened the flap, pulling out the pages, an old-looking envelope slipped out.

A smaller letter. It was also addressed to Grandma, but bore the sender's name: Nguyễn Hoàng Thuận—my dead uncle.

Grandma's eyes flew open. "It's Thuận's handwriting. Oh, my son, my son!"

My mother held on to Grandma's shoulders as I became dizzy.

"How the hell did he get this?" Auntie Hạnh voiced the question that was running wild in my mind. Uncle Đạt eyed the bed. Uncle Minh had turned away from us, his skin sagging from the bones of his back.

My mother took Uncle Thuận's letter from Grandma and read it aloud to all of us.

Đông Hà, Quảng Trị, 15/2/1972,

Dear Mama,

On the doorstep of this New Year of the Mouse, I think about you. Oh how I long to be with you, and with my brothers and sisters. How I long to sit next to the bubbling pot of *bánh chưng*, the perfume of those sticky rice cakes warming our home.

How are you, my dear Mama? How are Hương, Sister Ngọc and Sister Hạnh? Have you received news from Brother Đạt, Brother Sáng, and Brother Hoàng? If you haven't, don't worry. They're strong and skillful. Soon they'll join me in returning home.

Mama, I heard the bombings in Hà Nội are getting worse. Please take good care and stay in underground shelters. If you can, leave. Go to a village where it's safe.

I dream about the day when I can come home to you, Mama. All over Việt Nam, hundreds of thousands of mothers are waiting for their sons and daughters to return from the war. Tonight, I see the eyes of those mothers and yours lighting up Heaven above my head.

How are you celebrating Tết this year, Mama? Could you manage to buy sticky rice and pork to make *bánh chưng*? Do people still sell cherry blossom branches on the streets? Oh I miss watching those red and pink flowers bursting out from bamboo baskets or on the back of peddlers' bikes.

You would have loved our New Year celebration here in the jungle, Mama. We had a feast today, with fresh fish caught from a stream. You'd have enjoyed the *tàu bay* wild vegetable I cooked. And can you guess what I found yesterday on my trek? A branch of a yellow *mai*. Its budding flowers tell me this war will end, that I will soon come back to you. Come back to you and be your child again.

I miss you, Mama.

Your son,

Thuận.

P.S. My comrade is heading for the North on an assignment so I'm giving this to him. Please tell Hương, Ngọc, and Hạnh I'm halfway through my letter to them. I hope to be able to send it soon.

Tears stung my eyes. Uncle Thuận had loved *bánh chưng* cakes so much that he always insisted that Grandma make them for Tết. With him gone, Grandma had never made them again.

"My poor brother. He loved us and he loved his life," said Auntie Hạnh. She bent forward as if someone had punched her in the stomach. "It's people like him who killed Thuận." She pointed at Uncle Minh.

"Hạnh!" Uncle Đạt grabbed her arm, pulling it down. He eyed Grandma, who was cupping Uncle Thuận's letter to her face.

"He fought for the Southern Army," my aunt hissed. "I learnt this from his neighbors. So there's only one explanation, how the letter fell into his hands."

"Don't judge before you know all the facts." Grandma squared her shoulders. She gathered the larger envelope and its unread pages, giving them to me. "Hương, read clearly. Don't stop until you reach the end."

Nha Trang City, 16/12/1978

My dear Mama, Ngọc, Đạt, Thuận, Hạnh, and Sáng,

It's Minh here. I'm writing this twenty-three years since the day we last saw each other. Believe me, there have been many times when I started this letter, only to tear it apart. There're so many things I want to tell you, but didn't know how to begin. How could I pack all my longing for you into the smallness of words? It'd be better for me to talk to you in person but what if I'll never get to see you again?

Thuận, I got your letter in 1972, a few months after you'd written it. Holding your words in my hand, I laughed since you all had survived the Land Reform, and I cried because you had to fight in this bloodbath of a war. Oh my little brother, how are you now? Đạt, Sáng, Ngọc and Hạnh, did you have to go to the battlefield? Were you injured?

Mama, how did you manage to escape from those murderers? I'm so sorry I couldn't wait for you and take you with me as I went to the South. If I did, perhaps all of us would be in America right now, living in freedom, as a family. Oh how selfish and cowardly of me to have run away without waiting for you after my escape. As the eldest son in the family, I should have taken care of you. I failed in my responsibility. I'm so sorry.

My beloved family, there've been many things that happened since the day that tore us apart. Perhaps I can begin by recalling what happened to Uncle Công and me during that dreadful day. It's painful to remember, but I must relive those experiences, for they not only changed me but also explain the reasons for my actions later on.

It was a peaceful day, and we had been weeding a patch of rice field, remember, Mama? After you'd gone home to feed Sáng, I worked alongside Uncle Công. Suddenly, shouting voices boomed.

"Someone must have caught a thief," said Uncle Công, his back bent low above the rice. But the voices were getting closer. When I wiped sweat from my eyes and lifted my head, a group of men and women were charging at us, armed with bricks, knives, large sticks.

"Down with wicked landowners!" the crowd shouted, their weapons high in their hands.

Uncle Công begged for mercy, but those people overpowered him. As I howled and kicked, they pinned us down, tied us up, beat us, and dragged us toward our village.

I was terrified when I saw you, Mama. You were being flung down the five steps of the front yard.

Fear paralyzed me as I was gagged, pulled away from our home, and paraded around the village. Uncle Công and I had to walk under the rain of rotten eggs, rocks, brick shards, and angry words. Bleeding, we were led to the village river and bound with coarse rope to large trunks of trees.

We knelt, thirsty and in unbearable pain. As I struggled to free myself, Uncle Công leaned over to me. He couldn't talk, but in his eyes I read his sorrow and his love for me. Nearby, those who captured us had started a bonfire. They laughed raucously as they ate, emptied bottles of rice liquor, cheered, and shouted slogans. They challenged each other to deliver the worst punishment to the wicked landlords.

When the heat of the discussions among the men was intense, they unbound Uncle Công. They demanded that he kiss their feet. When Uncle Công refused, they kicked him, calling him the dirtiest of names. I tried to shrink into a ball when they dragged out a lidded bamboo basket—the kind used for transporting pigs."

At this, I had to stop. Across from me, Grandma was biting her lip so hard that it was white. I wished I could make the words vanish so that they wouldn't inflict additional pain on her.

But Grandma's eyes told me to go on.

"Admit you are a wicked landlord who exploits poor farmers!" one of the men shouted at Uncle Công.

My dear uncle shook his head, and they pushed him into the basket, closing the lid.

Howls gurgled in my mouth as the basket was hurled into the river. "Tell us you're a wicked landlord and we'll release you!" the mob chanted as they dunked the basket repeatedly.

I tried to break away from the tree. I wanted to strangle each person there with my bare hands, but the rope held me back. My eyes had been emptied of tears by the time Uncle Công's lifeless body thudded down on the ground next to me. I wriggled, craned forward, and managed to reach him with my foot. I nudged him repeatedly, but there was no response. As time passed, his body grew cold and stiff.

Dead—my uncle who had taken care of me like a father. Dead—the man who had taught me about kindness and hard work. My uncle was murdered in front of my eyes and yet I wasn't able to do anything for him.

The men continued to drink and shout their slogans. I was sure they left me alive to punish me in the coming days, for all our villagers to witness. Occasionally, they stood up, went to the tree, and pissed on me. They kicked me and laughed at me. I bit my lip until it bled. I hadn't known about hatred, even when my father was taken away from me, but now I tasted hatred on my tongue. I vowed to take revenge for my father and uncle as long as I live.

Late in the night the men became so drunk, they crumpled into heaps around the withering fire, their snores and snorts breaking the silence of the hour. I struggled but was powerless against the rope. I lost all my hope as the fire died down.

A soft voice. My heart jumped. Mr. Hải and his son had come for me. They hurried to untie me, then led me onto a road. Everything was dark as coal; I didn't know where I was.

"You have to leave, Minh. . . run far away. Stay here and they'll kill you," whispered Mr. Hải.

"How about my mother, my family? Shouldn't I wait for them?" I asked.

"I'll tell them that you've escaped, and they, too, should flee. Go now, else they'll catch you." Mr. Hải's hands trembled on my face. "Good luck, Minh. They have a quota of how many people to execute. My son will take you to the national highway. I'm going to your mother." His footsteps disappeared into the night.

At the national highway, his son's urgent words buzzed in my ears, telling me to try hitchhiking, to run fast.

After he'd hugged me good-bye, I stumbled along the road. Shouts and drumbeats from afar sent tremors from my head to my toes. I told myself I had to survive. I was nearly eighteen. I could take care of myself. I had to, but a part of me begged to go back home, to look for you, my dear Mama, to look for you, my beloved brothers and sisters.

As I wandered on the national highway, I ran into a Catholic family who were fleeing—Mr. Cường, his wife, and their two daughters. They'd managed to secure travel passes for the national highway and were waiting for their buffalo cart. Looking at my bleeding wounds, cut by the rope, they felt sorry for me. They shared with me their medicine, food, and water. They asked what had happened and offered to hide me inside the cart. They knew it'd be dangerous but decided that God had arranged for them to meet me, and that it was their duty to help.

Turning back to our village and seeing only fear and death, I let those kind people cover me with straw. They surrounded me with bags of belongings and fixed a wooden board above me. As I was pulled away from my birthplace, I felt my limbs were being ripped apart from my body.

After days of traveling, Mr. Cường's family drew back the board. I emerged into the light to find myself in Hải Phòng, a city Mr. Cường said was around 120 kilometers east of Hà Nội. I looked back at the road we'd just traveled. It was filled with black coal dust. I saw no future for me there.

Mr. Cường told me he planned to cross the border by sea and head south, and I decided to go along. The South meant freedom from the Communists. Once I got settled, I would send news to you and perhaps help you escape. The thought cheered me up.

Mr. Cường was an influential trader who knew quite a few people in Hải Phòng. One of them took us into his home. When night fell, he led us to a deserted part of a river, where a fisherman and his boat were waiting. We got into the boat, flattening ourselves onto the wet floor, and the fisherman covered us with nets and rowed us away.

It was well into the next day when the fisherman removed the net. On immense water stood a gigantic ship, with tiny fishing boats bobbing around it. The ship was packed with people and was about to head south. Mr. Cường's family had arranged tickets for themselves.

Mr. Cường told me to wait as he went aboard. A short while later, he appeared on the tall deck together with a man in white uniform. He convinced the man that I'd be a strong, good worker.

On the ship, I shoveled coal into burning furnaces. I worked furiously, trying to exhaust myself so I could fall asleep during breaks. There was no turning back, no land in sight, just the wind, the water, the sun.

It took more than a week for us to reach Nha Trang. I left the ship, black with coal dust, but bright with new joy in my heart. I'd found friendship in Linh, Mr. Cường's eldest daughter. Together we grieved for our lost homes, but at the same time we were excited about the future ahead of us—a future free of terror, we thought.

The Southern government was trying to encourage people to flee the North. They provided free accommodation and means of support to newly arrived Northerners. I stayed with a group of young men in the same neighborhood as Mr. Cường's family. During the day, I worked as a laborer for a construction project. In the evenings, I attended classes. I wanted to get a good job, earn money, to be able to bring you to the South, my dear Mama, Ngọc, Đạt, Thuận, Hạnh, and Sáng.

I often found myself wandering around Nha Trang port, staring at the streams of people pouring out of ships and boats. I hoped you had been able to go south like me. I wrote many letters, but found no way of sending them. There was no longer a North–South postal service. No one I knew would risk their lives by going back to the North. Still, the hope for our reunion burned inside of me and gave light to my dark days.

I finished high school, with Linh by my side. I went to church with her and found peace in listening to God's words. I found new strength in my faith. I was baptized and vowed to be a good Catholic.

But being a good Catholic isn't easy. God asks me to forgive those who harmed me. But how could I ever forgive those who murdered my father and my uncle and tore our family apart?

I studied hard, got into university, and graduated with a law degree. I specialized in criminal law, determined to help undo injustice. On my graduation day, while my friends laughed, I cried because you were not there to celebrate with me. On the first day that I worked as a practicing lawyer, I didn't cry, though. I smiled because I knew you would be proud of me.

My job paid well and I was able to borrow from the bank to buy a small house. My first house, can you imagine?

I wish you could have been there at my wedding. Linh looked just like an angel. Our son, Thiện, was born one year later, followed by our daughter, Nhân. You would have loved to meet your grandchildren, Mama. They know you well because I told them stories about you every day. I didn't ever want them to forget their roots.

The war intensified. Fighting took place on the outskirts of our city, but sometimes artillery exploded in our neighborhood. We lived in fear because anyone could be a disguised Việt Cộng, hiding a hand grenade inside their pants or shirt.

The American government had sent their troops to help, and I was convinced we were going to defeat Hà Nội. Once that happened, the first thing I'd do is to return to our village and find you.

I wanted the Communists to fall, but still, when the draft notice arrived, I was stunned. I looked up at Jesus and prayed to him. I wanted to safeguard the freedom we had in the South, but if I went to the battlefield, I would face death and Linh could be left alone with my children. If I went to the battlefield, I would risk fighting against my brothers and sisters.

My father-in-law came to see me. He said it'd be difficult for me to escape the draft, but he was ready to bribe. Or he would bribe to get me an office job with the government. Our Southern regime, unfortunately, was so corrupt that you could almost buy anything with money. I despised such corruption and didn't want to support it.

That night, as I tried to make up my mind, I remembered how white the funeral bands were on our heads as we wailed in front of my father's coffin, how wicked the laughter of those who'd killed Uncle Công, and how bitter the hatred I'd tasted on my lips. And I remembered my vow of revenge.

So, in 1971, I joined the Army of the Republic of Việt Nam, the ARVN.

Oh, my brothers and sisters, I had to be the man who stands up for his beliefs, but I knew then that I could be facing you in the battlefield. Sixteen years had passed, but your faces were imprinted in my mind. If we were to meet each other, would you shoot at me? I wouldn't. But what if one of my comrades had his gun pointed at your forehead? Would I kill my brother in arms to save my brother in blood?

Those questions were alive in my mind during my four years in the Army. I slipped through the fingers of death many times. And though I never saw you, I often found myself by the side of the dead enemy. As I looked at their faces and inspected their belongings, I feared the worst.

I thought I'd find satisfaction seeing my enemy dead, but the sight only made me empty and sad. I realized that blood that is shed can't make blood flow again in other people's veins.

I had expected us to win the war, but the Americans withdrew their troops one year after my oath to fight alongside them. They swallowed their promise to help protect the South from Communist invasion. And our ARVN had been weakened by the weevil of corruption. When the Northern Army and the Southern Việt Cộng won battle after battle, my commander fled with a helicopter. Some of my comrades committed suicide. The rest deserted their posts or surrendered.

The day my hometown, Nha Trang, was taken over, I wept. By then, I'd abandoned my weapons and come home. We dug a shelter at the back of my house for me to hide, but after several weeks living underground as an animal, I crawled out. The radio was telling us that the new government was working toward reconciliation. They asked all former ARVN soldiers to turn ourselves in. They promised not to punish anyone. They sent people who were former ARVN soldiers to our home to talk to my wife and children. Those soldiers said that they'd been treated well; Northerners or Southerners, we were all brothers and sisters now.

Linh and my father-in-law accompanied me when I first turned myself in. We worried I'd be arrested, but the officers who spoke to me were friendly. They asked me to write a report about things I'd done during the war. Afterward, they told me to go home and report back every week for the next three months, and that this was only for administrative purposes. That night, we celebrated. I decided that as soon as my three-month time was up, I would try to find you.

But nothing is certain in life. When I reported to the authorities the next week, I was immediately ushered into a crowded truck, which took me to a reeducation camp many hours away from Nha Trang, high up in the mountains. I didn't even have the chance to say good-bye to my loved ones.

The camp was a harsh labor prison. We had to clear away

bushes and hoe rocky land to turn it into rice paddies. Without medical care and enough food, many people died. Malaria nearly killed me several times. What made me more miserable, though, was the fact that I didn't know what had happened to Linh and my kids—or to any of you.

The two years at the camp felt like centuries. Upon release, I came home to see my wife and children struggling. Linh couldn't find a job and had had to sell her jewelry, clothes, and our furniture to be able to keep Thiện and Nhân at school. They were labeled Ngụy—"the Illegitimate"—and suffered extreme discrimination. For the next two years, I wasn't entitled to my rights as a citizen. I couldn't work. I didn't have an ID card. I wasn't able to vote. Every week for the next many months, I had to report to the authorities.

My father-in-law had built himself a business empire in Nha Trang but lost nearly everything after the war. While I was in prison, his houses, assets, and business were nationalized. He and his wife had to spend one year in the Lâm Đồng New Economic Zone. The mountainous conditions there were harsh, and every night they had to gather and sing songs that praised the new government. One night, my father-in-law grabbed his wife and sneaked out of their hut. They escaped, went home, and dug up the gold ingots they'd buried in their garden. They bought a boat and within the next many months, secretly prepared to cross the sea to America.

It'd be a dangerous journey. "But I'd rather die than live the life of the unwanted," my father-in-law told me. My wife and children decided to get on the boat. They begged me to come, and I wanted to, but my mind turned to the North. I'd lost you once. I couldn't do it twice. I had to go back for you first.

Watching my wife and children depart was the hardest thing I ever had to do.

Alone, I returned home. I rented a rickshaw, stood at street corners and waited for customers. I also waited for the moment I could contact you. I kept believing things would soon change, that I could soon travel back to our home village. Unfortunately, prosecutions against those like me continued. If I sent you letters or came back to see you, I would bring you serious harm.

I longed for news about Linh, Thiện, Nhân, and my parents-in-law, but only terrible stories reached me. Stories about boat people being robbed, raped, and murdered by pirates at sea; stories about boats running out of food, water, and petrol, being capsized by storms. I could do nothing but pray.

When I fell ill, I tried to convince myself that it wasn't serious, that it was only caused by my worries. Then I threw up blood and couldn't get up anymore. I had to sell my house to finance the treatments.

Now, I am in this shack, hoping to get better, longing to see you and tell you how much I've yearned for you.

So, I have tried to explain the reasons I couldn't contact you any earlier. There's another question that must be burning in your minds: How did Thuận's letter come into my possession?

It was a miracle.

It happened in 1972, after a bombing raid. My unit was searching a forest where the enemy had been hiding. Near a bomb crater, I found the body of a soldier whose uniform and hat bore the Communist stars. I searched his knapsack. Among the usual things were a bunch of handwritten letters.

I was supposed to give the letters to my commanding officer but couldn't resist going through the addresses on the envelopes.

Addresses of villages, districts, towns, cities. Addresses of mothers, fathers, sisters, grandparents. I studied them quickly.

Suddenly my heart jumped. "Gửi Mẹ Trần Diệu Lan, 173 Phố Khâm Thiên, Hà Nội." The letter was addressed to you, Mama, and the sender was Nguyễn Hoàng Thuận—my brother. I quickly hid the letter and, once I was alone, opened it, devouring each word. Tears wet my face. For the next years, the letter stayed inside my breast pocket. It gave me hope for another miracle, that I would be united with my family.

I'd wanted to see you in better circumstances, when I had a job, when I was surrounded by my loving wife and children. But once again, fate has reduced me to a loser, a sick man. A man who has nothing to give, except for his burden of pain and sorrow.

Mama, Ngọc, Đạt, Thuận, Hạnh, and Sáng, if you meet me before I die, please find the strength inside of you to look past my pitiful appearance and see a fire inside of me. It burns for you, for our ancestors, and for our village. It burns, asking for your forgiveness. Please forgive me, for I haven't been there for you. Please forgive me, for I have fought in the war. But I didn't fight against you, I fought for my right to freedom.

Always and always,

Minh

I put down the letter, exhausted. I couldn't believe Uncle Minh had decided to become a soldier despite the chance to escape the draft. On the other hand, he'd suffered injustices. And he, like Uncle Đạt, hated the war.

Grandma pushed herself up, wobbling like a shadow toward the bed.

"Perhaps he lied." Auntie Hạnh eyed Uncle Minh, who now wept in Grandma's arms. "Maybe he killed Brother Thuận. That's how he got the letter. That's why he didn't dare contact Mama."

"Thuận said that he was sending his letter with a comrade who was traveling North," said Uncle Đạt. "That matched with what Brother Minh wrote. Our eldest brother, I know, would never lie to us."

My mother's eyes welled up with tears. "But he did fight alongside the blood-thirsty American imperialists and alongside those monsters. . . ."

"Sister, it was the stupid war," said Uncle Đạt. "Remember the Southern soldier who rescued you? And the door gunner who spared my life? Not all those who fought on the other side were bad."

My mother bit her lip.

"Sisters," my uncle continued, "don't forget how wonderful Brother Minh was to us. He was the one who defended us from bullies. Remember the guy who used to throw rocks at us on the way to school? And how Brother Minh faced him for us?"

"He built rafts and rowed us out on the village pond," whispered my mother. "Once I wanted a *gạo* flower high up on the tree, he climbed to pick it for me. The branch broke, he fell . . . he fell down so hard. I ran to him, to find him laughing. He said he got a good massage on his bum. He gave me the flower, perfectly intact." She cried harder.

"That's Eldest Brother Minh," said Uncle Đạt, "He's our brother. Don't let anything change that."

"Those childhood memories mean nothing." Auntie Hạnh shook her head. "Even if he didn't kill Thuận himself, his comrades did." She looked at her watch. "I can't stay. The last train is leaving for Sài Gòn in half an hour."

"But we just got here," my mother and Uncle Đạt exclaimed in one voice.

"I can't carry the burden of this family a minute longer," said Auntie Hạnh. "For years I've tried to do the best for everyone, but no one cares what I've gone through. If Brother Minh is so great, tell him to fight the bullies at my children's school. The bullies who've been calling my kids *Bắc Kỳ ngu*—"stupid Northerners." The bullies who've been saying that we invaded the South, taking away their parents' jobs."

"I'm sorry, Hạnh," my mother said. "Why did you never tell us about such things?"

"You've been so lost in your own problems, Sister. And what could you do to help, huh? Everyone thinks I have a perfect life, but life is never perfect. Do you know that because of my past, my husband has to prove his loyalty to the Party time and time again? He's under watchful eyes. If they find out my brother is a *Nguy*, there'll be serious implications."

"Hạnh," said Uncle Đạt. "I understand how you feel. But *một giọt máu đào hơn ao nước lã*—One drop of familial blood outranks a pond of water. It's our brother we're talking about, and he's dying."

Auntie Hạnh's shoulders slumped. "As I've told you, Tuấn asked me to leave if Brother Minh is a *Nguy*. I promised him I would. And I can't break that promise."

Lying on the mat, I hugged Grandma's back. She'd cried until exhaustion overtook her. I put my face against her shirt. The trembling of her body made my throat dry. She'd tried so hard to reunite our family, only for it to be torn apart again.

Auntie Hạnh must be on the train. Was she still crying as hard as she'd been when she left us? For years I'd both envied her and wished to be like her, but now I knew I wouldn't want to be in her position: torn in her loyalty between her family and her husband.

Uncle Minh's chest was rising and falling rhythmically. What had run through his mind as Auntie Hạnh said good-bye? I'd expected him to beg her to stay, but he just clutched her hands, smiled, and thanked her. He must have guessed the real reasons for her departure, but didn't ask.

I'd feared that Uncle Minh fought for the Southern Army, so his letter wasn't such a big shock to me. Still, I wondered if he'd faced my father in the battlefield, and if he'd set up those land mines that blew up Uncle Đạt's legs.

I wished Tâm were here to tell me everything would be all right. If I could lean on his strong shoulder, even for the briefest moment, I wouldn't feel so shaken.

Tâm had always been there for me. He'd unfailingly been the first to read my poems, and he persuaded me to learn English. Under the light of our oil lamp, he'd sat by my side, translating with me the last page of *Little House in the Big Woods*. And with the book whole again, I could hear Laura's father sing; somehow her father resembled my own.

"Tâm." I said his name and woke up. Uncle Minh and Grandma were still fast asleep. It was late in the afternoon, yet the air was bursting with heat.

My mother and Uncle Đạt had gone out and now they returned. At the back of the shack, they showed me all the food they'd bought. My mother unpacked a paper bag filled with Western medicine. They'd been to the local hospital, trying to persuade the doctors there to readmit Uncle Minh, but no bed was available.

Uncle Minh woke up and vomited blood. My mother listened to his lungs and gave him the pills. Grandma fed him porridge. He pinched his nose and drank another bowl of herbal medicine. Grandma stayed by his side, her voice rising.

"À à ơi, làng tôi có lũy tre xanh, có sông Tô Lịch uốn quanh xóm làng.... À à ơi ..."

Childhood lullabies. She'd sung them to me.

Uncle Đạt sat down on the bed. "Brother, what can I do?"

Uncle Minh touched the wooden legs. "I'm sorry," he mouthed.

"I'm sorry, too, Brother. I should have run after Uncle Công and you. Maybe I could have helped you when you were alone by the river."

Uncle Minh shook his head. He grabbed Uncle Đạt's hand, putting it on his heart.

The next day, Uncle Minh was particularly alert. He insisted on talking. There was no word of anguish on his lips, just joyful memories about his childhood, being Grandma's son and the brother of his siblings. And happy memories of his own family in the South. He insisted that all of us sit next to him, hold his hands, and tell us as much as we could about life in the North.

When he showed us the pictures of his wife and children, I wept. I gazed at a photo where my uncle had one arm wrapped around my Auntie Linh, who was laughing, and the other arm around my beautiful cousins, Thiện and Nhân. *Thiện Nhân* meant "good person." My uncle had tried all his life to retain the goodness he was born with, and I hoped his family succeeded in carrying his hopes and dreams across the ocean and in planting them in the garden of their new home.

Uncle Minh grew tired. His priest came and prayed for him. "Your son has helped shoulder Christ's cross through the stations of life, and now he's free to join Him in Heaven," he told Grandma.

I woke up next morning to the sound of Grandma's sobs. Uncle Minh lay silent in front of her, his body limp.

I knelt with Uncle Đạt and my mother next to the bed, our hands in front of our chests. Grandma closed her eyes, the stick in her hand knocking rhythmically against her prayer bell. *"Nam Mô A Di Đà Phật, Nam Mô Quan Thế Âm Bồ Tát."* We joined her in the prayer.

A noise. I turned. The tin sheets rattled as the front door opened, letting in a torrent of light. I squinted at a tall, thin shadow.

In an instant, I was on my feet. "Uncle Sáng, you've come!"

Grandma enfolded him in her arms.

"I'm sorry, Mama," said Uncle Sáng, but she pulled him toward the bed.

I looked out to the road, hoping to see Auntie Hạnh, but only emptiness met my gaze.

Standing behind Uncle Sáng, I noticed his white hair for the first time. I wondered which strands had turned white grieving for his dead daughter, which ones lost their youth due to his marriage's breakdown, and which ones changed color due to his fear of the Agent Orange Devil. I hadn't cared before, but now I wanted to know. And it was time I got to know the undercurrents of Auntie Hạnh's life, the undercurrents that threatened to pull her away from us.

When Uncle Minh died, I took my notebook to the back of the house. Squatting on the ground, I wrote for an uncle I'd been robbed of, who was a leaf pushed away from its tree, but at its last moment still struggled to fall back to its roots. I wrote for Grandma, who'd hoped for the fire of war to be extinguished, only for its embers to keep burning her. I wrote for my uncles, my aunt, and my parents, who were helpless in the fight of brother against brother, and whose war went on, regardless of whether they were alive, or dead.

Facing the Enemy

Nghệ An, 1980

I sank into the softness of dry rice straws, the rice straws of Vĩnh Phúc Village. They unfurled around me. I inhaled their faint fragrance and understood why Grandma, when she'd told me her life story, called it the perfume of her sleep.

Grandma, my mother, and I had arrived in the village of my ancestors earlier this evening. Mr. Hải, his wife, his children, and his grandchildren were having dinner when our buffalo cart pulled up at their gate. They rejoiced and made us join their simple meal. As Mr. Hải scooped rice into my bowl, I was overcome. How could I ever thank him enough for rescuing Grandma from the hands of Wicked Ghost and for saving her life from angry villagers?

We talked late into the night. Grandma told Mr. Hải about our trip to Nha Trang and about Uncle Minh.

"I'm sorry." Mr. Hải's voice trembled. "I should've done more . . . so that Minh could have met up with you somewhere along the way when you escaped."

I bit my lip. The turbulent events of our history had not just ripped people apart, they'd imprinted on them a sense of guilt about things over which they had no control.

"Uncle, you did your best," said Grandma. "You saved our lives. One day, Minh's wife and children will return. They'll come here to thank you."

We hadn't heard any news about Auntie Linh, Thiện, and Nhân, but Grandma believed they'd survived their rough trip at sea, that they would try to find us. I hadn't told Grandma yet, but Tâm and I were looking into ways to search for them, using their pictures. I wanted to be like Grandma: Never give up hope.

Grandma had hoped Uncle Sáng would change, and he didn't disappoint her. Now, he visited our home from time to time. He joined Grandma, my mother, and me in visiting Auntie Hạnh in Sài Gòn. During the last Mid-Autumn Festival, he taught me how to make a star lantern for the Light Parade.

I held up the Sơn ca, listening to its silent songs. I wished my father could be here right now, to join us in visiting Tâm's family tomorrow. Wherever my father was, I knew he loved Tâm, too.

From the living room, the murmurs of Grandma, my mother, and Mr. Hải flowed toward me. "Tâm's uncle visited me a few weeks ago," said Grandma. "He told me Tâm would like to marry Hương next spring."

Heat rose to my face. We were young, Tâm and I. We still had to finish our education but didn't want to wait. In Tâm, I knew I'd found the love of my life.

"That's excellent news," said Mr. Hải.

"I haven't said yes since we must know more about his family," Grandma whispered.

"I have no worries though," said my mother. "He's a nice boy, so he must come from a good family."

Like my mother, I had no doubt. I could hardly wait to meet Tâm's parents and sister. I felt anxious about his grandfather, though. I hoped he would come out of his room to meet me and that he'd approve of me.

"How can he not like you? Everyone does." Tâm had raised his eyebrows when I told him my concern. "Besides, if he has a problem, he'll have to live with it. He's a stranger to me anyway." Tâm pulled me close, his lips on my ear. "I love you, and you'll soon be my wife."

Closing my eyes, I saw myself drifting down a river on a sampan boat, Tâm beside me. The boat rocked and swayed against the fast current. There were rocks and whirlpools ahead of us, but I felt safe. I knew whatever perils awaited us, we would face them, together.

A ROOSTER'S CROW pierced the earthen walls, pulling me away from the last flicker of my dream. I opened my eyes. I had fallen asleep on the straw nest, but now I was on a bamboo bed, empty but for two sunken pillows. Grandma and my mother must have carried me up here, but where were they?

Lifting the mosquito netting, I crawled out, changed my clothes, and hurried outside. The night had faded into gray. The air, cold and fresh, glided against my skin.

A layer of mist lingered in the front yard. On tree branches, birds gossiped back and forth.

My mother, Grandma, and Mr. Hải were sitting on a straw mat on the floor of the veranda, steaming cups of tea in their hands.

"What were you doing, Hương? You slept in the straw nest," Grandma said.

"I was searching for the perfume of your sleep," I said, smiling, receiving a cup from Mr. Hải. The tea tasted as fresh as the country air.

"Perfume of my sleep?" Grandma laughed. "Found it?"

"Bet the mosquitoes found her first." My mother studied the many red dots on my legs. She fetched another cup of tea, blew it to cool, and rubbed the liquid on my mosquito bites. The itching eased. I leaned against her, becoming a child again in the warmth of her body.

The sun rose from a curtain of cloud, painting the sky with a rosy hue, scattering soft rays onto the yard.

"Everything has changed so much," said Grandma. "I'm afraid I'll feel like a stranger out there."

My mother finished her cup. She took Grandma's elbow, helping her stand up. Mr. Hải and I hurried to put our sandals on.

My feet felt light on the village road I knew so well from Grandma's story. We passed the pagoda with its roofs curving like the fingers of an exquisite dancer, the clanging of its bell rippling in the cool air. The ponds stretched out in front of us, their surfaces as calm as silk sheets. Thick canopies of green bamboo swayed, giving shade to the low houses that lined our path.

Several villagers greeted Mr. Hải. An elderly lady froze in her path. "Diệu Lan, is that you?" she asked. The wrinkles on her face deepened when Grandma nodded.

The lady put her baskets down. "I'm . . . I'm sorry about the things that happened."

"It's good to see you, Sister," said Grandma. "Let bygones be bygones. I wish you all the best."

We watched the lady stagger away, her bamboo pole braced across her bony shoulders.

"She was shouting those ugly slogans and pumping her fists," said my mother. "I'll never forget her bitchy face."

"Try to forgive and forget, Ngọc," said Grandma. "If you bear grudges, you're the one who'll have to bear the burden of sorrow."

Mr. Hải shook his head. "It was appalling, though. Your parents saved her during the Great Hunger. Then she turned her fists on you."

We arrived at a dirt road, pocked with holes. "The path to our home," gasped my mother.

"Our home, our home," said Grandma tenderly. Following her gaze, I saw a thick fence guarding a large estate.

We arrived in front of a gate. I peered inside, expecting to see an impressive *năm gian* house with five wooden sections surrounded by lush gardens. Instead, my heart sank at the sight of neglect and abandonment.

"Seven families live here now." Mr. Hải led us through the open gate. He raised his voice, "Anyone home?"

Grandma, my mother, and I clung to each other, stepping into the slippery front yard. Once paved with redbrick tiles, it was now punctured by pockets of greenish water and scattered with rubbish. The longan tree was no longer there. Wild grass and green moss had overgrown every possible space and corner.

And the house! Where were the doors bearing exquisite carvings of flowers and birds, the dark lacquered shutters that gleamed in the sun, the ceramic dragons and phoenixes that danced atop the curving ends of the roof?

I thought I'd expected the worst. But not this. Not a rickety-looking building stripped naked of all doors and windows. Not rotting walls with propaganda posters about family planning and drug addiction plastered on them; not makeshift partitions poking out of the house's floor, like bones of a fish.

The smell of rot drifted to my nose. The garden was now a patch of brown earth harboring large holes, over which clouds of green flies were buzzing.

"Open toilets." Mr. Hải sighed. "Fertilizers are expensive; human dung is now gold." He waved away some flies. "When the families moved into this house, they fought and fought about the division of dung. Finally, each dug their own toilet."

"This used to be heaven on earth." My mother clenched her fists. "Let us go, Mama. I can't stand it."

But Grandma was tearing herself away from us, hurrying toward the house's door. There, an elderly woman had just appeared. Her hair was white. She felt her way across the large veranda with a walking stick. Arriving at the five steps that led down to the yard, she threw the cane aside, crouching down on her hands and knees, crawling like an animal.

"Let me give you a hand." Grandma helped the woman to her feet.

Stepping closer, I gazed at the woman's face. A protruding forehead. Teeth that looked like those of a rabbit. The butcher-woman. She'd viciously attacked Grandma and had been determined to catch her. She was the one who'd driven my family out of our ancestors' home so she could take it over.

If Grandma loathed the woman, she didn't show. She held the woman's hand, guiding her down the steps.

"Who are you?" The butcher-woman gazed up at Grandma with her white eyes. Her withered hand reached up to touch Grandma's face. She sniffed at her.

"I'm visiting a friend in the village," said Grandma in her Hà Nội accent.

"No wonder you smell nice, not like the rats that live here." The woman winced. "Oh, my bones hurt." She thumped her back with her fist. "Lead me to the toilet closest to the kitchen, won't you? I must produce my daily quota, else my bastard of a son will punish me with his rod."

Grandma led the butcher-woman to her toilet. For the pain Grandma had suffered, she could've pushed her former enemy into the hole filled with human waste, but she helped the woman secure her footing and left her there.

As we turned to go, I looked back at the white-haired woman squatting on the ground, a cloud of flies her company. "Heaven has eyes," I said. "Cruelty dispensed, cruelty returned."

A BUFFALO CART arrived. Grandma loaded it with bundles of flowers, bags of fruits, and incense sticks. Mr. Hải got onto the cart, pulling us up. We waved good-bye to his family, then moved off in silence.

Nam Đàn Forest opened its green arms to receive me as we got off the cart. Grandma found a bush where flowers were showing off their petals. "*Sim* berries." She handed me a couple of the purple fruit. I put one on my tongue; its sweetness melted into my mouth.

The deeper we walked into the forest, the lighter I felt. The path became narrower, surrounded by tall, swaying trees. We pushed through a thicket, and I found myself in an open area ringed by shrubs. Wildflowers spread out their red, yellow, white, and purple petals, leading my eyes to five mounds of earth—the graves of my great grandparents, Grandpa Hùng, Great Uncle Công, and Mrs. Tú. Grandma had moved all of them here, so they could be together in death.

Grandma knelt, her palms in front of her chest. She brought her head to touch the ground and stayed there for a long while. I followed her, tears warming my eyes.

My mother and I arranged the flowers in front of the graves. We unpacked the bags, heaping the fruits on large plates.

Mr. Hải lit a bunch of incense. Receiving smoldering sticks, I raised them high. Their smoke unfurled toward Heaven, bringing my prayers to my ancestors. Their death and suffering taught me about love and sacrifice.

"Please help us find my father," I whispered. Whether he was alive or dead, I needed to know.

WHEN WE REACHED Tâm's village in Hà Tĩnh, we found him standing outside the lane of his house, waiting for us. He was wearing a shirt I'd sewn for him, using some of the skills I'd learned from my *nữ công gia chánh*—homemaking class. His face lit up when he saw me, and I knew why I loved him. Over the years we'd known each other, he'd grown into a tall man. The sight of him still made my knees go weak.

He helped everyone else off the cart, then turned to me, picked me up, twirling me around. As heat rose to my face, he whispered, "I've missed you."

I begged him to let me down. Children had gathered around us, their hands over their mouths, giggling.

Tâm guided us through the winding lane. "My parents are so excited to see you." He squeezed my hand. A man and a woman appeared under the bursting colors of bougainvillea outside a brick house. *"Chào bà, chào bác,"* they greeted Grandma and Mr. Hải.

Tâm's mother reached out to my mother and embraced her. "I'm so happy you could come, Sister. Your daughter has your beautiful features." Her eyes shifted to my face, and I blushed.

"Come in, please come in," Tâm's father told us.

"Thank you for the gifts you sent us," said Grandma. "I'm glad to meet you at last."

The coolness of Tâm's house welcomed me in. It was a friendly home. Plants flowered next to sunlit windows; tasteful paintings adorned the walls.

"Lành, the trouble maker," Tâm introduced me to his sister. I liked her smile instantly. On her hair was the pink headband I'd sewn, as a gift for Tâm to give his sister. She looked to be of my size, and perhaps I could try to make a skirt for her.

In the kitchen, pots were steaming; pans were sizzling. Tâm's mother returned to her stove. I rolled up my sleeves and joined Lành in washing vegetables. Surprisingly, I wasn't nervous at all. It was pleasant to talk to Tâm's mother and his sister. Their laughter relaxed me, and I found myself laughing, too.

After the food was ready, we first offered it to Tâm's ancestors. We arranged plates on a copper tray, decorating them with red roses and white lotus etched out of tomatoes and onions. Tâm carried the tray to the living room where his father was serving tea to my mother, Grandma, and Mr. Hải.

I helped Tâm put the food on the table in front of his family altar. He edged next to me. "Today I'll ask my ancestors to accept you as my wife. I can't wait until next spring."

I pinched him. "Don't be so impatient."

He pinched me back. "Be a good wife."

As we tried to hide our giggles, Tâm's mother walked past us, arm in arm with an elderly man. He was stooped, his hands and legs trembling. He looked to be in great pain.

"My father," Tâm's mother introduced him to Grandma, my mother, and Mr. Hải.

Grandma looked up. Her lips parted. *"Ôi trời đất ơi!"* She called for Heaven and Earth. She looked terrified. More terrified than I'd ever seen her.

"Ôi trời đất ơi!" Mr. Hải exclaimed, and the next thing I knew, Grandma had collapsed onto the floor.

ON TÂM'S BED, my mother massaged Grandma's forehead.

"Wake up, please," I begged.

Grandma's eyelashes fluttered. But what was happening? Why was she crying?

Her body shook. "No, it can't be true," she whimpered.

I wanted to reach out for her hands, but Mr. Hải pulled me away from the bed. "Hương, give her some time."

I stood shivering next to the wall, watching my mother trying desperately to comfort Grandma.

Mr. Hải paced back and forth.

"Great Uncle, what's going on?" I asked him.

"Hương, I'm not sure . . ." He shook his head.

"What? Tell me." I clutched his arm.

"I'm sorry."

"For what?"

Mr. Hải looked at me. His eyes were wide. The corners of his mouth twitched. He brought his hands to my shoulders and held me for a long moment. Then he pulled me to him. "I'm really sorry, Hương. . . . Tâm's grandfather . . . Tâm's grandfather is Wicked Ghost."

"No!" I pushed him away. "You're wrong."

"I wish I were, Hương. I worked for him. I knew him—"

I backed away from the room. I ran, passing Tâm, his parents, and Wicked Ghost. I darted under the flowers and out to the village road.

"Hương . . . Hương . . ." Tâm was behind me, his voice above the wind. But I raced faster. I couldn't go back to him. I could no longer love him. He was the flesh and blood of Grandma's worst enemy.

WE LEFT FOR Hà Nội the next day, much earlier than planned. The public bus was packed with people. I felt empty. My mother tried to console me, but her words couldn't give wings to the sorrow heavy in my heart.

Did Tâm know about Wicked Ghost and not tell me? Had he lied to me?

Back home, I placed the Sơn ca on the family altar. Kneeling, I bowed, my forehead touching the ground. I prayed for my father's soul to come home. I accepted now that I'd never see my Papa again. I accepted now that those I loved so dearly could be taken away from me so suddenly.

Tâm came to see me. I turned away from him. He began to follow me home from university. I ignored him. I said nothing when he told me he'd been ignorant of his grandpa's past. I gave him my silence in return for his words of apology.

No matter how hard I tried, though, I found myself mumbling Tâm's name whenever he was not with me. I missed our talks, our laughter, our fights. At the same time, I feared that if I accepted Tâm back, it would be a betrayal of my grandma.

Summer departed, then fall, and winter arrived. Tâm braced against the cold, cycling alongside me. He talked to me as if nothing had changed. He told me about the results of his research; he was studying rice. Farmers in his province were planting a new variety that he'd developed. I wished I could tell him about my writing. Without him, my new poems lay silent in darkness.

One cold, rainy day Tâm wasn't waiting for me outside my class. I hung about, expecting to see him turning up late, his smile lighting up the rain and his voice wrapping me in its warmth. Night came, but the night didn't bring him. The roads home were long and colorless.

Time seemed to stop moving. I could hear my own heartbeat. The slightest noise startled me. I saw Tâm's face everywhere I looked, but when I reached out for him, he was nothing but thin air.

SIX DAYS WENT by. I cycled home alone. Winter never felt so cold. It was colder than that November day many years ago, when I hid with Grandma from the bombs, muddy water up to my waist. I was frightened then that I would die. Now I was terrified that I would have to live on without my soul mate and best friend.

I pedaled slowly through my silent neighborhood, where brick houses had replaced the tin-roofed shacks. Our *bàng* tree had grown tall.

Pushing my bike inside the house, I found Grandma sitting by the dining table, her palms cupping something in front of her. So lost in her thought, she didn't even look up when I came in.

I sat down next to her. "Grandma, are you all right?"

"Tâm and his parents . . . they were just here to see me."

She opened her palms. A magnificent necklace.

I reached for its gold chain. The ruby glimmered in my hands. Grandma's story came rushing back. "Great-Grandma had this in her pocket," I said. "Wicked Ghost took it from her. It's our family treasure."

Grandma nodded. "That terrible man, he stole it and kept it all those years. He only told his daughter the truth about his past before he died. Tâm's mother . . . she found out about the necklace and insisted that it be returned to our family."

"Wicked Ghost died, Grandma? When?"

"Last week. Yes . . . he's dead. He's dead, and it's impossible to undo his sins. Wicked Ghost didn't just hurt other people, Hương, he inflicted pain on his own family. He used to beat his daughter so savagely. Many people in our village thought she wouldn't survive his beatings."

I thought about Tâm's mother, her smile, and her tender words. She was a beautiful lotus flower that had risen from a pond of mud.

Grandma shook her head. "I couldn't believe it when she handed the necklace over to me. She could've gotten a fortune for it, but she said it's important we have it back. She said she wished to be able make it up to us, for the misery her father had caused. I told her it was not her fault. She was his victim, like us."

Grandma reached for my hand. "Hương, I've been thinking . . . Tâm has nothing to do with what happened. I used to believe that blood will tell, but blood evolves and can change, too. Young people can't be blamed for what their ancestors did." She smiled. "Tâm is a good man, Hương. I've seen how he made you happy. He told me today you mean everything to him, and he won't give up on you."

"He did?"

"Yes, in front of his parents, so that says a lot. I understand how difficult this has been for you. But I also know that true love is rare, and once we find our true love, we must hold on to it. What I'm trying to say is, Hương, my darling, if you want to see Tâm again, you have my blessing."

A light radiated from Grandma's eyes. Even her wrinkles were soft. There was no longer sorrow on her face. She looked peaceful and calm; as peaceful and calm as Buddha.

I stood up. I drew Grandma to her feet. I hugged her.

My Grandmother's Songs

Nghệ An, 2017

I place the Sơn ca in front of Grandma's grave. The children kneel down next to me. Tâm strikes a match, igniting a bundle of incense. He turns and beams at me.

"I know Grandma is proud of you. I am too, my love," he says as the smoldering incense wraps us with its fragrance.

"You helped make this possible, Tâm." I hold out a stack of paper, thick and sturdy. It is my family's story, told by Grandma and me.

"Can Great-Grandma read this in Heaven?" asks our son Quang, his hands patting the cover.

"When we burn it, the smoke will send it to her," our daughter Thanh says. She believes it because she loved to listen to Grandma as much as I did.

I raise the copy of my manuscript above my head. Grandma once told me that the challenges faced by the Vietnamese people throughout history are as tall as the tallest mountain. I have stood far enough away to see the mountaintop, yet close enough to witness how Grandma became the tallest mountain herself: always there, always strong, always protecting us.

I close my eyes. Grandma's gentle face appears before me. *I'm glad you wrote down what we went through, Guava. I can't wait to read it.*

"I miss you, Grandma."

Fire flares up in Tâm's hands. Our children help feed the pages to the flames.

Wisps of smoke curl upward. And in the twirling ash, I see the Sơn ca moving. It is flapping its wings, craning its neck, calling my grandma's songs toward Heaven.

ACKNOWLEDGMENTS

*T*he *Mountains Sing* is inspired by the experiences of my own family and those around me. I am grateful to my parents, my relatives, and many other Vietnamese who have shared with me their personal stories and continue to inspire me with their courage and compassion.

I am indebted to my teacher—*thầy* Trương Văn Ánh—from whom I first learned English in eighth grade. I didn't know that one day, it would be English, not my Vietnamese mother tongue, that would give me a voice when it comes to historical fiction. My husband, Hans Farnhammer, believes in me and encouraged me to quit my salary-earning job to become a writer. Peter Conners, BOA Editions, and the Lannan Foundation paved the way for my international career with the publication of my poetry book *The Secret of Hoa Sen,* which I translated from Vietnamese, together with the poet and professor Bruce Weigl. A scholarship from Lancaster University's M.A. in Creative Writing program granted me the chance to research and write this novel. I am grateful for the guidance of my mentor Sara Maitland and the feedback from other writers at Lancaster, especially

Philip Caveney, Zoe Lambert, Graham Mort, Anne O'Brien, Laura Morgan, Michelle Scowcroft, Mary Chism, Joe Lavelle, and Suzanne Conboy-Hill. Insights from the war veterans Đinh Văn Tùng, Nguyễn Văn Bảo, Trần Minh Quang, Bruce Weigl, John Havan, Wayne Karlin, and Tracy French have been invaluable.

Master John Havan, who was himself a novelist, taught me Kick-Poke-Chop self-defense. He had invented this technique for surviving real-life attacks. Helle Kafka journeyed with me from the start of this novel. Beth Phillips expanded my reading horizons by giving me a job at the library of the American International School Dhaka, Bangladesh. Special thanks to Mr. Cường Nguyễn and Mrs. Thảo Đỗ, for the inspirations they provided me. The talented and generous novelist Viet Thanh Nguyen gave me much-needed encouragement and introduced me to my wonderful agent Julie Stevenson, who heard *The Mountains Sing* despite the distance of many oceans between us. My sister-in-writing, Thanhhà Lại, worked with me over late nights and early mornings translating Vietnamese proverbs. Paul Christiansen and Dr. Eric Henry gave input to my translations of complicated Vietnamese words and phrases.

I am incredibly lucky that *The Mountains Sing* finds its home at Algonquin Books. My editor, Betsy Gleick, is brilliant, warm, and very supportive. It has been my honor to work with her, as well as with the many other capable and caring people at Algonquin, including Brunson Hoole, Michael McKenzie, Anne Winslow, Randall Lotowycz, Elisabeth Scharlatt, Stephanie Mendoza, Debra Linn, Lauren Moseley, and Kendra Poster. This novel also benefited from the keen and careful reading eyes of Chúc Mỹ Tuệ (Teresa Mei Chuc), Eva Maaten, Abby Muller, and Chris Stamey.

I am grateful to organizations and individuals who lent me strength when I needed it most, especially the Australia Awards scholarship program, the Diasporic Vietnamese Artists Network (DVAN), the Djerassi Resident Artists Program, Rick Simonson, chị Tuyết Nga, and the amazing writers who read and provided such heartfelt blurbs for my novel.

To my children, Clara Quế Mai and Nguyễn Minh Johann: Thank you for being my light during the years I wrote *The Mountains Sing*.

THE MOUNTAINS SING

❧ ❀ ❧

Climbing Many Mountains
An Essay by Nguyễn Phan Quế Mai

Questions for Discussion

Climbing Many Mountains

An Essay by Nguyễn Phan Quế Mai

In 1983, when I was ten years old, I went secretly to the post office in my hometown to mail a letter to Hà Nội. The letter contained my entry for a writing competition. When a notice arrived announcing that I had won a prize, my parents were shocked. Due to the long history of Vietnamese writers' experiences in my country, my parents reminded me of their wish that their only daughter would not become a writer.

I had to put aside my dreams of writing to do a variety of jobs to earn a living and help support my family. But the writer in me always listened to other people, always asked questions about their experiences during the war, and memorized their stories. In my teenage years, I began to travel to my parents' villages to talk with our elder relatives and family friends so I could imagine how life had been for my grandparents, who had either died or been killed before I was born. Gradually, the more I began to understand Việt Nam's painful past, the more people shared with me the events of their lives.

Unbeknownst to me, at that young age I was already carrying out the research for *The Mountains Sing*. It was only with time and distance and my ongoing academic research that I could comprehend the complexity of Việt Nam's history and its relation to other nations. My extensive exchanges with Vietnamese and American combat veterans, as well as volunteer work with victims of the war, has expanded this understanding.

The Mountains Sing embodies my yearning to know my grandmothers, and to bring to life the underrepresented women and children who often suffer the consequences of wars the most but must hide their sorrows to become pillars of strength and comfort for returning soldiers. Through Grandma Diệu Lan and her granddaughter Hương in the novel, I could talk to them, trace their footsteps, and imagine their dreams and hopes.

It may seem ironic that I have chosen to write this novel, by far my most personal work to date, in English, which is also the language of invasive military powers and cultures. But this language has given me a new voice and a way to fictionalize the turbulent events of my country's past, including those that have not yet been sufficiently documented in Vietnamese fiction, such as the Great Hunger or the Land Reform. I am also responding to Hollywood movies and novels written by those Westerners who continue to see our country only as a place of war and the Vietnamese as people who don't need to speak—or, when we do, sound simple, naïve, cruel, or opportunistic. The canon of Việt Nam war and post-war literature in English is vast, but there is a lack of voices from inside Việt Nam.

When I first learned English in eighth grade, I didn't know that one day it would be the language that would save *The Mountains Sing*. Khương Dụ, the small northern village where I was born, did not have an English teacher. Bạc Liêu, the southern town where I grew up, didn't have many people who could speak English. For me, a student who also worked as a rice farmer and street vendor, the Western world was mysterious, existing only in the black-and-white movies I would occasionally catch a glimpse of while selling cigarettes in the town's cemetery, which also served as our only open-air movie theater.

I didn't know any English words until well into secondary school, when one afternoon my eldest brother brought home a notebook. He told me he had just learned English from someone and would teach me. I was so excited I could barely swallow my dinner. That night, after I had lit the oil lamp (we had electricity only occasionally) and put on long pants and a long-sleeved shirt to ward off the zillions of mosquitoes, my brother solemnly brought out his notebook. He opened the first page and pointed at a strange-looking word. "Sờ cu lờ," he said, and then looked at me, expecting me to repeat after him.

"Sờ ... sờ ..." I said, and brought my hand to my mouth.

"Sờ cu lờ," he said again.

"Sờ ... sờ cu ..." I repeated and burst out laughing. I couldn't help it! The words that had just escaped my mouth sounded like the Vietnamese phrase for "to touch a male's genitals."

So ended my first English lesson. Because I hadn't been able to stop laughing, my brother slapped his notebook shut and stormed out of the room. His face was as red as a gấc fruit.

"Brother! Teach me, please," I called after him, but he didn't turn back.

Later, much later, I found out my brother was trying to teach me a very important word: "school."

I didn't dare ask him to teach me again, but occasionally I would steal his notebook when he was gone, hide under the mango and coconut trees that circled our fish pond, and stare at the English words. I sensed that behind those strange-looking words existed some magic doors, and if I managed to push them open, I would be able to enter the big, wide world.

And now, with *The Mountains Sing*, I am taking my baby steps into that world. It took me seven years to write and edit, hundreds of revisions, many sleepless nights, tears, and countless moments of doubt. I doubted that I was a good-enough storyteller. I doubted my ability to express complicated thoughts and emotions in English. But I never doubted my decision in 2006 at the age of thirty-three to return to my dream of becoming a writer.

By turning to the first page of *The Mountains Sing*, you will open the door into an authentic Việt Nam where proverbs are sprinkled throughout daily conversations, where lullabies and poems are sung. You will experience the colors, richness, and complexity of our culture, beginning with our Vietnamese names and language, which appear in full diacritical marks. Those marks might look strange at first, but they are as important as the roof of a home. The word "ma," for example, can be written as ma, má, mà, mả, mạ, mã; each meaning very different things: ghost, mother, but, grave, young rice plant, horse. The word "bo" can become bó, bỏ, bọ, bơ, bở, bờ, bô, bố, bổ, bộ (bunch, abandon, insect, butter, mushy, shore, chamber pot, father, mistress, nutritious).

Just like Hương in *The Mountains Sing*, for several of my childhood years, books were my only friends; they allowed me to escape from desperation and poverty. My family had moved from the north to the south of Việt Nam; it was just a few years after the war, and despite the country's unification, the north-south tension ran strong. While living amidst this tension I understood the deep wounds that divided our country and families. Many of these wounds have still not healed, even though nearly forty-five years have passed since the war's ending on April 30, 1975.

Tremendous progress has been made in terms of reconciliation between Việt Nam and the United States, but the wounds that divided our country and families, both at home and in the diaspora, remain profound and painful. For that reason, *The Mountains Sing* places our people at the center of the Việt Nam War in the hopes that we will be open to difficult but necessary conversations that can help one another heal. And at the same time, I hope the story of Hương and Diệu Lan helps international readers discover our common humanity, as in the words of Hương: "Somehow I was sure that if people were willing to read each other, and see the light of other cultures, there would be no war on earth."

Questions for Discussion

1. There are many major historical events featured in the novel. How much did you know about these events before you read *The Mountains Sing*? Did the story show you a new side to any events you were already familiar with?

2. Many of the characters in *The Mountains Sing* experience terrible things, and some of them must make difficult choices. Each of them handles their experiences differently. The Sơn ca helps Hương on her journey. What other objects, memories, people, or conversations help each character to endure and recover?

3. How does Grandma Diệu Lan help her children after their return? What might her relationships with her children reveal about family relationships in Vietnam?

4. War stories are often told from a male perspective. In *The Mountains Sing*, Hương and Grandma Diệu Lan take turns narrating their stories. How might this be a different novel if it had male narrators? Why do you think the author chose to have women and girls tell the story instead?

5. Which character did you feel the most sympathetic toward? The least? Is that different from which character you like the most and least, and if so, why?

6. In addition to descriptions of war and pain, *The Mountains Sing* features many descriptions of gorgeous landscapes, interesting city sights, and delicious foods. Were there any locations that you would like to visit? Any foods you would like to try?

7. According to Hương, proverbs are the essence of Vietnamese wisdom, passed orally from one generation to the next, even before the written Vietnamese language existed. For example, two are *Trong cái rủi có cái may* (Good luck hides inside bad luck) and *Ác giả ác báo* (Cruelty dispensed, cruelty returned). Do these proverbs ring true for you? Were there other proverbs that resonated with you as particularly true or meaningful?

8. In *The Mountains Sing*, Vietnamese names and words appear with their full diacritical marks. For Vietnamese speakers, these marks are necessary to interpret meaning: for example, the words ma, mả, má, mà, mạ, and mã all have separate meanings (ghost, grave, mother, but, young rice plant, and horse, respectively). Nonetheless, it is unusual for an American novel to include the marks. Did their inclusion affect your reading experience? How?

9. Hương thinks that if people are willing to learn about other cultures, there will be no war on earth. Do you think Hương feels differently about America and American people because of her reading? What books have made your world bigger?

10. Grandma says, "If our stories survive, we will not die, even when our bodies are no longer here on this earth." *The Mountains Sing* is loosely based on the author's own family story. What stories do you know about your family? Do you know any fictional stories that remind you of your own family story?

11. When talking to Miss Nhung, Hương reflects that she finds words beautiful but doesn't know whether she's brave enough to be a writer. What are some of the censorship issues mentioned in the novel? Is censorship an issue in your country today?

12. Had you previously read other books from or about Việt Nam? How is the Việt Nam portrayed in *The Mountains Sing* similar to or different from the Việt Nam you already knew?

© VŨ THỊ VÂN ANH

Born into the Việt Nam War in 1973, **Nguyễn Phan Quế Mai** grew up witnessing the war's devastation and its aftermath. She worked as a street vendor and rice farmer before winning a scholarship to attend university in Australia. Upon her return to Việt Nam, Quế Mai contributed to the sustainable development of her homeland via her work with local and international organizations, including UN agencies. She is the author of eight books of poetry, fiction, and nonfiction in Vietnamese; *The Mountains Sing* is the first novel she has written in English. Her writing has been translated and published in more than fifteen countries and has received many honors, including the Poetry of the Year 2010 Award from the Hà Nội Writers Association, and she is the 2020 recipient of the Lannan Literary Fellowship for Fiction. Quế Mai has a PhD in creative writing from Lancaster University in the United Kingdom and currently divides her time between Indonesia and Việt Nam. For more information about Nguyễn Phan Quế Mai, visit her at www.nguyenphanquemai.com.